THE LAKE
at
UNION GAP

The LAKE
at
UNION GAP

═══ A NOVEL ═══

PEGGY
McCLURKEN

WATERMAIN

Published in the United States by

WATERMAIN PRESS
491 Eastern Isle Avenue
Summerville, South Carolina 29486

Tradepaper ISBN: 979-8-218-08900-9

Hardcover ISBN: 979-8-218-32462-9

Library of Congress Control Number: 2022919340

First Edition

1 3 5 7 9 10 8 6 4 2

Printed in the United States of America

"An Old Virginia Christmas" song lyrics
Copyright © 1999 by John and Peggy McClurken

Book Design by Watermain Press

Cover Photo by Ed Nelson

For JOHN
My One and Only

PART I

May 2017

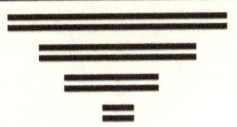

One

Happy O'Hurley stood on the Lakewalk outside Books Galore Bookstore. She shielded her eyes against the bright orange morning sun rising in the east and squinted toward the north side of Big Gap Lake directly opposite her. "Well I'll be a goose's caboose," she said out loud. Her little terrier-mix Pippy cocked his head and shifted from one leg to the other, whining softly. He was telling his mistress to hurry up and open the door. It was time for him to begin the day as official greeter at Books Galore, a job he took seriously. And, of utmost importance, it was time for his morning snack, a perk that came with the job.

Happy fumbled with her keys, dropping them twice before managing to open the door enough to let Pippy inside. She stayed in the doorway continuing to stare across the lake. She was focusing on the sprawling, three-storied stone, shingled, and shuttered Stonewall Mansion that sat on Jackson's Point. Like a beacon, the mansion always called attention to itself. And although it had an ominous air about it, it was a piece of prime lakefront property adjoining the gated community called The Gallery at Union Gap.

As Happy watched, two muscled and tanned young men in coveralls were carrying something big. *A desk maybe? A trunk?* They entered through the service door on the side of the house. Happy waited several moments until the duo exited through the same door and walked around to the back of the property and out of sight. She sighed, went inside the bookstore, hurriedly turned the sign on the door from "Closed" to "Open," then reconsidered and turned it back to "Closed." In her haste to get to the telephone on the service counter, she tripped over Pippy, who let out a surprised yowl and dashed to his hideaway under the counter.

"Sorry, Mr. Pips," she said. "Just give me one minute to make a phone call, then we'll open shop and get your snack." Happy dialed the number she knew by heart, but the call went to voice-mail, where her best friend's abrupt voice told the caller to leave a message. Happy cursed good-naturedly and spoke into the phone, "Maggie, you ole busy-body, where the dickens are you? I need to know what's going on. Call me!"

Happy began the process of opening the shop—turning the sign back to "Open," readying the cash register, setting out displays, and going through the mail, which she'd picked up from the Union Gap Post Office on her way in as she did every morning. She started toward the inside door that connected Books Galore to the Mean Beans Bistro. Pippy, who had been patiently waiting, happily came out from his cubbyhole under the service counter. The daily visit next door, he knew, meant one thing to him: breakfast.

Happy unfastened the two latches with an excited Pippy at her heels and started to open the door when another thought occurred to her. She rushed back to the counter and rummaged through the assortment of dog-eared business cards, coffee-stained notes, months-old receipts, and other odds and ends. She was about to end her search when she spotted the napkin from Creekside Café on which Maggie had written her new mobile phone number.

Maggie was a newspaper person from back in the days when she always had a pencil behind her ear, a reporter's notebook in hand, and used a special shorthand that only she could decipher. She scoffed at modern gadgets like smartphones with their Internet access, downloaded applications, and the new language of texting.

She was slow coming to terms with the new digital technology, to say the least.

Happy punched in the number on the napkin while Pippy sighed heavily and laid back down, head on his paws. On the fifth ring, an irritated voice demanded, "What?"

"Whoa, Mags! Don't bite my head off. Where are you?"

"Knee deep in dog shit if you must know. Literally. Sorry, I didn't mean to growl, no pun intended." Maggie was petulant. "What's up?"

Before Happy could respond, Maggie proceeded to give her friend an earful. "I've had it with those 'Pee-ughs' and that so-called dog that's the size of a small horse. Takes a crap wherever he feels like it and they just leave it."

She was referring to the Pews, pronounced like the bench seats in churches, and their 200-pound Great Dane, aptly named Trojan.

"Your dog poops, you scoop," Maggie grumbled. "That's the rule. Written into the almighty HOA by-laws and all. Can't tell you how many times I've complained to that snooty Petrinka Boggs. Calls herself president of The Gallery Homeowners Association. Fancy-schmancy title. But when it comes to enforcing the rules, she's like, 'Margaret, my dear...' She knows how I hate to be called 'Margaret', just says it to irritate me. 'Honey, we don't want to make waves. The Pews are a fine dues-paying family'."

Maggie went on. "Gimme a break. The Pee-ughs are a fine family of stinkin' no-class riffraff. The almighty association should have by-laws banning such ill-mannered types. But what does our esteemed Bitch Boggs have to say about that? 'Oh, dear, we certainly don't want to make waves, now do we?'"

Happy had heard enough. She wanted to get down to the business at hand but knew better than to interject, and anyway her friend didn't give her a chance. When Maggie was on a heated roll, it was best to allow her to keep rolling.

"Yep, I stepped right in it," Maggie announced matter-of-fact-ly. "Out minding my own business, taking Bowser for his morning walk and trying out these so-called enhanced texting features— 'L-O-L'—on my new 'smartass' phone. Passed the Pee-ughs and their horse-dog on Trout Run Trail. Is it my responsibility to be look-ing down for a pile of poop the size of a small mountain right in the middle of the trail?"

Happy wanted to say something about the perils of walking and texting at the same time, but refrained.

"Smelled it though, that's for sure," Maggie continued. "Bent down to try to scrape it off my shoe with a twig, and wouldn't you know it, went down with my knee right smack dab into the crapola. Walking back home now, stink and all. Shit on my shoe. Crop pants are now crap pants. Oh, holy sweet moley, here comes the power walking queen, Miss Prissy Betty Porter."

As the other woman approached at a fast walking pace, hold-ing a two-pound weight in each hand, Maggie gave her a broad Cheshire cat-like grin through gritted teeth.

"Beautiful morning, isn't it, Maggie," chirped Betty, slowing down as she approached, ready for conversation. Then, "Oh my, oh my goodness!" Betty wrinkled her nose at the sight and smell of the other woman and scurried past. She resumed her speed-walk-ing stride with back straight and gaze directed forward, not at the ground. A moment later she let out a shriek. Maggie turned to see Betty standing on one leg, looking horrified at the crap she had just stepped in, the same pile Maggie had just stepped out of.

"And a shitty morning to you too, Betty," Maggie said into the phone.

"Mags!" Happy finally cut in. "I can tell this isn't a good time." She told Maggie to call her back after she got cleaned up and had cooled off.

"Oh, I'm okay, Glads. She didn't hear me. What's up?" She sounded a bit calmed down.

"Glads" was a nickname short for Gladys. Happy hated her given name and several years ago had shortened "Gladys" to "Glads." Somewhere along the line, Glads became Happy. It was a fitting reflection of her cheerful personality, and the Happy moniker stuck.

Most folks who knew them saw the two women as the classic odd couple. Where Happy was kind-hearted, helpful, and always politically correct, Maggie was hard-drinking and tough-talking, with a trademark dour mood and rough-around-the-edges demeanor. Only Maggie still called her old friend "Glads" and Happy let her get away with it.

Happy told Maggie what she'd seen across the lake, in Maggie's neighborhood. Stonewall Mansion had been the scene of a gruesome murder four months earlier. Most folks expected the mansion would remain empty for some time, if not indefinitely. With the homicide unsolved and the primary suspect on the lam, a rumor was circulating that the mansion was haunted by the restless soul of the murder victim, Ruby Rosa. The scuttlebutt was repeated by patrons in Mel's Barber Shop, by shoppers at Union Gap Grocery Mart, and by churchgoers at all the Sunday services.

"Looks like someone's moving in," said Happy. "What are your people saying, Mags?"

Maggie was uncharacteristically taken aback. It was unlike her to not know what was going on in her neighborhood. As a semi-retired investigative print journalist and crime reporter, she remained the go-to candidate for breaking news. Once a reporter, always a reporter.

"Uh, Glads, let me get back to you. Need to get home and

cleaned up. How about joining me and our new intern, Ally, for lunch today? She's going to be staying with us this summer, and Mac's asked me to take her under my wing, so to speak, show her around town, and teach her everything I know about working in a newsroom. His words, not mine," she chuckled. Mac was Maggie's husband, Ralph McGuire, owner and publisher of the *Lakeside Ledger*, Union Gap's weekly newspaper.

"We're meeting at Creekside at noon, and I'd really like you to join us."

"Why me?" asked Happy. "I don't want to intrude."

"Don't be silly, Glads. You're the unofficial historian of Union Gap, and you're on my short list of people for Ally to meet."

Happy hesitated. She often left the bookstore in the capable hands of her nephew Kyle Kalahan, and she wasn't concerned about letting him mind the shop while she went to lunch. However… Happy wasn't sure she was up to suffering through Maggie's three martini lunch and gin-infused babble.

But her curiosity won over and the odd couple agreed to meet at Creekside Café at noon. Happy knew that her friend would have some news of the goings on at Stonewall Mansion by the time they met.

Lunch plans made, Happy O'Hurley and a very happy Pippy Shortstocking O'Hurley went next door to the bistro. It was finally snack time.

Two

The Mean Beans Bistro started out as an unpretentious coffee house with a gawdawful tongue twister of a name: The Mean Beans Caffeine Canteen. Its claim to fame had been offering 50 flavors of coffee. But nothing else. With a dwindling customer base, the establishment was finally brought from the brink of bankruptcy to its present-day status as a favorite stop in Union Gap by Fern Finfrock. It now had a simpler name and a scaled down coffee menu. It also offered home baked breads and pastries, fancy fresh salads, and gourmet deli sandwiches.

Because the community of Union Gap was uber-dog friendly, the bistro included a special "Bone Appétit" menu for its furry four-legged customers, who were always welcome.

A recent addition to the cafe's menu was the daily "Wined Down" on the outdoor Lakewalk patio, where locals gathered after work to de-stress with wine and cheese, socialize, and take in the spectacular sunsets at the west end of Big Gap Lake. Fern Finfrock had performed a miracle in the rebirth of the once ailing establishment, thanks in part to the initial help of her father.

Back in the early days of the revitalization of Union Gap, Fern's father, life-long resident Cletus Finfrock, came into a sizable chunk of money as the result of a horrific accident that took the life of his wife. It left him a well-off but none-too-merry widower with a 10-year-old daughter to raise alone.

His wife, Willa Dean Davis Finfrock, was a big-boned woman

with a sturdy physique that lent itself well to manual labor. While working on the local construction crew that was contracted to assist in preparing the waterfront for The Lakewalk at Union Gap, the backhoe she was operating was broadsided by a fully loaded runaway dump truck. Willa Dean and her 15,000-pound backhoe as well as the 35-ton dump truck and its driver all went over the embankment and into the lake.

The autopsy revealed that Willa Dean's back was crushed and she was likely paralyzed but quite possibly conscious and helpless as she lay drowning. The dump truck driver survived with a skull fracture and several broken bones. He went on to testify that his brakes malfunctioned, causing his vehicle to go barreling down the hill toward the waterfront. This was later substantiated by the teams of heavy machinery experts sent by the insurance companies and lawyers for all involved.

It was determined the malfunction was due to the fact that the aging dump truck's brakes had been manually adjusted so many times that the clutch mechanism was severely worn. A contributing factor was the prolonged application of the brakes as the truck made numerous downhill treks while loaded to capacity or beyond with gravel, eventually causing them to fail completely.

The dump truck was owned and the driver employed by Loneworthy Development, Inc., a high-profile commercial real estate developer out of Northern Virginia. Loneworthy had an impressive reputation for building communities and shopping centers and had partnerships with several well-known consulting firms and financial groups. The company also had an unimpressive safety record with numerous OSHA citations and Workers Compensation claims.

Loneworthy's legal team immediately grasped the liability as well as the potential damage to the company's reputation through prolonged media exposure. The firm's insurance company offered Cletus two million dollars to settle out of court.

Cletus was a man of small stature and limited education. He came from a family of honest, hard-working folk who owned a large farm on the outskirts of Union Gap. He'd dropped out of school in the tenth grade when his father, Grady Finfrock, became gravely ill and bed-ridden with late-stage lung cancer. Cletus and his older brother Dabney worked the fields, milked the cows, and tended to the chickens for the nine months Grady lingered.

Because the family had no health insurance and limited resources, Cletus's mother Dorothy became her husband's full-time caregiver as he died a slow and agonizing death. Shortly thereafter, the older son, Dabney, enlisted in the Army and never returned to Union Gap even when Dorothy took sick and died two years later.

Cletus assumed sole ownership and continued farming, the only job he'd ever known and ever wanted to know. He met Willa Dean Davis at church, married her after a brief courtship and loved her dearly. They complimented each other perfectly. Where Willa Dean was strong-willed and capable, Cletus was soft-spoken and dependable. Cletus leaned on his wife and relied on her.

When Cletus turned to his friend from church, the lawyer Henry H. Livermore, for advice about the settlement proposal, he was told, "You know, Cletus, you could probably get more money, a lot more, with a jury trial."

But Cletus said no. A man of simple means, he knew that no amount of money would bring back Willa Dean. He had his daughter Fern to think about and couldn't stomach the thought of going to court. With the farm and a two-million-dollar settlement, he and Fern would be just fine.

And fine they were, father and daughter, during the next decade. Fern's teenage years were unremarkable. She adored her father, loved animals, and liked to read, in that order. Throughout high school, she had no interest in boys, preferring instead to work beside her father on the farm. She earned spending money for books and grooming supplies for her pony Misty by working as a barista at the Mean Beans Caffeine Canteen. In her free time, she'd saddle Misty, take a book, and set off across the fields with the farm's working dog, a border collie named Molly, trotting alongside. They always went to Fern's special place along the Dominion River where she would sit beneath the big weeping willow tree and escape into the adventures she lived through her books.

Cletus doted on Fern, a sensitive child. He tried his best to compensate for the fact that she'd lost her mother. The seven-figure settlement was invested with the assistance of his lawyer friend Henry, and a substantial portion was placed in an interest-bearing bank account where it was readily available for Cletus to draw on anytime the need or a want arose. Truth was, Cletus had no idea what to do with the money, and it remained in the bank untouched, except when it came to Fern.

On the first anniversary of the death of Willa Dean, Cletus found his daughter curled up in an empty stall in the barn, sobbing softly and clutching a book, with Molly by her side.

Cletus sat down next to her. Neither said a word for several moments. At last, Fern broke the silence.

"I miss Mom," she sniffled.

Cletus was heart-broken to see his daughter so sad. "I miss her too," he said. He wondered what he could do to make her feel better. "You know," he said, "you have a birthday coming up in a couple of weeks. Have you been thinking about what you want? You name it. Anything."

Fern pulled up the neck of her T-shirt and wiped her nose. Like her father, she had little interest in material possessions beyond what was needed to live comfortably, and she rarely asked for anything. So, Cletus was surprised when Fern held up the book she had been clutching and hesitantly asked, "Can I have a pony?"

Unlike his daughter, who at a young age had inherited a love of books from her mother, Cletus had always struggled to read. He looked at the book Fern had brought home from the library. On the cover was a palomino tobiano pinto pony foal. He saw the title, *Misty of Chincoteague*, but couldn't make out the word Chincoteague.

He sat while Fern patiently told him the story of the wild ponies that roam the island of Assateague Island off the coast of Virginia, the yearly roundup, pony swim, and the auction where the ponies are sold. She teared up as she spoke of the two children in the book who lived with their grandparents on nearby Chincoteague Island and their efforts to buy a wild mare named Phantom and her new foal, Misty.

"They were orphans, Daddy," she said of book's young Paul and Maureen Beebe.

Cletus's heart melted seeing the empathy his sensitive and soft-hearted daughter felt for the orphan children and how she related to their dream of owning a pony. "No promises sweetheart," said Cletus, "but we'll see about that pony."

A dairy farmer all of his life, Cletus knew everything there was to know about cows but not a lick about horses. He'd never owned and never wanted to own a horse or a pony. As a young boy, he had gotten a good kick in the shin by a mule his father had leased from a neighboring farm to help plow the fields. Ever since, he shied away from anything equine.

So, he paid a visit to the Books Galore Bookstore in its original location, the converted garage adjoining Happy O'Hurley's house.

He knew Happy would be able to help him sort things out. This was the first time Cletus had come to her bookstore. She was delighted to see him.

"Cletus, how are you? And how is Fern?" Happy spoke with genuine interest. She knew Cletus and Fern from pot luck dinners she often attended at their church and had been good friends with Fern's mother. Willa Dean had shared Happy's passion for books and came to the monthly book club meetings at Books Galore. Newly widowed herself, Happy was delighted to step in after the death of Willa Dean and help with "girl stuff" like taking Fern shopping for school clothes. She loved Fern like a granddaughter.

"Fern's goin' through a rough time right now, Happy, with it bein' the anniversary of Willa Dean's death and all," said Cletus. "But the reason I'm here is 'cause she's got a birthday comin' up. You know how she loves to read. I was wonderin' if you have any more of them *Misty* books. She told me all 'bout the first one and said there are more."

"Well, let me see," said Happy. "Those are older books, from the 40s and 50s." She pulled up her inventory list on the computer. "Sorry, Cletus, I don't have any in stock, but I can order some for you. Should have them within a week."

Cletus said that would be fine and Happy ordered *Stormy, Misty's Foal, Misty's Twilight,* and *Sea Star: Orphan of Chincoteague.*

Then, Cletus had another request.

"Well," said Happy, "Let's get to work on that. Fern is going to be one happy little birthday girl!"

In the days leading up to her birthday in mid-July, Fern kept pumping her father for information. Had he made a decision yet about her having a pony? But Cletus remained non-committal, telling her he was still thinking about it.

The day of her birthday, Fern was excited. She was sure she and her father would walk down to the barn together, hand-in-hand, and there would be the pony of her dreams in the empty stall. She practiced how she would act surprised.

After lunch, Happy pulled up in the driveway and began unloading balloons, birthday cake, ice cream, and presents from her van. Fern was polite and appreciative as she opened presents from both her father and "Gramma Happy." She loved the *Misty* collection from her father and the *Goosebumps* mysteries from Happy. She showed genuine appreciation for the shorts and shirts and jeans to finish out the summer and start school in the fall. She blew out candles and ate cake and ice cream. Afterwards, her father said, "Let's take a walk." Fern was ecstatic. She was sure her pony would be waiting, just as she'd pictured it over and over in her mind.

But when they got to the barn and Fern ran to the empty stall, it was bare except for a miniature stuffed palomino tobiano pinto pony that looked like the Misty illustration on the book cover.

But no real live pony.

Fern swallowed hard. She picked up the stuffed pony, smiled tightly, and holding back tears, hugged her father. "Thank you, Daddy," she said softly.

Happy, who had been standing nearby, asked, "What's that?" She pointed to a piece of cardboard barely visible through the straw.

"Better see what that is," said Cletus.

Fern hesitantly started pawing through the straw and uncovered a giant poster with colorful wording. She screamed with delight and cried and hugged her father, then Happy.

"Read it out loud," said Cletus.

Through sniffles and with her voice pitching excitedly, she read,

"Fern Finfrock, you are going to Chincoteague!" Then, "Don't come home without a pony." Attached were pictures, a brochure about the Wild Pony Auction, and room reservations in Chincoteague for the last week in July when each year the ponies are rounded up to make the swim across from Assateague Island and be sold at auction. That was two weeks away.

Happy had helped Cletus download the information, make the arrangements, and map out the route. Cletus Finfrock, who had never been farther away from his home in southern Virginia than the 50-mile trip to Roanoke, for the first time withdrew money from his interest-bearing account in the Bank of Union Gap. He hitched his two-stall livestock trailer to his pickup truck and set out with his daughter, heading out of the mountains, bound for Virginia's Eastern Shore.

With enough money for Cletus to outbid others for the pony his daughter wanted, Fern Finfrock came home with a palomino tobiano pinto yearling that she named Misty.

During Fern's senior year of high school, Cletus began agonizing about the future for his daughter. Fern was book smart but shy. She never spoke of any plans after graduation. Cletus approached the subject of college first with Happy, and after careful consideration, Happy suggested that Fern should attend Virginia Tech University. It was close to home, in Blacksburg, with a renowned veterinary school, which Happy thought Fern, with her love and concern for animals, might be interested in. Happy downloaded information and made printouts for Cletus.

"No!" Fern was adamant. "I'm not going anywhere," she said firmly when Cletus tried to talk to her about his and Happy's plan for her. "I have everything I need right here in Union Gap. I'm not leaving you."

End of conversation.

Cletus was just as adamant. His daughter was not going to follow in his footsteps and become a farmer. She was much too smart for that, and he'd already decided that the family farming business would end with him. "What're you gonna do here, Fernadina?" he asked, using his pet name for her.

"Actually, I've been thinking about it, Daddy," she said. She got quiet and Cletus waited. She wasn't sure how to approach the subject, so she just came right out and said it. "I want to buy the Mean Beans Caffeine Canteen, Daddy."

Because his daughter never asked for anything, Cletus was taken back to when the little 11-year-old girl sat in the straw in the empty stall in the barn and asked ever so humbly if she could have a pony. He was surprised by her new request. The Mean Beans was going bankrupt. Certainly, she could see this was not a good investment. Fern was a smart girl.

Fern smiled. "Oh, Daddy, believe me, this is an excellent investment. With the building in foreclosure, we can get it cheap, and I have big plans to turn it around."

She told her father how she'd tried and tried, without success, to get Janet Maples to expand her menu and upgrade the shop's interior and exterior. "This is a prime location, Jan," Fern had told her employer. "Right on the waterfront and with room along the Lakewalk for outdoor seating. Folks want breakfast sandwiches and pastries with their morning coffee."

But Janet refused. She didn't want to admit it but the truth was, she had been steadily losing money, had no resources to invest, and no clout with the banks.

"Best of all," Fern told her father, "the Mean Beans building is right next door to Happy's bookstore." Happy had moved her business from her garage to the waterfront location after the stores along The Lakewalk at Union Gap were ready for occupancy.

Cletus never ceased to be amazed by his daughter. Yes, she took after him physically, small in stature to the point of being delicate, and yes, she had inherited his shyness and sensitivity. But when it came to smarts, Fern was Willa Dean's daughter and Cletus could not be more proud. For only the second time since the insurance settlement he went to the Bank of Union Gap and withdrew money from his interest-bearing account, enough to buy the Mean Beans Caffeine Canteen for his daughter and refurbish the business according to her plan.

And that's how Fern Finfrock went from barista to business owner, and the Mean Beans evolved from a floundering caffeine canteen into a popular bistro.

"Mornin' Fern," chirped Happy as she and Pippy came over from the bookstore after her phone call with Maggie. Fern was checking and refilling the coffee urns in the self-service alcove. As usual, by the nine o'clock hour, the urn containing the Mountain Mama Blend was almost empty.

The blend was a special creation that combined Fern's preferred smooth-blended gourmet mountain roast with the hearty flavor of the Jamaican Blue Mountain Bold. Blending the two was the suggestion of the bistro's kitchen manager, Jamaican-born Clover Battersby, who had been recruited by Fern from the Gabby Penwell School of Culinary Arts in Roanoke. Both Fern and Clover agreed that Mountain Mama Blend had a unique "sophistication," and they'd decided to market it as "Rich, but with a hint of natural sweetness and an eye-opening intense aroma." It was a morning favorite of locals, that was clear.

Fern turned toward her surrogate grandmother. "Happy, I was starting to wonder where you and Mr. Pips were. It's not like that little guy to be late for breakfast."

"We had a little distraction this morning," said Happy, pointing outside. "Something's going on across the lake."

"Tell me about it," replied Fern, tilting her head toward the front of the dining room where a small group had gathered.

"Pippy will have his usual, Betty," Happy said to the plump, gray-haired woman behind the counter. The "usual," was an Egg McMutt Tin and a side of sausage-flavored dog biscuit. Both came from the small dog section of the Bone Appétit menu, which touted "Freshly made recipes of tasty, wholesome, natural ingredients for dogs, featuring long grain and wild rice, vegetables, eggs, cheese, and meat flavorings. No artificial ingredients, soy or fillers."

A sign on the wall behind the counter featured a caricature of a happy dog face with an exaggerated grin. The sign boasted, "Our canine friends get only the best when they come to Fern's Mean Beans Bistro."

"And for you, Miss Happy?" Betty asked with her crisp British accent.

"I'm just going to have coffee, thanks Betty, as soon as Fern finishes refilling the Mountain Mama urn."

Pippy took his place in the little hallway that connected the Mean Beans with Books Galore, waiting for his order to be served. Per health department rules, dogs weren't allowed inside the restaurant although "well-mannered" pets were warmly welcomed on the outside patio. Pippy was an exception and a regular inside, and no one ever complained. Even the local health inspector, Horace Orndorff, was on board.

If Pippy happened to be in the bistro during one of Horace's inspections, the "roach patrol," as he was called, turned his head until one of the workers or customers had time to hustle the little dog back to Books Galore. To be prudent, though, Pippy took his meals just outside the dining room in the hallway close to the bookstore into which he could make a hasty retreat if necessary.

There was a loud conversation taking place near the front of the dining room, and Happy hurried over to see what the commotion was all about. Four familiar faces from the Lake County road crew were taking their morning break. Kenny Spickler was looking through binoculars at Stonewall Mansion while Bumper Presgraves, Buzz Cook, and Jim Mason stood nearby, waiting for Kenny to tell them what he was seeing. Another group had gathered outside on the Lakewalk.

"What's going on?" asked Happy.

"Somethin's happenin' over at that haunted house," offered Buzz. "Folks movin' in and out and all around and all the shutters bein' throwed opened."

"Shut your clucker," said Kenny. "Someone just came out onto the upstairs balcony." The group moved outside to have a better look. A male figure was now standing on the balcony overlooking the lake. He was dressed in black, and Kenny, through the binoculars, reported that he had white hair and a neatly-trimmed Van Dyke beard "kinda like Colonel Sanders."

As the crowd started pointing, the man in black raised both hands into the air. He first cast his gaze skyward, then lowered his head and slowly scanned the lake, stopping to stare directly at the group of oglers outside the Mean Beans. He held his stare long enough to make the onlookers uncomfortable. With his hands still upraised, he closed his fists, with the exception of one long finger of each hand pointed upward. The onlookers gave a collective gasp and shrank back. The figure then abruptly spun around, sweeping a black cape around himself in the process, and ducked back through the French doors into the mansion.

Bumper Presgraves, not one known for his tact, declared, "My sweet ass! The fuck was that?" Seeing Happy's scowl of disapproval, he added, "Sorry Miss Happy."

"He gave us the finger," said Buzz.

"Actually," said Happy, "I believe I saw the index fingers raised on each hand, not the middle ones. It's a theatrical gesture given as a signal of appreciation to his fans."

"But, who in crap's name is it?" asked Kenny.

"If I'm not mistaken," said Happy, "that was the elusive and eccentric Hobart Castlebury."

Three

Big Gap Lake was a natural mountain lake nestled between two ridges of the Allegheny Mountains, the Dominion Ridge to the west and the River Ridge to the east. The Dominion River meandered along the mountain range, then snaked down River Ridge. The lake's main artery was Sneaky Creek, which flowed from the Dominion River.

Creekside Café sat alongside Sneaky Creek at the stone bridge that crossed the creek and connected the town of Union Gap on the south with the Gallery, a gated community, just to the north. The lake was narrowest, about a quarter mile across, at the Sneaky Creek point of entry but gradually ballooned toward the west, encompassing 500-plus acres in all.

As Happy pulled into the café parking lot at twelve o'clock for her lunch date with Maggie, her friend was already seated at a table on the outside patio sipping her first martini. Sharing the table, Happy guessed, was Ally the intern. Maggie stood and extended her arm, waving Happy over. The two women greeted each other with a friendly hug. Maggie introduced Happy to Allyson Murphy, an attractive young woman with a pale complexion, long dark auburn hair, and emerald green eyes that were framed with bookish reading glasses she wore while studying the menu.

While Happy ordered an iced tea, Maggie focused on her martini and Ally sipped a diet cola through a straw. All three were enjoying the early May day and admiring the mountain and water views. On certain still days like this, the water of Big Gap Lake was smooth as glass with reflections as vivid as life. Even the few boats on the water appeared respectful, moving in slow motion, or not at all. "Postcard Perfect" was the way Ally, the newcomer, described the scene.

Maggie explained that Ally was from Roanoke and a fourth year multimedia journalism student at Virginia Commonwealth University in Richmond. Mac and Maggie knew her family from the days when Mac was publisher of the *Roanoke Daily Record*. Tim Murphy, Ally's father, was a partner in the law firm of Griffin & Murphy and a member of the Saponi County Board of Supervisors. He was one of the few friends who had stayed loyal to Mac in the wake of a scandal that drove the newsman and his reporter wife out of Roanoke and into seclusion in the mountains.

Tim and his wife Ann loved Union Gap and Big Gap Lake. They were frequent weekend guests at the McGuire home in the Gallery. During one such visit, Tim approached Mac about the possibility of an internship for his daughter.

Ally and her college roommate, Monica Doyle, had taken a semester off from VCU the previous year to spend a few months in Europe with Monica's family. Her father was the "D" in RMD Technologies, Inc., and had relocated to London for a year to start up a new division of the corporation there. Now, Ally was playing catch up at VCU and needed internship credits as she prepared to finish out her senior year in the fall. Mac readily agreed to take her on.

Like most city slickers, Ally was in awe of the mountains, the small town, and the lake. She pointed to the westernmost end of the Big Gap and commented as to the fact that it was largely undeveloped.

"Well," said Happy, "it's a long story, but if the townspeople have their way, it will remain as you see it now."

"What's the story?" asked Ally.

Maggie commented that this girl was going to make a great reporter, always asking questions. "Be prepared," she told Happy.

Their waitress, Deb, had returned, and Happy said, "Let's order, then I'll tell you all about the underhanded tactics of Leon Loneworthy." She used her fingers to make air quotes to emphasize underhanded tactics. All three ordered the special of the day, Creekside's signature tomato basil bisque along with a crab cake sandwich on toasted sourdough with homemade jalapeño tartar sauce. Maggie pointed to her empty glass, indicating she was ready for her second martini.

Ally returned to the topic Happy had introduced. "Tell me about the, quote 'underhanded tactics' of what did you say his name was? Mr. Lonewolf?"

Happy laughed. "Leon Loneworthy," she corrected. "But it's funny you said 'Lonewolf' because that's what they called him. The lone wolf in sheep's clothing."

Union Gap had been a sleepy little town off the beaten path for more than a century, Happy related, when Loneworthy stumbled on it while participating in an annual black bear harvest with his son Preston and fellow members of the Fish Paw Hunting Lodge. A successful real estate developer, Loneworthy immediately recognized the potential for Union Gap to become a popular mountain resort town.

"He envisioned luxury cabins, a lodge, restaurants, shops, fishing charters, parasailing, jet skis, perhaps an equestrian center and even ski slopes." Happy stretched out her arms to demonstrate that Loneworthy's plans encompassed the whole lake.

Ally seemed entranced and peppered Happy for more details. Maggie, on the other hand, looked toward the restaurant, impatient for her drink refill. Happy continued her story.

Loneworthy arranged several meetings with then Mayor Richard "Ducky" Duckworth and the town council but kept the big picture to himself. He wanted to develop the waterfront, he told the local governing body. Put in a lakewalk and a row of shops. A "beautification project" he called it.

A series of town halls was scheduled. The townspeople were excited. They embraced Loneworthy and were eager to get the beautification project started. Meanwhile, Loneworthy fully expected that once the revitalization was underway it would be a simple matter to outsmart the local yokels and move ahead with his plans for a full-blown mountain resort town.

"What happened?" asked Ally. "Considering the lake is still largely undeveloped."

Happy beamed. "Mr. Loneworthy underestimated the resilience of the residents of Union Gap," she said proudly.

Their food arrived, and Happy waited while everyone was being served before continuing. A now grumpy Maggie again pointed to her empty glass. Fortunately, just as Deb was apologizing for the delay, a second server from the bar appeared with Maggie's refill. Sighs of relief were breathed all around.

"This soup is delicious," said Ally, and all agreed. "But, Happy, please go on. I can't wait to hear more about the lone wolf."

To gain the trust of the residents, Happy continued, Loneworthy established what he called a partnership agreement. He would employ local residents and businesses to assist in the construction and provide them with jobs afterwards in the new businesses. It would be a win-win situation for Union Gap, transforming it from a small poor farming town to a beautiful waterfront community and thriving weekend getaway destination where visitors could take time out from the busy rat race of their lives to browse the quaint shops and relax at a lakewalk café.

"The visitors would bring in money," Happy continued, "which would go in the pockets of the townspeople."

"That was a good thing, wasn't it?" asked Ally.

"It was until it wasn't," said Happy. "The first setback came early in the development process with the tragic death of Willa Dean Finfrock."

Happy gave Ally an abbreviated version of the accident, pointing out that while Loneworthy was quick to offer a generous settlement to Willa Dean's husband Cletus, rumors began circulating that the company was operating with substandard equipment and ignoring safety requirements. The incident caused a rift and many of the townspeople wanted out.

"At this point, Loneworthy got tough," Happy continued. "There would be no pulling out. Construction was underway and under contract for development of a mile long stretch of waterfront property on the south side of Big Gap Lake."

Worse, the developer started making known his true plans. Phase One included not only the waterfront revitalization project, which would be a strip of shops along what was called The Lakewalk at Union Gap, but also a lodge, and further down, a campground for RVs, plus cabins and a bathhouse.

Loneworthy had also secretly entered into negotiations to purchase the Jackson property directly across the lake for Phase Two of his development plans. Happy pointed to Jackson's Point, which was prominently visible from where they sat. "He quietly obtained permits from the Lake County Development Authority for the property to be plotted for a hundred and sixty single family homes within an exclusive gated residential community."

"The Gallery," noted Ally.

"Right," said Happy.

Large waterfront homes in the million dollar range were being built around Jackson's Point, leaving Stonewall Mansion intact as a focal point and historical landmark. Inland, clustered neighborhoods featured medium-sized single-family homes and smaller villa-type residences referred to as cottages. There were recreational amenities for dues-paying residents that included a beach and swimming area, a boat launch and small marina, a clubhouse, a nine-hole golf course, and hiking trails.

To the residents of Union Gap, who thought they were only signing on to a small lakefront beautification project, Loneworthy was suddenly a shyster.

"This was how he became known as the lone wolf in sheep's clothing," Happy explained.

The townspeople held town halls and wrung their hands, and complained to the Lake County Development Authority, all to no avail. Construction commenced. Officially, there was nothing they could do. Once the Phase One Lakewalk was complete, Loneworthy hired a public relations firm to promote the picturesque mountain lake community as ideal for family getaways. Professionals were paid to post glowing reviews.

Tourists began flocking to Union Gap. The locals who had been hired to run the campground, the lodge, the eateries and shops were used to a slow-paced, almost lazy lifestyle and were ill-prepared for the influx of noisy, demanding intruders.

Between mouthfuls of sandwich and comments about the generous portion of jumbo lump crab and the zippy sauce, Ally asked more questions. "But, what could they do? The poor locals?" She wanted to know.

Happy was clearly enjoying this captive audience of one and delighted in continuing her story. At the end of the first summer season, the residents were up in arms. Some were in tears. During the next several months, construction continued on the houses at the Gallery, and sales were steady. But enough was enough. Behind closed doors, Mayor Duckworth met with the community elders, the so-called movers and shakers of Union Gap. A plan was hatched and the mayor's covert "Duck Brigade" was dispatched.

The following year, the tourist season began with spring break and the arrival of unruly students from the nearby colleges and universities who saw Union Gap as a perfect party town with a sleepy two-man police force. After two days of drunken carousing, trashing the campground, vomiting and passing out on the Lakewalk, whooping it up, yelling and running noisy jet skis at all hours of night, the Duck Brigade, members of which had formed a volunteer posse, rounded up the lot of them on drunk and disorderly charges, and placed them en masse in the community center. The next morning, as they were sobering up, they were given an ultimatum.

"They could leave and the charges would be dropped," explained Happy, "or they could stay and be prosecuted."

Collectively, the group agreed to leave, but one detainee, Anders Spencer of old money and a sense of entitlement befitting his Northern Virginia preppy pedigree, angrily pointed a finger at the deputized townspeople and vowed that he and his wealthy college cronies would never return.

"You won't get any more of our business," Spencer proclaimed, "and we're going to tell all of our friends to boycott this swamp hole."

Perfect! Just what the Duck Brigade had hoped would happen.

As the summer season commenced, the tourists were shocked to discover that the linens in their rooms at the lodge were not changed, they had to beg for fresh towels, restaurant meals were overcooked or cold when served, shops were closed for long lunches taken by employees, shelves were not restocked, boat charters were canceled, trash accumulated at the campgrounds, and the townspeople in general were rude, or at least not friendly.

"Social media was soon aflood with bad reviews," said Happy.

Ally smiled. "I love it! Then what?"

Happy continued. Loneworthy, the lone wolf, was befuddled. The developer was in the planning stages of Phase Three, which included acquiring much of the undeveloped property around the lake and building another golf course surrounded by condominiums, plus developing a ski resort on a portion of Dominion Ridge overlooking the lake. Instead, at the close of the second summer season, tourism had all but dried up, the townspeople were angry and uncooperative, and investors were no longer interested.

While the original residents of Union Gap joyfully celebrated good riddance to the unwelcome tourists, they came to develop a fondness for the new residents across the lake in the Gallery. Unlike the visitors, these folks were not only good neighbors and now members of the community, but they had money.

"And that saved the town," said Happy.

Back in Northern Virginia, at the head office of Loneworthy Development, Inc., corporate bigwigs had decided to cut their losses and move on. They offered to gift all of their own financial interests in Union Gap to the town.

"Wow!" said Ally. "That must have been great news."

"Well, yes and no," continued Happy. "There was enough interest among the townspeople to assume the outstanding bank loans on the businesses. With Loneworthy and company gone, they intended to make customer service a number one priority. But there was still one sticking point. Before anything could be signed over, hundreds of thousands of dollars in property taxes had to be paid, and Loneworthy had made it clear, he had no intention of paying up. If the town was unwilling or unable, all Loneworthy property would be abandoned for the county to foreclose on. The locals certainly didn't have that kind of money."

"But the Gallery people were willing to pay the taxes?"

Maggie, who up to now had remained silent, content to sip her martinis and let Happy tell the story, butted in. "Willing my ass. We, the so-called wealthy class of glorified over-priced cottages, are paying out the caboose in HOA dues for whatever the high-and-mighty Board of Directors decides for us. Damn bloodsucking personal fiefdom. That's what it is."

"Maggie, so nice of you to join the conversation," said Happy. "Now, tell us what you found out about..." She gestured toward Jackson's Point.

As they all looked across the water, a figure in a hooded black robe was coming down the stone stairway from the mansion. They watched as he went out onto the boat dock, looked around, removed his black robe, ran full speed and cannonballed into the lake buck naked except for a black balaclava covering his head and face. The huge splash disrupted the stillness of the lake. A pair of loons foraging nearby, took to flight, expressing their displeasure with gull-like wailing sounds.

"That," said Maggie, "I believe, is our newest resident freakin' weirdo. Union Gap's first-rate and finest."

"Hobart Castlebury?" asked Happy.

"Yes, and now sole owner of the infamous murder mansion."

"Murder mansion?" Ally was wide-eyed and open-mouthed.

"Stonewall Mansion. It's where Hobart Castlebury's wife was murdered four months ago," chimed in Happy.

"Oh, please," begged Ally, "I want to hear all about it."

"I need another drink," Maggie said.

Four

Hobart Castlebury was born Alfred Kowalczyk. The oldest of four children of Polish immigrant working-class parents, he grew up in the Greenpoint neighborhood of Brooklyn. From a young age, Alfred detested everything about his life. He hated his name. He hated his nationality. He hated his lowly social status, his neighborhood, his bleak future. His family's crowded apartment was always cold and dark and full of anger. Alfred was strikingly attractive but not a likable child. He thrived on bullying other kids and defying rules.

Despite his dour personality, young Alfred had a mentor in Father Joseph "Papa Joe" Ryan. As youth coordinator at St. Francis Xavier Catholic Church, Papa Joe saw potential in Alfred if, and only if, that hostility could somehow be channeled through a positive outlet. Papa Joe thought he knew just where that might be.

The Back Street Theatre Company in Brooklyn was established as a venue for oppressed and troubled youth of Greenpoint and soon became a popular theater troupe. With a personality that craved attention, Alfred readily embraced the stage. He thrived on the applause. With a dazzling smile and magnetic stage presence, he was a natural; he knew it and his audiences loved him.

During his teenage years, Alfred started hanging around small off-off-Broadway theaters where he would help with stage setups and tear-downs and run errands. Occasionally, he would receive a tip, but mainly he was in it for the thrill of watching and learning.

He managed to graduate from high school, just barely, and he was ecstatic when the Wayside Playhouse, one of his hangouts, invited him to join their traveling theater troupe as a paid stage hand and backup performer for a summer tour through New England.

Hitting the road, the kid who started out in life with a chip on his shoulder now welcomed each day as a new adventure. As he embarked on this new journey, "Alfred Kowalczyk" was left behind and "Hobart Castlebury" came into his own.

"Hi, Mr. Castlebury, my name is Ally Murphy from the *Lakeside Ledger*. I just learned that you're the new owner of Stonewall Mansion. Congratulations! I would love the opportunity to properly welcome you to the community and interview you for a feature story for our newspaper. Could you please call me back at..."

As she was finishing, someone at the other end picked up the phone. "Begone!" bellowed the voice. Ally was disconnected.

From the next desk over, where she had listened to the exchange via speaker phone, Maggie chuckled. "Ouch!"

"Ugh!" said Ally. "I really didn't think the elusive, erratic Mister C would be agreeable, but it was worth a shot."

Maggie had filled Ally in on what she knew about the murder, which wasn't much. Stonewall Mansion at the time was an events venue. According to news reports, Ruby Rosa, a well-known New York theatrical producer and performer had rented the mansion as a getaway to work on a screen play. She was accompanied by Levi Eriksson, whose stage name was Erik Reno. Ruby called Erik a "close family friend, confidant, and highly valued collaborator."

Six weeks into their stay, the mansion's weekly cleaning crew found the lifeless body of Ruby propped up in her French Louis XVI boudoir chaise lounge with her hands crossed over heart, pressing a red rose against her chest. It was determined that the body had been staged soon after death. The cause of death was ruled strangulation. Ruby's husband, Hobart Castlebury, was in New York at the time and cleared of any involvement in the murder. An all-points bulletin was issued for Levi Eriksson, aka Erik Reno, who, four months later still remained at large.

Ally was captivated by the case and devoured every newspaper report she could find. She wanted to meet Hobart Castlebury and was discouraged by his initial rejection.

"Ally, my dear intern," said Maggie, "any newspaper woman worth her paltry reporter's salary goes after the story like a bloodhound on a trail and grabs hold like a pit bull with steel jaws and doesn't let up. We're going right to Plan B. Let's go see Happy."

"I think that's a great idea," chirped Happy. "Mags, I do like this kinder gentler side of you."

"Glads, I thought you knew me better than that. Of course I have ulterior motives. And Ally here is my partner in crime." Maggie winked at her intern.

"Well, regardless, let's bring Fern into this little venture."

Happy left to go next door and request the presence of her business neighbor for a powwow. She found her nephew Kyle and Fern at a table huddled over *Brain Drain*, a trivia crossword puzzle game they played all the time. Pippy, who had settled in under the table, perked up when he saw his mistress.

"Happy," asked Fern, "what's two words, seven letters for *Sexy Lady Vaudevillian who said, 'Sex is emotion in motion'?*"

"Any letters?" asked Happy.

"Ends with *t* as in *thwart* using the *t* from the clue *prevent*. I got that one," beamed Kyle.

"Yeah, well you didn't know that *hinny* is cross between a male horse and female donkey," chided Fern.

"*Mae West,*" interjected Happy, getting back to the original question. "Famous for her double entendres and clever comebacks. And yes, I'm that old. Now, Fern, 'Team Scheme' is calling a meeting and your presence is requested. Can you come over and meet with Maggie, her new intern Ally, and me in our Board Room?"

"Sure," said Fern. "I can do that. This is our mid-afternoon lull, and I won't be needed until the after-work crowd comes over for Wined Down. Patio business is picking up now that the weather's getting warmer."

"Perfect. And Kyle, I'll need you to come over and mind the store for a while."

"Yes, boss lady," said Kyle, good-naturedly. "But please boss lady, don't beat me no more."

The three were laughing as they locked arms and two-stepped their way back over to Books Galore Bookstore, with the little terrier Pippy right behind.

The Board Room was an area in the upstairs section of the bookstore that had been set up with comfy chairs and tables for board and card games and refreshments during book club meetings. And, for Team Scheme conferences when the need arose.

At the urging of Maggie, Ally started things off. She introduced herself to Fern and gave a recap of her phone call to Stonewall Mansion and the brusque rebuff she received when she attempted to leave a voicemail to set up an interview with Hobart Castlebury.

"I'm the new kid on the block," she said. "I really want to get this scoop. It's such a fascinating story: the 'haunted house', scene of a murder, eccentric new owner...So, Maggie had this idea." She turned toward her mentor.

"It's really Happy's plan," said Maggie. "I'll let her explain it."

Happy was, in a word, happy. As a born storyteller, she described the successful approach they'd come up with once before to solve a difficult problem and how they might be able to use a scaled-down version of it again.

"Back in the days of the 'lone wolf'," she began, "everyone was mad at everyone. The townspeople were mad at Loneworthy. The tourists, were mad at the lack of service. The new residents of the Gallery were mad at the deceit. It was bad all around."

It was true, she conceded, that the developer offered to gift the property to Union Gap, but only with the provision that the town pay the sizable backlog of taxes. Most of the original residents were of meager means and not in a position to absorb the tax burden. And, the residents of the new, exclusive gated community across the bridge stood to lose big in property values. Everyone was concerned that if the developer abandoned ownership and defaulted on taxes, all the Loneworthy holdings would become the property of Lake County to do with as they pleased.

After meeting with their attorney, the Board of Directors of The Gallery Homeowners Association voted to secure a loan to pay the taxes, then repay the loan through a series of yearly special assessments on residents of the gated community. That the Gallery residents took on the tax burden, albeit some begrudgingly, was a tremendous relief, and the townspeople owed their neighbors a debt of gratitude. Happy led the effort to show their appreciation.

"We called it 'Bridging the Gap'," she said.

Five

With Maggie and Fern chiming in, Happy explained that Bridging the Gap had been a community-wide effort. Union Gap boasted people of many talents, and now with the addition of the waterfront Lakewalk, there was a diversity of specialized shops with niche and novelty merchandise. The townspeople had all contributed and feted the northside guests to a large, lively shindig with food, entertainment, and gift bags. It was the start of a union, "bridging the gap" between the Gallery on the north side of Big Gap Lake and the town of Union Gap on the south, with the two sides bonding in friendship.

"So," said Happy, "we thought we could do a scaled down 'Welcome Wagon' type version of Bridging the Gap for our newest neighbor, who also, don't forget, is grieving the loss of his wife. We can gather gifts and present them to Mister C along with an invitation to a special 'Sunset Social' on the Lakewalk in his honor as a way to properly welcome him."

"I love it," said Ally. "It will also give us an opportunity to learn more about him and maybe get new details of the murder."

"I'm in it for the dang scoop," said Maggie. "Getting an exclusive story that will make our little *Lakeside Ledger* a force to be reckoned with."

"Let's do it," said Fern. "I particularly like the idea of reaching out to offer our condolences on the tragic death of his wife." She sounded mournful. "I'll start by commissioning Clover to bake her award-winning Caribbean Key Lime Pie." The creation was always a hit on the Mean Beans' dessert menu. Customers raved about the coconut crust and had fun trying to guess the other ingredients in the top-secret recipe.

As the group dispersed with each team member given instructions for her role, Happy returned downstairs and went to her regional book section where she kept titles by local authors and those with local appeal. She picked up her favorite and held it affectionately.

The Lake at Union Gap was a book by Liam O'Hurley, Happy's late husband and former Professor of History at Virginia's Loudoun Hall College. After his diagnosis at age 44 with Amyotrophic Lateral Sclerosis, commonly referred to as ALS or Lou Gehrig's Disease, Liam and Happy retired to the small town of Union Gap for the clean mountain air and a simpler life.

As a specialist in Virginia history, Professor O'Hurley found the little lake community fascinating. He spent his final years researching and writing about the early settlers who came to the region where the farming was good and the hunting and fishing exceptional.

As the disease weakened his muscles and he lost the ability to move his limbs, the professor dictated the final findings of his research into recordings, which Happy transcribed. Over time, much less time than the couple had hoped for, the muscles in Liam's chest and respiratory system started to fail until the disease proved fatal. *The Lake at Union Gap* was published shortly before Liam's 52nd birthday. The professor died six months later, just about the time Leon Loneworthy and company were moving in on the town with their big dreams and schemes for a thriving mountain resort town.

While Happy was holding the copy of *The Lake at Union Gap*, which she planned to contribute to the Bridging the Gap project, and fondly reminiscing about the man she adored, Daphne Simpson entered the store. At the sound of the bell chiming, Pippy came out of his hideaway under the counter and welcomed her with a wagging tail, doing his job as official greeter.

Daphne was a slim woman in her mid-forties with long dark curly hair, long painted fingernails, a wardrobe of long colorful skirts, and a large collection of long dangling earrings.

"Well hellooo Mr. Pips," she sang rather than said, "And Kyle, how are you?"

Before Kyle could respond, Daphne pressed on. "Is Happy around?"

Happy, who had heard the door chimes and Daphne's voice, stepped out from the regional book section and greeted her friend. "Daphne, how are you, my dear, and how's business at Waterside Treasures?"

"Gettin' ready for the big Memorial Day kick off of summer season. I just received this new shipment of mugs and am hoping you might be willing to put a few on display in your store. You know, send business down my way." Daphne took out the new mugs from her tote bag and placed them on the counter for review. As with most of the inventory in her gift shop a few doors down, the mugs all had a catchy lake theme. *Go Jump in the Lake...On Lake Time...Lakeaholic...*

"Of course I will," agreed Happy, "These mugs are delightful." Then, in her sweetest voice, "And I have a favor to ask of you." She told Daphne about the Bridging the Gap venture underway to welcome Hobart Castlebury, offer condolences on the loss of his wife, and coax the eccentric new resident out of his exclusive shell, namely the spooky mansion.

"These two *On Lake Time* mugs will be perfect to add to the gift basket." She didn't pose it as a question and didn't leave much room for anything other than Daphne's terse, "Of course" response.

Kyle, from his vantage point behind the counter, shook his head and winked at Happy. She gave a conspiratorial wink in return. Pippy, sensing the playful mood, retrieved his favorite toy and began shaking it back and forth. He stood in front of Daphne, wagging his stump of a terrier tail and looking up at her hopefully as if to say, *Wanna play 'Funky Monkey' with me?*

"Sure, why not Mr. Pips?" said Daphne, engaging the little dog in a frisky tug-of-war. "After all, we're living *On Lake Time.*"

Convening the next morning in the Board Room, the four members of Team Scheme reported on their progress in collecting items for the Hobart Castlebury gift basket. They were calling it their version of a swag bag, "Stuff We All Give."

In addition to *The Lake at Union Gap* and the two *On Lake Time* mugs from Daphne, Happy had found a coffee table book of photographs that chronicled the Union Gap waterfront development. And, she'd secured a promise from Gus Tanner that his trio of River Ridge Boys would provide bluegrass music on the Lakewalk when the special Sunset Social event took place.

Fern reported that Clover's special key lime pie was in the works, and she'd prepared a personal invitation, requiring an RSVP, for Hobart Castlebury to attend the Sunset Social on the Lakewalk the following week on Friday evening, nine days away. Maggie and her husband Mac were contributing a six-month subscription to the *Lakeside Ledger.*

Ally had visited the remaining businesses along the Lakewalk and came away with an assortment of gifts and gift certificates, which she assembled on a table in the Board Room. A bottle of

River Ridge Red wine from the Virgin Glen Vineyards outlet store. A half-pound of Double Dark Dare chocolate fudge from Mandie's Candies. Four coupons for complimentary appetizers, beers, or desserts at Jack McKay's Publick House. And, a T-shirt from husbands Lenny and Donald Bailey, owners of Tee Time Lake Apparel.

Fern gave Ally a fist bump. "Very nicely done for the new kid on the block," she said, admiring Ally's haul.

"This new kid," said Maggie, pointing to Ally, "also scored an unlikely win. Show them what you got from 'Ole Man Grimm'."

Ally smiled quizzically at Maggie's reference to Milton Grimsley, the owner of the Generation Gap, a gallery of antiques and vintage gifts and novelties. She produced two decks of collector playing cards that she hoped would appeal to someone in the theater. The first deck was Marchen: Hamelin Edition, celebrating the Germanic culture of the Brothers Grimm with fairy tale images of evil kings, mysterious maidens, and vengeful monsters. The second deck was a custom set inspired by the Victorian era. The images were common animals dressed in period regalia, and each card represented an actual historical figure from Queen Victoria's reign.

"Wow! I am so impressed," grinned Happy, with a look of approval.

"Way to go, girl!" echoed Fern, giving Ally another fist bump.

Ally beamed. "I think these vintage playing cards are perfect for a person with Mister C's theatrical background. But, why do you say this was an 'unlikely win'? Help the new kid out here."

Maggie, Fern, and Happy exchanged knowing grins.

Maggie, never one to beat around the bush, cleared her throat. "Milton Grimsley is a crusty old curmudgeon, a stubborn, ill-tempered sourpuss, to put it bluntly."

Happy took a somewhat gentler tone. "Mr. Grimsley is pretty tight-fisted, never negotiates, never comes down on a sale price, and has never been one to give anything away."

Fern was a little more specific. "Milton won't even hand out candy at Halloween."

All three looked at Ally. "How did you manage to butter him up?" asked Happy. "Did you…"

Maggie interjected, "Well, you know, the old goat is reputed to have an eye for pretty young girls in short sleeveless sundresses."

Ally blushed and crossed her bare arms over her chest. "Well, he did ask if he could have a dance at the Sunset Social if he donated the cards. I said sure. Was that a mistake?"

"Oh, he's harmless," laughed Fern. "The old guy has an ogling eye, and he might try to cop a feel if given half a chance but he responds well to the 'back off' gesture." She assumed the female stance and got Ally to be her male dance partner.

"As soon as you feel him getting too close, put your hands on his chest and push yourself back firmly." She demonstrated. "Hopefully, Ole Grimm gets the hint and you won't have to resort to the nuclear option."

"The nuclear option? You mean…?" asked Ally, wide-eyed.

"Yep, the old standby, a hard and fast knee to the groin."

"Ouch!" Ally voiced what they all felt at that moment, and they all laughed except Happy.

"Fern," clucked Happy, "You sound like you're talking from experience."

"I learned all that on YouTube after I had my own Grimm dance experience," retorted Fern. "Love you Gramma Happy, but I'm not 10-years-old anymore."

"So I've noticed," muttered Happy.

Six

Team Scheme wrapped up their session and agreed to meet back in the Board Room at two o'clock that afternoon to set their plan in motion. There was some discussion about whether to call ahead to the mansion or just show up. After Ally's earlier phone call and the abrupt disconnect, they all agreed it would be best not to give Hobart Castlebury an opportunity to dismiss their attempt at Bringing the Gap. They would just show up.

After they disbanded, Happy set out to run some errands. As she drove, she thought about Fern's declaration that she was not 10-years-old anymore. It was a bittersweet moment for Happy. Although she'd never been a mother herself, she felt the pangs she believed all parents must feel when they realize the child they had lovingly nourished through the years was asserting their independence. At the same time, she was proud of the young woman Fern had become. Fern was pretty, not beautiful like Ally, but attractive in her own way. She was inherently sweet and instantly likable, and sensible, with an admirable level of confidence and competence.

Caught up in these thoughts, Happy was smiling as she pulled into the parking lot of JD's Dockside Station, Union Gap's version of a Wal-Mart Supercenter. She parked across from the banner displaying the store name in big bold letters along with the slogan, "Stop in! Stock up!" and the iconic image of the Union Gap's trademark logo, a jumping largemouth bass.

Dockside Station was owned by John Douglas Stockman, who

had taken a cue from the successful chain of Shop-to-Shore stores he had worked for up and down the East Coast of Maryland and Virginia. Having started out as a part-time shelf stocker at two locations while a student at Salisbury University's Perdue School of Business, he remained with the parent company after graduation. He steadily worked his way up to regional manager of the store chain that catered to vacationers with not only groceries, but also a large array of beach and bay supplies.

JD, as he was known, was an avid fisherman, and while he enjoyed trolling the waters of the Chesapeake Bay near his home in Annapolis, he returned to Union Gap every year with his two sons for some fresh water angling and two weeks of laid-back bliss. He had followed closely the development of the area from the beginning stages to the subsequent downfall of Leon Loneworthy's venture in Union Gap. He was not disappointed to see the collapse of Loneworthy's grand scheme to turn the mountain lake community into a high-profile tourist destination. In fact, he considered the resulting Union Gap just about perfect with its quaint new waterfront Lakewalk and an upscale residential community across the lake while keeping the greater part of the land surrounding the lake untouched.

On one of his visits, he learned that the town's aging community center building was going to be replaced with a new modern civic center adjacent to the town hall. He saw in this an opportunity to escape the fiercely competitive rat race of his life for a simpler lifestyle.

JD had mulled over the pros and cons of buying the community center building, converting it, and becoming a full-time resident of Union Gap. He didn't think about it for long. Rather, John Douglas Stockman, age 48, divorced, two teenage sons with shared custody, cashed in his company stock options and made the bold move to turn a dream into reality. With the establishment of Dockside Station and a personal commitment to more relaxation, JD went from being a full-time merchant and part-time fisherman to the enviable role of part-time merchant and full-time fisherman.

"Happy, how good to see you. How've you been?" JD was in the front of the store posting weekly sale advertisements in the window.

"Been good, thank you, JD. How's business?"

"Can't complain." Pleasantries out of the way, JD asked, "What are your people saying about the goings on across the pond?"

"You mean at Stonewall Mansion? Everyone's talking about it."

JD nodded. "I saw the strangest sight over there a couple of days ago. I was out on the water getting my boat ready for the big bass fishing tournament coming up Memorial Day. I wasn't close enough to get a good look, not that I wanted to, I swear, but I saw a hooded naked man run down the dock and make a big splash. Then, I watched as he hauled his bare butt out of the water and up the stone steps to the mansion."

Happy laughed out loud, but was non-committal. "I did hear something about that. Our reporter gal Maggie's on the story, and hopefully we'll have more news soon." She looked at her watch and feigned surprise at the time. "Gotta run…Take care," she said and scurried off.

Happy traversed the narrow aisles, encountering townspeople who stopped her along the way. Everyone, it seemed, had heard something and wanted to know what was going on at Stonewall Mansion. Word had gotten around about a character in black on the upstairs balcony. But Happy was vague in her responses, hinting she may have some news soon.

She continued through the different sections: kids clothes, fishing gear…groceries, fishing gear…electronics, fishing gear…At every turn, the store reflected JD's passion for fishing, with displays of rods and reels, lures and tackles, nets and special buckets…You name it. In addition, the entire back wall of the store was devoted to, Yep! fishing.

Finally, she found what she was looking for, a small wicker basket, just about the right size to hold the gifts the team had accumulated. She hurriedly checked out and left. On her way back to the waterfront, she stopped at the visitors' center in the town hall and collected brochures about the area's places of interest, things to do, and maps. These, she thought, would make nice fillers.

"I just don't think it's a good idea."

Kyle was pacing around the front of Books Galore Bookstore. Happy had just walked in on an argument and saw the agitation on his face.

"Happy," said Fern, "please tell Kyle to stop worrying. We're simply making a neighborly visit to a new resident, who also happens to be in mourning over the tragic loss of his wife."

"A new resident who by all accounts is an eccentric old fool and who may or may not be involved in the murder of his wife." Kyle emphasized the word murder with air quotes. "A murder, I might add, that took place in the very house you're planning to visit. A monstrous old house that's as creepy as its new owner."

Happy set down the wicker basket and interjected. "Kyle, you've been listening to too many ghost stories…"

Kyle cut in. "Not ghost stories, Aunt Gladys, a real live un-solved murder." Referring to Happy as "Aunt Gladys" was Kyle's way of showing displeasure. "At least let me go with you girls."

"Nonsense!" Happy was adamant.

"Us 'girls'?" Fern was offended.

"What about us girls?" asked Maggie, wearing her own look of aggravation as she came in with Ally.

"I'll fill you in on the way over," said Happy. "We're running late. Let's get packing."

They arranged the gifts in the wicker basket while Fern filled Maggie and Ally in on Kyle's concerns about "us girls" heading over to the spooky Stonewall Mansion and encountering the fright-ful Hobart Castlebury without the protection of a male escort.

"Ugh!" Ally was aghast. "Men! Maggie, tell them about the encounter we had on the way over here."

"Don't get me started," said Maggie. But then, she began to rant. She and Ally had gone from the *Ledger* office to the McGuire house in the Gallery for lunch, and had started back to reconvene with Team Scheme.

"We were just driving along minding our own business, and that sneaky little roving rent-a-cop, Darrell Dumbass What's-His-Name, jumped out of the bushes, right in front of our SUV, pointing a gigantic gun at us. I about piddled my panties."

"What?" gasped Fern.

Ally quickly jumped in. "It was a radar gun," she clarified. "And the little guy, well, yes, he actually is a little guy, is part of the Gallery's roving security patrol."

"Little guy with delusions of grandeur," grumbled Maggie. "Said I was speeding. Wouldn't even let me explain that we were running late for an extremely important engagement, and doing 45 in a 25 zone was no big deal. Kids are in school, or supposed to be, and we're paying top dollar for state-of-the-art walking trails for pedestrians. Damn homeowners 'ass-o-ciation' needs to mind its own business. But, snooty President Boggs and her Board of Degenerates have determined that we, the so-called privileged, deserve security, and paying Little Darrell, he better produce at least one fifty-dollar citation every hour."

Maggie was on a roll, and Happy needed her to end it. "Okay, ladies. Show time!" she called.

"Dumbassery! That's what I call it," said Maggie, making sure she got in the last word, like she always did.

The foursome gathered up the loot they were delivering. Maggie and Ally carried the basket while Happy gave last minute instructions to Kyle as they went out the door. Happy had offered to drive, but Maggie insisted, arguing she had the bigger vehicle to carry the four of them plus their precious cargo. Fern didn't say anything, but considering Maggie's account of earlier roadway shenanigans, she decided to carry Clover's secret-recipe key lime pie on her lap to ensure it arrived unscathed.

After crossing the stone bridge and making an immediate left turn, they followed the quarter-mile private access road that led directly to Jackson's Point, the strip of land that jutted out into the lake, where Stonewall Mansion prominently sat. All except Ally had been to the mansion on previous occasions for events and were familiar with the layout. Maggie pulled into the old visitor parking lot and killed the engine.

Fern, who earlier had been outraged when Kyle tried to persuade her not to go, now felt a little queasy. *Maybe we should have called first,* she thought. *Maybe this wasn't such a great idea after all.*

Stonewall Mansion dated back to the Civil War era and had weathered many attempts to be placed on the National Register of Historic Places. Not wanting to be regulated or limited in what they could do, the chain of owners through the years had all rejected efforts by historic preservationists to nominate the property for inclusion. Instead, the mansion was kept afloat as a private events venue even though keeping up with the maintenance of the aging structure was an ongoing challenge.

With Maggie and Ally carrying the basket, Fern clutching the key lime pie, and Happy leading the way, the foursome made their way toward the front entrance. A massive wrought iron gate that blocked entrance to the brick walkway leading to the porch still stood, but years of exposure to the elements left it rusted and in disrepair. When Maggie tried the latch and gave a slight nudge, the screws holding the upper hinge broke free. The gate teetered and swayed before sagging in an unsteady state of lopsidedness.

Fern gasped with a sense of foreboding like a naughty child in big trouble. "Deep doo-doo," she could hear her daddy say. Ally was examining the gate, optimistic that they could prop it back into place, then continue on as though nothing had happened. Maggie, a seasoned, tough-as-nails investigative reporter who had been in scrapes far more sticky than this, merely laughed. Happy, for her part, was mentally making plans to visit Herb at Lewis's Hardware and make arrangements to have Herb's handyman, Alejandro, replace the gate's hinges.

"Shall we proceed?" asked Happy. "I'll let Mister C know that this'll be taken care of."

Continuing down the brick walkway, then up a flight of six stairs, they stood at a large rustic double door entrance. A doorbell with a loud Beethoven's Fifth ringtone announced their arrival. After what seemed an eternity, static woke up the video intercom adjacent to the door.

"Speak!" The command was full-throated, deep, resonant.

"Mr. Castlebury? I'm Gladys O'Hurley, here with Maggie McGuire, Allyson Murphy, and Fern Finfrock. We're your friendly neighborhood welcoming committee. We'd like to drop off some gifts from the community and offer condolences on the tragic death of your wife. May we come in?"

"I should say not! Where are your manners? Do you not believe in announcing your visit like civilized society instead of just showing up, uninvited? What did you say your name is?"

"I'm Gladys O'Hurley. But people call me 'Happy'."

"Happy, huh? I'll be the judge of that." The faceless speaker guffawed at his own joke.

Ally cut in. "Mr. Castlebury, I'm Ally Murphy, remember? I did call you, with a very polite request I might add, to meet with you. And your very brusque response? 'Begone!'"

There was a pause, then, "Oh, yes…Step in front of the video camera, please."

Ally felt uncomfortable with the request, but obliged, looking straight into the lens.

"So, the fair maiden of the phone, as I imagined her to be, is in fact a fiery redhead, cheeky and impertinent. Sly little shrew, are you not? Trying to lure me into the arena of public scrutiny."

"Not at all," Ally stammered. "You're much admired, a brilliant master of the stage."

"My dear, *'All the world's a stage, and all the men and women merely players. / They have their exits and their entrances; / And one man in his time plays many parts'*."

"*Hamlet?*" asked Happy.

"Lady Happy," said the voice. "It's a quote from *As You Like It.* Act 2, Scene 7."

Ally countered Castlebury's rebuke: "I am most certainly not a 'sly little shrew'. And, I was not at all attempting to compel you into doing into anything against your will."

"'*The lady doth protest too much, methinks*'," quoted the voice.

"More from *As You Like It*?" asked Happy.

"*Hamlet*, Lady Happy. *Hamlet*. Act 3, Scene 2."

Fern broke in, trying to bring the conversation back to why they were there. "Mr. Castlebury," she said, "We'd like to express how very sorry we are for the loss of your wife. Please accept these gifts along with our condolences."

"Leave them. And begone with you now."

"There you go again," huffed Ally, "with that 'begone' stuff. And, for the record, my hair is not red, it's auburn. There's a difference."

"'*When red headed people are above a certain social grade their hair is auburn*'," said the voice.

"Is that Shakespeare again?" asked Happy. "Doesn't sound like it to me."

The voice laughed. "Very good, oh Happy one. Actually, it is indeed not Shakespeare but in fact Mark Twain."

"If you please, Mr. Castlebury," said Fern, "my pastry chef, Clover Battersby, at the Mean Beans Bistro across the lake made her special Caribbean key lime pie with coconut crust. It shouldn't remain out here long. May I bring it in and put it in your refrigerator? Please?"

"Young lady, stop babbling for heaven's sake. With all due respect to your pastry chef, this is not a good time. I am a very busy man. Leave it, as well as the rest of your good will offerings. I can assure you the pie will receive proper refrigeration."

Maggie, who'd remained uncharacteristically quiet thus far, had not forgotten the real reason she was here. She was a newspaper reporter on a mission, determined to get an exclusive interview and was not going to be dismissed so easily.

"Mr. Castlebury," she said, "we also bring an invitation from the community. Union Gap would like to host a get-together in your honor next Friday evening on the Lakewalk. May we report back that you accept? We've included a formal invitation in our welcome basket."

The big double doors flew open and a figure stood in the entryway. It was not the white-haired Colonel Sanders look-alike with the neatly-trimmed goatee Happy remembered from the balcony scene. This person was clean shaven and dark-haired with the distinguished but casual look of perhaps an elder statesman working at home. He wore a long sleeved pale blue shirt with the sleeves rolled up above the elbows and open necked, showing off a paisley, multicolored ascot.

"My response to your formal invitation," he announced, "will likewise be formally delivered, post haste, I assure you. Now leave me to my important work."

The four visitors stared in awe at Hobart Castlebury and found themselves a bit ill at ease to be in the presence of this commanding figure.

"And for your brazen fiery lady of the auburn hair," he continued, "who doth protest my use of 'begone' as brusque, I shall politely ask, '*Wilt thou be gone?*'"

"*Romeo and Juliet!*" announced Ally. "Much better."

"Just one more matter," said Happy. "Your front gate, I'm afraid, did not take kindly to our entrance. It came apart at the hinges. With your permission, I'll send a handyman to replace the hardware. I can assure you, it will be 'up to snuff', to borrow a line, I believe, from your *Hamlet*."

"You believe!" said the voice, exasperated. "The phrase '*up to snuff'* is spoken in *Hamlet Travestie* by Hamlet's friend Guildenstern."

"You indeed are a brilliant master of the stage," said Happy, admiringly. "I thank you for educating such a mere mortal as my wretched self."

"'*Lord, what fools these mortals be!*'" barked the voice. "And before you ask, Lady Happy, the answer is no, I am not quoting *Hamlet.*"

"*A Midsummer Night's Dream!*" exclaimed a jubilant Happy. "Act 1, Scene 1. And don't try to tell me I'm wrong!"

There was a pause, then the master of the stage turned and stepped back into the house, letting the big double doors slam loudly behind him.

Seven

Ally was at her desk at the *Lakeside Ledger*. She was trying to concentrate on editing and designing the layout for six obituaries, the weekly submission received that morning from Humphrey's Funeral Home in the nearby county seat of Dominion Mills, but she wasn't having much luck. She was distracted, talking to herself, reliving the visit to Stonewall Mansion the previous day, and remembering what Hobart Castlebury called her.

"Fiery redhead!"

"Cheeky and impertinent!"

"Sly little shrew!"

The words stung.

"Screw you, Hobart Castlebury! You self-righteous old goat!" She was venting loudly.

"Excuse me?"

Ally froze. She hadn't heard the visitor come in. She slowly turned and took in the handsome, well put-together man. Thirtyish, she guessed, with a polished look of professionalism: tousled short pompadour of thick dark blond hair that looked effortlessly casual but, Ally knew, was expensively styled; tasteful, well-trimmed facial hair, on the shorter side; eyes so blue they almost didn't look real peering from behind trendy tortoise shell glasses; tailor-made suit; sexy...Oh, yes, definitely sexy!

Ally blushed. "Oh," she said. "I hope you weren't listening to my little rant. Yesterday was, simply, unbelievable. Can I help you?"

The visitor gave a slight smile, and Ally thought she may have caught a hint of a wink. "Are you Allyson Murphy?"

"Yes." She looked uncertainly at the visitor. "And you are?"

"George Rothman. I was asked to deliver this to you." The visitor held out a white envelope closed with a gold wax seal.

Ally took the envelope. Admiring the seal, she noticed it was monogrammed in what appeared to be Edwardian Script, a calligraphic typeface. She gave a slight gasp. "HC?" She looked questioningly at George Rothman. "Hobart Castlebury?"

The visitor gave a slight nod. "I understand you and your 'Welcome Wagon' friends need a response to the invitation extended to my boss." He emphasized Welcome Wagon with air quotes.

Ally opened the envelope and read the hand-written note:

> *Mister Hobart Castlebury accepts with pleasure your*
> *kind invitation for Friday, the twelfth day of May, in the year*
> *MMXVII at sunset on the promenade (commonly referred to*
> *by locals as "the Lakewalk") by the side of Big Gap Lake in*
> *Union Gap, Virginia.*

Ally smiled with satisfaction, then frowned, embarrassed, as she remembered her rant about Hobart Castlebury while this George Rothman person was listening.

"You said Hobart Castlebury is your boss?"

Rothman nodded. "I'm Mr. Castlebury's personal assistant."

"Hobart Castlebury's who? What?" Maggie was wide-eyed and uncharacteristically at a loss for words. She and her publisher husband were in Mac's office where they had been reviewing the financials for the *Lakeside Ledger*. Mac seemed equally bemused.

"His 'personal assistant'," Ally whispered. She did a downward gesture with her hands in front of her, signaling they should keep their voices down. "George Rothman. He's waiting out front."

Shaking her head and lowering her voice, Maggie asked, "What does he want?"

Ally handed Maggie the envelope with the monogrammed gold wax seal and the handwritten invitation response inside. "He delivered this on Mr. Castlebury's behalf. The elusive Mister C accepts with pleasure."

"And?"

"And, he wants to take me to lunch, at Mister C's request, to make amends for his mean behavior yesterday."

"Where does he intend to take you?"

"He said the place of my choosing. He's new in town. I was thinking the Mean Beans. We can sit outside. I think he wants me to fill him in as much as I want to pick his brain."

"And just what do you hope to get from him?"

"Maggie, I hope to get an exclusive. You know…the scoop? So, can I have an early and extended lunch today?"

"Did you finish those obituaries?"

"Umm, no," Ally stammered. "But I'll stay late today to get them done."

"Well see that you do," said Maggie, a bit too harshly.

"Don't mind her," Mac chimed in. "Maggie's just jealous that you got invited and not her."

"Short. Sleeveless. Sundress…" mumbled Maggie, dismissing Ally with a wave of her hand.

"Kyle, check this out!" Happy was looking out the front

window of Books Galore. "That's Ally sitting at the table close to the water, but who's the man? Have you seen him before?"

Kyle joined Happy at the window. He shook his head. "No idea, never seen him."

Happy dispatched Kyle to the Mean Beans to see what he could find out. Always ready for an excuse to visit with Fern, he didn't protest. As he started toward the door connecting Books Galore with Mean Beans, Pippy, ever optimistic that a visit next door might result in a snack, came bounding out of his cubbyhole under the counter and followed closely at Kyle's heels. After they were gone, Happy wasted no time calling Maggie.

"Mags, what the darn heck is your intern up to."

Maggie was still in a foul mood at being passed over for the lunch date with the attractive, mysterious stranger. She filled Happy in on the man called George Rothman, who claimed to be Hobart Castlebury's personal assistant, who'd delivered a formal acceptance to their invitation, and then invited Ally to lunch.

"Back in the day," she said, "I was the tart young hussy who got the guys and the story. I could wiggle my butt with the best of them. Sources would follow me around like I had them on short chains with rings through their noses."

"I'll bet you could. But Ally's not like that. She takes her career very seriously."

"Like I don't?"

"Still," Happy marveled, "Mister C has agreed to grace us with his presence. That's big."

"Should be a hoot," Maggie shot back.

"He's a fascinating character," said Happy. "I could banter with him all day about Shakespeare."

"Ally, so nice of you to stop by for lunch." Fern smiled quizzically at her new friend. She was so curious when she saw Ally and her handsome companion had seated themselves outside, she'd taken the menus from her lunchtime waitress, Phoebe, announcing that she'd see to Table Number 6 herself.

Fern handed a menu to Ally, then introduced herself to Ally's companion as she handed one to him. "I'm Fern Finfrock, owner of the Mean Beans Bistro. Welcome!"

"George Rothman," he said, rising and extending his hand, which Fern shook. She stood waiting, hoping for more information.

Ally was clearly enjoying this. After a few awkward moments of silence, she smiled broadly. "Fern, George is Hobart Castlebury's personal assistant."

The announcement had the effect Ally expected. Fern was at a loss for words.

"George," Ally continued, "Fern was part of our little welcoming committee that delivered the gift basket yesterday."

"Oh yes, of course," said George. "The bearer of the amazing key lime pie. My boss shared it with me. I must say we ate, devoured actually, nearly the whole pie. I must give my compliments to your pastry chef. Is she available?"

Fern stammered. "Umm, I'll see. Would you like...can I get you something to drink. Do you want to order, I mean hear about our lunch specials?"

George laughed good-naturedly. "For now, I'll just have a glass of Cabernet Sauvignon." He invited Ally to join him for a glass of wine, but she declined.

"I'll have a diet cola, thanks Fern." To George she said, "I am, after all, supposed to be working."

"I hope this afternoon won't be all work. I am, after all," George said mockingly, "supposed to be making it up to you for the dastardly behavior of that 'self-righteous old goat'."

Ally gasped and covered her face, embarrassed that Hobart Castlebury's personal assistant was quoting her snooty words about his boss. George smiled and winked, having a little fun of his own. Fern, who was taking all this in, finally excused herself to get the drinks.

"I was hoping," said George, "that you might have some time after lunch to show me around a bit. I expect I'll be sticking around these parts for a while."

"My pleasure. And, while we are in this 'hoping' frame of mind, I sure would like to get a story for the *Ledger*, to prove myself as a lowly intern. This is a big deal. Hobart Castlebury, a giant of the stage, new owner of Stonewall Mansion, the murder..." She stopped herself. "Oh, I'm so sorry. How terribly ill-mannered of me, letting that slip. Of course, the murder of his wife is very personal."

"Well, yes, it is. And while I do appreciate your passion as a young reporter, certain topics have to be off-limits. And, yes, one of those topics is the murder. It's still under investigation, and Mr. Castlebury is not at liberty to discuss the case, even if he wanted to."

"Please..." Ally attempted again to apologize, but George held up his hand and continued, "That said, Mr. Castlebury also wishes to convey his apologies for his brusqueness when you called. Believe it or not, he actually does have a soft side, but he can be rough around the edges."

Ally was eager to continue the conversation, but at that moment Fern returned with the drinks and a heavyset, dark-skinned, pleasant-faced, apron-clad, clearly reluctant woman in tow.

"Mr. Rothman, umm, George, this is Clover Battersby, my all-around kitchen wizard: head cook, kitchen manager, creator of that award-winning secret-recipe Caribbean key lime pie, as well as architect of our very own special Mountain Mama Blend coffee."

"Yuh a too kind, Miss Fern," responded Clover. Diffident by nature and self-conscious about her heavily-accented Jamaican English, Clover shied away from situations that required her to converse with Americans. She often reverted back involuntarily to her native Patois dialect, which was not easily understood by non-Jamaicans. She turned to George and awkwardly asked, "Howdeedo?"

George understood her perfectly. "I'm well, ma'am" he said, rising to his feet, taking her hand and kissing it in a gentlemanly gesture. "Miss Clover, I bring compliments of the highest order from my boss, Hobart Castlebury, on your heavenly key lime pie. As I was telling Miss Fern, Mr. Castlebury and I consumed nearly the entire pie in one sitting last night. You are indeed a masterful chef, and I look forward to enjoying more of your creations."

"Thenk yuh," said Clover. "Yuh a kind man, Mista George." She turned to Fern with a look that bespoke her desire to escape back to the comfort of her kitchen. Fern nodded approval.

"Mi gaan now, Mista George," she said as she turned leave.

"Good-bye to you, too, Miss Clover. Take care."

Both Fern and Ally were duly impressed by this interesting new man in town and his courtly manners.

"So, you also speak Jamaican?" teased Ally.

"Actually," said George, "English, Jamaican English, is the official language of Jamaica. But, many Jamaicans don't speak English as their native language. They learn it as a second language with Jamaican Patois being first."

"Actually," said Fern, "Clover speaks English very well, although with a thick accent. But, in unfamiliar situations, like now, she gets nervous and automatically reverts back to Patois, where she's more comfortable."

Ally, eager to move on, prompted Fern, "Tell us about your lunch specials. I'm starving."

"Me too," said George.

Fern recited the list of daily specials. Ally ordered a cup of pureed pumpkin soup and a salad of romaine hearts with grilled chicken and a creamy anchovy dressing. George went for the smoked turkey sandwich on ciabatta with asiago, baby spinach, and a sun-dried tomato aioli spread.

After Fern left, Ally turned the conversation back to where they left off when they first sat down. "So," she said, "we were talking about our 'hopes', as in my human interest story for the *Ledger*."

George laughed. "I believe we were talking about topics off-limits, and by that I mean, if they come up, not for publication."

"Okay, one is the murder, I get that. What else?"

"First, let me explain that while Hobart Castlebury has a very public image, his personal life is very private. He bought the big house and moved to Union Gap to get out of the spotlight and hole up here in the mountains. For personal reasons."

"Ally, my goodness, fancy seeing you here."

Ally looked up to see Happy, smiling broadly. "I was just passing by, on my way to see Daphne at Waterside Treasures and get some more of those delightful mugs and some other things to complete the display in the bookstore. And to see if she would do the same for me with a few best-sellers that just came in."

"Happy, good to see you," muttered Ally, with a tight smile that indicated she was not at all pleased and did not believe for a minute that Happy just happened to be passing by.

Turning to George, Happy extended her hand and introduced herself. "I'm Happy O'Hurley. I own the bookstore next door. Are you new in town?"

Ally's irritation didn't go unnoticed by George, but he assumed his charming persona nonetheless. "George Rothman, Ms. O'Hurley, personal assistant to Hobart Castlebury, who just moved into the big house on the point, directly across the lake."

"Oh, please call me Happy, and I am a big fan of Hobart Castlebury. I was, in fact, part of a welcoming committee that dropped off a gift basket there yesterday, along with Ally here, and I am delighted to meet you, and, oh my, please forgive my babbling and my intrusion."

Happy made no effort, however, to leave, and George, gentleman that he was, encouraged her stay. They talked about her late husband's book, *The Lake at Union Gap*, which had been included in the welcome basket, and about Happy being taken to task over quotations from Shakespeare by the stage meister Hobart Castlebury.

Ally was mentally willing Happy to be on her way, when Fern arrived, thankfully, with their lunch.

"Well, I best be moseying along," said Happy. "Again my apologies for intruding. Enjoy your lunch."

As Fern served the food, Ally shook her head at the stunt Happy had pulled. She knew darn well that Happy and Maggie had talked prior to Happy's "accidental" meeting.

"Oh yeah, she just happened to be passing by," Ally snorted.

Fern, eager to be a part of this conversation, confided how Happy had sent Kyle over to the Mean Beans to find out what was going on. "You've become quite the Union Gap sensation," Fern said to George.

"At least among the nosy townspeople," mumbled Ally.

George was clearly enjoying this exchange. "So, how many others were part of this 'Welcome Wagon'?" he asked, smiling.

"Well, much of the town contributed," said Ally, "but just four of us delivered: Happy, Fern, me, and my boss Maggie."

"Speak of the devil," said Fern gesturing toward a familiar face coming their way.

"Oh Ally, here you are." Ally looked up to see Maggie coming over to the table.

"I wanted to let you know that Bobby just dropped off his draft of the town council meeting last night. I left it on your desk. Please proof it and clean it up when you get back to the office after you finish up with those obituaries." Bobby Hinkleberry was a stringer for the *Ledger*, a part-timer who reported on events as needed.

Maggie continued, "I'm heading over to Town Hall to see what's on the agenda for Memorial Day. Not that far off you know." She turned to George and said, "I'm Maggie McGuire, Managing Editor of the *Lakeside Ledger*, and you must be George Rothman, Hobart Castlebury's personal assistant."

"Oh my, that looks good," Maggie said, eyeing the plates of food in front of Ally and George. "Mind if I join you for a quick lunch? I'm starving." Without waiting for an answer, Maggie pulled up a chair from an adjoining table and turned to Fern to take her order for a bowl of soup and glass of wine.

Having been interrupted twice already while they were eating, Ally again asked George about the off-the-record topics. George reiterated, for Maggie's benefit, that the murder was off the record for personal reasons and because of the ongoing investigation. "Another issue I am not to discuss is Mr. Castlebury's health."

"What about his health," asked Maggie, ignoring the fact that George had just said he couldn't discuss it.

George held up his hands in a back-off gesture, and Maggie, unperturbed, focused on her pinot grigio.

"What else?" asked Ally.

"Finances."

"Finances?"

"As Mr. Castlebury's personal assistant, I'm working with him to straighten out some issues with his late wife's estate." He again held up his hands when he saw Maggie getting ready to ask another question. "It's all very confidential," he said.

"Okay, what can we talk about?" asked Ally.

"Well, for starters, let's talk about how to refer to and how to address Hobart Castlebury. He dislikes being called Mr. Castlebury. He prefers 'Hobart'. Or..." George said with a wink, "'Hobart the Great'!"

"I love it!" declared Ally.

Maggie wanted George's take on the strange behavior they'd seen and heard about at Stonewall Mansion.

"Well," said George, "Hobart is eccentric, no denying that. More so since the murder of his wife. He loved her very much."

George went on to tell them the story of the young Alfred Kowalczyk, growing up in Brooklyn, poor, defiant and angry, until he was introduced to a local youth theater company where he thrived on being in the spotlight, then later ran away with a traveling theater troupe, changed his name, and never looked back.

George was a skilled story-teller. Both Ally and Maggie were entranced as he took them through the Alfred-to-Hobart transformation. Maggie looked at her watch, gave Ally her *Ledger* credit card, said her good-byes, and with a "Nice to meet you George," she hurried off.

Fern had stopped by to clear away the dishes and returned with two complimentary cups of Mountain Mama Blend coffee and Clover's dessert of the day, Jamaican Rum Cake. They were raving about the dessert and enjoying the moments they finally had to themselves when Happy came bustling back from her visit with Daphne. She stopped at the table and held up a tote bag of "stuff," as she called it, to show that her trip was a success.

"Oh my," she said, "is that Clover's Jamaican Rum Cake?" She plopped herself down in the chair Maggie had just vacated and asked the waitress Phoebe, who was clearing other tables, to bring her a slice of cake and cup of coffee. Then, almost as an afterthought, she asked, "Mind if I join you?"

"Wow!" exclaimed Ally when she and George had finally gotten away. "I am so sorry about the intrusions."

George was good-natured about the interruptions, but admitted he was glad to be free of the attention, which he noted was all from the so-called welcoming committee.

To which Ally replied, "Some coincidence, huh?"

They walked down the Lakewalk, past the LakeView Lodge at Union Gap, and into the LakeShore Campground where they found a picnic table and sat on top.

"So," queried George, "what else does the esteemed newshound wish to know?"

"Oh, so much!" exclaimed Ally. "I was especially intrigued about Ruby Rosa. Not the murder, I know that's off-limits, but the love story. Who was she? How did she and Hobart meet? What was their marriage like?"

"Oh, it was inevitable that the paths of Ruby Rosa and Hobart Castlebury would intersect," said George.

"Can I write about that?"

"Come with me," said George, taking Ally by the hand.

Eight

Ally was finally back at her desk at the *Lakeside Ledger*. It was six o'clock and eerily quiet for the usually bustling newsroom. Everyone had gone home for the day, and on her desk she found a pile of printouts of electronic files with instructions. She rifled through the stack and glanced at the Post-it Notes. "Please proof this." "Need the obits in final form, laid out, and ready for Mac first thing in the morning." "This needs serious editing. See what you can do to fix it."

Ugh! Ally sighed. Where to start? Her head was spinning. She went to the break room and made herself a cup of herbal tea. Having been out of the office most of the day, she knew she needed to get to work right away, but first she just wanted to unwind and think back on her afternoon with the mysterious Mr. Rothman. The delightful Mr. Rothman. The oh-so-funny Mr. Rothman. *Just five minutes,* she told herself.

George had given her the green light to write a feature story about the Hobart Castlebury and Ruby Rosa love connection and had provided her with reference materials as well as personal anecdotes.

After leaving the campground that afternoon, Ally was surprised when they stopped at the Union Gap Public Library. With its columned portico, brick walls, and ivy-covered façade, it had been the home of a founding father of Union Gap and was one of the town's oldest and most recognizable buildings.

"The library?" she asked.

"You'll see," said George.

Leading her into the reception area, he inquired at the desk where to find the reference section. They were directed to the second floor by a librarian with short dark hair, a big smile, and a tag that read, "*Hello, my name is* **Susan**. *I am a Bibliophile.*"

On the mezzanine, midway between the first and second levels, George and Ally were ushered up a short flight of stairs by an older, bespectacled, woman, this one unsmiling, wearing a tag that read "*Hello, my name is* **Ethel**. *I am a Bibliophile.*"

George walked slowly through the aisles, with Ally close behind. He finally found one of the works he was looking for: *Offstage: A Behind the Scenes Look at Celebrated Theater Personalities.* He took the book and led Ally to a table in the back. As he thumbed through the pages, he explained that little had been written about Hobart's life with Ruby. Both were well-known in their own right but their private lives were largely a mystery. *Offstage* delved into the non-public aspects of big name personalities.

The book was a reference work and couldn't be checked out, so George summoned Ethel-the-Bibliophile and asked her where he could copy some pages. The chapter, "Hobart Castlebury and Ruby Rosa: Romance Behind the Scenes," was 34 pages long, all of which he planned to copy.

Ethel-the-Bibliophile directed him to the copier room, telling him it was twenty-five cents per page, and the copier only took quarters. After Ethel had retreated back to her desk, George filled Ally in on what was in the material. He told her that it could be cited as a reference for parts of the Hobart and Ruby love story he was about to tell her.

Ally wished she had a tape recorder or even a pen and pad to take notes, but George waved her off.

"Let's just chat," he said. "Where should I start?"

"Well," said Ally, "I know about Hobart's background, the bad boy from Brooklyn and his love of the stage. Tell me about Ruby. Who was she?"

"Ruby Rosa was the stage name for Rosa Maria Talone, the oldest of six daughters born to Tony and Maria Talone and a granddaughter of Joey Talone, a capo in the Talone Crime Family of New York."

"No way!" exclaimed Ally, eyes wide. "Can I quote you?"

Ethel-the-Bibliophile was arranging books on a shelf nearby. She looked their way with a scowl and put her finger to her lips to signal "Quiet."

"It's all in the pages that we're going to copy," George said softly. "I prefer that you don't mention me. I wasn't there."

Ally lowered her voice. "This is fascinating."

She sat entranced while George told the story of how the Talone Crime Family eventually broke up when the feds began investigating their string of restaurants and auditing the books for money laundering. Before any indictments were handed up, the restaurants were sold or closed and most of the Joey Talone Crime Family disappeared. It was rumored they fled to the Caribbean, out of reach of the FBI, and lived off money they'd stashed away in offshore bank accounts.

Meanwhile, back in New York, the Tony Talone family was dabbling in various business ventures.

"Like what?" asked Ally.

"One of the family businesses was a colorful but short-lived operation they started called *Widgets & Whatsits: Where Thoughts Become Things*. You may have heard of it. Or maybe not."

Ally shook her head no.

George explained that *Widgets & Whatsits* was analogous to the more widely promoted *As Seen on TV*. Both gave unknown inventors an outlet for their products.

"You mean like 'But wait, there's more…?'" Ally asked, being overly dramatic, speaking low but miming a booming voice.

"Hey, you could be a pitchman," said George, a bit too loudly.

Ally snorted, unable to help herself. She put her hand over her mouth in an attempt to muffle her laugh.

Ethel-the-Bibliophile was now strongly tsk-tsking her disapproval before turning and leaving in a huff, headed back to her mezzanine reference desk.

"And," continued George, "to answer your question, yes, it was similar to *As Seen on TV* but the Talone family business never became that popular, mainly because the family shied away from being seen on TV. Rather, they pitched their products solely in their small chain of *Widgets & Whatsits* stores."

"Great story," said Ally. "Thanks for sharing. But…" she giggled, "I have to say, a mob family selling widgets? Too funny."

George chuckled in agreement. "Now," he said, "let's get those copies made. How many quarters do you have?"

Ally checked her change purse and found only two. George had four.

"I guess," ventured George, "one of us will have to ask the old sourpuss for change."

Ally still had the *Lakeside Ledger* credit card she had been given when Maggie left the Mean Beans earlier. "I'll go," she offered.

Presenting the card to Ethel-the-Bibliophile and asking for ten dollars' worth of quarters, Ally was summarily rebuffed. "No credit cards," Ethel asserted with a scowl.

Ally pulled out a twenty.

"You want twenty dollars' worth of quarters?"

"No," said Ally, "just ten."

Ethel-the-Bibliophile sighed heavily. "Well I don't have change for a twenty, except in quarters."

Besides the twenty, Ally only had two ones in her wallet, and walked back to the table with eight additional quarters plus the two she already had. "What an ordeal," she said to George.

"Let me see what I can do," he offered, getting up and heading over to the reference desk.

"Better put on your body armor," Ally called out to him as he walked away.

In all, they ended up with forty-two quarters to make copies. With a few pages lost due to copier jams, Ally got the thirty-four pages printed, but just barely.

"Now," said George, "I'll give you a brief rundown on the Ruby and Hobart love connection, then send you on your way. I understand you have some obituaries waiting for you."

"Ugh, yes! You waltzed in and whisked me away from one of those dreadful tasks reserved for lowly interns, and for that I thank you, brief though the reprieve may be."

"Glad to be at your service, fair lady."

"Guess that's better than being a 'fiery redhead'."

"Oh, I have a feeling you are that too."

Back in the newsroom, Ally snapped out of her day dreaming with a start. She sat up straight in her chair and looked at the wall clock. Ten minutes to seven. She had been sitting there for nearly an hour. Her work pile sat untouched, and she was hungry, really hungry. She went back to the break room and found a frozen chicken stir fry dinner, heated it in the microwave, and carried it back to her desk, intending to eat while she worked on the obituaries.

The first one was easy, following the *Ledger's* format, and she entered the death notice for Herman Whitacre into the publishing software with only minor edits. A JPEG head shot, which Ally guessed to be at least 20 years younger than Mr. Whitacre's stated age of 78 had been included, and Ally placed it next to his name, then wrapped the notice around it.

The second obituary, for Lenora Crites, was less straightforward. A side note from the funeral home indicated that the decedent's family insisted on using the notice that Ms. Crites had written herself.

> *Lenora Amelia Crites left her earthly home in Dominion Mills on May 1 and traveled across the mystical Rainbow Bridge connecting earth with pet heaven to be greeted by her beloved Boston terrier, the late Buster Crites, who had been patiently waiting for her for five years…*

"Ugh!" Ally blurted out loud. She read the rest, which included references to Lenora's lifelong passion for collecting bird feathers, now numbering in the thousands, which decorated the walls throughout her house. A list of survivors included her loving, long-haired cat Fluffy and her neighbor's parakeet Kirby, who she had taught to say "Hello Cutie" and "Bye-bye Sweetie."

Seriously? Ally shook her head and rolled her eyes. She pulled out her AP Stylebook. Mac was a stickler for adhering to Associated Press usage, and the stylebook was his Bible. If the Crites family didn't like the standard format, they'd need to submit the obituary as a paid advertisement. She laid "Lenora Crites" aside for Maggie to decide how to proceed.

Ally tried to focus on the next obituary, but the copied pages from "Hobart Castlebury and Ruby Rosa: Romance Behind the Scenes," kept calling her.

According to George, at the same time Alfred Kowalczyk was growing up a bitter young Polish kid in Brooklyn, Rosa Maria Talone was struggling with her own identity issues across the river on the Lower East Side.

Her family was always fighting while they schemed to make money any way they could: the drug trade, illegal gambling, loan-sharking, all the typical crime family operations. The money was laundered through family businesses, mainly restaurants. After the FBI investigations started, Rosa's immediate family ventured into new, legitimate businesses in an attempt to distance themselves from the rest of the criminal Talones.

Rosa hated it. All of it. To placate her, Rosa's parents encouraged her love of show business with dancing, acting, and singing classes. In her twenties, Rosa put aside her disdain for her family's ill-gotten gains and accepted enough money from her father to start an off-Broadway theater company in the East Village. Her Ruby Slipper Center for the Performing Arts was where Hobart Castlebury, the former Alfred Kowalczyk, met Ruby Rosa, the former Rosa Maria Talone.

"As I said," George had told her, "it was inevitable that the paths of Ruby Rosa and Hobart Castlebury should cross. Their symmetry was too great for them not to. When they did, it was a match made in heaven."

Ally was eager to know more. She picked up the pages from the library. Skipping through the early years, she continued where George had left off. Ruby was enamored with Hobart, recognizing a talent and passion for the stage that equaled her own. She was captivated by his good looks and charming demeanor. Together, the couple's chemistry was magic. They became the darlings of the stage.

Soon, the couple married and Ruby made Hobart a business

partner. Off-stage and on, they were a dynamic power couple. Each having a keen eye for talent, they recruited the best and brightest, coaching new talent into rising stars of the stage.

They discovered Levi Eriksson when he was a young gifted teen, a boy wonder some might say. "Our wunderkind," Ruby and Hobart called him. Hobart saw in Levi a young version of himself. Like Alfred Kowalczyk, Levi was captivated by the theater. He was a natural on stage. He blossomed under the tutelage of his mentors. This charismatic young man, Ruby and Hobart felt sure, was their ticket to fame and fortune.

Growing up, Levi had lived in an imaginary existence, play-acting and struggling to find his place in the real world. He had been the child of a broken home, often left in the care of relatives who were absorbed in their own lives and too busy to pay attention to this strange child who constantly craved attention.

To Ruby, Levi was the child she was never able to have, and she showered him with praise and motherly affection. Here, Levi felt at home. At his request, Ruby and Hobart went to court and were awarded guardianship of the teenager, who promptly changed his name to Erik Reno.

There were some black and white pictures of the threesome, on stage, behind the scenes at the Ruby Slipper and at the Obie Awards where they were honored more than once for their work in off-Broadway theater. That was where the pages from the library ended.

Ally was curious and went online see if she could find more about Ruby, Hobart, and Erik. She was rewarded with a fairly recent entry about an award for a musical entitled *An Old Virginia Christmas* by Hobart Castlebury, Ruby Rosa, and Erik Reno.

The play was adapted from a song with the same name, written by a Virginia couple, Anne Martin and Ryan Marks, who had attended a Ruby Slipper performance during a visit to New York. On their way out, they were greeted at the door by Hobart and, on a whim, asked him if he and Ruby might be interested in a song they had written. Hobart said "Sure," and when they returned to Virginia they emailed a copy of their song, "An Old Virginia Christmas," to the Ruby Slipper.

The song was loosely based on the Martin-Marks' own experiences of growing up in a small Virginia town, then each going their own way but always nostalgic for their hometown at Christmastime. Hobart and Ruby loved the song and the story the lyrics told, and together with Erik they wrote a play, which was a hit, running for nearly a year at the Ruby Slipper. A Los Angeles screenwriter in the audience approached them about turning it into a movie for the Holiday Movie Network.

According to the online article, the movie was currently in the works. Ally wondered if the screenplay Ruby and Erik had been working on at Stonewall Mansion was *An Old Virginia Christmas*. She made a mental note to ask George, then looked at the clock and let out a shriek. *Yikes! Ten-twenty.* With her eyelids heavy and her body protesting the prolonged sitting position, she turned back to her obituary file. She was so sleepy, so very sleepy. Her head dropped to the desk and her eyes closed.

Nine

The town of Union Gap was abuzz. It was the day before Friday's Sunset Social honoring Hobart Castlebury. Happy O'Hurley was at the helm, spearheading the arrangements. She had met with all the merchants along the Lakewalk and most had agreed to participate.

The Mean Beans Bistro would be setting up tables with assorted hors d'oeuvres, including Clover's Jamaican jerk chicken. There would be wine tasting at the Virgin Glen Vineyards Outlet, and assorted bon bons and truffles at Mandie's Candies, including a new recipe Mandie was making special for the occasion: champagne and white chocolate earth-balls, which she christened "Mandie's Passion." At Jack's Pub, Jack McKay would be offering craft beers on tap, meatballs in chimichurri sauce, and his Happy Hour *Wingin' It* assortment. Both Waterside Treasures and Tee Time Lake Apparel were preparing gift bags for door prizes.

Happy was in charge of preparations for the River Ridge Boys, who would be providing bluegrass music in front of her Books Galore Bookstore. At the Generation Gap, when asked if he wished to contribute, Milton Grimsley told Happy "Yes," he would be bringing himself.

Back at the *Lakeside Ledger*, Ally Murphy was breathing a sigh of relief, having a week ago dodged a bullet, so to speak, following her outing with George Rothman. She'd awakened at four in the morning, still at her desk and realized that her work assignments, due in just a few short hours, remained largely untouched. She'd jumped up, run to the bathroom and splashed water in her face, made herself a super-sized cup of Mountain Mama Blend coffee, and returned to her desk.

Rested and alert, and operating on adrenaline, she'd tackled her work list. She chuckled as she proof-read Sarah Sanderson's weekly column "Around the Gap", which this week was a humorous piece focusing on the reported sightings around Stonewall Mansion and the rumors surrounding its eccentric new owner. Ally breezed through the remaining obituaries, writing occasional questions for Maggie or comments for Mac in red.

Bobby Hinkleberry's draft of the Union Gap Town Council meeting was more challenging. Maggie's assessment was on the mark. The article needed "serious editing," but Ally's specialty was rewrites and she actually enjoyed plunging into the revisions.

When Mac arrived promptly at eight, Ally was sitting at her desk reading the online version of the *Dominion Daily News*. She'd just finished her work ten minutes earlier, but she didn't share that detail with her publisher boss.

"Morning, Mac," she said cheerily.

"Morning to you. I would say you're early this morning, but Maggie and I noticed that you never came home last night."

"Yeah, I came back to the office to finish up the work Maggie asked me to take care of, and I fell asleep at my desk. And, that's the truth."

"I believe you." Mac laughed, good-naturedly.

Maggie, arriving an hour later, was not so forgiving. "Well, well, look who's here," she chided. "Did you and 'Gorgeous George' enjoy your all-night tryst?"

"No," stammered Ally. "It wasn't like that. I came back here..."

"Oh, spare me," snapped Maggie. "You're staying with us

during this internship, which makes Mac and me responsible for you, and you tramping around all night with a fancy-dressed, pompadoured, smooth-talker who just rolled into town is not part of the bargain." She slammed her fist down on Ally's desk.

"I'm sorry," whimpered Ally, who was now in tears.

Mac raised his voice. "Maggie! Cut it out! Ally came back here, finished all her work, and fell asleep at her desk. You've no right to talk to her like that."

Now, a week later, Maggie was cheerful and even apologetic to Ally. She'd been working with Ed Berger, the photography instructor at Lake County High School, lining up two senior photography students, who were now in the newsroom of the *Ledger*, along with a couple of the paper's regular freelancers. All were receiving instructions from Maggie for tomorrow's event. The stringers were told to mingle, get photos and comments from the attendees along the Lakewalk, and, most importantly, keep their eyes on "the prize."

"Hobart Castlebury, the new owner of Stonewall Mansion will be guest of honor," Maggie informed the group. "Be discreet, but get all you can."

"Can we question him about the murder?" asked Leanne Smallwood, an aspiring journalist, who was starting her freshman year at Virginia Commonwealth University in the fall.

"Absolutely not!" responded Maggie. "The murder is off-limits. In fact, any questioning of Mr. Castlebury will be done by me or Ally." She added, "Sorry, but those are the ground rules."

As the group was departing, Maggie called aside Justin and Bradley, the two photographers. "If possible," she told them, "get pictures of me with Mr. Castlebury." She winked and told them there'd be a bonus if they did.

Maggie had also contacted Helen Overington, the president of the Lake County Historical Society, who agreed to be interviewed about Stonewall Mansion for a special edition of the *Lakeside Ledger*. Maggie had considered giving this assignment to her intern, but after Ally filled her in on the article she was working on about the Hobart Castlebury and Ruby Rosa love connection for the special edition, she smiled approvingly.

"Nice work," she said, giving Ally a thumbs up. "Yes, by all means work on that. I'll handle the Stonewall Mansion angle."

Ally was beaming at being back in Maggie's good graces.

"By the way," continued Maggie, "What's going on with George Rothman these days?"

Ally had been purposely mum on anything about George after Maggie's dressing her down last week.

"Well," she said, "I haven't seen him, but I did talk to him the other day. He confirmed, on the record, that Ruby Rosa and Erik Reno were at Stonewall Mansion working with a Los Angeles screenwriter on the final draft of a movie script, adapted from their play, *An Old Virginia Christmas*."

"This screenwriter was with Ruby and Erik at the mansion?" asked Maggie. She started thinking of another angle, a third person at the scene of the murder.

"I'm not sure about that. I don't know if he was actually here."

"Maybe you can confirm that with George tomorrow at the Sunset Social. Be sure to wear one of your cute little sundresses."

Ally ignored the slight. "Actually," she said. "George is in New York handling estate matters for Hobart and won't be there."

"That's a shame, but Hobart's still coming, right?"

"George assured me he is, and in fact is looking forward to it."

Ten

Townspeople began showing up on the Lakewalk long before the Sunset Social's start time of seven o'clock. They milled about outside and browsed inside the stores, getting in the way of the people setting up. Finally, the shop owners all agreed to close. They announced they'd reopen at seven.

Happy was outside Books Galore overseeing the assembly of the makeshift stage for the River Ridge Boys. She knew next to nothing about stage assembly, but she was trying to look authoritative until an exasperated Gus Tanner told her, "We've got this Miss Happy," hoping she would take the hint and leave the maintenance crew to their task. A miffed Happy retreated inside to cool off and was greeted by Pippy, whose tail was wagging excitedly. The little dog knew something big was afoot and had taken up a position in the bay window where he could keep tabs on everything.

Next door at the Mean Beans, Fern and Clover were busy in the kitchen while Susan and Phoebe were setting up and decorating the dining room and the outside patio. Kyle, who had ventured over to help out, was given a clipboard and tasked with checking off items on the to-do list, a polite way of telling him to stay out of the way.

"Cletus, how good to see you. How've you been?" Happy was back outside mingling as the evening's crowd started to assemble.

Pippy, ever the social animal, not unlike his mistress, was making his rounds, greeting attendees as they arrived.

Cletus, sitting at a table Fern had saved for her father outside the Mean Beans, smiled broadly at Happy. "Never better," he said. "I am one proud papa, and I owe so much to you, taking Fern under your wing the way you have." His eyes welled up as he looked around.

"Fern's a remarkable young lady," said Happy. "Smart, business-savvy, delightful to be around. You've raised her well, Cletus. You deserve to be proud."

"Well hellooo Cletus." Both Happy and Cletus recognized the sing-song voice and turned around to see Daphne Simpson, decked out as usual in an ankle-length multi-colored hippie-style flowing skirt and off-the-shoulders top, with several long beaded and tasseled colorful necklaces added for good measure.

As usual, Cletus was at a loss for words. He greeted the bubbly Daphne shyly, with a terse "How do," not quite able to make eye contact. Daphne, never at a loss for words, invited herself to join him at the table.

Happy excused herself, leaving Cletus in the uncomfortable position of being alone in the company of a woman. She moseyed along the Lakewalk, welcoming newcomers and chatting with the regulars. A group of fishermen were gathered around the bar that had been set up outside Jack's Pub, devouring wings and meatballs, washing them down with the free-flowing beer on tap, and swapping fish stories. Bumper Presgraves and Cecil Moomaw were arguing about which of them should lead the parade of boats out into the lake for the start of the Memorial Day Bass Tournament.

"Shit, Moomaw," sputtered Bumper through a mouth full of meatballs, "you'll be lucky if that sorry-ass rust bucket of yours makes it to the starting point."

"Screw you, Bumper. Don't forget that me and my 'rust bucket' won last year and I hold the all-time record for catching the biggest, baddest-ass bass in Big Gap Lake."

"Yeah, well that sorry-ass bass you keep boastin' 'bout was older than my Granny, and any one of us could have reached down and scooped it up with our bare hands."

"Boys!" Happy came up behind them. "This is a family event and a profanity-free zone. Please keep it clean."

"Yes, ma'am," responded Bumper. "Sorry 'bout that."

"Sorry my ass, you son-'a-bitch," Cecil mumbled under his breath.

"I heard that," Happy admonished over her shoulder as she was walking away.

Maggie, Mac, and Ally were just arriving, and Pippy greeted them excitedly, bouncing about with little dog yaps and wildly wagging his stump of a tail. Ally, still stinging from Maggie's rebukes about her short sundresses, was wearing black slacks and a long sleeved white cotton button-down shirt. She had on her thick-framed reading glasses, and her hair was pulled back in a pony tail.

Happy waved them over, and they all stood at the Lakewalk's three-foot-high wall, staring across at Stonewall Mansion, looking for any sign that Hobart Castlebury would follow through with his promise and honor them with his presence.

The River Ridge Boys, who'd been warming up, began playing, starting things off with a couple of old favorites, first the bluegrass classic "Rocky Top," followed by "Great Balls of Fire." Then, the band was joined by Gus Tanner's daughter EllaJane, who began singing the Patsy Cline hit, "I Fall to Pieces." The crowd cheered wildly. Patsy Cline was a folk hero in these parts, remembered for her gifted voice and mourned for her tragic death at age 30 in a plane crash. Many locals had visited the Patsy Cline Historic House in Winchester, just a few hours' drive north on I-81 to pay tribute to the Virginia girl who they claimed as one of their own. As EllaJane's voice belted out the lyrics, the crowd started grabbing partners and swinging, swaying, and twirling up and down the Lakewalk.

Ally was thinking back to her own feeble attempts at karaoke at the Pizza Pit in Richmond where she and her college friends hung out. She wished she could sing like EllaJane. Milton Grimsley, undeterred by Ally's lack of a short sundress, snuck up behind, grabbed ahold of her and got right down to business. He pulled her close, twerking his hips as he did so. He began mouthing the lyrics in her ear. Ally managed not to gag trying to remember what Fern had told her about dealing with the old "Grimster."

With the sun just setting, the music abruptly stopped. All eyes turned toward the bandstand. An imposing figure, impeccably dressed in a white dress shirt, black vest, black coat, black dress pants, black Oxfords, black cape, white gloves, and a signature white half mask, had jumped on the stage, grabbed the microphone, and in a commanding voice addressed the crowd:

"Slowly, gently, night unfurls its splendour.
Grasp it, sense it, tremulous and tender.
Turn your face away from the garish light of day,
turn your thoughts away from cold, unfeeling light,
and listen to the music of the night!"

"Who is that masked man?" came a voice from the crowd.

"It's the Phantom of the Opera!" someone shouted.

"It's Hobart Castlebury!" yelled another. The crowd let out a collective gasp. Everyone was mesmerized.

The masked man, aka Phantom of the Opera, aka Hobart Castlebury, turned toward the River Ridge Boys and told them, "Carry on with the *'music of the night'*." He then descended the stairs into the crowd, saying:

> *"Why so silent, good monsieurs?*
> *Did you think that I had left you for good?*
> *Have you missed me, good monsieurs?*
> *I have written you an opera!*
> *Here I bring the finished score.*
> *Don Juan Triumphant!*
> *Fondest greetings to you all."*

"Cheers!" The unmistakable voice of Bumper Presgraves rang out, and the merriment grew. The Phantom was working the crowd in gentlemanly fashion, shaking the hands of the men and kissing those of the ladies. He graciously posed for selfies and politely responded to questions, even answering with humor those that seemed out of line.

"Whatcha hidin' under that there mask?" asked someone.

"*'This face which earned a mother's fear and loathing...'*" he responded.

Milton Grimsley again grabbed Ally as she was attempting to walk away. "Sweetheart, you promised me a dance, 'emember?"

"Not now, Mr. Grimsley," Ally pleaded. "I need to sit down." She tried to pull away.

"You owe me, darlin'. Think I gave you them 'spensive collectors 'cards for nothin'?" His mouth was close to hers, and Ally was close to gagging. His breath smelled like stale beer, and his spittle was hitting her in the face.

"Let me go, you old coot," she said loudly.

As she was trying to free herself, she felt a gentle tap on her shoulder and heard a kind voice ask, "May I have this dance?" and she was staring into the face of the masked man. Before she could respond, she was whisked away. To her great relief!

Ally thought she must be dreaming. A moment ago she was fighting off a disgusting lecher pawing at her, and now she was being waltzed. Waltzed? With the Phantom of the Opera? *My god,* she thought, *what must he think*? Befitting the occasion, a fairy tale phrase came to her mind: "damsel in distress."

Ally didn't realize she had said aloud those words, but the man behind the mask seemed amused. "No my dear, not a 'damsel in distress'. Rather, the 'fiery redhead' I saw back there."

Ally laughed. "Well, Mister Phantom, tonight you may call me what you wish. I am most appreciative of you rescuing me from that troll. Tonight I dub you my 'Prince Charming'."

Milton Grimsley was shuffling away, muttering expletives to himself, when he spotted Fern standing outside the Mean Beans Bistro. He beelined in her direction and was a few feet away when a young man appeared at her side and put his arm protectively around her shoulders. "Don't even think about it, Pal," said Kyle Kalahan, staring down the menacing look in Grimster's eyes.

"C'mon, Milton, time to go home," said Darrell Dempsey, who appeared out of nowhere and began escorting a very grim Milton Grimsley away. Darrell was employed by the security company across the lake at the Gallery and was the person who'd caught Maggie speeding a short time ago. He'd been hired to work security for tonight's event on the Lakewalk. Although small in stature, he wore his security guard uniform with pride and projected himself with an air of authority.

Milton bristled and grumbled and spit out a few more expletives, but didn't resist when Darrell led him away.

Daphne was making her rounds, handing out ticket stubs for

the door prizes soon to be awarded. Earlier, she'd found a captive audience in Cletus as she told him in dramatic detail about fleeing from an abusive husband in Tennessee and hiding out with a Melungeon family in the Cumberland Gap area of Southwest Virginia. Cletus had heard stories of the mysterious Melungeons and wanted to know more about the family that took Daphne in.

"They called themselves 'Portuguee' and even claimed to be descendants of shipwrecked Portuguese sailors," said Daphne. "They didn't want to be called Melungeons, but I could tell they were. They had that distinctive dark skin and blue eyes and mountaineer roots."

"Why'd they not wanna be Melungeons?" asked Cletus.

"Melungeons are said to be mixed-race. Back in the early days, it was against the law to mix the races. So, they claimed to be Portuguese in order to remain free and have the privileges that came with being white. Didn't matter none to me. These were good folk and they were grateful for my renting a room from them as much as I was glad to have a place to hide out."

"Why was you hidin' out?" asked Cletus shyly, not wanting to pry but nonetheless curious.

Daphne was more than willing to share. "My husband, Larry Toliver, was a well-to-do merchant, but a mean son-of-a-beach," she said. "I cleaned out a couple of our joint bank accounts on my way out of town."

"Ain't you afeared he'll find you here in Union Gap?"

"Oh, believe me, I was scared when I ran away with the money. I knew he'd be mighty mad. But, don't have to worry no more."

"Why so?"

"He's dead. Asthma." She said it matter-of-factly.

"Asthma?" Cletus sounded surprised.

"Yep. Succumbed during Asthma Peak Week. That's the third

week in September every year. Comes like clockwork. High ragweed season. Seventeen different species of the wild green plant filling the air. The perfect storm."

"I'm sorry," said Cletus, not sure what else to say.

"No need. I don't mean to sound uncaring, but Larry Toliver's death, my freedom. You know? Then I saw the ad for the lakefront store for sale in Union Gap. It was just what I was looking for. So, with my retail experience working with Larry and what was left from the money I got from our joint accounts I landed here."

Cletus wasn't sure what to make of this free-spirited woman, but he found himself enjoying her company. Daphne was a wealth of information he may never have a need for, but he appreciated how she did all the talking so he didn't have to. When she got up to attend to door prize business, he was sorry to see her go.

The evening was winding down. The band was packing up and folks were departing. Many said that this was one of the best times they'd ever had.

The Phantom was standing alone at the Lakewalk's three-foot wall looking across the water. After returning Ally to her table, he'd graciously smiled for the camera with his arm around Maggie as her freelance photographer Bradley snapped several pictures. He'd bowed to the entreaties of the ladies to dance with them. He'd taught them waltz moves, and they taught him the Texas Two-Step. He'd joined in line dances and found himself doing the Electric Slide and the Macarena with the best of them. He'd danced to "Y.M.C.A." and even took part in the Chicken Dance.

Tonight, the curtain had gone up on Union Gap's Sunset Social with Hobart Castlebury in the starring role, unscripted and unrehearsed. He was feeling quite pleased with his evening's performance. He was the Phantom of the Opera just having fun.

"Hello, Hobart."

The Phantom froze. He recognized the voice and was not pleased. Slowly, he turned around.

"Gianna," he said.

Eleven

The hour was late. The Lakewalk shop owners were closing up, and cleanup was underway. There'd been a lot of chatter about Hobart Castlebury and the hit he made with the townspeople. Aside from the incident with Milton Grimsley, some colorful language here and there, and a few folks whooping it up a bit too much, the crowd overall was well-behaved, and everyone had a great time. The *Lakeside Ledger's* stringers, Leanne Smallwood and Emily Cowherd, were roving among the attendees as they were leaving, getting departing comments. All agreed, the evening was a big success.

Happy was chatting with members of the River Ridge Boys, who were packing up their instruments and taking down the portable stage. She thanked them for an outstanding performance.

"Did you know about the surprise entrance of the Phantom on stage?" Happy asked.

"Man," said Gus, "that was wild. We didn't know what to think. I figured it musta been part of your plan, and I wondered why you didn't give us a heads up."

"No, no, I had no idea."

"Quite the character, that Hobart guy…"

"Hey, careful with that!" Happy cut him off, directing her attention to Lennie Metz, who had just dropped a stage panel with a loud thud.

"We got this Miss Happy," said Gus.

Happy took the hint and said her good nights, leaving the

River Ridge Boys to finish up without the benefit of her supervision.

Next door, Clover was in the kitchen of the Mean Beans cleaning up. Ally was helping Susan clear tables outside while Fern and Kyle were taking the cleared tables and stacking them in the storage room, along with the chairs. Phoebe was sweeping up.

"Ally," said Fern, "I am so sorry about that 'Grimm' experience you had. I feel kind of responsible since I told you he was generally harmless. The old goat was in rare and wretched form tonight."

"Oh Fern, I'm over it," replied Ally. "My only regret is that I didn't get to use your 'nuclear option' on that bad boy. That would have given him a wake-up call."

Everyone laughed, and Phoebe turned the subject to the Phantom. "He certainly seemed to take a liking to you," she said to Ally.

Ally experienced a slight sensation of excitement as she remembered being swept away from the horrible Mr. Grimsley and the playful exchange she had with the Phantom about her being the damsel in distress and him her Prince Charming. "Talk about being in rare form," she said. "Who would have expected to see the Phantom of the Opera making such a hit with the townspeople and enjoying every minute of it?"

They all nodded in agreement and continued their cleanup.

Meanwhile, Maggie and Mac were talking to the four stringers, thanking them for their great work. "Let's get together first thing Monday morning at the *Ledger*," said Mac. "We'll go over what you've got and see what to use for next week's issue and what to save for the special edition coming up later."

They all said their good-byes as Maggie and Mac were getting ready to leave. Up and down the Lakewalk, the other shop owners had closed up. At the end of the strip of shops, with Milton Grimsley having long departed, the Generation Gap was dark. But there, in front, Maggie saw a strange woman approach the Phantom and noticed how startled he looked. He said something, then took the woman by the shoulder and walked her around the corner of the Generation Gap.

"Mac," she said to her husband. "I just thought of something I need to do. You go on home. I'll catch a ride with Ally."

"Hobart, you don't seem very pleased to see your ex-sister-in-law."

Gianna Talone was the younger sister of the late Rosa Maria Talone, aka Ruby Rosa. Not as pretty, not as talented, not as famous, she'd always lived in the shadows of her larger-than-life big sister.

"What are you doing here, Gianna?"

"I think you know very well what I'm doing here, Hobart 'Mister Phantom of the Opera' Castlebury. The diamonds. It's now been four months. You promised me you'd hand over the family jewels that had been given to my sister for safe keeping. You've been stalling long enough. I'm here to collect what's mine, what belongs in my family."

"Of course, Gianna. I have no need nor desire for your family's ill-gotten gains. You'll get the jewels as promised. The sooner the better as far as I'm concerned. As we speak, my personal assistant is in New York working out the details of my dear Ruby's estate..."

"Cut the crap, Hobart!" Gianna was now raising her voice. "You know very well those diamonds aren't part of her estate."

"Gianna, I implore you to please return to New York and be patient. We're searching. You have Hobart Castlebury's promise, your family jewels will be turned over as soon as we find them. For all we know, Erik Reno may have run off with them after he murdered my wife. For now, please return to New York and trust me."

"Fuck you! I am here for the diamonds, and the sooner I get them, the sooner I'll be on my merry way."

With that, Gianna turned on her heels and stormed away.

With a heavy sigh, the Phantom of the Opera turned and rounded the corner of the Generation Gap. As he did so, Maggie slunk deeper back into the shadows. She'd positioned herself in front of the Generation Gap behind a life-size statue of Elvis sitting on a stool, strumming his guitar. She had listened to the conversation, committing what she'd heard to memory, like any good, investigative reporter would do.

Twelve

It was the morning after and the McGuires were relaxing on their backyard veranda, enjoying their Mountain Mama Blend and appreciating the quiet while Ally was off walking Bowser, their standard-size schnauzer.

"No way, Maggie!" Mac said irritably. "Absolutely not!"

"Mac, listen to me. This is big news, dammit! A mysterious 'Gianna' appears at our event honoring Hobart Castlebury. She's seen and heard discussing the 'family jewels' with him. Diamonds of questionable origin. Diamonds that may be missing. Diamonds that may have disappeared with Erik Reno, the prime suspect in Ruby Rosa's murder. This is information that may not even be known by the authorities, information that certainly hasn't been made public."

"Yes, it's a fine bit of bloody snooping, Maggie, but get real. You're not a detective. If anything, you should report what you heard to the authorities."

"Oh sure, and make myself a part of the crime case. No thanks."

"Well, the information is hearsay, and we're not going down that road again."

"You call it snooping. I call it good investigative reporting. And if you insist on bringing up what happened in Roanoke, may I remind you, you were part of it too. And, dammit, Mac, we were right. We just couldn't prove it."

Maggie got up and stormed back into the house to fix herself a Bloody Mary to calm her nerves and ease her growing irritation. "Chicken shit," she said under her breath as she walked away.

Alone on the veranda, Mac thought back to the incident that caused him to resign in disgrace as publisher of the *Roanoke Daily Record*, move to Union Gap with Maggie, and accept his less-distinguished place in the world of print journalism as owner of a small town weekly newspaper.

Back then, he'd learned from a confidential source that Saponi County Administrator Allen Armbrewster had hatched a scheme to channel money through the Department of Family Services to support a human sex trafficking operation. A rural property leased by the county for use as an emergency shelter for families in need was instead housing eight immigrant women, some underage, from Nicaragua. The women were being forced into prostitution. Armbrewster and his partner in crime, Director of Family Services Terrence Allamong, were allegedly receiving hefty kickbacks from the traffickers.

With the help of the paper's lead investigative reporter, namely Mac's wife Maggie, and her contacts, they were able to obtain emails and financial records that showed expenditures for "emergency housing" at the address where the women were being kept.

Maggie, fluent in Spanish, made a visit to the premises, and struck up a friendly conversation with "Annya," a slight-built girl who claimed to be 16. Annya described how she and the other women were lured with promises of decent jobs and better lives. She burst into tears as she described how she was forced against her will to perform sexual acts and endure physical abuse. She said the women were often beaten and raped. Frequently, they were deprived of adequate food. The traffickers at times threatened to kill or harm members of their families. Strangers in a strange land, the women were trapped by their inability to speak English, their immigration status, and their lack of knowledge of where to go for protection. Maggie left Annya with a promise that she was going to help her and the other women.

Back in the newsroom at the *Roanoke Daily Record*, Mac shared Maggie's outrage when she told him about the operation. He contacted the FBI, reporting alleged violations of the Bureau's Crimes Against Children and Human Trafficking Program. Not long afterward, he was told that search warrants had been issued for the Saponi County Administrative Offices.

When Mac received a tip that an FBI raid on the house where the women were being kept was underway, he made the editorial decision to immediately break the story that he and Maggie had kept on hold. The story detailed the operation going on at the house, the FBI involvement, and the role of county officials in the illicit scheme.

The story was posted immediately on the online version of the *Daily Record* and had been readied for the night's press run of the morning's print version.

The first blow came as the McGuires were sitting in Mac's office celebrating with glasses of champagne. It was after midnight when the phone on Mac's desk rang. The couple were expecting to hear that the raid on the premises was successful, that the eight women were taken into protective custody, that arrest warrants had been issued for Armbrewster and Allamong and the traffickers.

But, Special Agent Glenn Faulkner was calling to tell them that when they raided the house, it was abandoned. Whoever had been there departed in a hurry with clothes left behind and food in the refrigerator.

Mac quickly took down the online version, then phoned downstairs to the press room. Trying to keep his voice calm, he asked Neil Campos, the second shift press operator, to hold the presses.

"Holy shit!" shouted Neil above the roar of the presses running in the background. "Mr. McGuire, we've already run off twenty thousand copies, and the press is spittin' them out rapid fire. The first delivery vans have already loaded and left. Still want me to shut 'er down?"

"Let me think," said Mac. "I'll let you know."

"Well, with all due respect, Mr. McGuire, shuttin' down ain't quick. And, those delivery folks standin' by waitin' will be hoppin' mad."

"Thank you, Neil. You're doing a great job. Carry on."

Mac slumped in his seat. "We should have waited…we should have waited, let the feds complete the raid first…Why did I have to be so fuckin' quick to get a scoop? The implications for this paper… The danger we may have put those women in…"

Maggie was quick to defend him. "Mac, look, we're in this together. Let's talk it out. First, the implications. Okay, the traffickers got wind of the impending raid. We'll address the 'how?' later. For now, what we have is a story that the feds were conducting a raid on a county-leased property where a sex trafficking operation was suspected. The house turned out to be abandoned. That's how we'll re-post the online version, then put out an update tomorrow for the print copies."

"But," interjected Mac, "your interview with Annya, her allegations…the women were recruited, held against their will, abused, forced into sex slavery…My god! What's going to happen to them?"

That thought made Maggie sick to her stomach. She'd promised Annya that the women would be safe. She'd been careful in her reporting to not identify anyone by name. "Still," she offered, "we have the evidence against Armbrewster and Allamong. They can be made to talk. Right?"

But, in the days and weeks that followed, the case against the county executives crumbled, bit by bit. Mac's source, another high ranking county official, had spoken and produced the emails on the condition of anonymity. Fearing for his job, he refused to allow his identity be known, and Mac was duty bound to respect and protect his source.

The financial records showed only that the house was leased by the county as emergency housing and payments were made for utilities and food. Terrence Allamong insisted he'd interviewed the families who said they were referred to him by a pastor, whose name and affiliation were unknown. The supposed families, consisting of four parents and six children in all, claimed to have entered the country as penniless Nicaraguan refugees. As Director of Family Services, Allamong found that the house and funds were available, and of course he couldn't refuse these needy families the services.

The director contended he last had contact with the families about a week prior to the raid, that they had given no indication they were planning to leave and had left no forwarding address. Allamong stopped short of accusing Maggie of conjuring up the story of sex trafficking; however, if the house was being used for any purpose other than what he claimed, he insisted he was totally unaware of it.

Based almost solely on the *Roanoke Daily Record's* reporting, Armbrewster and Allamong were initially charged with conspiracy and aiding and abetting in the commission of the human trafficking. But, the charges were later dropped for lack of credible evidence. Any disciplinary action against the two would be the responsibility of the county.

In the aftermath, Armbrewster and Allamong sued the *Daily Record* for defamation of character; the paper settled out of court for an undisclosed sum; and Ralph McGuire was asked to submit his resignation.

Ally's father, Tim Murphy, a member of the Saponi County Board of Directors, stood by Mac. He had no doubt the allegations were true and that Armbrewster and Allamong had received substantial kickbacks from the traffickers and possibly from other illicit operations as well. The two had taken their families on lavish vacations and treated themselves to a new 35-foot Catalina sail boat, which they kept in a slip on the Rapppahannock River and took out on the Chesapeake Bay.

During his years as a successful publisher of large newspapers, Mac had benefited from generous performance bonuses, profit sharing payouts, and aggressive investing. He walked away with resources enough to move to Union Gap with Maggie, buy a nice mid-size home in the Gallery, lease a small commercial building in town, and start a weekly newspaper with his wife. They were living a comfortable, mostly stress-free life, and Mac was content.

Now, on this quiet morning, as he relived that nightmare, he told himself, true or not, no way was he getting his little *Lakeside Ledger* sucked into some wild story. The murder…the mansion…the Phantom of the Opera…the mysterious Gianna…missing family jewels. A rabbit hole of odd and disturbing proportions, he told himself.

Mac shook his head and hollered in to Maggie in the kitchen.

"Hey, Hon, would you fix me one of those Bloody Marys while you're at it? And make that a double."

Thirteen

—————◆—————

While Maggie and Mac were enjoying their Bloody Marys, Ally and Bowser the schnauzer were ambling along one of the Gallery's nature trails. Ally was basking in the glow of the successful Sunset Social the night before. So wrapped up in thought was she that had she not smelled it, she would have stepped smack dab in a pile of dog doo-doo. She looked down and managed to side-step it just in the nick of time.

"Trojan!" she said out loud, remembering what Maggie had told her about the horse-sized dog that did his business wherever he pleased and his owners who blatantly ignored the HOA rules to clean up after their pets.

Bowser, being a normal dog, was quite interested in the pile and would have preferred to stay and sniff for a while if Ally hadn't jerked on the leash to pull him away.

Newly leafing trees and springtime foliage enveloped the trail. With the Trojan detraction behind them, she let Bowser take his time checking out scents. With each new tree, it seemed, he lifted his leg and added his mark for future dogs to know he'd been there.

"Quite a night last night, wasn't it?" came a voice from the woods.

Ally jumped and almost screamed. She hadn't seen or heard anyone on the trail and was startled that someone had snuck up behind her. She turned to see Darrell Dempsey, in all of his security guard grandeur, step out of the brush.

"Darrell Dempsey! You scared the crap out of me," Ally said angrily.

"Sorry," Darrell responded apologetically. "Just making my rounds. Never know what trouble might be brewing along these secluded trails."

"Yeah, well just go back there a few hundred feet and you'll see a big pile of trouble—trouble most foul—right in the middle of the path."

"Aha! Trojan!"

"Yes, Trojan. Can't you do something about that? It is after all an HOA infraction, right?"

"Yes, ma'am, it shore is. Them Pews been warned, but nothing the Compliance Committee can do 'lest they're caught in the act. I carry my camera around just in case, but I always seem to just miss them."

"Well, the Gallery is lucky to have you, Johnny-on-the-spot Detective Dempsey." Ally had resumed walking, and Darrell fell in step beside her. He chuckled.

"Not 'detective', not yet anyway. But, I'm taking online courses in police officer training and have my sights on getting into the Roanoke Police Academy."

"That's great Darrell, but, isn't there a height requirement?" As soon as she spoke, Ally wished she could take her words back. "Oh, I'm sorry, that was rude of me."

Darrell's five-foot, four-inch, 130-pound physique was a frequent topic of conversation around the Gallery, but he shrugged it off. "I talked to Chief Hawkins over at the P.D., and he said having grit—you know, courage, strength of character, passion, all that—is more important than size. So that's what I'm working on. Grit."

"Back to your original question," said Ally, "yeah, last night was quite an event. And thanks for helping out with the old 'Grimster', carting him off the way you did. That took 'grit'."

"Aww…thanks Miss Ally. Glad to assist. Milton Grimsley can be quite a handful."

When they came to a clearing, Bowser stopped and stood at alert, hackles raised. On the other side of a wooden rail fence was the rear of a ramshackle house. Virginia creeper vines aggressively clung to the siding, and trees with branches like craggy witch fingers surrounded the structure. The place looked unwelcoming and unloved. Ally shuddered at the sight of it. Suddenly, she was grateful to have Darrell Dempsey's five foot, four inches of determined grit beside her.

"Spooky," she said out loud, and took hold of his arm.

"What we're lookin' at is the back yard of Stonewall Mansion," said Darrell.

"Wow!" gasped Ally. "I didn't realize the mansion abutted the Gallery property. But, now I do remember Happy saying the Gallery was built around Jackson's Point, leaving Stonewall Mansion intact." Ally stared, open-mouthed. "This place gives me goosebumps," she whispered.

Darrell was basking in his new role as protector of a beautiful young lady.

Suddenly, they heard the sound of tires on gravel. A white van had turned into the service entrance at the mansion. Ally saw the Creekside Café logo on the passenger side door as the van circled to the back side of house. The logo read *"Waterfront Dining and Catering"* with the image of an anchor in between a knife and fork.

Ally and Darrell watched as the van stopped near the back porch. Ally recognized Deb, one of the daytime employees at Creekside, who got out on the driver's side, removed a large box from the back and placed it on the porch. Back in the van, she gave a short toot of the horn as she pulled away.

Ally remembered George Rothman telling her that he and Hobart had most of their meals delivered from Creekside because neither of them cooked. They usually ordered enough food for three or four days, ready-made meals they only needed to pop in the microwave.

As she was explaining this to Darrell, the back door opened and a figure clad in a long regal red robe with a collar of fur and royal blue sash came out. It was Hobart Castlebury. He stood for a moment, scanning the clearing. Then he picked up the box and started back toward the door just as Bowser let out a low growl that broke into a full round of barking.

Startled, the figure in red set the box down and looked out over the clearing. Ally thought of her dance with the charismatic Phantom the night before. She stepped out of the trees and waved.

"Hobart, it's me, Ally from last night. Just out walking the dog. Didn't mean to startle you. Bowser, be quiet." Ally pulled the dog's leash tighter in an attempt to make him stop barking.

Castlebury held out both hands in front of him, palms up. "Stop!" he barked. "So, the fair-lady-turned-fiery-redhead returns. Uninvited. Again. Caught lurking in the nearby woods. Spying. Prying. Intruding. What savage beast is that you bring, snarling and drooling at the mouth. Come no closer. What sayeth you, wench?"

"Mr. Castlebury...Hobart. I am most assuredly no wench. We're just out for a morning walk with a family dog. Hardly a savage beast."

"'Fair is foul, and foul is fair.'"

"I don't understand. Last night you charmed the townspeople of Union Gap. You were my personal Prince Charming, rescuing me from the pawing hands of that nasty Mr. Grimsley. Now you attack me with insults. I don't deserve it."

Hobart stared at her, contemplating her words. "All is not as it appears, I venture to say. You dare to sneak around, trespassing on my personal domain, unsummoned and unwelcome. The foulest of the fair, a sly little shrew indeed."

"Mr. Castlebury, that's enough!" Darrell Dempsey stepped forward, standing as tall as his five-foot, four-inch frame would allow and speaking as forcefully as he could.

"Who the bloody hell is that?" bellowed Hobart.

"Never mind," shouted Ally, now close to tears. "We're leaving. Come on Darrell."

"Then begone with you. *'Screw your courage to the sticking-place'.*"

Ally retorted: "*'Double, double toil and trouble / Fire burn, and cauldron bubble.'* Take that Hobart Castlebury! I know Macbeth too. And, for the record, my hair is auburn."

Hobart cackled loudly. Now he seemed to be enjoying the kerfuffle. He turned back toward the door but before opening it, lifted his robe, bent forward, and exposed his bare buttocks.

Ally had already started walking away. She started to turn back around when she heard the guffaw, but Darrell took hold of her elbow and steered her forward. "You don't want to see that," he said.

"What?" asked Ally.

"You were just mooned by the great Hobart Castlebury."

"Oh, gawd!" gasped Ally. "That's more than eccentric. It's bizarre."

"And it weren't purty neither."

Fourteen

Fern was in the barn hanging horse tack on the wall pegs, and with her back to the door she didn't hear Kyle come in. "Good morning beautiful," he whispered in her ear while slipping his arms around her waist from behind. Her body quivered with excitement as he nuzzled her neck. She turned around slowly. The two embraced and kissed.

The romance between Fern Finfrock and Kyle Kalahan had been evolving slowly. They tried to make it look casual for the sake of appearance, but those who knew them had already figured out it was getting serious.

The night before last, at Friday's Sunset Social, Kyle had asked Fern to go with him on an overnight get-away and help him look for a place to rent. He loved his Aunt Happy dearly and was grateful for her hospitality by allowing him to stay with her and work at the bookstore, but it was time to start looking for his own place. After taking the current semester off from college, he'd be student teaching at Lake County High School in the fall, rounding out his final year as an English major at James Madison University in Harrisonburg. He'd also started writing a book, a historical novel set partly in Virginia during the Civil War. He needed a quiet place to work and hopefully have some alone time with Fern, away from Happy's perpetually prying eyes.

Fern had unequivocally said yes to Kyle's invitation, and the two were planning to set off later that day. "You're sure?" Kyle asked, breaking the embrace and looking into her eyes.

Fern nodded with a smile. She'd just returned from a workout with the Tennessee Walking Horse she was fostering and was still dressed in her riding gear: breeches, dressage boots, schooler helmet, and gripper gloves.

Merryfield's Magic was one of more than a dozen horses rescued from a cluster of Kentucky training stables where they were kept in filthy conditions, underfed, dehydrated, and subjected to a painful practice called soring. Despite laws banning it, horse soring was still very common, with breeders, owners, and trainers intent on producing high-stepping gaits in the showrings of Tennessee Walkers.

When Fern heard about the rescue and the neglect and torture of the horses, she immediately submitted an application to become a foster. Accompanying her application were a dozen letters of reference from townspeople attesting to her stellar character and compassion and caring for animals.

After a visit by representatives from the Mid-Atlantic Tennessee Walker Equine Rescue (TWER) and approval to become a foster, Fern enlisted her father Cletus to hitch up the old two-stall livestock trailer to his new Ram truck, and the two set off for Kentucky. They returned with a new stablemate for Misty, her Chincoteague pony, and a monumental task of healing the physical wounds and restoring the spirit of a magnificent solid black Tennessee Walker Stallion.

During the application process, Fern had learned that Magic's life as a sored horse was filled with fear and pain. He was often left in his stall for days at a time with his legs subjected to caustic chemicals and sharp objects. He wasn't allowed to go out in the fields to graze or socialize with other horses. In training, his sored ankles were wrapped in chains, which slid up and down, further irritating the already painful areas. Each step Magic took was filled with excruciating pain, resulting in the high-stepping gait that was rewarded in showrings.

Magic, Fern learned, was one of the more severe cases of abuse. When the stables were raided, based on the inside tip of a sympathetic stable hand, he was found lying down in his stall, malnourished and moaning in pain. Fern's heart broke when she heard the story. She assured the rescue group TWER she was up to the task of making him whole, and she meant it.

"How's Magic doing this morning?" asked Kyle, stepping away to rub the nose of the black stallion, who was loosely tethered to a wall bracket, waiting for his post-exercise rubdown.

"We're making progress," said Fern, taking her dandy brush and whisking away loose dirt and hair from the stallion's coat with short flicking motions. "This morning, he took a few steps around the paddock with a saddle on his back and me in the saddle."

Fern handed a body brush to Kyle and showed him how to work his way along the areas she had covered, using long sweeping strokes in the direction of hair growth to smooth down the coat for a luxurious shine.

"Remember when Magic first came to the farm?" asked Fern. "How traumatized he was, nervous around people and fearful of anything having to do with his legs?"

"Yep. I remember how he snorted and stomped his foot, trying to pull away."

When he could, Kyle had joined Fern and Cletus as they worked together to soothe the horse's frayed nerves and gain his trust enough to apply medicine to his sore ankles. His physical wounds responded well to the salves provided by Union Gap's only veterinarian, Dr. Johansson, but his emotional state needed much more time and patience. "Baby steps" was how Fern described it. First, slow-walking Magic outside, then placing a saddle on his back, and finally sitting astride him, all on his own terms.

"Surprisingly," she told Kyle, "Misty has had a positive effect on Magic." The palomino and tobiano pinto that Fern and Cletus brought back from Chincoteague as a yearling was now twelve years old. Fern described how he had taken on a protective role toward his new stablemate.

"When I let Misty out into the field in the mornings, Magic whinnies and tosses his head and paws at the floor of his stall. The past couple of days, I've let him go and he follows Misty's lead. I've even caught them nuzzling each other. They've really bonded."

As if he knew Fern was talking about him, the black stallion turned his head and nuzzled her shoulder affectionately. Kyle, who had worked his way around front laughed, and Magic responded with a head butt to Kyle's chest. "Yeah," said Kyle, "I would say he's doing much better."

Fern forced a weak smile and said, "Kyle, you know how much I love seeing Magic's progress, but..." She hesitated.

"But?"

"It's been six weeks, and Doc Johansson is almost ready to declare him eligible for adoption."

"Fern, you've submitted your application to adopt him. With what you've done, it's obvious you're the perfect candidate to give him a forever home here in Union Gap. He's part of the family now."

Fern shook her head. "I have my doubts. TWER has a long waiting list of qualified adopters who would love to own a champion show horse." Her eyes started watering. "It's not fair," she said. "The rescue had very few applicants willing to take on the responsibilities of fostering and caring for a badly-damaged horse, but now they're lined up wanting to claim him for the prestige of owning such a beautiful animal like this one."

Kyle put his arms around her as her tears rolled softly onto his shoulder. He loved her big heart and her love for animals.

"I know they told me before I took this on that fostering was not adopting. But, Kyle, I can't bear the thought of Magic being put back in showrings. Not after all he's been through. I just want to see him live out the rest of his life as a free spirit."

"We'll figure it out, Fern."

Happy, Maggie, and Ally were sitting at a table outside the Mean Beans Bistro. On Sundays, Happy attended Mass in Dominion Mills and didn't open the bookstore until one o'clock. Today, Maggie and Ally would be meeting Mac at the *Ledger* early in the afternoon to review the digital photos from the freelance photographers. Tomorrow they'd be laying out the spread of the Sunset Social. But now they just wanted to enjoy something from Clover's Sunday brunch menu over some girl talk.

Ally had already told Maggie about the encounter with Hobart during her walk yesterday morning. Now she was telling Happy about the abrupt change in his personality. "How could he be so charming Friday evening, then turn into such an ill-tempered ogre overnight?" She nibbled on a pumpernickel bagel spread with a generous topping of cream cheese with chives.

"Have you talked to George Rothman?" asked Happy.

"I left him messages yesterday, but haven't heard back."

"Maybe the great Hobart got up on the wrong side of the bed,"

Happy volunteered with a laugh.

"Well, there was certainly something eating at him," said Ally.

Maggie snorted, remembering the conversation she'd eaves-dropped on between Hobart and his sister-in-law.

"Yes?" said Happy, looking at her friend. "You have something to add, Mags?"

Maggie took a bite of her crab and asparagus quiche, then washed it down with a big swig of mimosa, her second since sitting down. She started to say something about the conversation she'd overheard, but instead changed the subject. "Well look who's here," she said, waving to the couple who had just arrived on the Lakewalk, beckoning them over.

Fern and Kyle walked to their table, smiling, and greeted the threesome with high fives. "I'm hungry enough to eat a Mean Beans Killer Skillet," said Kyle. He was referring to Clover's version of Jamaican Omelette Olé, which was a complete meal, made with six eggs, three cheeses, and loaded with potatoes and fresh vegetables, then topped with hot pepper sauce and cut and served like a pizza.

"I'll share it with you," said Fern, "And that looks good too," she added, pointing to the fresh fruit compote in front of Happy.

"Then, by all means, pull up a couple of chairs," said Happy. "Actually, Kyle, I want to go over a couple of things with you before you take off this afternoon."

Kyle rolled his eyes in exasperation. "Aunt Gladys!"

"For heaven's sake, Kyle, relax. I'm talking bookstore business. What did you think I was referring to?"

Kyle sat, relieved but also embarrassed. Ever since he'd asked his aunt for a couple of days off and told her that Fern was going with him on his house-hunting excursion, he'd been expecting his overzealous Irish Catholic aunt to lecture him, old school style, on the evils of modern day loose morals. Or worse, she might feel compelled to tutor him on the temptations and consequences of seemingly innocent coquetry. He smiled at that last thought trying to picture Fern with a coquettish grin.

"I'll go place our order," said Fern. "I need to go over a few things myself with Clover and the staff." Walking away, she turned back and with a sly, playful smile added, "Bistro business."

"Well, Fern certainly seems chipper this morning," said Happy.

"Not really," said Kyle. "This Magic situation is weighing on her." He told them about how Fern was worried that her application for adoption would be passed over by TWER in favor of applicants higher on the waiting list.

"That's a crock of holy crap!" Maggie said loudly. The mimosas were kicking in. "They might say they have a waiting list they're bound to honor, and they might pass themselves off as non-profit, but it's all about the mother-truckin' money, and, believe me, that means rewarding their hoity-toity donors."

"But, what can we do?" asked Kyle. "Aside from kidnapping and hiding a champion show horse."

Ally's phone rang. She looked at the contact ID and excused herself to take the call just as Fern was returning with a tray of food.

"Who's kidnapping a horse?" Fern asked. When she saw the serious faces, she shook her head. "No, we're not kidnapping Magic."

"We may not have to," said Maggie, downing the last few drops of her second mimosa and signaling Phoebe for a refill. "As a crusty old newspaper reporter, I have a few ideas."

"Some would call you an old curmudgeon when it comes to news reporting," said Happy. To the others around the table, she elaborated, "Mags has ink in her veins."

Maggie chuckled. "The newspaper business is not for the faint of heart."

"Yep," responded Happy, "and I'll never underestimate you.

Now, let's hear your ideas, and I pray they don't involve any Wild West type antics."

Maggie cleared her throat. "My good friend Glads here knows I've been in some shitty situations. But, my crimes don't rise to the level of horse-rustling. Here's what I'm thinking..."

"George, I'm just saying, something is not ringing true here. I wish you could have seen Hobart at the Sunset Social, dancing and charming the townspeople as Phantom of the Opera." Ally told George Rothman how delightful his boss had been on Friday night, then Hobart's abrupt about-face when she saw him by accident the next morning.

Rothman sighed heavily. "Ally, if you remember, I told you certain topics were off-limits. In particular, the matter of Hobart's health. I'm going to tell you something, but this is strictly between you and me. Understood?"

Ally was making her way down the Lakewalk, putting distance between herself and her friends back at the table. "Of course, George. I won't betray your confidence. Is Hobart ill?"

"In a sense, yes. Physically, he's the picture of health, but mentally...I don't know how to put this. He has serious mood swings."

"You mean like bipolar?"

"He's not been diagnosed, but in my opinion he does have a personality disorder. When he's on stage, performing, like you described him at the Sunset Social, he's in a state of high energy. It's almost like he loses touch with reality when he steps into a role. But, then there are the depressive episodes. He has no interest in day-to-day activities, is intolerant of others, and has angry outbursts."

"Is he taking medication?"

"He's on medication, and it helps, but someone needs to make sure he takes it. I probably shouldn't have left him alone, but he'd been doing so well and was pumped about the Phantom role. I thought he would be fine on his own for a few days. One of the things I've been doing here in New York is checking into a live-in caregiver. I didn't think we were at that point yet, but maybe that's going to happen sooner rather than later. He may also need some psychotherapy sessions."

"Do you think he'll be okay until you get back? When are you coming back, by the way?"

"Hoping to wrap up my business tomorrow, and I may be able to catch a late flight back to Roanoke. If not, Tuesday for sure."

"George?"

"Yes?"

"Thanks, and let me know if there's anything I can do."

Back at the Mean Beans, the brunch bunch was breaking up, and Kyle walked back to Books Galore with Happy. Once inside the store, she started peppering him with routine questions. Bookstore business. How was the automated indexing project coming along? Was he caught up with the mail orders? Did he have a chance to look over the past month's financials?

Kyle politely answered all of Happy's questions, but was getting fidgety. His thoughts were on going next door, collecting Fern, stopping to pick up his travel bag, computer, and briefcase from his room at Happy's house, then a stop at Finfrock Farm for Fern, then, finally, be on their way.

"Ahem! Earth-to-Kyle, come in Kyle."

"Sorry, Aunt Gladys. What were you saying?"

"Oh, never mind. Kyle, I promised myself I wasn't going to lecture you or Fern. I just want you to know…"

(*Uh-oh, here it comes…*)

"Kyle, I just want you to know that you and Fern are two of my favorite people in the world. I know you care about each other very much."

(*But?*)

"Just take care of her, Kyle. Take care of each other." Happy started to tear up. "Now, go," she said, shooing him out and turning her back to hide her tears.

"The pictures look great," said Mac, pulling up the digital file and displaying the images in grid view. Ally nodded approvingly. "These are going to make a great spread. Do you want me to start working on a layout?"

"Let's wait until we meet with the stringers tomorrow. I want them to be included."

Maggie was feeling woozy from her three mimosas and accepted Mac's assessment of the photographs without really knowing what she was agreeing to. She kept thinking about the conversation between the Phantom and…what was her name? The mysterious woman. Gina? The Phantom's reaction…

"Maggie! I can see you're not going to be much help here. Let's go home." Mac took hold of her arm and started walking her out with Ally following.

Maggie was still trying to clear her head enough to put the

pieces of the heated exchange back together. No, it was Gianna, she remembered, sister of Ruby Rosa. The murder. Something about family jewels. The Phantom had been displeased...

What did it all mean?

Fifteen

evi Eriksson, aka Erik Reno, entered the lobby of LakeView Lodge at Union Gap. He had buckled the belt of his trench coat at the waist and pulled his purple Patrick Henry Patriots baseball cap down low on his forehead. He gave a half-nod to the front desk clerk and walked with purpose to the elevators. It was 10 p.m. and the clerk, passing time on this slow Sunday night by scrolling through her cell phone, barely acknowledged the visitor, assuming he was a registered guest.

Earlier, he'd called Gianna Talone, disguising his voice and saying he was George Rothman, personal assistant to Hobart Castlebury. He was just back from New York, he told her, and Hobart had asked him to meet with her to update her on the estate.

Erik knew that George Rothman wasn't expected back from New York for another day or two but Gianna wouldn't know that. She told him she was expecting George's visit. She hoped he had good news about the Talone family jewels and invited him to Room 232.

He got off the elevator on the second floor. Making sure to keep his head low so as not to be identified through the peephole in the door, Erik knocked and called out, "Gianna, it's George Rothman." He heard her remove the security chain as she opened the door.

Erik moved fast. He pushed the door open and sent Gianna sprawling. She looked up and instantly recognized him. "You!" she screamed, a look of utter fear on her face. "My sister's killer!"

These were the last words she spoke. With the door slamming shut behind him, Erik jerked Gianna to her feet. Looking into her terror-stricken eyes, he smiled, enjoying the moment. He spun her around and placed her in a rear naked chokehold, the same technique he'd used on her sister Ruby Rosa. Erik's right arm encircled Gianna's neck and grasped his left arm biceps. He brought his elbows together and in a matter of seconds Gianna was rendered unconscious. He maintained the hold until he was sure her death by strangulation was complete.

He lifted her lifeless body and laid it on the bed. Then he positioned her hands across her heart and from the inside pocket of his coat he retrieved a single black rose, which he pressed in her hands.

"You meddling old biddy," he said, standing over her and admiring his work. "Just couldn't leave it alone, could you? You're most certainly not like your sister. I loved Ruby Rosa. She loved me. If anyone deserves those diamonds, it's me, and I intend to claim what's mine. Rot in hell, you greedy bitch."

Tears were now streaming down Erik's face as he thought of Ruby. He wiped them away with the cuff of his two-thousand dollar Burberry beige trench coat and walked out into the hall. He looked up at the nearby security camera without concern. Levi Eriksson, aka Erik Reno, was already a wanted man, a suspect, person of interest, whatever they wanted to call him, in the death of Ruby Rosa.

Gianna's body would be found tomorrow, and Erik would be identified as the alleged killer. So be it. He was smart. He was a master of deception. A student of the brilliant sovereign of the stage himself: Hobart Castlebury. He had eluded authorities for more than four months. His masterful plan was close to reaching fruition. He felt none of the remorse he had when he laid his beloved Ruby Rosa to rest. In fact, he was surprised at his quivers of elation. Squeezing the life out of that worthless Gianna felt like redemption, like he was making things right. "I've outsmarted everyone," he said to himself. "For you, my darling Ruby."

He took the elevator down, this time holding his head up and shoulders erect. With a cheerful, flirtatious "Have a good evening, Gorgeous" to the desk clerk, who was still engrossed in scrolling through her phone, Erik Reno strode across the lobby and walked through the doors, out into the night.

Sixteen

Fern was sitting in the oversized Adirondack chair on the deck of their cabin at the Treetop Lodge, high in the mountains. Wrapped up against the morning's mountain chill in the lodge's plush hooded throw blanket, she was enjoying the quiet when Kyle stepped outside and handed her a steaming cup of coffee, Mountain Mama Blend, of course. Kyle kissed her lightly on the cheek, then took the empty chair beside her. They sat quietly, enjoying their morning brew and admiring the stunning views of Union Gap and Big Gap Lake below.

Before heading out yesterday, they'd stopped at Finfrock Farm for Fern to collect her overnight bag and check in one last time with Cletus. "Are you sure you'll be okay working alone with Magic?" she'd asked her father.

"Don't you worry none," Cletus had said. "I'm an old pro with horses now. You've really turned me 'round." He was referring to how he'd always shied away from all things equine after a childhood encounter with the backside of an angry mule. "Magic and I are…what's that term you young 'uns use for best friends?"

"BFF, Dad, 'best friends forever'."

"Yep, that's us."

"Well then, we'll be on our way." She wrapped her arms around him and laid her head against his chest, "I love you, Daddy."

Cletus choked up. "I love you too, Fernadina."

They both knew she was embarking on a new chapter in her

life. For Cletus, it was a bittersweet moment. He turned to Kyle and took his hand. "You take care of my little girl," he sniffled.

As they drove down the long path, then turned onto West Ridge Road, Fern shot Kyle a questioning look about the direction they were headed. She'd thought they'd be driving to Dominion Mills.

"A little surprise," he said. "Since we're not meeting with the realtor until tomorrow, I thought we could make this evening special with a moonlight tryst on the mountaintop."

"Oh, I love a man who has a way with words and surprises up his sleeve." Despite her trying to be nonchalant, she was actually anxious. She liked that Kyle was lightening the mood, and she was enjoying the suspense.

"As an English major, I plan to woo you to boredom with my grandiloquence."

Fern laughed. "Your what?"

Kyle spelled the word for her and told her it meant extravagantly colorful language.

"Oh, really, Mister English Major. Do you know how to spell 'pompous'? It means irritatingly self-important."

Kyle laughed out loud. He loved that she could give it right back. "You are badass, Fern Finfrock, and I mean that in the slangy way of saying you're awesome to the extreme."

"You ain't seen nothin' yet Kyle Kalahan."

"Is that a threat or a promise, my dear?"

"Any way you want to take it, my darling."

Springtime in Appalachia was a place of scenic beauty. Fern couldn't get enough of the wildflowers growing along the winding roads leading up the mountain and the wooded areas that occasionally opened up to pastoral farmlands where sheep and cattle grazed. Kyle had just read *The Lake at Union Gap* and told Fern about Professor O'Hurley's historical account of the early settlers who came to this mountain region in the 1700s. Fern tried to picture their frontier way of life.

They were in Appalachian country, and much of the tradition, she knew, still existed. As she looked out the window, she pointed to the pokeweed, which grows in the spring. She told Kyle about the annual Appalachian Cultural Days celebration every June in Union Gap, where pinto beans are slow cooked in big pots and served with corn bread and "poke salad."

"Poke salad?" Kyle was intrigued.

"Yep, poke salad," Fern repeated. "Although, it's actually poke 'sallet'." She spelled it for Kyle and explained that the out-of-towners are always shocked when they learn that they're eating not just a weed but one that can be harmful or even deadly if not cooked properly.

"Then why on earth eat it?" asked Kyle.

"Not to sound like a commercial endorsement," said Fern, "but pokeweed is actually high in nutrients. It also has cleansing properties. Because it's a springtime plant, it's said to help the body with 'spring cleaning'." She held up her fingers in air quotes to emphasize.

Kyle thought that was funny. "You actually do sound like you're selling it. Do you eat it?"

"Sure, it's delicious."

The conversation turned to Appalachian culture. Kyle had heard about large uneducated clans of toothless people who lacked ambition and lived off welfare in crude mountain shacks. Fern rebuked him for stereotyping. She countered with personal stories of folks she knew, people who were hard workers but also gentle dulcimer-players, soft spoken, and unpretentious.

"Well," said Kyle, "that's a relief. I was starting to picture you in your later years as a cute mellow old soul, folk-singing and chewing on weed with a mouthful of bad teeth."

Fern swatted him in the arm with the map she was holding. "Pokeweed is not *that* kind of weed. Go ahead and tease me about my Appalachian roots, but at least I'll be spring-cleaned from the inside out!"

They both laughed.

"Darn it," said Kyle, suddenly changing the subject. They'd been having so much fun that he realized he'd missed his turn.

After checking into the Treetop Lodge and dropping their bags in their cabin, Fern and Kyle did some exploring. Fern was ecstatic that Kyle had brought her to this place she'd only heard about and always wanted to visit. They spent the rest of the afternoon hand-in-hand on the hiking trails, enjoying the quiet and being close to nature. It was a welcome get-away from Union Gap. They stopped to admire spring wildflowers like the common blue violets with their palmately-parted leaves that Fern said reminded her of a bird's foot. When they thought they were alone, they embraced and kissed, only to discover they were being watched by several deer peeking at them from behind trees. In one clearing, they found dead wood and decaying tree trunks that formed a scene resembling a couple of dragons fighting. Kyle asked Fern to imagine young boys' adventures being played out in this forest.

"Only boys?" asked Fern.

"Okay, let's say bumbling adolescent boys trying to impress brave dragon-slaying pretty girls."

"That's more like it!"

Kyle had reserved a window table for dinner in the Valley View Restaurant at Treetop Lodge. They arrived early and waited in the Hawk's Nest Pub, relaxing with a glass of white zinfandel for Fern and an American pale ale for him.

The evening sun was setting. To ward off the mountain chill, a fire had been lit and flames were dancing in the big stone fireplace. With the smell of wood burning and the crackling sound it made, the setting was warm, cozy, and inviting.

"A very romantic scene, wouldn't you say?" asked Kyle.

Fern felt suddenly shy and averted her eyes. Kyle reached across to her chair and placed his hand over hers. "Are you okay?"

Fern looked up and stared into his eyes. She nodded, then took a sip of her wine and smiled. "Perfect," she said.

Sitting in front of the fire, sipping their drinks, savoring the ambiance, they talked about life in Union Gap, Fern's bistro, Kyle's upcoming student teaching, Happy's bookstore, Finfrock Farm, Hobart Castlebury's mansion. At their table, they continued the small talk over a dinner of blackened rockfish, wild rice, and steamed asparagus. From their seats, they had a picturesque view of the night lights in Union Gap below. Big Gap Lake was bathed in moonlight.

"Moon Lake," marveled Fern.

"Moonglade," offered Kyle.

Fern frowned. "Is that even a word?"

Kyle beamed. "Of course. It describes just what we're looking at, the bright reflection of moonlight on water."

"Smarty Pants! Is this another example of your promise to woo me to boredom with your grandio...what did you called it?"

"Grandiloquence. And, I do intend to do some wooing, but of

a different sort tonight. Just hope I won't be too boring."

"I doubt that." Fern smiled.

They shared a dessert of chocolate mousse, and it was so delicious Fern said she was going to talk to Clover about occasionally adding it to the Mean Beans menu.

Back in their cabin, Kyle poured two glasses of merlot from a bottle that had sat untouched at dinner. The cabin was chilly, and he started a fire with the logs that had been stacked beside the small fireplace.

Fern had retreated to the bathroom to freshen up, and came out with her bathrobe wrapped tightly around her. Kyle handed her a glass of wine and excused himself to "freshen up" as well. While he was gone, Fern took small sips of her wine and stared into the fire. She was amazed at how comfortable she was with Kyle, how easy their conversation was. Her earlier feelings of nervousness were gone. She was savoring the moment.

Kyle came out wearing gym shorts and a black T-shirt with "Big Gap Lake" in gold lettering, and the image of a largemouth bass jumping out of the water. Fern laughed and opened her robe to reveal her own bedtime shorts and exactly the same tee but in shades of red, white, and blue.

"Great minds think alike," she said.

"True, but it looks a lot better on you," Kyle responded, admiringly.

During her teenage years, Fern was a serious student in high school and a hard worker at her part time job at the Mean Beans Caffeine Canteen. She was also a good daughter, keeping house for her father and staying out of trouble. She had no time for or interest in boys and found their antics annoying. Then, in the years right out of high school, she was too busy building her bistro business to think about dating.

Now, lying in front of the fire on a soft, plush sherpa throw blanket Kyle had brought, she was feeling a deep emotional connection. Kyle was gently caressing her in places where no man's hands had been before, and Fern was experiencing sensations in her body she had never felt before.

"You know, don't you," whispered Kyle while nuzzling her neck, "that I am insanely and wildly in love with you?" He buried his face in her neck.

"Is this the part where you're wooing me?" Fern whispered back.

"May I? Woo you?"

"Yes, please…And Kyle?"

"Hmmm…?"

"You know, don't you, that I am in love with you too? Madly…" She paused and caught her breath. "…and crazily."

The couple was slow getting up in the morning. They playfully snuggled, sappily professing their love for each other. But then Fern decided she needed to get serious. "I need to get something out of the way," she said.

"Hmmm…me too," teased Kyle."

"I'm trying to be serious, boyfriend."

"Don't you think I deserve to be upgraded from mere

'boyfriend'?"

"Maybe. What would you like to be?"

"Hmmm…How about 'lover'?" Kyle pulled her close.

"Maybe." Fern giggled and snuggled closer. "But, I think I might need some more wooing before I'm sure."

"That will be my pleasure."

Sitting outside now, Kyle broke the silence. "You had something to say earlier? Something serious?"

"You mean before you so saucily interrupted me?"

"'Saucily'? Nice word, but you're the 'saucy' one. And I mean that as a compliment. I didn't know exactly how saucy you can be."

"Ha ha…"

"Don't get me wrong. I love it. I love you. I love us."

"Okay, as I was saying earlier before you, shall we say, so 'suavely' interrupted me. In all seriousness…"

"Suavely?"

"I mean that in a slangy kind of way of saying 'delightfully… romantically'."

"Hmmm…"

"Seriously, though…" She was searching for the right words. "Our relationship…"

Kyle waited, wondering where this was going.

"I'm not sure where it's going, but…"

"Fern," Kyle interrupted her. He was serious now. "Wherever this is going, we're going together. I need you to know that. I'm in love with you."

"But you know, don't you, that I will never leave my father?"

"I would never ask you to."

"But, your career…It's just taking off."

"I have no plans to leave Union Gap. After I finish my student teaching, I expect to get a job at Lake County High School. That's my goal. I love it here."

"And if you don't get that teaching job here? What if you get a great job offer somewhere else? An offer you can't refuse? I never want to hold you back."

"Who says I can't refuse? But, okay, for the sake of argument, let's say I get offered that dream job. Let's say I'm offered United States Secretary of Education. I imagine it would be pretty rude to tell the president no. In that case, we just might have to pack up Cletus and take him with us."

"Not going to happen!" Fern punched him in the arm, but she was laughing. "I love your sense of humor. I love you, and you'll always be my boyfriend. I don't care how high and mighty and lovey-dovey you get."

"Pinkies?" Kyle extended his little finger to Fern.

"Pinkies," she said wrapping her own little finger around his.

"More coffee?" Kyle got up to go back into the cabin. Then, "What the…?" He was looking down the mountain.

"What?" Fern stood to get a better look. They both saw a barrage of flashing lights.

"What is it?" asked Fern.

"Something's going on down along the waterfront." Kyle went in and came back with binoculars. "Looks like something's happening at the LakeView Lodge. All kinds of emergency vehicles, Lake County Sheriff, Union Gap police cars, ambulance.

"Let me see," said Fern, reaching for the binoculars.

Seventeen

Mid-morning on Monday, Mac, Maggie, Ally, and the freelancers were gathered in the small conference room at the *Lakeside Ledger* going over photographs and notes from Friday's Sunset Social. The pictures were great, they all agreed, capturing townspeople laughing, dancing, and having fun in the company of Hobart Castlebury as the Phantom of the Opera. Maggie had singled out some of Bradley's photos of the Phantom posing for the camera with his arm around her. She was trying to decide which ones put her in the most flattering light.

The weekly edition of the *Ledger* came out on Thursdays, and Mac had been running numbers to determine how much space they could devote to the Sunset Social. He decided it warranted a prominent place on Page One, above the fold, with a jump to a two page spread inside. He was going to approach the owners of the businesses along the Lakewalk about advertising on those pages where they'd be featured in photos and credited for their contributions.

"Ally," he said, "I want you to work with Maggie on this."

"Sure," she responded. "I'd love to."

"Good," said Maggie. "You work with Leanne and Emily on assembling the quotes they collected, and you can write the first draft of the story. I'll work with Bradley and Justin on selecting and prepping the photographs we'll use."

Her eyes returned to the images she'd set aside of herself with the Phantom. As she was trying to decide which one should be on the front page, they heard the *Ledger's* police scanner crackle awake with static.

Maggie took her pen and notepad and hurried into the newsroom where the box was located. She was a scanner-savvy reporter, familiar with law enforcement jargon. She could tell this was something big for the little town of Union Gap. Stopping at her desk, she grabbed her personal camera, phone, and a few other items. She managed to call out a few words to the team as she rushed out the door. "Dead body…possible foul play…LakeView Lodge…."

"Keep us posted," Mac yelled to her backside.

Maggie gave a thumbs up.

"Can I go with her, please?" begged Ally.

"No," said Mac. "I need you here and I need us to focus. Maggie knows what she's doing."

Ally was stung by his words: *Maggie knows what she's doing.* Clearly, Mac believed that Ally did not. She sulked through the rest of the meeting, and then told Leanne and Emily she'd review all their notes. If necessary, they'd meet again tomorrow.

After the stringers left, Mac explained to Ally why it was not a good idea for her to tag along to a crime scene like this. "Ally, I know you're upset. I know you wanted to go with Maggie…"

"I just want to learn everything I can. Isn't that why I'm here?"

"Yes, of course. But an active crime scene is not the place for learning the ropes. Bystanders aren't welcome, and that includes reporters-in-training. Crime scenes are tightly controlled. Only a few people are allowed in. There are rules and boundaries that journalists need to understand and respect."

"I get it, but I could just watch, couldn't I?"

Mac sighed. "Maggie lives for this. It's in her blood. She knows how to navigate. When she has the time and feels you're ready, she'll bring you in."

After Mac's explanation, Ally felt a little sheepish. "You're right. I appreciate all you and Maggie are doing for me."

Her phone rang. "Hi Fern. What's up?"

"Sorry to bother you, Ally, but what's going on down along the waterfront? Kyle and I saw a gazillion flashing lights."

Ally wondered where they were to see a "gazillion" lights but didn't ask. "Fern, we don't know much yet, but something's going on at the lodge. Maggie's says it's a crime scene. She's there now."

"Wow! Keep me posted, please?"

"Sure thing. Are you and Kyle having fun?" It was obvious that Ally was fishing for juicy details.

"Yes, life is good. Can't wait to tell you all about it…Well, maybe not all."

"I get it, girlfriend." Ally smiled. "Talk to you later."

Maggie didn't take well to being boxed into roped off areas with bystanders. She was always one to push the boundaries. She'd been forced to stay with the crowd of onlookers in front of the LakeView Lodge, but she kept inching her way closer to the crime scene command post. Like a good reporter, she was jotting notes in her writing pad, descriptions of the surroundings, the number and types of emergency vehicles and the comings and goings of officials. But what she really wanted was to eavesdrop, to get the straight poop on what was going on.

She pulled a small earpiece from her pocket and tucked it behind her right ear, out of sight beneath her hair. Then she took her "smartass" phone and clicked on an app that Ally had loaded after her arrival. It was a test version of something called "ListenUp!" which two of Ally's computer science major friends at VCU were developing.

The app, in some ingenious way, turned the phone's speaker into a microphone and used Bluetooth to transmit the sound to Maggie's small earpiece. It still needed a lot of work to produce good sound, but after Maggie had turned it up as far as it would go, she was able to zero in on a heated conversation between Union Gap Police Chief Odell Hawkins and Lake County Sheriff Linwood Farley. The sound was choppy, but Maggie could hear them arguing over jurisdiction.

"The body...discovered within town limits," said Chief Hawkins. "...no indication the death occurred anywhere else...our case."

"...you and your ragtag crew," countered Sheriff Farley, "don't have the know-how or resources to..."

Maggie couldn't make out the rest, but judging from Hawkins' reaction, she suspected it must be pretty vile. He was in Farley's face, spittle flying. "It's our case and if I need your fucking help I'll ask for it," he yelled. Maggie heard that, loud and clear.

"Screw you, Hawkins," Farley fired back.

Turf war, Maggie thought. She was shaking her head as a mobile crime lab pulled up. Two people, one male and one female, got out and approached the command post. Shielded now by the big unit, Maggie stepped closer and was hearing much better.

"I'm Special Agent Vicki Shepard, and this is Special Agent Adam Maloney. We're from the Virginia State Police Bureau of Criminal Investigation, Field Intelligence Unit. We've been ordered to take over the crime scene." They each handed a business card to both Hawkins and Farley.

"Ordered by who?" demanded Farley. "Yeah, who?" echoed Hawkins.

"We were dispatched by the Office of the Governor of the

Commonwealth of Virginia," said Shepard. "We'll be doing the initial crime scene investigation. Then, we'll turn it back over to you locals for the ground work. I assume your two departments have jurisdictional matters sorted out?"

Having their roles minimized, Hawkins and Farley could only nod.

Les Turner, the lodge manager came over to announce that the security tapes for the past 24 hours were ready for review. As they turned to walk into the lodge, Hawkins asked, "So, the state police are taking over jurisdiction of this case?"

"Not exactly," said Maloney.

"Well then, who is officially in charge?"

"The Federal Bureau of Investigation."

"What the heck?" asked Mac, dumbfounded.

Maggie had returned to the newsroom, and was relaying what she'd overheard.

"So," said Ally, "we have the town police, then the county sheriff's department, the state police, and now the FBI all wanting a piece of the action. And, we don't even know who the victim is or any of the circumstances."

"I waited 'til they brought the body out in a body bag and loaded it in the meat wagon," said Maggie. "Then Odell, he's the police chief, Odell Hawkins, came out carrying something, maybe the security footage. I tried to catch him as he was walking back to the station. But, he waved me off, said we'd know more later today."

Eighteen

The combined law enforcement agencies had scheduled a press conference for four o'clock that afternoon, and the trio from the *Lakeside Ledger* arrived early at the Union Gap Civic Center. They were mingling with the other print and broadcast journalists who had come from Roanoke and surrounding areas. Camera crews were setting up and reporters were laying claim to seats as near to the front as they could get. At ten minutes past the planned start time, a spokesperson from the Lake County Sheriff's Media Relations Unit approached the microphone and announced that there would be a delay. She waved off questions and announced a new time of six o'clock.

Some of the attendees grumbled while others decided to make the most of the free time. Todd Harmon, a reporter for the *Dominion Daily News*, announced that Jack's Pub had an awesome Happy Hour with reduced price craft beers and complimentary wings. This was met with a loud chorus of cheers, and a small crowd fell in behind Harmon as he happily led the procession toward the Lakewalk for some *Wingin' It*.

Maggie was one of those grumbling. Not that she wouldn't have enjoyed joining the Happy Hour crowd, but Mac decided they needed to return to the *Ledger* and get some work done. With the discovery of a body and the involvement of the state, and possibly the feds if Maggie had heard correctly, they needed to regroup and rethink Thursday's edition.

"If it's a homicide, we'll need to be prepared to lead off with that," he said. "Let's figure out how that's going to impact the Sunset Social."

Back in the newsroom, Maggie retreated to the break room and returned with her own makeshift version of Happy Hour, Sinatra style. Three clear plastic cups each held three ice cubes, two fingers of Jack Daniel's, and one splash of water, Frank Sinatra's drink of choice. She handed a cup each to Mac and Ally and then took a sip from her own.

Mac tried to hide his annoyance and managed to keep his voice calm. "Maggie, go easy on this. We still have the press conference at six. We need to keep our wits about us." Nonetheless, he took a sip of his drink, then another. It seemed to calm him.

"This is wild," said Maggie. "We go weeks scrounging around for real stories in this sleepy little town, then bam! Just like that we're hit with a double whammy."

Ally had set her drink aside and was focusing on incorporating additional quotes into the Sunset Social story she'd started to write. "Here's a good one," she told Maggie. "'That Phantom dude is one smooth character. He can waltz me away anytime.'"

"Who said that?" asked Maggie.

"Beulah Marples."

Maggie scoffed and downed the remainder of her drink. "The only place Beulah Marples will be waltzing to is one of those pie-eating competitions she's famous for winning around these parts."

Mac scowled.

"Makes good reading, though," Maggie added. "Use it. Without my unsolicited commentary of course."

Ally's phone rang, and she saw it was George Rothman. "Hey," she said. "What's up?"

"That's exactly what I want to ask you. Hobart called me and he's pretty upset. Said he saw all kinds of lights and commotion down along the waterfront. Then, the police chief called him and wants to ask him a few questions. Hobart hung up on him."

"Oh my," said Ally. She filled him in on what she knew and told him about the press conference. "But, why would they want to talk to Hobart?"

"I have no idea, but can we get together tomorrow morning? I'm at the airport now arranging for a charter flight back to Roanoke, then an Uber to Union Gap. Should get in late tonight."

"I'll be in the newsroom bright and early, and most likely all day. Busy week for us. But you can stop by if you want." They said their good-byes and disconnected.

The three continued their work on a new layout until Maggie pointed to her watch and motioned that it was time to head back over to the civic center.

The room was abuzz with chatter when the trio from the *Ledger* walked in. Almost every seat was taken. Sarah Sanderson, the paper's "Around the Gap" columnist, stood and waved them up front where she had saved three seats as Maggie had asked her to do.

A small group was on stage. Union Gap Police Chief Odell Hawkins and Lake County Sheriff Linwood Farley stood side by side at the lectern in a show of solidarity. Motioning for quiet, Farley was the first to speak, introducing himself and others sharing the stage, starting with Hawkins and State Police Special Agents Vicki Shepard and Adam Maloney. He then turned to a newcomer. "And, just arrived from the FBI Field Office in Richmond, we have Special Agent Lincoln Stryker." He turned toward the dark-complected man in a business suit.

At the mention of the FBI, some in the audience murmured. Sheriff Farley motioned for silence. Ally was struck by how handsome Special Agent Stryker was with his olive complexion, thick dark hair, and piercing hazel eyes. Maggie caught her staring and elbowed her.

Farley continued. "We're investigating a suspicious death at the LakeView Lodge, which at this time, we're treating as a homicide. As you can see, we've assembled an impressive task force.

"I know y'all have a lot of questions. Questions about *who?*, questions about *what?*, about *when?*, *where?*, *why?* We're going to give you some information, we'll try to answer some of your questions, and in return ask for your help.

"First of all, the *who?* I can confirm that the body has been identified as 49-year-old Gianna Talone, a resident of New York, who checked into the lodge three days ago."

Maggie's face went white. Her eyes went wide. Her jaw dropped. She started wringing her hands. Mac leaned across Ally and placed his hand on Maggie's thigh. He looked her in the eyes, held up his hand, and shook his head "no," his way of telling her to keep quiet. Ally looked from Maggie to Mac, then back to Maggie. She was surprised enough to hear the name Talone, as in the Talone Crime Family she'd learned about recently from George Rothman. And now, she was confused by this weird exchange between Maggie and Mac.

Maggie only half listened to the press conference speakers. She was recording the session and not particularly worried about missing something important. She just needed time to gather her thoughts. She returned to the conversation she'd heard Friday night between "Gianna" and Hobart Castlebury. Now one of them was dead. Was it possible…could it be that Hobart Castlebury, the captivating Phantom of the Opera who had charmed the townspeople only days earlier murdered Gianna Talone?

Or, was she getting ahead of herself?

Sitting beside her, Ally was listening closely to the proceedings. Sheriff Farley was still speaking.

"We have established that the victim was the sister of Rosa Maria Talone, also known as Ruby Rosa."

The audience gave a collective gasp.

Farley held up his hands. "Ruby Rosa, if you recall, was murdered four months ago in the mansion on the other side of Big Gap Lake."

A question was shouted from the crowd: "Hobart Castlebury's wife?"

"Please," responded Farley, clearly irritated. "Hold your questions."

Then Chief Hawkins started to speak, but Farley talked over him. "Chief Hawkins and his fine police department are investigating this as a homicide that occurred in their jurisdiction. My office, the Lake County Sheriff's Department in Dominion Mills, will provide homicide detectives and experience that is beyond the scope of this small town's manpower."

Hawkins was trying to maintain a dignified presence while seething at Farley's obvious slights. How dare he fail to show the Union Gap Police Department proper respect. He was formulating an in-kind response, but before he had the chance to deliver it, Farley announced he was turning the microphone over to the state police. Hawkins had no choice but to take a step back with Farley.

Special Agent Shepard kept her remarks brief. She and her partner, Special Agent Maloney, took turns explaining that their team of lab technicians, photographers, and forensic experts had taken charge of the crime scene. They were collecting fingerprints for analysis, taking photographs, measurements, and notes. Agent Shepard ended by stressing the importance of teamwork.

"We appreciate the support of the local authorities in giving us free rein to carry out this part of the investigation. As soon as we have the results, they'll be shared with Chief Hawkins, Sheriff Farley, and the FBI. In closing, I just want to say that every person involved in this investigation plays a vital role. A homicide investigation requires teamwork. It's no place for egos."

Ouch! thought Ally. Was that last comment directed toward Hawkins and Farley? Had Agent Shepard picked up on the friction? In contrast, it was refreshing to see the two state police agents sharing the spotlight as professionals without trying to upstage each other.

Special Agent Lincoln Stryker then came forward. Ally noticed how he carried himself with an air of confidence. She was star struck watching him as he explained why the FBI had been brought in to the case.

"Ordinarily, the FBI has no authority in a local homicide investigation. In this case, however, the initial evidence points to a specific suspect, namely Levi Eriksson, also known as Erik Reno. There's an all-points bulletin out for his arrest."

Gasps went up from the crowd as Stryker signaled to an AV technician. A stock photo of Erik Reno, smiling and obviously taken in happier times, appeared on an overhead screen.

"Erik Reno, as many of you know, has been a person of interest in the murder earlier this year of Ruby Rosa and remains at large. Aside from the fact that both homicides occurred in Union Gap, there are a number of other similarities, which I'm not at liberty to divulge at this early stage of the investigation. I can, however, reiterate that both victims, Ruby Rose and Gianna Talone, were sisters."

A number of hands shot up.

"I know you all have questions," continued Stryker, "and we'll get to those shortly. First..." He signaled to the tech and directed everyone's attention to a new, this time grainier, image that appeared on the screen.

"Fortunately, the LakeView Lodge has excellent video surveillance. This image was taken from footage captured last night in the second floor hallway. The entire stream shows a male forcibly pushing his way into Room 232, where Ms. Talone was staying, and exiting about thirty minutes later. Here you see the person we've identified as Erik Reno looking right into the camera. This, as well as other facts, indicate that he's not particularly concerned about being identified.

"You're all probably wondering why the FBI is involved in this case. Simply put, we believe we have a serial killer at large, a person who may be operating in more than one state. And, we feel it's important to get this information out quickly. Erik Reno is a cunning fiend. He should be considered armed and dangerous. Now, we'll take a few questions."

There was a steady stream of hands.

"Do you know the cause of death?"

"Do you have any leads on the whereabouts of Erik Reno?"

"What are the authorities doing to catch the suspect?"

"What steps are the local police and sheriff doing to ensure the safety of the citizens of Union Gap?"

"What can ordinary citizens do?"

Most of the questions were answered with short responses. "An autopsy is being performed to determine cause of death..." "An APB is being distributed to multiple agencies across multiple jurisdictions to get the word out…" "We've also issued a BOLO—Be On the LookOut—for Erik Reno…" "The local authorities will have extra patrols in and around Union Gap…" "If you see something, say something…" "We're setting up a tipline for citizens to call in, anonymously or not, with information."

Todd Harmon from the *Dominion Daily News* asked: "Is Hobart Castlebury believed to be involved in any way?"

There was a brief discussion on the stage, then Chief Hawkins stepped forward, brushing aside Sheriff Farley with a comic air of self-importance. "Ladies and gentlemen, I can assure you that nothing and nobody is being ruled out. However, at this time, we have no reason to believe that Hobart Castlebury is connected to this homicide. We do have questions for him, though, and will be following up on that."

Ally turned and whispered in Mac's ear. He listened, nodding a few times, then gave her a thumbs up. Ally raised her hand, but was passed over three times.

Finally, Chief Hawkins spotted her to his far right, toward the end of the front row. He pointed to her, and she stood up.

"Allyson Murphy with the *Lakeside Ledger*. I have a question for Special Agent Stryker."

Stryker stepped up to the mic and looked at Ally.

"Agent Stryker, the Talone family has known ties to organized crime. Do you see a connection between that and either or both of these homicides?"

Stryker stared at Ally with his piercing eyes. His face was expressionless. He hesitated before answering, then responded, slowly and deliberately. "That's not a question I can answer at this time." He looked out into the crowd, summarily dismissing Ally. "Next question?"

Ally's question about a possible connection to organized crime, elicited a new show of hands and follow-up questions.

"Agent Stryker, can you confirm that the Talone family does in fact have ties to organized crime?"

"Agent Stryker, is the suspect Erik Reno believed to be connected to organized crime?"

"Agent Stryker, Is Hobart Castlebury considered a part of a Talone Crime Family?"

Each question was answered with a terse "No comment." Stryker's eyes again landed on Ally. He stared intently. She started to squirm, wondering if she had waded into unsanctioned territory. Mac gave her knee a reassuring squeeze.

Maggie remained strangely silent, still lost in her own thoughts.

Nineteen

The press conference adjourned and the crowd was dissipating. Mac, Maggie, and Ally were walking back to the *Ledger*, where they'd left their car. They were laughing about an exchange they overheard on their way out the side door as they passed the room where the speakers had gathered. Farley had called Hawkins "prickly," and Hawkins responded in kind, calling Farley a "blustering blowhard."

"I agree with Chief Hawkins," said Ally. "Sheriff Farley was trying to steal his thunder."

"Small-town, small-minded rivalries," quipped Maggie. "Farley's a dickhead. I don't know how he got elected."

The three were looking forward to getting home, settling in, kicking back, and discussing what they had learned and what had been left unsaid. Mac suggested they call ahead to the Creekside Café and get takeout to pick up on the way home.

"Ms. Murphy!"

Special Agent Stryker was walking fast to catch up with them. "Ms. Murphy, do you have a minute?" He sounded out of breath.

"Agent Stryker," Ally said, turning around to see who was calling to her. She felt uncomfortable that the FBI agent wanted to talk to her after the look he'd given her earlier.

"Can I ask you a few questions?"

Mac spoke up. "Agent Stryker, Ally's our intern at the *Lakeside Ledger*. I'm afraid if you want to question her, you'll have to include my wife and me. We own and operate the *Ledger*." He extended his hand and introduced himself. "Mac McGuire. This is my wife Maggie."

Stryker shook both their hands. "Is there someplace nearby where we can talk?

"Do we need a lawyer?" asked Maggie.

"No, no, nothing like that, I can assure you. I just have a few questions."

"We're heading over to our office," said Mac. We were hoping to get in our car and head home. It's been a long day. But, I suppose we can give you a couple of minutes. If you want to join us at the office, it's just over in the next block."

Stryker fell in alongside them.

Back in the newspaper office, Mac ushered everyone into the small conference room. Maggie was in a huff. FBI agent or no agent, she announced that she was fixing herself a "stiff" one. "Would anyone like to join me?"

Mac asked for his usual. Stryker shook his head. "I wish, but I'm on duty." Ally declined Maggie's offer also, but said she'd go to the break room with her and get a soda. "Can I get you anything, Agent Stryker? A water? Soda?"

"A water would be good, thanks," he responded, "but please everyone, call me 'Linc'."

As they sat around the table with their drinks all eyes were on FBI Special Agent Lincoln Stryker, who was now asking to be addressed as "Linc."

"Am I in trouble?" Asked Ally.

"Ms. Murphy…"

"Please call me 'Ally'…since we're on a first name basis. 'Linc'."

Linc smiled. "Ally, you're not in trouble. But I was a little surprised by your question and I'm curious where you got your information about the Talones being a crime family."

Ally hesitated. She didn't want to involve George Rothman after he'd specifically asked to be kept out of anything she wrote. "Research," she said. "From the library." She explained that the *Ledger* was planning to do a feature on Hobart Castlebury and Stonewall Mansion.

"Where'd you find anything about the Talone family's involvement in organized crime? So little has been written about it."

"Wait here." Ally left and returned with the pages she had brought back from the library. "These are from the book, *Offstage: A Behind-the-Scenes Look at Celebrated Theatre Personalities.* The chapter is 'Hobart Castlebury and Ruby Rosa: Romance Behind the Scenes.' I can run off copies for you if you like."

"Can I ask you how you found this obscure book? Has someone talked to you about the so-called Talone Crime Family?"

Ally was uncomfortable with the question. She looked at Maggie, then Mac.

"Hold on," said Maggie, "Ally has done nothing wrong, and we don't reveal our sources, if in fact there is a source. Period."

"I understand," said Stryker. "I'd like to explain what I'm getting at. Can we talk off the record?"

Maggie looked at Mac, who was carefully weighing the question. "Let's first agree on some ground rules," he said. "Are you asking that nothing you say during this conversation be used in any way? Or, are you saying we can take this on background but can't attribute any of it to you? I mean, it's a little unusual for a federal agent wanting to give us information."

"Good points. No, you cannot quote me. Not even as an

anonymous source. Beyond that, technically, I can't stop you from shopping around to get information from other sources, but I'd ask you to hear me out and consider the implications."

"Okay," said Mac, skeptical. "Proceed."

Stryker began: "You only heard part of the story at the news conference this afternoon."

It was now almost eight o'clock. Linc said he needed a break and left for the restroom. While he was gone, Maggie, Mac, and Ally conferred. It had been a long day. They were tired and hungry. The meeting with Linc had already lasted well beyond the few minutes Mac had agreed to. Yet, they all wanted to learn what the agent had to say.

When Linc returned, Mac suggested moving the conversation to their house. "Not sure what your protocol is here, Linc, but these chairs are not the most comfortable and we'd like to get something to eat. We can order carryout and pick it up on our way."

Linc hesitated, but only until Ally mentioned that Monday's special at the Creekside Café was chicken pot pie. That won him over. Ally called and ordered four, and they wasted no time closing up and heading out. They dropped Linc off at the LakeView Lodge, where he was staying, so he could get his car and follow them.

At the house, they sat around the dining room table where the atmosphere was more relaxed. Maggie and Ally had transferred the meals from the carryout containers to china plates and replaced the plasticware with flatware. Maggie brought a bottle of Cabernet

Sauvignon to the table for herself and Mac, and Ally filled two glasses with cold sparkling water for herself and Linc.

"Thank you all for having me," said Linc. "This is great. I wasn't sure what the meal options were in town."

"Aside from the Creekside Cafe, not much once the sun goes down," said Maggie. "If you like pub grub, wings and burgers and such, Jack McKay's Publick House, better known as Jack's Pub, is pretty good. How long are you staying in town?"

"Hopefully just a day or two. I was surprised to get a room at the lodge with the crime scene still being active, but the first floor rooms are still available for guests while the second floor is sealed off."

"They also serve a decent breakfast, from what I've heard," offered Maggie.

Small talk out of the way, Linc cleared his throat. "So, first of all, you're probably wondering how and why us outsiders, state and feds, got involved in this case so fast."

Nobody spoke, but all three looked at Linc intently, waiting for him to continue.

"Actually, we've had Gianna Talone on our radar for some time. When the field office in Richmond heard this morning that she was found dead under suspicious circumstances, we asked the state police to send a mobile unit to secure the crime scene. Nothing against the locals, but the Commonwealth has the advanced technology that we need in this case."

"Okay," Ally interrupted, "but why was Ms. Talone under surveillance?"

"Ally, your question at the press conference was right on target, but it would not have been appropriate for me to veer off topic then. To answer your question, though, the Talone family has for a long time dabbled in organized crime. It was rumored that after the capo Joey Talone absconded, the family went clean. But they're still very active in organized crime, not the least of which involves interstate transportation of stolen property."

Ally interjected. "Was Ruby Rosa part of this? I heard that she hated that life."

"You heard correctly. Ruby Rosa, at the time of her death, was working with our office. Which brings me back to my original question. Where are you getting your information?"

"Not yet," Ally smiled, teasingly. "I have more questions. You had no comment earlier when asked if Hobart Castlebury might be involved. Can you explain?"

"I believe it was Chief Hawkins who said we have no reason to believe he is involved. Mr. Castlebury was cleared of involvement in the murder of his wife. He was not here when it happened, and he passed a series of lie detector tests. With this second Talone murder, we have more questions for him."

Maggie had been content to let Ally ask questions, and was enjoying watching her intern. One of the most difficult skills for a young reporter to master, she knew, was interviewing. Ally appeared confident and comfortable, conducting it more like a conversation, letting each answer flow into another question. Now, though, as the conversation turned to Hobart Castlebury, she felt uneasy, remembering the conversation she'd overheard him having with the now-deceased Gianna Talone.

"Linc?" asked Maggie, "How does Erik Reno factor into these two murders? What's his motive?"

Good question, thought Ally. Now she could see why Maggie was a pro. She looked at Linc to see how he would respond.

"We don't have all the answers," said Linc, "and unfortunately, what we do know I am not at liberty to discuss."

Mac had been sitting quietly, letting the conversation unfold on its own, but now he turned to his wife.

"Maggie, tell Agent Stryker—umm, Linc—what you overheard. I think it's relevant."

Both Linc and Ally stared at Maggie. The agent's eyes were piercing; the intern's look was questioning. Maggie actually felt relieved as she told them about the exchange she'd heard between Hobart and Gianna. But she omitted the part where she'd been hiding in the shadows behind the life-size statue of Elvis sitting on a stool, strumming his guitar.

"Well," Linc finally managed to say after a long pause while everyone at the table sat in silence. "Thanks, Maggie. This is very helpful."

This was the first Ally had heard about the secret conversation, but she recovered quickly enough to ask Linc what he knew about the "family jewels" that Maggie had just told them about.

"I suspect the 'family jewels' are in fact stolen goods, and may be a motive, but I'm speculating. Anything else?"

Ally had started clearing the table, and Linc joined her, helping to carry the dishes into the kitchen. "You might want to talk to George Rothman," she said.

"Who's that?"

"Hobart Castlebury's personal assistant."

They exchanged phone numbers.

"Thanks," said Linc.

"And, thank you for all the background information."

"My pleasure."

Linc was holding his gaze as he looked at her a bit longer than necessary. *Odd thing for him to say*, thought Ally. Was it her imagination, or was Special Agent Lincoln Stryker flirting with her?

Twenty

Erik Reno sat in his hideaway, sipping his evening Cognac out of a brandy snifter and staring into the warm light of the stone fireplace. He was fancying himself in the role of a nobleman, wearing a smoking jacket and reclining in an expensive leather chair in a well-appointed study, contemplating a dilemma. The dilemma was real.

A person who prided himself on always being prepared, Erik had not anticipated that the FBI would be interested in Gianna Talone. She was, in his mind, insignificant. Sure, there was bound to be some excitement in this shitty little town with two Talone sisters murdered, but he hadn't expected that bumping off Gianna would be of any serious consequence.

Sitting near the back of the civic center at the press conference earlier that evening, hearing himself being described as "cunning," Erik was enjoying the fact that none of these dimwits had an inkling the killer was in their midst. An accomplished stage actor, he'd made himself up to be an older female reporter, curly-haired wig, red lipstick smeared a bit, pancake makeup, reading glasses positioned on the tip of his nose, and an ample fake bosom. He had a flowered lanyard around his neck with a crudely-fashioned press card attached. He purposely kept the straps twisted backwards, correctly predicting that amid all the hubbub, no one would actually want to see his credentials. He held in his lap an open reporter's notebook into which he doodled, pretending to be taking notes.

Erik Reno relished being called cunning. He was amused that he should be considered armed and dangerous. He'd love to give that pompous federal agent a dose of the lethal strong-armed medicine he'd given Gianna, who deserved it, and his beloved Ruby, who didn't, but who, regrettably, had given him no choice. He would get immense pleasure seeing those piercing eyes popping wide as the agent's final breath was being choked out of him.

Ruby Rosa, who he'd loved like a mother, even though he sometimes secretly fantasized about her being his mistress, didn't get nearly the attention in death as that bitch Gianna was receiving today. Gianna Talone was a nasty nobody.

He thought back to the press conference when the person sitting next to him asked a question. "Are you talking to me?" he'd inquired in the slightly higher-pitched female voice he had perfected. Turning sideways, he saw two hideously-injected oversized lips moving while a pair of humongous black eyelashes flitted his way. He lowered his eyes to see a veritable mountain of cleavage on display. *Egad!* He pictured this floozy sitting at some anchor desk, all tarted up, presumably to improve ratings. He cringed.

"Yes, ma'am!" mouthed the huge puffy lips. "I was asking if you caught the name of that FBI guy who's speaking."

When Erik didn't respond, her "Daffy Duck" mouth, as he pictured it, started moving again. "He's kinda cute, don't you think?"

What a bimbo, thought Erik. *Like we're two tweens engaging in girl talk about the latest teen idol.* "Yeah," he said, "that's Agent Fuckface."

"Huh?" The mouth became pouty. "How would you spell that?"

Erik had forgotten he was supposed to be keeping a low profile. He got up, flashed the bird to the birdbrain, and amid the stares of onlookers, no doubt surprised at the behavior of this frumpy middle-aged female reporter, he walked out into the street.

Now as he sat looking into the dancing flames, he bemoaned the unexpected attention that was interfering with his game plan. But wait, a new, maybe even better, scheme was starting to take form.

He smiled. "Erik Reno," he said to himself, "you devious devil. You are so clever, a regular rollin'-in-the-aisles rascal."

Twenty-One

aggie was in the newsroom uncharacteristically early the next morning, having driven in by herself to work on her story about the murder. Because Union Gap's *Lakeside Ledger* was a weekly paper and would be coming out three days after the fact, she was struggling a bit. She was used to reporting on big news as it was breaking, writing the article while it was still fresh and the facts were unfolding. Most of the details surrounding the Gianna Talone homicide would already be known when the *Ledger* came out on Thursday. As she started writing, she focused on how that event was affecting the lives of the townspeople.

The little town of Union Gap was rocked this week by the high-profile homicide of Gianna Talone. The 49-year-old New York native and sister of the slain Rosa Maria Talone, was staying at the LakeView Lodge, where her body was discovered in her room Monday morning by housekeeping. The killing has sent shock waves through the community as local, state, and federal authorities joined forces to investigate what they believe to be the work of a serial killer. A warrant has been issued for the arrest of Levi Eriksson, aka Erik Reno, who is wanted in connection with the deaths of both Talone sisters.

With her lead paragraph done, Maggie began typing a list of what to include in the rest of the piece and realized the story had several different angles. There would be a summary of the crime scene from her personal perspective as a resident of Union Gap and a rundown of the press conference. She needed to include topics of local importance like the authorities pledging extra patrols in and around town and a tipline being set up for the public to provide information.

She made herself a note to follow-up on whether there would be a crime-solvers reward for information leading to an arrest and conviction. And, she would need to get pictures of Gianna Talone and Erik Reno and updates on the forensic results from the crime scene.

It would also be necessary to provide background on the murder of Rosa Maria Talone, aka Ruby Rosa, at Stonewall Mansion earlier this year and the relationship of the suspect to both victims. Then there was the connection between Stonewall Mansion and Hobart Castlebury. Lastly, during the press conference, Ally had introduced a possible link to organized crime, and Maggie wondered whether that should be included. And, she needed to remember to avoid the off-the-record topics discussed with Federal Agent Lincoln Stryker last night.

Maggie was on her fourth cup of coffee, but otherwise working on an empty stomach when Ally burst in with pastries from the Mean Beans Bistro.

"'Bout time you decided to roll in," Maggie chided, taking the box from Ally and helping herself to a butter almond bear claw.

"Sorry Maggie, I got waylaid by Fern. Of course, she wanted a rundown on what happened yesterday while she and Kyle were away. I told her things were crazy busy and I had to run, and I broke away as soon as I could. I promised her we'd get together as soon as possible. I want to hear about her get-away too."

"Okay, okay," Maggie held up her hands. "Thanks, at least, for the sweets. Gawd, I need this sugar. And, a break. And, a brain re-boot."

Mac came in next, grabbed two plain donuts, and closed himself in his office to write his weekly editorial. This was certainly not a typical week, and he was mulling over how he would write about the recent events. Union Gap was grappling with a grisly homicide not far from the site of a joyful celebration a few days earlier. If there was anything positive in such a contrast, it was the way a small town comes together in good times and bad. *Coming Together*. That would be the theme, Mac decided.

Sarah Sanderson arrived with her column, "Around the Gap," which this week was a witty piece entitled "Who Was That Masked Man?" She described Hobart Castlebury as a man of many moods and master of all. She recounted the way in which he announced his arrival in town with a flashy display of raised middle, or index, fingers, depending on point of view, and a bare-butted plunge into the lake. Then, she shifted to the charismatic actor who charmed the townspeople with his out-of-the-blue portrayal of the Phantom of the Opera in feats of boot scootin' and boogyin', slidin' and shufflin' along the Lakewalk.

Mac caught sight of Sarah and came out to coax her into staying to help out with obituaries and copy editing. Bobby Hinkleberry, the stringer who covered local government, police, and the courts on a part time basis, would be bringing in any indictments handed up today by the grand jury in Dominion Mills. He was excellent at gathering information, but his grammar and spelling were atrocious. His work always needed a major editorial overhaul.

When George Rothman walked in shortly before noon, the newsroom was in overdrive. Maggie was on the phone. The door to Mac's office was closed, but he saw through the window the publisher staring at his computer in deep concentration. Sarah Sanderson was at Ally's desk typing with a sense of purpose. No one seemed to notice him. He wandered around and found Ally and Leanne Smallwood in the conference room poring over photographs and snippets of copy that were spread over the table.

"Knock, knock," he said.

Ally looked up. "Oh, hi George."

"Not busy, are you?" he joked.

"Ha ha," Ally mock-laughed. "Funny guy, this one," she said to Leanne.

"Can you break away for lunch? He asked. "You do have to eat, don't you?"

"Actually," Ally responded, "Mac is having sandwiches delivered from Papa Don's Corner Deli and expects all hands in the break room for a working lunch meeting…" She looked at the clock. "…In just about ten minutes."

"How about this afternoon?"

"George," Ally cast a rueful grin, "I can't. Maggie's devoting all her time to the murder, so I've been given the responsibility for the entire Sunset Social—write-up, pictures, layout—along with Leanne here helping me." Introductions were made.

"Hi Leanne." George offered his hand and gave her his trademark wink. Turning back to Ally, he said, "I really need to talk to you. When will you be free?"

Ally mulled over the question. "Okay, why don't we plan to meet around sixish at Jack's Pub? After today I'll be ready for a cold one."

After the working lunch, Maggie headed over to the police station for a one o'clock sit-down with Chief Odell Hawkins. She was surprised to find Special Agent Lincoln Stryker in the chief's office. The two were looking at his computer monitor.

"Come on in Maggie," said Odell, pointing to an empty chair. "Pull up a seat. Agent Stryker and I have been going over some footage of the audience at the press conference, trying to identify attendees. Maybe you can help."

"Ah!" said Maggie. "You think maybe it's like the killer returning to the scene of the crime?"

"It's worth a shot. We haven't come across anyone resembling Erik Reno, but we did find an interesting dust up between two women toward the end of the press conference."

The chief fast forwarded to the sequence he was looking for. The video wasn't great. With the cameras positioned in the front of the room aiming outward, they were looking at some sort of confrontation between two women near the rear doors.

"Now watch this," said Odell. The three looked at the screen as the older woman got up, gave the younger one the finger, then hustled out. "Little unusual, wouldn't you say?"

"Very strange," agreed Maggie.

"Do you know either of them?" Odell asked.

Maggie asked Odell to go back and freeze the screen at a place that showed the women in full frontal view. She stared at the screen intently, then said the younger woman looked familiar.

"She's with a TV station in our area. I can't remember which one. Mac would know, He gets all gaga over her big..." Maggie stopped.

"Lips?" Odell finished her sentence for her.

"Umm, yeah. That too. I don't recognize the older lady." She took a closer look at the hair, the glasses, the overdone makeup, the red smeared lipstick, and the dress. The woman was wearing a mid-length loose fitting dress in light blue with bold floral print in shades of hot pink. She had a bulky off-white sweater draped across her shoulders.

"I can't picture her as someone who'd be in front of TV cameras. Maybe she's a print journalist but not from anywhere around here. Too bad we can't see her badge. Can I get a copy of this still shot? I'll shop it around."

Odell buzzed his administrative assistant. "Darlene, can you send Ozzie in, please?" Ozzie was the department's technical go-to guru.

While they were waiting, Maggie texted Mac, who knew right away who the sometimes-anchor with the supersized body parts was as well as the name of the TV station where she worked.

Linc jotted down the information. "I'll follow up with her," he told Odell.

When the police chief rolled his eyes, Stryker added, "Well, it *is* outside your jurisdiction, right?"

A thin, heavily tattooed youngish man came in. He wore a dark cuffed beanie on his head, below which long stringy hair hung over his ears. Squinty eyes peered out from behind vintage gold wire-rimmed John Lennon type glasses. He sported Chuck Taylor All Star Hi-Tops and a baggy, wrinkled Star Trek T-shirt.

"Whatcha need, boss?" he asked. Ozzie provided computer support and technical services for the department. Despite his appearance, he was a real whiz kid, according to the chief.

"Hey, Oz, can you run off a couple of still shots of this woman flashing her middle finger?" Odell pointed to the computer screen.

"Gotcha. Gimme a few."

"He's fast," said Odell when Ozzie had left. "While we're wait-ing, what else can I do ya for?"

"The forensics," she said. "Anything back yet?"

Odell turned to Stryker. "You want to give her what we've got?"

Linc cleared his throat. "Some fingerprints are back. Erik Reno doesn't have a criminal record, so there are no prints of his on file. However, we compared these new prints with the ones taken from the scene of Ruby Rosa's murder."

Maggie waited. "And?"

"Perfect match. It shows that the suspect was at the scene of both murders. Once again, it looks like he didn't care about cover-ing his tracks."

"Anything else?"

"There are similarities in the two crime scenes; however, we're not at liberty to make those known yet."

"Cause of death?"

"We're awaiting the results of the autopsy."

"Can you speculate?"

"Off the record?"

"Okay, off the record."

"We believe the cause of Ms. Talone's death is strangulation, just like her sister. And, I'm asking you not to divulge that informa-tion until we get the official results."

"As Ozzie would say, 'gotcha, boss'. How about DNA?"

"Nothing so far."

Ozzie popped back in with the printouts, and Maggie asked if she could also get images of the suspect. Odell reached into a folder on his desk and handed over copies of the photos of Erik Reno that were shown at the press conference.

As Maggie started to leave, the chief said, "Let me know if you find out anything about the mystery lady at the press conference."

Maggie gave him a thumbs up, and headed out the door.

It was almost six-thirty when Ally walked into Jack's Pub and looked around. The Happy Hour crowd was out in force. Every stool at the bar was taken. Other customers were gathered at the "Fixins Station" for "Taco Tuesday." George was standing at the end of the bar and waved her over.

"It's noisy in here," she said. "And crowded."

"I know. I reserved us a table in the regular dining room. What are you drinking?"

Jack McKay, owner of the pub and the evening's bartender, came over. "Hey Ally! Good to see you."

Ally introduced Jack to George and asked for a Corona with lime. "Make that two," said George.

"And, those tacos smell great," added Ally. "Can we order from our table in the dining room?"

"Not a problem," said Jack. He handed them their beers, and they walked through the bar into the restaurant section to a booth in a quiet corner.

"So," said George, "you've had some excitement around here while I was gone, huh?"

"You could say that. It's all so bizarre. First, the Sunset Social, which was an unbelievable success. As I told you on the phone, Hobart was captivating, charming, engaging…I wish you could have been here. It's hard to describe."

"Hobart Castlebury is a pro. It's like he has an on-off switch. When he's turned on, he performs and does so masterfully. But, as I said, he also has a down side, mood swings, erratic behavior. And, now he's overwrought with the news of Gianna."

"So, you know about the murder and you know the victim is Ruby Rosa's sister?"

George hesitated, then said, "I've been following it in the news."

The waitress came over, introduced herself as Margie, and asked if they were ready to order. Neither had looked at the menu, but, it being Taco Tuesday, Ally ordered a taco salad. George ordered the same and two more Coronas.

"Sure," said Margie. "Chips and salsa, too?"

"Yep, and guacamole too," said Ally. As an aside to George, she added, "I'm hungry."

When Margie left, George asked, "Are there any new developments?"

"Well, we had a chat with Agent Stryker after the press conference, and Maggie told him about the conversation she overheard, but that's not being made public."

George stared at her. "Conversation?"

"Oh, I guess you don't know. There's so much going on, and I'm having a difficult time keeping everything straight. Who knows what and when? Maybe I shouldn't say anything."

George was stone-faced, his tone jarring. "What conversation?" he asked coldly. Ally was taken aback by his sudden seriousness. She started to feel uncomfortable.

"Friday night, as the Sunset Social was breaking up," she stammered, "Maggie overheard a conversation between Hobart and Gianna. Something about 'the family jewels'." She filled George in on the little she knew about the conversation.

"What was this FBI guy's reaction?"

"Agent Stryker said the so-called family jewels might be stolen diamonds, maybe connected to the murders. But he also said they have no reason to suspect Hobart at this time. They just want to talk to him. They're focusing one hundred percent on Erik Reno. George, how well do you this guy Reno? What do you know about these jewels?"

"Ally, I appreciate you telling me this. Sorry if I came across a little harsh. I think it helps explain why Hobart is so upset." George was back to his easy-going self, and Ally relaxed. "Truth is," he continued, "I know *about* Erik but have never met him. Hobart hired me after Ruby's death to handle his affairs. Erik had disappeared by then. Hobart was hopelessly lost and very depressed. He had a pile of estate matters and personal business that needed attention. The family jewels, if they in fact exist, are not part of the estate, and I know nothing about them."

Margie came over with their food and drinks. There was a lull in the conversation as they ate. Mostly, Ally ate and George picked at his meal and sipped his beer.

When they finished, Ally tried to lighten the mood, telling George how the federal agent chased them down after the press conference with questions about how Ally knew about the Talone Crime Family.

"So, I pulled out the pages we got from the library and told him the truth: I was doing research for a feature story. Remember Ethel-the-Bibliophile? Wasn't that funny?"

George wasn't laughing.

"George, I didn't mention you, just like you asked. Although, I told Agent Stryker, or Linc as he wants to be called, that he may want to talk to you. Is that okay?"

"Linc?" George rolled the name over his tongue. "Federal Agent 'Linc' is it?"

Uh-oh, Ally wondered. *Is George jealous?*

Twenty-Two

The next morning Special Agent Lincoln Stryker paid a visit to Stonewall Mansion. George Rothman punched in some digits on the landline phone and played a recorded message. "You need to hear this," he said. "And, I have to tell you, it's disconcerting."

Hobart Castlebury, you know who this is. By now you should also know how dead serious I am. I'm out of patience. I'm tired of playing games. I want what was promised to me. What rightfully belongs to me. You know what I'm capable of. When I say I'm dead serious, I mean cold, stiff, lifeless serious. Let that sink in. Get the goods ready because I'm coming for them. Them or you.

"When did you say you received this call?"

"I got home around ten last night and saw we had a voicemail. The call log says it came in at twelve minutes after nine."

"And Mr. Castlebury was here then?"

"Yes, he was asleep. I haven't told him about it. He's been quite distressed over all of this and is taking medication."

"Play it again," said Stryker. "I'm going to record it, then I'll get the phone company to get me an actual copy."

Stryker listened again. The voice was filtered and sounded altered. Then he checked the Caller ID and tried the *69 redial option, both of which George said he'd done already. The display showed *No Caller ID*. Star 69 provided a number, which Stryker jotted down.

"Did you try calling this number," he asked George.

"No. I thought you'd want to make that determination."

"Good. It's probably the number of a burner phone that's most likely been discarded by now. Or, if the caller is technically savvy, he may have software that changes the number you got from Star 69. 'Spoofing'. Widely used by scammers. I'll check it out."

"And, in the meantime?" asked George. "Are Hobart and I expected to just sit here waiting for this homicidal maniac to strike?"

"Do you have a home security system?"

"No."

"I'll see what I can do from my end. Unfortunately, in most cases, police agencies aren't obligated to provide protection to private citizens."

"Well, that sucks!"

"That doesn't mean they can't. They get to make the call, and because this is a special situation maybe they will. In any case, I'll need to talk to Mr. Castlebury."

"That's not possible right now. As I told you, he's under heavy medication and not always coherent."

"Okay, so take me through your evening hours yesterday."

"Why? Am I a suspect?"

"No, Mr. Rothman, I'm just trying to establish background and a timeline."

"I went into town shortly before six. I met a friend for drinks and dinner at Jack McKay's Publick House."

"Your friend's name?"

George hesitated, but decided to do some fishing of his own. "Ally. Allyson Murphy. She works at the *Lakeside Ledger*. But you already know that, right? She told me that you had an interest in her."

Stryker remained expressionless and ignored the question.

"Please continue," he said.

"Actually, Ally said you might want to talk to me. Which, in addition to the phone call, was another reason I called you. Anyway, she left around eight-thirty or nine. I walked her to her car, then I took a walk along the Lakewalk, it was a beautiful evening. Then I walked myself home. I like to walk, Agent Stryker."

"How well do you know Ms. Murphy?"

George recoiled. "What is this?" he demanded. "I called you over here to tell you about the phone call and to help however I can. Not to be interrogated about my relationship, or lack thereof, with Allyson Murphy. And, for the record, I find it unusual that you 'chased her down' after the press conference. Yes, she told me that."

Stryker again ignored Rothman's comments. "I do have more questions about the case."

"Well, right now, I'm asking you to leave. I'll see if Hobart can be available this afternoon."

Stryker got up and offered his hand. "Thank you, Mr. Rothman. I'll be waiting to hear from you." He handed George his card.

"You're welcome, Agent Stryker. May I call you 'Linc'?" he said with a derisive tone.

Ally was sitting at a small table outside the Mean Beans Bistro, enjoying the warm, sunshiny day and waiting for Fern to join her for a quick lunch and some catching up. Things at the *Lakeside Ledger* were winding down for this week's edition, and Ally was given the go-ahead to take a lunch break with the stipulation that she return in time to help put the paper to bed. The *Ledger* was printed in Dominion Mills, and the digital print files had to be there by four o'clock so the paper could be run off before the evening print run of the *Dominion Daily News*.

The past couple of days had been grueling at the little weekly, where the small staff was accustomed to a leisurely, relaxed pace. First, the Sunset Social meant rethinking the usual go-to layout. Then, the murder required additional juggling: budgetary considerations, news allocation, layout and design.

Maggie's reporting of the murder, with accompanying photos, was given the entire news space above the fold on the front page, with a jump to the second page. The Sunset Social occupied a smaller space below the fold before jumping to a two-page inside spread. With room only for one front page photo of the Sunset Social, Ally had opted for an action shot showing the Phantom of the Opera, front and center, doing a spirited rendition of the Macarena with several townspeople. It was a surreal scene.

The completed section had been given a big thumbs up by Mac and, begrudgingly, by Maggie, whose photograph with the Phantom had been moved to one of the inside pages where it was among the many featured shots. Ally was given a coveted byline for her write-up, and the freelancers were credited in an endnote as contributors.

Fern appeared with diet sodas and two plates of whole-wheat Greek salad wraps.

"Yum! These look delicious," said Ally, eyeing the chopped tomatoes, cucumbers, red onion, kalamata olives, bell peppers, chick peas, prosciutto, and feta cheese.

"And healthy," added Fern. "How are you holding up?"

"It's been quite a learning experience, but...Wow! I have my own byline for the spread on the Sunset Social. I'm so excited to add it to my portfolio."

"I can't wait to see it."

"And, I am dying to hear all about your getaway with Kyle."

"It's not nearly as exciting as your news. But, the time with Kyle was special. Well, actually more than just special."

"Fern, you're blushing."

"It's just...Kyle is sweet and kind...And we have this special connection, like a secret language that only we understand, and a silly sense of humor...And I've never..."

Ally's phone rang. She saw it was George Rothman and let it go to voicemail.

"Fern, I'm so happy for you, really truly delighted to see you so happy. Do you know you're glowing talking about Kyle?"

"I am happy. In love kind of happy."

"Okay now, I don't mean to get personal. But, I'm dying to know...Where did you guys go?"

Fern told her about Kyle's surprise change of route and the drive up the mountain to the Treetop Lodge. She described the nature walks, dinner at the Valley View Restaurant, and the stunning views looking down at Union Gap and Big Gap Lake.

"Ally, it was all so magical," she said. "Kyle is so easy to be with."

Ally smiled. "Fern, when you called me the next morning..."

"Yeah, we were sitting outside our cabin, drinking coffee and getting ready to head down the mountain to meet with the realtor. We saw all the flashing lights down along the waterfront. When we got to Dominion Mills, everyone was talking about a suspicious death at the LakeView Lodge. Big news in these parts."

"And," added Ally, "it just kept getting bigger as the day went on." She told Fern about the press conference, the unexpected involvement of the state police and the FBI, the similarities in the two local murders, and the identification of Erik Reno as a suspect and possible serial killer.

"Wow!," exclaimed Fern. "That's scary. I'm so looking forward to reading this week's *Ledger*, and getting Maggie's perspective."

"Now, back to you," said Ally. "Did Kyle find a rental?"

"Well, yes, but it almost didn't happen. We looked at apartments in Dominion Mills, and a couple of small houses in the area. Nothing seemed to suit him, and we were about ready to give up. Then Donna, she's the agent, suggested we might want to check out the rental cabins along the river, halfway between here and Dominion Mills. You know, those cute log units that are short term rentals mainly for hunters and fishermen?"

"I've seen them. They look pretty small."

"Yep, just a combo kitchen area and living room with small fireplace, tiny bedroom and a bathroom with shower. There's also a deck across the back, screened in, just steps from the river. Not much, but Kyle said it's perfect, just what he's looking for. Privacy for his writing."

"Sounds...cozy."

"It's pretty bare bones, but Dad and I have lots of extra dishes, cookware, towels, bedding, and stuff at the farmhouse. It'll be fun helping Kyle furnish it. Also, it's just a few miles south from there to the high school where he'll be student teaching. A*nd* just a few miles north from there to our farm."

"What about a rental agreement?" Ally asked. "I thought the cabins were for short term, like weekend get-aways or vacations."

"We talked to the rental agent, and he agreed to a six-month lease with option to renew. He gave Kyle a good discounted monthly rate since he won't have the hassle of people checking in, checking out, cleaning, advertising, and all that."

"Sounds great." Ally grinned.

"What?" asked Fern, noticing Ally's grin.

"I'm picturing you sneaking out your bedroom window, climbing bareback onto Magic and galloping across the fields for a midnight rendezvous."

Fern laughed. "You're funny!" Then she got a serious look.

"What?" asked Ally.

"Oh, it's just Magic. I'm not sure we'll be doing any galloping across fields. I can't stop thinking about what's going to happen with his adoption. He's making so much progress, and that's good, but it's also the downside. There's only a couple more weeks before he'll be ready to be rehomed. That'll devastate him."

"Fern, Maggie and I were talking about doing a feature on you and Magic. You can tell his story of abuse and your story of his rehabilitation. You can talk about not just his physical recovery, but also his emotional scars. What do you say?"

"Ally, I don't want to make this about me."

"But it is about you. It's about why Magic needs to stay with you, why he deserves to be right where he is now."

"Do you really think it will do any good? We're up against big money in horse country."

Ally's phone rang again. She saw it was Linc. *Not now*, she thought and again let the call go to voicemail.

"Hello, ladies!" Happy stopped at their table with a very peppy Pippy Shortstocking O'Hurley at her side. "I'm just on my way to the bank and Fern, would mind very much returning Pips to the bookstore when you finish your lunch? It will do him good to spend a little time outside here. I left Kyle minding the store while I run a few other errands."

Fern and Ally both caught Happy's mischievous wink before she bent down, gave Pippy a pat on the head, told him to be a good boy, then sauntered off.

"What was that about?" asked Ally.

"The gist of it is, now that Kyle and I are officially an 'item'," said Fern, using air quotes around the word *item*, "she's going overboard in a doting grandmotherly kind of way. This Pippy episode is her way of saying she's giving us her blessing by bringing the two of us together when I take him back to the store."

"Well, I think that's sweet, and I'd love to stay and chat longer, but I gotta run or risk the wrath of Maggie."

Back at the *Lakeside Ledger*, Ally sat at her desk to listen to her voicemail messages. She clicked on the first one.

Hi Ally, it's George. Listen, I met with Agent Stryker this morning. I'm a bit concerned about the way he kept wanting to bring you into the conversation. I just want to tell you to be careful. I think this guy has ulterior motives. Let me know if he makes you uncomfortable. Take care. I'll talk to you later.

Ally wrinkled her brow and shook her head. *That's kind of strange,* she thought. She went to the next message.

Ally, this is Linc—Agent Stryker. I wanted to let you know I met with George Rothman this morning as you suggested. He hinted at having a relationship with you, but was evasive and almost hostile when I questioned him. I'm good at reading people, and there is something about this guy that seems off. Please be careful, and let me know if you have any concerns.

Oh no, thought Ally, rubbing her temples with the fingers of both hands. The last thing she wanted was to be in the middle of whatever was going on between these two.

At Stonewall Mansion, George Rothman was listening to a voicemail on his landline without picking up.

Mr. Rothman, this is Agent Stryker. I've not heard back from you and need to know what time you plan to have Mr. Castlebury available to talk to me. Please call me back as soon as possible.

Back in his room at the LakeView Lodge, Lincoln Stryker had a voicemail on his room phone.

Agent Stryker — Linc — this is George Rothman. I regret that Mr. Castlebury will not be available to meet with you today.

Stryker was having none of it. *We'll see about that*, he said to himself.

Stryker pulled into the parking lot of Stonewall Mansion. The place looked and felt deserted, and Linc always trusted his feelings. Getting out and walking up close, he saw the curtains on the front windows were pulled shut. He walked through the massive wrought iron gate and noticed with interest that the hinges had been recently replaced. He continued down the brick walkway, up the six stairs onto the porch, and stood in front of the large rustic double doors. He rang the doorbell and heard the Beethoven's Fifth ringtone while simultaneously banging several times on the huge brass lion head door knocker. He waited a few minutes, then went back down and around the side of the house. He noticed all the side windows were tightly shuttered.

Following the driveway around to the back, he peeked through the windows of the detached garage. No vehicle. He went up the steps to the back porch and looked through the door window. All was dark and lifeless inside. He turned around to leave and saw a note taped to the top of a small utility table. It was folded and addressed to the Creekside Café. He unfolded it and read: *Please discontinue food deliveries until further notice. You may add the cost of this delivery to my account. Mr. Castlebury and I are away on business. Thank you!* —*George Rothman.*

Stryker replaced the note, cussed under his breath, and kicked a metal trash can, which toppled over with a loud rattling thud.

"Son of a Bitch!" he said out loud.

Twenty-Three

Happy O'Hurley was at her breakfast table with the weekly edition of the *Lakeside Ledger* spread out in front of her and her little dog Pippy on her lap. She was reading Maggie's reporting of the murder of Gianna Talone while she took bites of an English muffin topped with cherry preserves. Pippy was on crumb detail, always alert and ready to clean up muffin morsels that fell into his mistress's lap.

Sipping a cup of Mountain Mama Blend, Happy thought back on how so much had happened in their small town in just a few months. The murders, first Ruby Rosa and now her sister Gianna Talone; Erik Reno, the alleged killer of both sisters; Hobart Castlebury, the husband of one of the victims and brother-in-law of the other, and now the owner of Stonewall Mansion. *How does Hobart fit in to all of this? Or, does he?* Happy wondered.

She was remembering a time when Ruby and Erik were staying at Stonewall Mansion several months ago. They kept to themselves, but then one early December day Erik came into the bookstore. He was good looking, polite, and charming. "I can tell you're not from around here," she'd said with a welcoming smile. Erik introduced himself, said how much he loved Union Gap, and complimented her on her beautiful eyes. Happy had never considered her eyes anything but ordinary.

Erik had browsed through the section on local history, then asked Happy if she had any books that included information about

Stonewall Mansion. Happy told him no, nothing in stock, but said she'd see if she could find something.

Happy watched out the window as Erik exited the bookstore and walked across the Lakewalk toward a woman standing at the three-foot wall, looking out across the water. Long tresses of coal black hair cascaded down her back. As Erik approached, she turned toward him and linked her arm in his.

The woman, thought Happy, was striking in a way that commanded respect. Against the cold early December day, she wore high heeled boots and a long black leather coat with a lush fur collar and cuffs. Next to Erik, the woman carried herself with an air of superiority as they walked along the waterfront. She exuded an aura of mystery.

Ruby Rosa, thought Happy, with a sigh of reverence. Wife of Hobart Castlebury and star-of-the-stage in her own right.

After they were out of sight, she'd called Helen Overington, the president of the Lake County Historical Society. Helen told her they had a number of documents and photos related to Stonewall Mansion in the society's archives in the basement of the Lake County Court House. Mr. Reno was welcome to come by and look them over if he wished.

Erik never returned to the store, and Happy didn't feel comfortable intruding on whatever business was going on at Stonewall Mansion so she never relayed the information.

Now, Ruby Rosa was dead, and Erik Reno was wanted for two murders. With all this going on, Happy wondered if Mayor Merv might cancel the annual Memorial Day celebration, which was less than two weeks away. Not only was Happy a member of the town council and deputy mayor, but she was also chairperson of the town's Special Events Committee. She'd scheduled a committee meeting for that evening at the town hall to finalize plans. She decided to drop in on Mayor Merv this morning.

Happy moved on from the murder to Ally's coverage of the Sunset Social. She smiled seeing the pictures and remembering how much fun it had been for the whole town and how charismatic Hobart Castlebury had been as the star of the show.

"Come on Pips," she said, laying the paper aside. "Time to go to work."

Pippy jumped down from her lap and started running around in circles, yipping and wagging. Going to work, he knew, meant bookstore business, and with that came breakfast at the Mean Beans Bistro, the little terrier's favorite time of the day.

At the *Lakeside Ledger*, the three-person staff was high-fiving and having a celebration of sorts with champagne.

"Well done team," said Mac, raising his glass and clinking it against Maggie's and Ally's. They each took a sip. "This edition is our best ever. The answering machine was full when I came in this morning. I saved the messages for you guys to listen. Lots of positive feedback on our coverage of both the murder and the Sunset Social."

"We make a damn good team," Maggie agreed.

Mac put his arm around Maggie and kissed her on the cheek. "Maggie," he said, "you're the best reporter in the state. Too good for this little rinky-dink weekly in 'Nowheresville'."

"Stop!" said Maggie, pulling away. "Sure, this week reminded me how I sometimes miss my old world of big time investigative reporting. Actually, I may not always show it, but I like our laid-back lifestyle here. And, don't you dare give me all the credit." She held up her glass. "Cheers to Ally. Look at how our intern stepped up.

The coverage of the Sunset Social was excellent."

Ally beamed. "Thank you both for giving me this opportunity. It helped to have great photos to work with." Ally had talked Mac into purchasing design and layout software for the paper. It had paid off in the placement of the photos for the Sunset Social section.

"And while we're handing out awards," Ally continued, "I nominate Mac for a Pulitzer for his editorial. I wish I could write like that."

"You will, Ally," said Mac. "You're on your way. Maggie and I are very proud of you."

"Mac," said Maggie, "I think we should enter this issue in the Virginia Press Association Awards. They have a category for weeklies."

"I'll check into it," said Mac. "Now, before our heads get too big, let's get a jump on next week's edition."

"Ugh!" Both Maggie and Ally groaned. "Slave driver," teased Maggie.

"Just a lineup," said Mac. "Let's divvy up assignments, then we'll shut down the office for the day and head over to Dominion Mills for a long leisurely lunch at that new Italian restaurant everyone's talking about. How does that sound?"

Special Agent Lincoln Stryker walked into the TV station in Siler Mills, 40 miles southeast of Union Gap, and requested to speak to Cassie Curoso. When asked what this was concerning, he showed his badge. "Official business," he said. He was ushered to a conference room, and someone was sent to retrieve her.

When Cassie entered the room, her heavily-lashed eyes went wide. "I know you," she said. "You're that FBI guy from the press conference in Union Gap. What's this about?"

"Just a couple of questions." Stryker introduced himself, and from his leather attaché case pulled out a copy of the photo Ozzie had produced. "About the press conference...You were sitting beside this woman. What do you know about her?"

"Who is she?"

Stryker ignored the question, and looked at her, waiting.

Cassie began chewing her oversized lower lip. "I don't know her, I swear."

"What were you two talking about?"

"Nothing special. She was rude."

"How so?"

"You were talking, and I just asked her who you were. She got all obscene on me."

"What did she say."

Cassie thought about that. She looked at Stryker, then down at the table. "I don't want to tell you."

"Ms. Curoso, what did she say?"

"She called you..."

"What?"

"Agent Fuckface. She called you Agent Fuckface. Then, she flipped me the finger and stormed out."

Stryker remained expressionless. "Anything else?"

Cassie debated whether she should mention her own comment about Stryker being cute. She decided against it and slowly shook her head no, then asked, "Agent Stryker?"

"Yes?"

"Can you tell my boss I'm not in trouble?"

He ignored her question and handed her his card. "If you think of anything else, please let me know."

Happy entered the town hall and gave the mayor's secretary, a cheerful hello. "Beautiful morning, isn't it, Dee?"

Delores looked up from reading the *Lakeside Ledger*. "Happy, you're here bright and early."

"I'm here to see the mayor. Can I go on back? It's about the Memorial Day Celebration."

The mayor stepped out of his office behind the secretary's desk and motioned to her. "Come on back, Happy. Always glad to see you."

Mervil Turnbull was to many around town the quintessential Santa Claus, with a big belly and a jovial demeanor. He liked to refer to himself as a pleasingly plump, jolly old Saint Nick. But instead of a long white beard, he sported a manicured handlebar mustache. When he'd first run for mayor six years ago, he won easily, and he was unopposed for reelection two years ago. Nowadays he was trying to convince Happy to run when his current term ended. She was already the deputy mayor and was well-liked around town.

"Merv," said Happy, as they walked into his office. "Have you been thinking about Memorial Day? I mean with all this murder business in town. Any thoughts of canceling the events?"

The mayor waved his hands in a gesture of dismissal. "Now, none of that talk, Happy. We're not going to let this Levi person, or Erik Reno, or whatever he calls himself, stop us. I know you have a meeting tonight. Tell the committee you've been given the green light to proceed with the plans. Now, give me a run through. What's my role?"

"Well, you know the day always starts off with our annual pancake breakfast at the fire hall, followed by the Moment of Remembrance at the gazebo in Union Square. That's where you speak, briefly."

"Oh my, yes, I've got my remarks already prepared. You know my brother Arlie was killed in action in Vietnam. It's a painful reminder to be sure, not just for me, but for all the families who've lost loved ones in service to our country. Oh, sorry to start musing. I get a little carried away. Please continue."

"Of course. We'll have the entire Lakewalk decked out with flags, then the signature event..."

"The bass fishing tournament!"

"Bingo! I'll be getting with JD to make sure he's got everything under control for the big competition."

"None too soon. I think our Billy's getting a bit anxious to go out and populate." The mayor chortled.

Billy, a largemouth bass, was Union Gap's reigning mascot. A few years ago, Cecil Moomaw, a member of the town's Lake Committee, had come up with the idea of a yearly mascot contest as part of the tournament. The winning largemouth bass would be kept for the ensuing year in a large aquarium in the town hall with a plaque showing the winning fisherman's name. Every year, when a new winner was declared, the retiring bass would go to a nearby fish and wildlife sanctuary to live out his or her days. If the winning bass was a male, it was always named Billy; if a female, Betty.

"Well," said Happy, "May through June *is* mating season for largemouth bass. So I imagine Billy *is* getting restless to be fruitful and multiply."

"Ha ha! Pun intended?" Merv laughed.

"Yep. Cute, huh?" Happy loved matching wits with the mayor, who was well-versed in biblical literature.

"Moving on," said Happy, "we're good to go with the annual afternoon barbecue at the campgrounds' pavilion. We've got Meat & Eat BBQ doing the smoking and grilling. And, the River Ridge

Boys will be providing live music as usual."

"Now, Happy, I take it we won't be having any surprise Phantoms jumping up on the stage." The mayor leaned back in his chair and chuckled. "*'Have you missed me, good monsieurs?'*"

"*'I have written you an opera!'*" Happy responded, now laughing herself. Apparently, the mayor was also a student of the opera.

"*'Don Juan Triumphant!'*" roared Merv.

"*'Fondest greetings to you all,'*" Happy belted out.

By now, both were laughing heartily.

Ally asked to be dropped off at the Lakewalk when they returned from lunch at Storia Italiana. She couldn't pronounce Gnocchi Alla Sorrentina, but nonetheless ordered it at the recommendation of Mac and Maggie, and it was delicious. She overate and drank too much good wine. She needed to walk it off.

Her phone rang, and she groaned when she saw it was Linc. She wasn't in the mood to be lectured. She had already called George today, intending to tell him the same, and was surprised when that call went directly to voicemail. She hadn't left a message.

"Hello, Linc."

"Hi Ally. Quick question...Do you happen to know where Mr. Rothman and Mr. Castlebury took off to? The house is dark and shuttered, and my calls are going directly to voicemail. I'm concerned because we were supposed to meet yesterday."

"Nope, sorry, don't know. And, for the record, I'm not George's keeper. The message you left me earlier was a bit off-putting."

"I apologize. But, if you hear from him, would you please let me know? It's important."

"Okay."

"Oh, and one more thing. Do you know if Maggie found out anything about the mysterious lady at the press conference? She was going to ask around."

"Linc, really, I don't know. Maybe you could ask her."

"Okay, sorry to bother you. Have a good evening."

Ally decided to leave her car in the *Ledger* parking lot and walk home. She needed to clear her head. She was just crossing over the stone bridge when her phone rang again. She didn't recognize the number and decided not to answer.

A couple minutes later, when she saw that the caller left a voicemail, she thought it was probably spam, but decided to listen anyway.

Ally, I realize you won't recognize this number, but it's me, George. Can you please give me a call and I'll explain?

Why me? thought Ally. Why am I in the middle of this? She felt like throwing her phone off the bridge into Sneaky Creek. Instead, she hit redial, cussing softly as she did.

George answered on the first ring. "Ally?"

"George, what's going on?"

"Hobart received some serious threats. He was already unnerved by the homicide of Gianna, and now he's a complete mess. He's been sleeping way too much and then, when he's up, he's pacing the floor, mumbling nonsense. I'm worried about him. Long story short, I'm checking him into a place where he can receive professional care."

"George, I'm so sorry. Where are you taking Hobart?"

"Ally, it's a very good facility, but I can't tell you where it is right now. Please understand, he received threats against his life."

"Have you reported this to the authorities?"

"For all the good it did…I had your FBI friend—'Linc'—listen to the threatening message left on our landline phone. All he wanted to talk about was you. I think he's got a thing for you and for some reason considers me a threat."

"That's ridiculous!"

"Tell *him* that."

"I don't like being in the middle. How long will you be gone?"

"Not sure how long Hobart will be staying at the facility. I'll be dividing my time between him, business in New York, and checking back on things at the mansion."

"What about your phone? Why did you call me from this strange number?"

"In my attempt to get Hobart calmed down and us on our way, I forgot my cell phone at the mansion. I got this prepaid mobile to use temporarily."

"Agent Stryker told me to let him know if I heard from you."

"Yeah, well maybe you could tell Agent Stryker to conduct his own investigation and leave you out of it."

Twenty-Four

Fern was showing Ally how she applied the medicated salve to Magic's ankles as part of their morning routine. "His wounds are just about healed now," she said, "but he's still skittish."

With the Sunset Social behind them, Ally was given the go-ahead to do a feature story on the abused horse Fern was fostering and her fears that she wouldn't be able to adopt him after weeks of nurturing him back to health.

"Thank you for doing this, Ally," she said. "Doc Johansson is on our side. When I told him that Magic may be adopted out to a big-money horse farm and possibly put back in the showring, he was as appalled as I am. He also agreed that Magic isn't ready yet, emotionally at least, to be rehomed. He said he'd wait a few more weeks before signing off."

"No thanks necessary," said Ally. "I'll do anything I can to help you keep him. Now, let's get some pictures out in the paddock, and you can describe the progress you've made in getting back in the saddle."

Cletus appeared at the barn door as they were walking Magic out. Fern motioned for him to join them. "Dad, tell Ally the story of how you were kicked by that mule when you were a kid and how Magic helped you get over your fear of horses."

Cletus chuckled and related the story of Bertha, the neighbor's mule, who was leased by his father to plow the fields. "We called her Big Bad Bertha. Not only extra-large in size, bigger than any mule I'd ever seen, but that old girl was mean. And bullheaded..."

"Stubborn as a mule," laughed Fern. "Imagine that." As an aside to Ally, she whispered, "Every time he tells this story, the mule gets bigger. And her temper gets meaner."

"Anyhow," continued Cletus, "I was behind the plow. Pa said I could go down to the river fishin' soon as I got the field plowed, so I was tryin' to hurry Bertha along. Wouldn't ya know, she just stopped dead in her tracks, turned her head around and hee-hawed, you know, the way mules try to imitate donkeys. She rolled back her upper lip, flashed a mouth full of big, ugly yellow teeth. I thought she was laughing at me."

By the time they got to the paddock gate, Fern and Ally were both laughing. Fern was trying to roll her upper lip. Cletus told her she looked ridiculous. Ally wanted to hear more about Bertha.

Cletus continued. "I went around to her face and looked her square in the eye and told her to start plowin'. She didn't blink. So, I went around to her backside and smacked her on the rump. That's when she lifted both back legs and walloped me a good one. Sent me flying, she did."

"Oh no," said Ally. "Were you hurt?"

"Mostly my pride. When I picked myself up, Big Bertha had taken off, haulin' ass and draggin' the plow behind her. Got herself all tangled up in the fence yonder, and I had to limp back to the barn and tell Pa."

"His Pa wasn't amused," said Fern. "But, it's a funny story now, right Dad?"

"Never wanted nothin' to do with mules, donkeys, horses, zebras, none of them. Then, wouldn't ya know, Happy was givin' me directions, sendin' me off to that Chincoteague place with little Fern and comin' home with Misty."

"Love you, Daddy," said Fern, wrapping her arms around him.

"That Misty was a cute little fella, and he's been good for Fern" said Cletus. "That's what matters."

"And now," said Fern, "you and Magic are best friends, right Magic?" She stroked the black stallion's forehead.

Magic nuzzled her shoulder then turned to Cletus. The stallion shook his head, rolled back his upper lip and gave a high-pitched neigh.

"He is such a clown," said Fern, and they all laughed.

"So, Stonewall Mansion was once a safe house within the network of the Underground Railroad?" pondered Maggie. She'd expected her meeting with Helen Overington to be boring, but she was fascinated with what she was learning. The president of the Lake County Historical Society was giving her background on the stately house for the *Ledger's* upcoming feature.

Meeting in the basement of Lake County Court House, Helen had produced documents from the local archives dating back to the mid-Nineteenth Century about how Jeremiah Jackson had laid claim to the acreage on the north side of Big Gap Lake.

"Jeremiah was the son of Joshua Jackson, a well-to-do plantation owner in South Carolina," she said. "He was also hopelessly smitten with Priscilla Ambrose, the daughter of a wealthy banker. Priscilla was a much sought-after southern belle."

She was also a fiercely independent thinker, according to Helen. "Jeremiah courted her faithfully, and she liked him well enough, but Priscilla told him she could never marry a man who owned slaves."

Maggie was enjoying Helen's spirited narration. "How did that make Jeremiah feel?" she asked.

"Oh, he was crushed," she replied. "He believed his chance for happiness with the love of his life was out of his grasp. However, fate intervened."

"How so?"

"Jeremiah's father, Joshua, died unexpectedly. That gave Jeremiah the opportunity to ask Priscilla's father for her hand in marriage. In doing so, he promised her that he would sell the cotton plantation, free the family's slaves, and move north with her."

"So," prompted Maggie, "what brought them here?"

"Well, the newlyweds were traveling through Appalachia, to parts unknown when they stumbled upon Big Gap Lake. The forward-thinking Priscilla envisioned a big house on the point in the undeveloped area directly across from the then little farming town of Union Gap. There, they would raise a family of at least six children."

Helen recounted how Jeremiah, with his inheritance and proceeds from the sale of his family's plantation, purchased one hundred acres surrounding and including the point on the lake.

"With Jeremiah's money, Priscilla's dowry, and her father's know-how, they established a bank and lived comfortably while building Priscilla's dream house on the site of what became known as Jackson's Point."

Maggie was examining the land documents, which showed that Stonewall Mansion was built sometime around 1850. But, according to Helen, the couple's life was not entirely as they had envisioned it. "After suffering a miscarriage and almost losing her life in the process," said Helen, "Priscilla was declared 'barren', a term she despised and a condition she agonized over."

Although they lived well and threw lavish parties for the small upper class population of Lake County, and while their stately "Stonewall Mansion" was a frequent leisure destination for their wealthy friends from South Carolina, Priscilla mourned the absence of children running around the lush grounds along the shore of the Big Gap Lake.

"At that time," continued Helen, "the Underground Railroad was well-established. Abolitionists and sympathizers had set up secret routes and safe houses to assist run-away slaves in escaping to free states up north and Canada."

Helen was now paraphrasing from Priscilla's diary pages in which she wrote of her empathy for the slaves and her desire to join the cause of assisting the fugitives in their passage to freedom. "Because of the secrecy surrounding the escape network, we don't have any official record that Stonewall Mansion was a stop on the Underground Railroad, but Priscilla's journals suggest it."

Priscilla wrote about her "guests," using their first names and describing them with clipped phrases, such as "Tobias, about 35, dark coloured, med size, intelligent. Wife Sary, about 30, med dark coloured, scared. Owned by Master Braxton." She recounted stories of the treatment from which they had fled, ranging from "badly at times" to instances of "abuse," "violence," and "flogging." She wrote of her joy when she and her husband and their "guests of colour" gathered around the long table in the dining hall, where they shared their experiences, their fears, and their hopes. All spoke of achieving liberty.

Maggie was struck by all this. "Helen, are you saying that the Jacksons, who hosted elaborate banquets, wining and dining the rich and famous, provided the same hospitality to the lowly "negroes," who provided slave labor to the wealthy?"

"So it appears," responded Helen.

"Amazing. How did this couple fare during the Civil War?"

"According to Priscilla's diary, they proudly claimed to be staunch unionists. In fact, at the time of the Civil War, rumors circulated that Jeremiah Jackson was a distant relative of Thomas Jonathan Jackson, better known as "Stonewall" Jackson, the legendary Confederate general. Even though they lived in a stately home they had named 'Stonewall Mansion', both Jeremiah and Priscilla disavowed any relationship to the Confederate general, and we've found no documentation to the contrary."

After their deaths, with no designated heirs to their estate, Stonewall Mansion was sold and in the ensuing years it passed through several owners. The owner before Hobart Castlebury was Mountain Crest Properties LLC, a company that leased the mansion out as an event venue.

"What information do you have about the size, the number of rooms, the floor plans of the place?" asked Maggie.

Helen went to one of the file cabinets, opened a drawer marked "Historic Blueprints" and thumbed through the folders. She took out one labeled "Stonewall Mansion" and brought it to the table. She put on a pair of white gloves and carefully held the centuries-old sheets encased in plastic.

Maggie asked, "Can I get copies of these and also some of the diary pages?"

"Unfortunately, we have no way to copy these oversized documents," replied Helen, "but you're welcome to photograph them."

Maggie wished she'd brought a wide lens camera, but nevertheless snapped some pictures with her "smartass" phone and began packing up to leave.

"Helen, you've been extremely helpful," she said. "I can't thank you enough. You've provided me with more than I could have hoped for. What a storied and colorful history. Why have these stories remained untold for so long?"

Helen shrugged. "Nobody asked," she said.

Special Agent Lincoln Stryker was back in his Richmond office. He was sitting at his desk deep in thought, twiddling a pencil, and feeling like he was being played. He thought "burned" might be a better way to put it. He'd just learned the latest phone number he had for George Rothman was no longer in service. In fact, the number was for a burner phone, which, in all likelihood had been disposed of by now.

He'd been given the number by Ally, who was clearly not happy about being put in the middle of this. "Linc," she'd huffed, "I'm a journalist. I'm not part of this story."

She'd told him what she'd learned, that George said he was taking Hobart to an undisclosed location, a facility where he would be kept for observation and treatment…for what?

Very convenient, Mr. Rothman, thought Stryker. *A key person wanted for questioning in a high-profile murder investigation is suddenly not available. Very convenient that you left your phone at home and made a single call on a burner phone. And, the number assigned to the burner phone is no longer in service. But, of course, as I'm sure you know, you can simply discard the burner phone and purchase a new one. They're cheap.*

But why, Mr. Rothman? Why are you going to such lengths to evade me? Is this a game?

His desk phone buzzed. "Yes, Pat?" he asked the branch secretary.

"You have a call on line 2."

"Who is it?"

"He said his name is George Rothman."

Twenty-Five

J ohn Douglas Stockman, or JD as he was known locally, not only sold all things fish in his Dockside Station store, he lived to fish, and through his piscine zeal he brought a new dimension of lake life to the community. He also loved to talk about his passion, and Happy O'Hurley was the perfect audience to listen.

With Memorial Day less than a week away, Mac had asked Happy if she'd be willing to write a "Special to the *Ledger*" article about the bass fishing tournament based on her meetings about the event with JD. Maggie was still covering the murder for this week's edition and working on her future feature story about Stonewall Mansion. Ally was concentrating on her write-up about Fern and her foster horse Magic.

Happy was delighted and suggested to JD that they meet at the Mean Beans, where they could sit outside and chat. They were watching the morning mist rising over the lake and enjoying hot cups of Mountain Mama Blend. Happy had intended only to get the basic details about Monday's annual tournament, but JD was providing her with much more information than that, and she was encouraging him.

He told her that after moving to Union Gap he'd begun educating himself about lake health, and he had ideas as well for recreational and sporting events on the water. "So," he said, "I approached the town council about forming a lake committee. I argued that as the focal point of the town, Big Gap Lake is a treasure that needs to be nurtured and protected."

His proposal to form a lake committee was well received, and with a large group of eager members, JD was named chairman.

"Well, you and your committee have come a long way," said Happy.

"We have," JD agreed. "We convinced the town council to hire a reputable lake management consulting company. It was their recommendation that we install those man-made floating islands you see in the coves that get run-off from heavy rains."

"I've wondered about those," said Happy. "What do they do?"

JD was happy to explain in great detail that the clusters of water tolerant native vegetation were designed to capture a portion of unhealthy phosphorus and sediment runoffs that would otherwise enter the lake.

Happy shook her head. "You've lost me," she said.

"Sorry about that Miss Happy. In simple terms, the runoffs trigger harmful algae blooms. You may remember a couple summers' back, we had that extended heat wave. There were clusters of foamy scum, changing the water shades of green, blue, brown, red, and maybe other colors."

"I do remember. The town council was very concerned about swimming, fishing, boating...And, those floating islands prevent these blooms from happening?"

"Well, they help. They also provide surface habitat for wildlife and underwater root structures for fish and water-based life."

"I had no idea. I thought they were just for eye appeal."

"That too," JD laughed. "Are you sure I'm not boring you?" he asked. "I can talk about this stuff all day."

"Not at all. But I can see I'm going to be expanding my article. Please go on."

"Well, you know the annual fish stocking is a big focus of the lake committee."

"Oh, how well I do know," offered Happy. "It's always exciting. When the Bragg's Fish Hatchery Truck rolls in, residents follow it around like puppy dogs to its various stops. The kids especially love their part in the stocking process, carrying their buckets to the water's edge and releasing the fish. How many fish get released?"

JD had those numbers at his fingertips. "On average, Braggs brings a thousand each of young smallmouth bass, crappies, walleyes, and largemouth bass each year. The walleyes and young bass are always 'catch and release'," he said. "That allows them to get acclimated to their new environment and start reproducing."

Fern appeared with coffee refills and a plate of cinnamon rolls. "Just out of the oven," she announced. "I thought you might enjoy."

"Oh yes indeed," exclaimed JD. "Thank you so much, Fern." He began pulling apart a still-warm section with icing melting down the sides. "My compliments to the chef."

"I'll pass that along to Clover," smiled Fern. "She'll be pleased. Is there anything else I can get you?"

"Not for me," said Happy, "but, would you mind taking a couple of these over to Kyle at the bookstore? I'm afraid I'm keeping him from his morning break."

"Of course," replied Fern, giving Happy a conspiratorial wink. "Anything for your handsome nephew."

"And, your handsome boyfriend." Happy returned the wink.

Back to JD, she said, "Let's talk about the upcoming Memorial Day tournament. That's actually what Mac wants me to write about. I love all the excitement, but I've never paid attention to the details. So, what are the rules?"

"For largemouth bass, the minimum length is fourteen inches, with a limit of five. Smaller ones have to be released back into the water. The first fisherman to bring back a largemouth of designated length without exceeding the limit is declared winner of the Union Gap Mascot Contest. His name goes on the plaque beside the large aquarium in Town Hall where the mascot is kept. Then, there's a second category for largest bass caught during the six hour period. At the end of the tournament, all the fish except the new mascot, are returned to the water."

Happy and JD shared a laugh about how Cecil Moomaw's idea of rewarding the winning largemouth bass with a lifetime reprieve had become such a hit. The townspeople always enjoyed stopping at the aquarium when they had business in the town hall building to check on "Billy" or "Betty."

"I never knew," said Happy, "that you could keep bass in an aquarium."

"Actually," explained JD, holding up three fingers, "keeping our mascot in an aquarium is completely ethical as long as the tank is big enough, we feed it properly, and take care of its environment." He expounded on all the regulations pertaining to size, habitat, timed lighting, temperature, maintenance, and diet. The aquarium had to replicate a natural habitat, and they had to keep a combination of fresh, frozen, and pellet foods. "The food can get expensive," said JD, "especially because bass eat so much."

"I had no idea," said Happy. "Who takes care of all this?"

"Lake Committee members take turns. Cleaning's a big issue, but they all seem to take it in stride."

Happy snickered. "Not quite. I remember Cecil talking to the boys one morning here at the Mean Beans. He was saying he had no idea bass could produce so much waste. Although, he was somewhat more specific in his choice of words describing the waste."

"I'm sure," chuckled JD.

"But, why bass? What's their appeal?"

"Happy, I can't describe it." He pointed out in the lake where people were casting off low-slung bass boats. "For sports anglers," he said, "bass are prized catches. And you gotta get out early morning like these guys or late evening. The bass don't like the sun and tend to find shelter during daytime hours."

"Is it year-round?"

"Bass fishing is best May through July in these parts, which makes perfect timing for our tournament."

Happy helped herself to a second cinnamon roll. "Okay, here's a tough one for you. How can you tell the difference between the Bettys and the Billys?"

"Good question, Happy. Sometimes it's tough, but one way to tell is females have bigger mouths."

"Hey, better watch it there, JD. I resemble that."

"Gotcha, Happy," he laughed. "Just talking fish here. But it is true that female bass are just plain larger in general."

"Okay, so while all of this is going on, what will you, the designated tournament official, be doing?"

"I'll be out and about in the water during the competition, spot checking to make sure the boats and participants are complying with all the rules."

"Such as?"

"Well, they can't have more than five fish at a time in their live wells. That's one thing I check on."

Happy looked again out at the fishermen and thought how relaxed they looked. "Well," she said with a slight rise in the pitch of her voice, "now that I'm all educated and know everything there is to know about bass fishing, I might just sign up for the tournament myself."

"Sure, why not? We'd love to have you join us."

"I was only joking, but JD?"

"Yeah?"

"Look out there across the lake at Stonewall Mansion. Do you see something in the middle upstairs window?"

JD squinted, then shook his head. "Nah. Why? Do you see something?"

"It looked like the curtains were ruffling, then a dark form was there. Must be my imagination cause I know both George Rothman and Hobart Castlebury are away."

"Now Happy, you're not starting to believe those ghost stories, are you?"

"Hmmm…"

In Richmond, Special Agent Lincoln Stryker was explaining to Special Agent in Charge Colin Hynes why he felt the need to return to Union Gap. "I have some leads I need to follow up on in the Gianna Talone homicide investigation. Some pieces just don't add up, and I have concerns that certain people may be at risk while Erik Reno is still at large."

"Such as?" asked Hynes, sounding a little skeptical.

"The mysterious woman at the press conference, for one. She didn't fit in. No one recognizes her. Very strange considering the media in and around Union Gap is a small circle, and at that early stage of the investigation not many outside the circle knew or cared about the press conference. The disturbance she made and the language she used were out of place." Stryker told his boss about the woman's comments to the TV reporter, Cassie Curoso, and her abrupt departure.

"So, this mystery woman referred to you as 'Agent Fuckface'? You wouldn't be taking this personally, would you, Stryker?" Hynes was doing his best to hide a smile.

"Sir, I can assure you, I have very thick skin. I've been called worse."

"What else have you got?"

"I also finally got a call from George Rothman." In his initial report, Stryker had explained the connection between Rothman, Hobart Castlebury, Erik Reno, Ruby Rosa, and Gianna Talone. He also reported that before he could question Castlebury, Rothman whisked the actor away.

"So, what did Rothman have to say when he called you?"

"Well, first of all, he claimed he was calling me from a second burner phone, which is suspicious enough. He apologized profusely; claimed he picked up a couple of prepaids after discovering he'd left his personal cell at home. Then, supposedly, he was having trouble with the first phone and disposed of it. I suspect he was swapping out SIM cards."

"Sounds pretty fishy," Hynes agreed.

"Anyway, Rothman said he'll be back in town this weekend, minus Castlebury, to check on the house. He said he'll make himself available to talk to me."

"Okay. How long do you expect to be away?"

"Well, it is Memorial Day Weekend, and I'd like a few days leave to see to some personal business while I'm there."

"Personal business? Might this have to do with that girl reporter in Union Gap whose name keeps popping up?"

"I'm concerned about her and her involvement with Rothman."

"Just concerned?"

"Okay, I like her."

"I thought so. For a stone-faced FBI agent, you suck at hiding your sappy side."

Twenty-Six

Erik Reno was complimenting himself on his brilliance. The threatening phone call to Hobart Castlebury's landline achieved the results he intended. The stooges of Union Gap all thought Stonewall Mansion was empty. He had the big house to himself without having to worry about some fuck-faced federal agent knocking on the door wanting to talk to Hobart "Phantom of the Opera" Castlebury.

From the second floor window, he peaked around the edge of the drapes to view the lake and the Lakewalk across the water. After yesterday, he was careful not to make himself seen. He had caught that woman they call Happy staring right at him. He was thinking how he would enjoy wiping that stupid perpetual grin off her face one of these days. But for now, he had work to do.

Erik had seen the diamonds Ruby Rosa had in her possession during their stay at Stonewall Mansion. Because she'd often referred to him as her adopted son and promised that she was naming him an heir to her estate, he had assumed that bequest included what she referred to as the "family jewels."

Then came the shocking news. She'd told him that she was going to the feds, to report her family for what Hobart called the ill-begotten gains and to hand over the jewels. How did she think he would react? As much as he loved her, as a surrogate mother and a fantasy lover, he couldn't, no wouldn't, allow her to do it. That cache he had seen was easily worth a million dollars. Now he just had to find her hiding place. He'd been unsuccessful so far, but he'd eventually find the treasure.

He remembered the days following her death. With Ruby's body laid out on her French Louis boudoir chaise lounge, hands crossed over her heart, red rose pressed against her chest, Erik had searched all the little nooks and cubbies, recesses and crevices, walls and loose floorboards, anyplace where she might have secretly stored the stash. He cursed the big old house, then just before the arrival of the weekly cleaning crew, he'd fled, a fugitive from the law.

The fact that he was the prime suspect in Ruby's murder didn't particularly concern him. He knew that any hopes of cashing in on her estate were gone, but he was confident he could abscond with the diamonds and live a life of luxury.

In those early days when he laid low and plotted, he had come up with another brilliant plan. He could outsmart all those dick-heads who fancied themselves to be crackerjack shamuses.

And that, he said to himself, *includes you, Agent Fuckface.*

Twenty-Seven

Maggie had just finished reading Happy's "Special to the *Ledger*" article. She hadn't expected the write-up on the upcoming bass fishing tournament to turn into a full-blown feature story on JD Stockman and his efforts to protect the lake and improve lake life in their community, but she was nonetheless pleased.

"Happy, you went above and beyond," she said. "This is an excellent lead-in to Memorial Day. Just need a couple of pictures to go with your article, but I'll take care of that."

Happy smiled broadly. "Thanks, Maggie. That means a lot coming from you. JD can talk about the lake all day long. I learned a lot."

"We just may have to add you to our roster of freelancers."

Maggie had completed her update on the murder investigation, which would be on Page One. The autopsy results confirmed the cause of death as strangulation in a manner similar to the death of Ruby Rosa. More details about the murder scene were emerging, including the fact that the room was elaborately staged with Gianna Talone's body placed, post-mortem, on the bed, hands crossed over her chest, similar to the murder scene of Ruby Rosa, but with one exception. Gianna clutched a black, instead of red, rose in her hands.

Quoting a horticulturalist specializing in the symbolism of roses, Maggie wrote that just as red roses can show eternal love, the black rose can signify hatred.

Beyond that, few reliable leads resulted from the tipline. Erik Reno was still at large, possibly armed, considered dangerous, whereabouts unknown.

Maggie turned to Ally. "And, how are you doing with your article on Fern and Magic?"

"Just giving it a final proofing, Maggie," said Ally. "I'd like you to take a look at it when I finish. I learned a lot working on this feature."

"Seems to be the week that we've all learned a thing or two." Maggie told Ally and Happy about her visit with Helen Overington and what she found out about the original owners of Stonewall Mansion.

"The Jacksons were abolitionists?" asked Happy, who appeared genuinely impressed. I don't think even Liam knew that when he wrote *The Lake at Union Gap*.

Ally chimed in, "Stonewall Mansion was part of the Underground Railroad? That is so cool."

"Yes," said Maggie, "but that's for another edition. For now, we need to get this week wrapped up and put this baby to bed."

It was a typical Wednesday at the *Lakeside Ledger*.

Ally, in fact, was struggling with putting the finishing touches on her story. It meant the world to Fern to be able to adopt Magic, and she wanted to get it right. After watching Fern work with the black stallion in the paddock, they had gone back to the farmhouse and sat around the kitchen table. Fern had done extensive research on the practice of soring. In her mind, there was no "good" to come of it, only "bad" and "ugly."

"It's all about greed," Fern said. "A prize-winning Tennessee

Walking Horse could be worth as much as a million dollars. Using soring to create high-stepping horses gives the appearance of a champion bloodline, but it's all a false characterization. I don't believe any horse can perform that way without abuse."

"Fern," asked Ally, "explain what soring is. I want to be able to quote you."

Fern had gotten up to bring cups and a fresh-brewed pot of Mountain Mama Blend to the table. She went to a file cabinet beside her desk in the corner of the adjoining dining room and retrieved a couple of folders.

"You can take these copies with you, Ally. They explain it in detail. Soring is a painful process of cutting and applying chemicals to the horse's legs to force the animal to step high. In show circles, it's called the 'Big Lick', but what it is really, is the horse reacting to the pain."

"That sounds so cruel," said Ally. "Isn't it illegal? Where are the animal rights activists in all this?"

"It's supposed to be banned under the Horse Protection Act, but apparently there are ways to get around it. I've written to our Virginia lawmakers complaining about it, and those who've chosen to reply agree that soring is a cruel practice that has no place in our society."

Fern handed Ally copies of the two responses she received. Both of the respondents were co-sponsors the PAST Act to "Prevent All Soring Techniques" during the 114th Congress.

Ally read silently, noting that the PAST Act would have added new unlawful practices to the Horse Protection Act as well as strengthening penalties for violations, increasing enforcement actions, and ending self-policing.

"So," said Ally, "apparently the PAST Act had 50 Senate co-sponsors, but was not brought before either the Senate or the

House for consideration before the 2017 Congress adjourned earlier this year."

"Right. Hopefully it will reintroduced, but I'm afraid it's going to be a hard sell."

Ally had tentatively headlined her article "The Magic Touch." The title appropriately described the lead paragraph she'd written.

> *Local resident Fern Finfrock believes that tender loving care can sometimes be the best medicine to heal physical wounds and restore a broken spirit. She has demonstrated that to be the case with Merryfield's Magic, a champion Tennessee Walking Horse rescued from a grave abuse situation at a Kentucky horse farm. Finfrock has been fostering Magic for the past two months and now her hope is that her application to adopt the stallion will be approved.*

Ally went on to recount the backstory of the abuse, neglect, and torture Magic and his stablemates had been subjected to at the training stables. She detailed how the horses were kept in unsanitary conditions, underfed, dehydrated, and secretly subjected to the painful practice called soring. She described how Magic was found lying down in his stall, malnourished and moaning in pain from the soring episodes. She meticulously explained the methods of soring and the sad truth that, despite laws banning it, the cruelty was still running rampant, with breeders, owners, and trainers intent on producing high-stepping gaits in the showrings of Tennessee walkers.

Ally included the story of Fern and Cletus traveling to Kentucky after Fern's application to be a caregiver was approved and returning with the solid black Tennessee Walker stallion. She described Magic's physical wounds that required healing and his broken spirit that needed to be restored. She explained how Fern and her father gently applied daily treatments to Magic's legs and how, slowly but surely, Fern gained the horse's trust. She wrote about the horse's progress and how, now that his physical health was improved, Fern feared that "big money" in the horse world would be the deciding factor in who would get to adopt this champion. She wrote about how Fern worried that Magic could be forced back into the showrings, despite his fragile emotional state.

Ally concluded with a quote from Fern:

> *Virginia is home to some of the most prized horses in the country. There are rich owners who care only about competing for blue ribbons. Their money speaks volumes. I care for this gentle horse, who deserves better. After all that he's been through, my wish is that Magic be allowed to live out the rest of his life as a free spirit on our farm here in Union Gap.*

"No," said Maggie, laying down the printout of Ally's article and running a diagonal red line through the first paragraph.

"No?" asked Ally, frowning.

"Ally, think about it. What's the purpose of this article?"

Ally thought for a moment. "Mainly, I want to highlight Fern's hopes to be able to adopt Magic."

"Too soft."

"Too soft?"

"Ally, you're not writing a fluff piece. You need fighting words."

"Fighting words?"

"Do you have to repeat everything I say?"

"Sorry."

"Ally, listen, Fern is not 'hoping' to adopt. Fern is 'fighting'. Your first sentence should reflect that. Try it."

Ally reread her first paragraph. "What about: *'Local resident Fern Finfrock is fighting to adopt the abused horse she has been nurturing back to health.'* Is that what you mean?"

"Sort of, but you also need to present Fern, right up front, as a person the town will recognize. Many folks don't know her name, but they sure know her as the face of the Mean Beans Bistro."

"So: *'Local business owner Fern Finfrock, known around town as the friendly face at the Mean Beans Bistro, is fighting against big money in the horse world to adopt the abused horse she has been nurturing back to health'.*"

"Yes! But I think that also needs to go in the headline." Maggie again pulled out her red pen and inked in: "Mean Beans Bistro Owner Fighting to Adopt Abused Horse."

"But, what about 'The Magic Touch'? I thought that was pretty clever."

Maggie thought for a moment. "We'll use that in the cutline for the photo where Fern is standing in the paddock with the healthy horse resting his head across her shoulder. You took a couple of great pictures, by the way."

"Thanks for letting me use your camera."

"I also like the one in the field where Magic is following Misty, and the old dog—what's her name?—is trailing behind the two."

"Maybe that one can be captioned "A Magic Moment."

"I like that too."

"What about the photo taken during his rescue, showing him lying in his stall moaning in pain? I've debated using that one."

"Yes, we want to use it to underscore the severity of the situation. I'm not above sensationalism in a case like this. Remember though,

Mac always has final say. Rewrite the lead paragraph. The rest is good. Great, actually. I'll make sure Mac includes the headlines and writes previews on Page One under 'Inside this Edition' for both your story and Happy's."

"Thanks. Honestly, I felt something was missing. You're so good at seeing the big picture. But, Maggie?"

"Hmm?"

"How exactly is Fern 'fighting'?"

"The petition."

"The petition? We don't have a petition."

"Then, let's get one going. Think outside the box for a minute. Memorial Day is one of Union Gap's busiest days of the year along the Lakewalk. A perfect time and just the place to set up a booth and get signatures."

Happy, who'd been sitting nearby talking quietly with Sarah Sanderson and simultaneously eavesdropping, chimed in. "I can help with that. I have a collapsible canopy we can set up with a table and couple of chairs. We can have big beverage coolers of complimentary lemonade and sweet tea…"

"And cookies," added Maggie. "Clover's mouth-watering Jamaican butter rums."

"And coconut drops," added Happy.

"Wait," said Ally. "Does Fern know about this?"

Happy and Maggie exchanged looks. Both slowly shook their heads no.

"Well, who's going to tell her," asked Ally.

Happy and Maggie both looked at Ally.

Twenty-Eight

Fern was needling Ally. The two were fixing Parmesan chicken and getting down to some serious girl talk. "Ally, I'm dying to know who this mystery dinner guest is."

Kyle had been kicked out of the tiny kitchen area of the cabin and was sitting at his computer on the screened-in porch, staring out at the river, hoping to get some inspiration for the novel he was working on.

"Well," said Ally, "I can tell you he's tall, dark, and handsome."

"Not good enough. Tell me more," implored Fern.

"Okay, his name is Lincoln Stryker."

Fern's mouth dropped open. "You mean the FBI guy who's working on the murder?"

Ally nodded. "Speaking of which, I think I hear him pulling up now."

Linc had called Ally the day before and asked if he could take her to dinner when he came to town Friday. "I want to make up for upsetting you the last time we talked," he had said. "Any place you want to go, it's your choice."

Ally told him she'd get back to him. She was excited but also nervous. She was still bristling about being put in the middle of whatever this clash was between Linc and George Rothman. When

Fern called later to thank her for the "awesome newspaper coverage" of her and Magic and invite her to dinner at Kyle's cabin Friday, Ally hesitantly asked if she could bring a friend, no questions asked. Fern was understandably curious but said sure. "And while we're talking, I have questions about this petition, which I only found out about from the article," she said.

"I'll fill you in tomorrow," Ally promised. She was relieved that she'd be seeing Linc without going solo on a first date-of-sorts with him. *Was this, in fact, a date?* She wondered.

She took off work early Friday and went shopping, looking for a housewarming gift. Technically, the cabin was Kyle's rental—Fern was still living at the farm with her father—but Ally suspected the two would be spending a lot of together time there. She stopped at JD's Dockside Station and browsed the aisles for novelty items. Fern and Kyle certainly had enough Mean Beans coffee mugs and Wined Down glasses and Books Galore books. And they seemed to have everything else they needed to set up housekeeping in the little cabin.

Most of the Union Gap collectibles were lake-related, but Ally found a shelf stocked with Dominion River keepsakes. A large throw pillow was embroidered with multi-colored patchworks of "River Rules" in various fonts: "Go Fishing" "Nap" "Read a Book" "Relax" "Canoe" "Take a Hike" "Laugh" "Make Memories"… *Perfect*, she thought, and put it in her basket. She was about to go to checkout when she saw a rustic cedar wood wall hanging etched with the saying "Welcome to our River Home" above a canoe and "Row with the Flow" below. She added it to her cart and decided to stop in the floral department. Ally was the first to admit that she was not a cook, so instead of offering to bring a dish for dinner, she decided to get a colorful arrangement of spring flowers as a centerpiece for the table.

Fern and Kyle had also both taken the Friday afternoon off. Fern thought they should spruce the place up a bit and do some advance preparation for dinner. In the small bedroom, while laying a bedspread donated from Happy's large collection, Kyle winked at Fern. "I think I could get used to playing house with you," he teased.

"Easy, boyfriend," she replied. "We have work to do."

Kyle took her hands and fell back on the bed, pulling her down on top of him. "All work and no play...You know what they say."

"Umm hmm..."

Ally and Fern walked together to the front door and Ally waved as Linc was getting out of the car. With a bottle of River Ridge Red in his right hand and an Apple Blossom White in his left, he introduced himself to Fern. "Hi, I'm Lincoln Stryker. I'd shake your hand but..."

"But...I can see you have your hands full. I'm Fern Finfrock, and I'll take those...with pleasure."

With his hands now free, Linc gave Ally a casual hug and light peck on the cheek.

"Come on in," said Fern. Leading the way through the small cabin and out onto the back porch, Ally introduced Kyle to Linc. Kyle had the same jaw-dropping look on his face that Fern had earlier.

"Agent Stryker," Kyle held out his hand, "welcome to our little home."

"Please, call me Linc. I'm off duty and looking forward to kicking back. I had to promise Ally no FBI business tonight. Thanks for having me."

"Kyle," said Fern, "Linc brought wine. Would you mind doing the honors. Then...not to be bossy or anything, but maybe you guys can get acquainted while Ally and I finish getting the main course ready for the oven."

Ally was grating mozzarella and Parmesan cheeses while Fern pounded the boneless chicken breasts with a wooden mallet, then sprinkled each with her special assortment of herbs and spices.

"So, girlfriend, what's going on here?" asked Fern. "I mean with you and Linc?"

"I honestly don't know," responded Ally. "I've sensed him flirting with me, but there's some bad chemistry between him and George Rothman, and I'm being put in the middle. George has been a good friend to me."

"But...?"

"But, Linc doesn't trust him."

"How do you feel?"

"George has always been a perfect gentleman. I like him well enough as a friend, but just between you and me, he doesn't make me tingle all over the way Linc does."

"Oh wow! Ally! Linc makes you what? Tingle?"

"Shhh..." cautioned Ally, putting a finger to her lips and suppressing a giggle. "Not so loud."

The girls glanced out on the porch where the two guys were attempting to mount the wall hanging Ally had brought. Kyle was holding it up against a wood panel between window screens, and Linc, with hand gestures, was indicating higher...now over to the right...just a tad lower.

Ally laughed. "That looks like something that needs female

input."

"Nah." Fern shook her head. "They'll work it out."

Fern dipped the chicken breasts in beaten eggs, then passed them to Ally to roll in a mixture of seasoned Italian bread crumbs and Parmesan cheese and place in a baking dish. Fern had been simmering homemade marinara sauce all afternoon, and now spooned it over the chicken and told Ally to top it with mozzarella.

With the chicken dish in the oven, the girls sipped wine and resumed guy-watching. Fern was admiring the plaque, which Kyle had finally hung to Linc's satisfaction. She said it was a perfect addition to the porch. Ally was admiring Linc. More to the point, she was noticing his sizable muscles stretching the sleeves of his polo shirt.

"Sorry Fern, were you saying something?"

Dinner was going surprisingly well on the porch where the four sat around a rustic pine wood table on bench seats. For the first course, Fern had put together a garden salad that she now tossed at the table with homemade Italian dressing.

True to his word, Linc seemed to be unwinding and enjoying himself. He also proved to be a skilled conversationalist. "So," he asked, "what's this I read about a petition?" He'd picked up a copy of the *Ledger* when he got into town and saw Ally's full page article on Fern and her foster horse with a sidebar announcing that a booth would be set up on the Lakewalk on Memorial Day for anyone wishing to sign a petition.

"Thanks for asking, Linc," said Fern, "It's my question exactly. Took me by surprise." She turned to Ally. "When I asked Happy about it, she told me to talk to you."

"Maggie's idea actually," said Ally. "With a huge crowd on the Lakewalk Monday for the festivities, she suggested we set up a table for people to sign a petition asking the equine rescue group to approve Fern's application to adopt Magic. We'll have cold drinks and Clover's cookies as an enticement to sign."

"Well," said Fern, "I'm glad we got that cleared up. I'll need to put Clover on cookie detail this weekend."

"And," added Ally, "I know you'll be busy with the bistro, so we all agreed to take turns manning the table."

"I'll be in town, and I'd like to help," said Linc. He then turned to Kyle and asked about the book he was writing.

Kyle said it was a historical novel set during the Civil War.

"I have a special interest in the Civil War myself," said Linc. "I'm curious. What made you decide to write about it?"

"For one thing," said Kyle, "I've got a lot of background information. Plus…Well, it's a long story."

"We've got all night," said Ally, "and I for one would love to hear it."

"I would too," said Linc.

Kyle began by telling them about growing up in a small town called Abrams Point outside of Chicago. "In school, our history classes always focused on the fact that Illinois was a Union state during the Civil War, and Chicago was a pro-Lincoln stronghold with a very vocal abolitionist community. Everything we were taught was one-sided. All I really knew was I was a Yankee."

"Until he came to Virginia," Fern chimed in.

"What brought you here?" asked Linc.

Kyle talked a little about his home life in Abrams Point, which was not ideal. He described his father, Ken Kalahan, as "a loser who abandoned his family" when Kyle was a baby and how his mother Sarah, Happy's sister, younger by twelve years, struggled as a single mom and made some bad choices.

"She got in with the wrong crowd and spent years in and out of rehab for drugs and alcohol," he said. "And while that was going on, I was in and out of foster care."

The bright spots in his life, he said, were the summers he spent in Union Gap with his Aunt Happy and Uncle Liam.

"They had met while attending the College of William and Mary," he said, "then later married, and Happy never left Virginia."

During those visits, while Professor O'Hurley's body was deteriorating from ALS, his mind was as sharp as ever. He loved history and the Civil War in particular.

"I'd sit with him for hours as he told me stories from both the northern and southern perspectives."

After the professor's death, Happy tried to get guardianship of then-12-year-old Kyle, but his mother always managed to get clean and thwart her efforts.

"I still visited whenever I could," Kyle continued, "and because of my interest in the Civil War, Aunt Happy took me around to places like Appomattox Court House, Harpers Ferry, Gettysburg, Antietam, and Stonewall Jackson's Headquarters, places she'd been to herself with Uncle Liam."

After graduating from high school, Kyle moved in with Happy in Union Gap and enrolled at James Madison University. "It's taken me seven years," he said. "Working my way through college, I've had to cut back to part time here and there and even take semesters off to earn money. I wanted to avoid huge student loans I'd have to pay back. I'm happy to say that after my student teaching this fall, I'll be finished." He gave two thumbs up.

"I'm so proud of him," said Fern, hugging Kyle as she got up to go check on the dinner in the oven.

"Me too," said Ally.

"That's a real accomplishment," added Linc. "I can imagine it wasn't easy."

"But getting back to your book," said Fern, "tell Ally and Linc how you got the idea."

"Oh yeah, the book" said Kyle. "Sorry for getting off track."

"No need to be sorry," said Ally. "I'm glad you explained the Happy connection. I was wondering."

"Anyway," Kyle continued, "from my conversations with the professor, and the sites I visited with Happy, and all the reading I've done on my own, I decided to write a novel that shows both sides of the Civil War. It's a story about two families, one from the north and the other from the south, and a romance that crosses the Mason Dixon Line."

"That's a good way to tell both sides," said Linc. "Who's on which side? Or is that a secret?"

"Actually," said Kyle, "I'm just in the early stages of developing the story line. I've been playing out the narrative both ways. It's tricky. One side's going to win, and the other's going to lose. And family feuds will have to be mended if there's going to be a happy ending. Not that I'm promising a happy ending, though."

"Well," said Ally, "while we're on this topic, I learned something about the Civil War myself this week." The others looked at her, curious. She started to tell them what Maggie had found out about Stonewall Mansion from Helen Overington.

"Hold on, Ally," said Fern, who was starting to clear away the salad bowls. "I want to hear this story too. Wait 'til I get back with the chicken."

"I'll help you bring it out," offered Kyle.

"Whatever it is, it smells wonderful," said Linc.

The cheesy, saucy chicken entrees were served with warmed crusty ciabatta. Ally broke off a piece of the bread and dipped it in a side dish of seasoned olive oil before starting her story.

Linc took a bite of the Parmesan chicken and gave it a rave review. "This is delicious," he said.

"Okay, Ally," urged Fern, "now we want to hear about what Maggie learned from the president of the Lake County Historical Society."

While they ate, Ally told the story of Jeremiah and Priscilla Jackson, their courtship and marriage, their move to Lake County, and the construction of Stonewall Mansion, where Priscilla dreamed of raising a large family along the edge of Big Gap Lake.

"Sadly," Ally related, "Priscilla wasn't able to have children. To fill the void, she and Jeremiah became abolitionists, sympathetic to the cause of fugitive slaves. According to her diaries, Stonewall Mansion became a 'safe house' along the Underground Railroad."

As Ally was telling the story, Kyle interjected, "I love this. Now I'm thinking I may have to work the Underground Railroad into my novel."

"Thanks for sharing it," said Fern. "I can't wait to read about it in the *Ledger*."

"Linc," said Ally, "You mentioned you have a special interest in the Civil War yourself."

Linc was silent for a moment before he spoke. "I have an ancestral connection to the Underground Railroad," he said.

"Wow," said Ally. "Care to share it?"

"I'd like to hear about it," said Kyle.

"Me too," said Fern. "I'll put on a pot of coffee and bring out the dessert. Fresh strawberry pie from the Mean Beans." As an aside to Linc, she added, "It was made by our pastry chef, Clover Battersby."

"You're in for a real treat, Linc," said Kyle.

Linc's family history on his mother's side, as far back as he knew it, began with his great great great grandmother Sadie Byrd-Smith in the mid 1800s. "As a disclaimer," he cautioned, "none of this is documented. It's a tale that's been handed down through the generations."

As it had been told, Sadie was a house servant on the Byrd-Smith plantation in Georgia, near Savannah. Her job was tending to the needs of the plantation mistress who, when she wasn't bedridden, was confined to a wheelchair with some crippling condition. The job was so demanding that Sadie slept on a pallet on the floor of the bedroom to be at her mistress's beck and call day and night.

Young female house slaves, Linc explained, were often subjected to the sexual advances of their male slaveholders and sometimes were even offered for pleasure to their houseguests. Sixteen-year-old Sadie was especially vulnerable, having a master whose wife was disabled.

"She was raped repeatedly, impregnated, and gave birth to a daughter, who she named Naomi. The baby proved to be a problem for Master Byrd-Smith."

"Why a problem?" asked Ally. "The slaves must have had babies all the time."

"Not only did Naomi have a light complexion," said Linc, "but her eyes were a shade of light blue, like her plantation-owner father. Now, understand that a white man in those days need not concern himself with being arrested for raping a slave, but Sadie overheard her master discussing getting rid of the child, lest the tongues of his wife's female friends start wagging."

Ally, Fern, and Kyle were hanging on to his every word as Linc described how Sadie and her baby, along with a small group of other slaves, ran away and made their way north with the help of Underground Railroad "conductors" who provided safe passage from "depot" to "depot." Sadie and her companions made it to Michigan. She and some of the others settled in a community that welcomed runaway slaves while others went on to Canada. Sadie later dropped the name Byrd-Smith and took the surname Lincoln, in honor of the country's president.

Linc thought he was finished with his story but Kyle wanted more. "Where does the story go from there?" he asked.

Linc continued. "Well, Naomi grew into a beautiful but head-strong young woman. The way my grandmother tells it, she was a wild child, half black, half white, with curly black hair, mesmerizing eyes, and a tawny skin tone."

Unable by law to marry a white man, Naomi became the pampered mistress of a wealthy merchant named Thomas Updike and often traveled with him to New York, where he introduced her around Manhattan as the daughter of a Cuban cigar manufacturer.

"Naomi and Thomas were the parents of a love child. Their son, Thomas Updike, Jr., was my great grandfather and a man who adored his grandmother Sadie and embraced his African heritage. He didn't get along with his flamboyant, attention-seeking father, and was angry at his mother because she'd denounced her ancestry."

Linc stopped the story while Fern and Ally went back into the cabin to bring out the rest of the pie for seconds all around and the pot of coffee for refills.

At the urging of Ally, he recounted how the younger Thomas took back his Grandmother Sadie's surname of Lincoln and spent much of his time in the "Espana Chica"—Little Spain— neighborhood of Manhattan. He married Isabella, a woman of Spanish-American descent and together they raised their children to understand and appreciate both the influence and culture of

Africans in America as well as that of Spaniards.

"Education was a top priority," said Linc, "and unlike most of the residents of Little Spain, Thomas and Isabella enjoyed certain financial advantages. Thomas owned a cigar factory, and they were well off enough to send their kids to Europe to be educated. That emphasis on education was passed down through the generations."

"What about your immediate family?" asked Ally.

"So," Linc continued, "on my mother's side, I have the African-Spanish-American roots I just described. My father's ancestors are all from Germany, and his German roots go back as far we've been able to trace them.

"What are they like?" asked Ally. "Your parents?"

"Very smart, very educated, but highly opinionated," joked Linc. "They both teach at Harvard. My mother, Lizbeth Lincoln, is an associate professor of Clinical Psychology, and my father, Stefan Stryker, is a professor in the Political Science Department. They met in college, and their marriage caused quite a stir in both households, which were not quite ready for a marriage of such diverse backgrounds. But, they've all worked it out."

"Do you have siblings?" asked Ally.

"I have an older sister, Lauryn Stryker, who's a pediatrician in Boston and married to her neurosurgeon husband Azaan Patel. They have a four-year-old son Neel. And now that I've bored you all to tears…"

"Not at all," said Kyle. "It's a powerful story. I loved hearing it."

"I have another question," said Ally.

Linc smiled at her, enjoying what seemed to be an endless list of questions. *Must be the reporter in her*, he thought.

Ally asked, "Hearing this story of the young mother, your ancestral grandmother Sadie, and what she endured, aren't you bitter? Even a little?"

"Ally, it's true, my heart aches when I think about the injustice. But, I can't change history or do my job if I'm filled with hate and anger. I can only do what I'm able to do to right the wrongs in our world today. That's the reason, more than anything else, why I went into law enforcement."

The evening was winding down, and the foursome had moved outside to watch the sun setting over Dominion Ridge to the west. The conversation had turned to Hobart Castlebury.

"Are you still doing the feature on him?" Fern asked Ally.

"I've got all the information," said Ally, "but the story keeps changing by the day. Right now we need to get through Memorial Day and the aftermath of the murder."

"Speaking of which…" said Kyle. "Linc, are you working on the investigation while you're here? Any new leads?"

"I'm following up on some loose ends. But, I promised Ally I wouldn't talk business tonight. I'm also taking a few days personal leave next week, hoping to relax and enjoy more of this Union Gap hospitality."

He turned to Ally. "And, I'm hoping that my free time is not part of our off-limits agreement."

Ally tingled.

Twenty-Nine

With his booming voice and a loud bang from a prop gun that fired a pop-out fisherman's flag featuring a large-mouth bass, JD Stockman signaled the start of the Fifth Annual Big Gap Lake Bass Fishing Tournament.

"Let the games begin!"

The starting lineup had been determined the evening before at Jack's Pub where half-price beer and all-you-can-eat wings lured the fishermen in. An arm wrestling contest had rivals jockeying for the lead spot. Newcomer Michael "Meatloaf" Malone handily won out over the contenders by the sheer brute force of his formidable biceps. His win unseated Bumper Presgraves, who had proudly led the anglers to the starting point for the past four years.

Cecil Moomaw, who had himself been beefing up in hopes of securing the coveted lead role, joined forces with Bumper in a trash-talking assault on Meatloaf.

"Why don't you drag your substantial, sorry ass back up that mountain where you came from?" Bumper lashed out.

"Yeah, 'Meathead'," Cecil joined in. "Go scarf down some more wingy-dingys, why don't ya."

Meatloaf lifted his hefty self off the bar stool and towered over Bumper and Cecil. "Which one of you dipshits wants to be first to get my ugly, size 16 foot up your lovely ass?" he bellowed. The two smaller guys shrank back as buffalo sauce spittle was showered on them.

"Okay, boys," shouted Jack McKay from behind the bar. "Take it outside. Don't make me call Chief Hawkins."

JD escorted the trio out onto the Lakewalk and had a few choice words of his own. "If you boys are not back home and tucked in bed in 15 minutes, you'll all be barred from the tournament. And, don't even think about bringing this ruckus to tomorrow's event."

Bumper started to protest, but JD cut him off. "I'm serious, Bumper. Now go!"

The three stumbled off into the night.

This morning they showed up at the marina hungover but laughing off the previous night's shenanigans and jostling good-naturedly about who was going to catch the winning bass. With the signal from JD, Meatloaf pulled his boat out in front, and the twelve other fishermen fell in behind. At the starting line, directly offshore from the gazebo at Union Square, they broke off on their own, each with a strategy and eyes on the prize.

On the Lakewalk outside the Mean Beans Bistro, Ally was sitting with her parents. They were taste-testing assorted pastries from a sampler platter and enjoying the excitement that was building around them. Townspeople were lined up along the Lakewalk's three-foot-high stone wall cheering as the boats headed out. Some of the anglers smiled, some waved, and others postured by raising their clenched fists in a show of bass-fishing dominance. Beulah Marples, the lone female angler in the competition, was hanging over the side of her boat, blowing two-handed kisses like a pageant queen.

Ally's mom and dad, Ann and Tim Murphy, were in town to enjoy a week away from the hectic pace of their busy lives in

Roanoke and to celebrate Ally's 22nd birthday, a few days away. As always, they were houseguests of Maggie and Mac.

With her parents' arrival on Saturday and Linc's work, the couple hadn't seen each other all weekend. But that didn't stop Ally from thinking about him, and when her phone rang at ten o'clock on Saturday evening, she was elated to see it was "Linc."

"Hey," Ally answered chipperly, walking outside onto the veranda for some privacy.

"Hey yourself," he responded. He said his reason for calling was to get contact information for Fern and Kyle to thank them for dinner the night before. "I really enjoyed their company, and yours," he said. "Thanks for inviting me."

"It was fun," agreed Ally. She told him she didn't want to give out the personal information without permission but offered to pass along his thanks to Fern and Kyle.

"Do you have a few minutes to talk?" he asked.

"Sure, what's up?"

"I want to know more about Ally. I told my life story last night, several generations back, in fact. Now, tell me about you."

Ally said, "I'm just a simple Virginia girl. I've lived here all my life and have a family tree that includes several generations of Virginians. My dad's a lawyer and on the Board of Supervisors in Saponi County, outside Roanoke. My mom works for the school board there."

Linc asked why she got into journalism. She told him that ever since she was a little kid she loved to write. "I used to create little books by folding sheets of typing paper in half and filling the pages with stories I'd write. Some even had crudely drawn illustrations, but I've since shied away from fancying myself an artist. Then, in high school, I was editor of our school paper, *The Bullhorn*."

"I'd love to see some of your early work."

Ally laughed. "It was always just for fun, and I never took it seriously until college. Now, all I can think about is a career in print journalism, hopefully with a big-league newspaper."

"And where might that be?"

"First choice, *The Washington Post*. I'd love to work in D.C. At least for a time. That would be my dream job."

"You know, don't you, D.C. can be pretty ruthless? I mean the competition there is fierce and the political scene can get ugly."

"I know. I'm trying to get toughened up. My roommate in Richmond—we have a small apartment close to the campus—is the quintessential 'alpha female'. She's been working on drawing me out of my comfort zone. Monica can be hard to take, but she has so much of what I lack. 'Chutzpah!'"

"You mean like always being out front?"

"Yeah, bossy, actually. Last year the two of us took the spring semester off and traveled through Europe." Ally explained that Monica's father was a bigwig with a tech company in Northern Virginia and was spending a year in England starting up a new division. "Monica and I 'technically' stayed with her family to study at the London School of Journalism, to 'bolster our resumes'. But we studied just barely enough to get by. Monica's main focus was on gaining what she called an 'international perspective'. And I was her sidekick."

Monica's parents, were totally cool about the girls' plan to travel around alone by train. "I can tell you, I was nervous. My parents would never have approved this plan. But, Monica turned out to be a world-savvy traveler, even if she was a world-class snob at times."

"A snob? Like how?'" asked Linc.

"Like when we were in Paris. Monica was particularly haughty about me wanting to see the Mona Lisa at the Louvre. She didn't want to be seen as a lowly sightseer. Well, I got in line with the tourists, anyway, and she stayed behind grumbling about having to wait for me."

"Hey," said Linc, "Isn't that something all Americans in Paris do? I did when I was there."

"Exactly! But, I have to admit there were times I was grateful for her street smarts." Ally told him about walking along the Seine and admiring the works of the artists who were set up at easels and selling their paintings along the river walk. "We had lunch near Notre Dame on one of those floating restaurant boats."

"Um-hum," said Linc. "A *Peniche*."

"Smarty pants!"

"Sorry," he said. "But go on. I want to hear more of your story."

She told him about being on the bridge outside the cathedral. She was trying to communicate with a woman asking for directions when Monica grabbed her arm and roughly jerked her away. "Didn't you see that guy over there?" her friend had scolded. She nodded toward a lone man leaning against the bridge wall. "He was coming right toward you while you were talking. Obviously, those two are working together. This place is a hub for pickpockets and scam artists."

She told Linc about another time when they were on their way to Amsterdam, and their train stopped dead in the tracks. Announcements came over the loudspeaker in German and Dutch, which neither of them understood. Passengers were all rushing to leave the train.

"So, Monica grabbed me by my backpack and said 'Run...follow him'. She was pointing to a man who had been sitting in front of us and was rushing to get onto another train that was stopped. We did the same and were crammed into the aisle with a gazillion other passengers, not knowing where we were headed."

Monica had just laughed it off and used the occasion to lecture her again about being alert to what was going on. "Anyway," Ally continued, "we continued our train travels through France, Germany, and the Netherlands, and the whole experience broadened my horizons in more ways than one. I've been focusing on being more like Monica."

Linc liked hearing her tell the stories in her modest, self-deprecating manner. "Bossiness aside, Monica sounds like a good friend," he said.

"Maybe you'll meet her in the fall when we're back in Richmond." Before Linc could respond, Ally apologized. "Sorry, I'm assuming...Maybe you have a wife or something back in Richmond," she teased. "Do you?"

"Umm...no."

"An ex?"

"No."

"Kids?"

"No." He Laughed. "Are you interrogating me? Payback?"

"In my line of work, we call it interviewing. How about a girlfriend? Do you have one?"

"Not at present. Now your turn."

"No husband, no ex, no kids, no boyfriend."

"Any more questions, Lois Lane?"

"Let me see...Just one more. Tell me something you *don't* want me to know about you."

Linc had to think about that. "Now wait!" he said. "That's a trick question. You go first on this one."

"Hmm...when you put it that way, I withdraw the question."

They both laughed. Suddenly, it was midnight. Ally's father came out and asked her if she might be coming in anytime soon so they could lock up.

The "few minutes" Linc asked for had turned into two hours.

Now, sitting outside on the Lakewalk on Memorial Day morning, Ally was thinking how Friday night had really been fun. She, in part had been testing Linc when she invited him to join her for dinner with Fern and Kyle at the tiny cabin. She'd wanted to see how he would fit in with her unpretentious friends in a simple, no-frills setting. She smiled as she relived the evening. He passed. No, he more than passed. Linc's enjoyment seemed genuine.

Ally had spent much of the weekend indulging her mom, who wanted to browse all the quaint shops and buy gifts for her co-workers at the school board office. Mac had spent much of his weekend with Ally's dad, who wanted to golf. Among the amenities at the Gallery was a nine-hole course, along with a pro shop and lunchtime grill. Mac wasn't really into the game and never played unless his old golfer friend Tim was in town. Then, he graciously went along for the ride. He didn't have to "let" Tim win; his friend was hardly a duffer.

Ally pointed across the water to Stonewall Mansion and was telling her parents about the eccentric Hobart Castlebury and his surprise appearance at the Sunset Social as the Phantom of the Opera.

"I would love to meet him," said Ann. "He sounds like quite a character."

"Hopefully, you will at some point," said Ally, "but now is not the time." She brought her parents up to date on the homicide investigation, and the toll it was taking on Hobart, as reported to her by George Rothman.

That gave Tim the opening he'd been waiting for. "I don't like this," he said.

"What?" asked Ally.

"You being here with that Erik Reno guy still on the loose. I don't like it at all."

Ally rolled her eyes and was relieved when Happy chose that moment to come over to the table and introduce herself. She'd enlisted a couple of teenagers to help her set up the canopy in front of Books Galore for the petition table. More specifically, the boys were setting-up, and Happy was supervising.

Happy began her trademark chattering, effectively steering the conversation away from Erik Reno. "Ally's been first-rate helping Fern. She wrote that great story about Fern's efforts to adopt her foster horse," she told Ann and Tim. "I'm sure you read it, right? Now we're all hoping this petition will help. Fern is like a granddaughter to me, ever since her mother got killed in that terrible accident. You've heard about that, haven't you? I helped Cletus, that's Fern's father, get her that pony from Chincoteague. Oh, there she is now."

Thank goodness, thought Ally, as Happy waved Fern over.

"Happy," said Fern, "I have the coolers of lemonade and sweet tea ready and Clover's wanting to know how soon you'll be ready for the cookies. She's still baking and wondering if she's made enough."

Happy yelled over to the teens. "How much longer, boys?"

"Just finishing up anchoring to the tent weights," a kid named Jackson hollered back. As he spoke, a big gust of wind whipped in and toppled the structure.

"Oh my!" exclaimed Happy.

As she hustled back over to take charge, Ally breathed a sigh of relief. "She's wound up today," she said to Fern. "I didn't think she was ever going to run out of steam."

Fern chuckled. "She loves these events." To Ann and Tim she

added, "Happy loves to talk." She looked around. Nearly all the tables that had been set up outside were taken, and Susan and Phoebe were bustling about, taking orders.

"Can I get you all anything else?" Fern asked, anxious to get back to work. They all shook their heads no.

"But," said Ally, "about tonight. Are you and Kyle going to be able to make it?" She was talking about a Memorial Day cookout at Maggie and Mac's house.

"We'll come by after closing up. Kyle is locking up the bookstore at five, and with everything else that's going on, I've canceled Wined Down this evening. We should be there around six."

"Speaking of which," said Ally, "here come Maggie and Mac now."

The McGuires had gone into the *Ledger* that morning to meet with the freelancers. With Ally's parents here for the week, they were outsourcing as much of newspaper work as they could. Maggie had been meeting with Leanne and Emily, who would be covering some of the Memorial Day events plus assuming major newsroom responsibilities, including writing, editing, and layout. Justin and Bradley had gotten their instructions as roving photographers for today's events.

"How are things down at the paper?" asked Ally.

"So far good," said Maggie. "Emily was assigned to the pancake breakfast at the firehall this morning, and Leanne covered the mayor's remarks at Union Square. They're working on their write-ups now. Justin should be here shortly to get pictures of the bass boat that returns with our new mascot."

Maggie saw Happy, who was busy instructing the teens in how to secure the canopy corners to the tent weights without the structure collapsing. "I'm going to pop over and see if Happy can get a few words from the winning fisherman," she said. "Mac and

I need to get to the grocery store, then home to start getting ready for tonight."

"We're heading back to the house shortly," said Ann, "and I'm available all afternoon to help."

"Me too," added Ally, "right after I take a turn sitting at the petition table. "How many people are you expecting?"

"About a dozen besides us," said Maggie. "And, by the way, Ally, I invited your Agent Stryker. He came by the *Ledger* a little while ago. Wanted to know if I found out anything about that mysterious woman at the press conference."

"*My* Agent Stryker? You invited him on my account?"

"Well, he is in town and doesn't know many folks here. I thought it was the polite thing to do."

Ally was smiling. "Actually, I was going to ask you if it was okay for me to invite him. Thanks!"

"Gotta run," said Maggie. "You can fill your parents in on your date night with 'Linc'." She emphasized the word "Linc" with air quotes, then scurried over to talk to Happy.

"'Your Agent Stryker? 'Linc'?" Tim was staring at his daughter. "Isn't he that FBI guy working on the murder? And, what's this about your 'date'?"

Ally blushed and silently cursed Maggie for her big mouth. "It wasn't a date," she stammered. "Not exactly." She told her parents about the get-together with Fern and Kyle, downplaying any romantic connection. *Was there a romantic connection?* She asked herself. *That two-hour phone call Saturday night...*

Her thoughts were interrupted when someone yelled, "Coming in!" Up and down the Lakewalk, people started clapping and cheering as one of the fishing boats was approaching. As it came into view, another voice shouted, "It's Bumper, and JD's comin' up behind." The crowd gravitated toward the marina, and

Ally, her parents, Mac and Maggie joined in. Justin, the freelance photographer, came running up, red-faced and out of breath.

They all watched as Bumper took a bow, then climbed out onto the dock. He handed his catch over to Merle Smirkley, the check-in official. Merle took the good-sized largemouth bass and looked it over. Next, he attached an official tournament scale and a mouth gripper that held the fish securely while he checked the weight. He laid the catch down and measured.

JD had come up onto the dock and was conferring with Merle. He picked up the fish and looked it over, then nodded. Turning to the crowd that had gathered, he shouted, "Okay, folks, we have a Betty! And, she's a big girl, ten pounds, six ounces, and twenty-six inches long."

The crowd clapped and cheered, while Bumper beamed. Justin went up on the dock and positioned the three men with Bumper in the middle, Merle on his left and JD on the right. All three held the new town mascot as Justin snapped the picture which would be on the front page of this week's *Lakeside Ledger*.

Thirty

In truth, the main reason Special Agent Lincoln Stryker had stopped in the newsroom that morning was to talk to Maggie about concerns for Ally. He asked her not to say anything, but wanted Maggie to be aware he wasn't comfortable with her relationship with George Rothman. He told her he'd met with Rothman the previous afternoon and came away with even more misgivings than he had before. He couldn't put his finger on why but he distrusted the man. The feeling was strong, and he trusted his feelings.

Linc told Maggie that on this visit to Stonewall Mansion, George had been oozing politeness. He'd acted the perfect host, offering Linc a drink, which he'd declined. When Linc had asked him about Hobart Castlebury's whereabouts, Rothman gave him a plausible explanation, something about having to take Hobart to a psychiatric facility because he was concerned his boss might be having a breakdown.

Rothman explained that he'd already been checking out possible caregiving options due to Hobart's rapidly deteriorating mental state. The death of Gianna Talone seemed to put him over the edge. He said that Hobart was at the facility for observation and treatment, but the location, as well as Hobart's condition, was being kept confidential for his privacy and his security.

"You know, George," Linc had said, "the HIPAA Privacy Law has exemptions for law enforcement investigations. I can seek a court order."

"I hope you won't go that route," said Rothman. "Hobart is not well, and especially with that threatening phone call I'm sure you can understand he's not safe as long as Erik Reno is on the loose."

"What can you tell me about the so-called family jewels, or diamonds, that Gianna was after? After the Sunset Social she was overheard telling Hobart that she was in town to get what was hers."

"All I know is what Hobart told me. He said he doesn't know much. He'd heard the stories of these so-called diamonds in the Talone family that were said to be obtained by some chicanery, and they were given to Ruby for safe keeping. She was supposedly the only member of the family who could be trusted. Hobart believes she wanted no part of it and was prepared to go to the authorities. He has told me he has no idea where the jewels are, if indeed they even exist. I'm handling Ruby's estate and can assure you they are not listed as part of it."

"Do you mind if I have a look around?"

George consented with a smile. "I don't know what you hope to find, but by all means, please do. However, you'll need a warrant if you intend to go through any private files or records."

"Nope," said Linc. "With these threats, I just want to see the layout and living arrangements."

"Most of our living," said George, "takes place right here in what I guess you'd call an old-fashioned sitting room, and in our office, right through there." He pointed to the adjoining room. "Upstairs, are our bedrooms, baths, and Hobart's costume and makeup room."

Linc gave all the rooms a cursory inspection and found nothing suspicious. The upstairs rooms used by George and Hobart were neat and orderly, with the exception of what looked like an actor's dressing room. One wall was devoted to makeup counters with linear arrays of bare incandescent bulbs surrounding mirrors.

An assortment of cosmetics, greasepaints, foundations, as well as hair dryers, curling irons, combs, brushes, and other styling aids covered the countertops and filled the cubbies. A small closet held a few elaborate costumes, while open racks, which Linc browsed through, were crammed with all types of less formal outfits. Two closed wardrobes, he assumed, contained accessories, but he chose not to go poking around inside.

Downstairs, he walked through the formal ballroom and a massive dining room, both of which appeared to be long unused, with drop cloths covering the furniture. A library contained wall-to-wall bookshelves. The few books that remained were covered in thick layers of dust. He concluded his tour in the kitchen.

"Find anything interesting?" asked George, who was standing beside the refrigerator.

Linc ignored the question. He noticed a narrow staircase leading up, and asked if it was perhaps intended for servants.

"I believe so," said George. "It appears that there once were servants quarters out back in what's left of those old outbuildings."

Beside the stairs, Linc opened a door to what he assumed was a pantry. He noted that the shelves on the left wall were completely bare and only a few packaged goods were scattered elsewhere. On the floor, against the right wall were several cases of bottled water.

George caught his look and grinned. "As you can probably tell," he said, "neither of us cooks." He opened the refrigerator to reveal only a few Styrofoam carryout containers. The freezer, however, was well stocked with a large selection of frozen meals. "We've become quite skilled at popping frozen entrees into the microwave. During our extended stays, Creekside Café drops off meals."

As the agent was leaving, George held out his hand. "So nice of you to stop by 'Linc'. It was a pleasure."

Linc was not buying into Rothman's contrived gentlemanly

charm. There was something niggling at the back of his mind. Something he was missing that he sensed was significant. But that "something" remained just out of reach. He left the premises thinking about Ally and hoping to see her again soon.

"Hey, Hon," shouted Mac, "do you and Ann have any more kabobs ready for the grill? A few latecomers just arrived."

The Memorial Day cookout at the McGuire house was in full swing, and Maggie's skewered Hawaiian creations were a hit, as always. She'd been marinating chicken pieces and shrimp all afternoon in her special juicy pineapple sauce, while Ann and Ally cut up bell peppers, red onions, and pineapple chunks. The three of them were working now to keep up with demand, threading the components to create colorful arrays on the skewers in preparation for grilling. Mac's burgers and hot dogs were taking a back seat.

"Coming right up," Maggie called back. She placed the last eight skewered kabobs on a platter and handed it to Ally to take out to grill. Mac was wearing an apron and matching chef's hat, both personalized with the words, "Mac's Grill" and "I'm Flippin' Awesome." Ally made him hold up his spatula while she snapped his picture with her phone.

For her part, Maggie was relieved to finally be finished with the kabobs. She was looking forward to a drink or two, maybe three, and mingling with guests. Ally met her at the patio bar where her dad was serving as bartender.

"Tim," said Maggie, "Be a sweetheart and fix me a martini. You know how I like it."

Ally said, "And, I'll have one of those fruity drinks you've been making. But, easy on the alcohol."

Tim handed Maggie her drink, then said to Ally, "Fruity thing coming right up. No alcohol."

"Ha ha, very funny, Dad. I didn't say 'none', just light."

"Well, since you are going to be an elderly lady of 22 in a couple of days, I'll prepare accordingly."

Ally saw Linc at the buffet table on the veranda, holding a beer and talking to Happy. Taking her drink from Tim, she walked up. "Having a good time?" she asked.

"Oh, Ally," said Happy, "Agent Stryker and I were talking about the petition. After you left, he stopped by and introduced himself and graciously volunteered to take a turn manning the table. I was just filling him in on the amazing results. All-in-all, we have more than 200 signatures. Kyle had to run off extra sheets."

"That's great!" exclaimed Ally. "Maggie's preparing a package to send to the rescue group. We're going to include the newspaper article and reference letters. I hope all this is enough."

"Oh," added Happy, "that TV reporter from the station in Dominion Mills stopped by and did a short vox pop with Fern. It should be airing tonight. I've set my TV to record."

"Vox pop?" questioned Linc.

"'Voice of the people'," explained Ally. "In journalism, it refers to short interviews with members of the public, kind of like 'man on the street' pieces."

"And," said Happy, "just look at this appetizer tray Agent Stryker brought." She pointed to a platter loaded with assorted cheeses, thin slices of prosciutto and salami, crackers, strawberries and grapes, pickles and olives.

"Wow! I'm impressed," said Ally.

"Hold on," laughed Linc. "I wish I could take credit for creating this masterpiece, but I have to confess, I called earlier and ordered it from the Creekside Café and picked it up on the way over.

And, Happy, please call me Linc."

Fern and Kyle came over, each carrying a plate of kabobs, just off the grill. "Fern," said Ally, "did you hear about the petition results?"

"Umm, no," replied Fern. "We were so busy at the bistro today, I barely had time to catch my breath."

Happy filled her in on the signature count, and Fern was near tears. "You guys are so great. I love you all."

Fern's dad, Cletus, and Daphne Simpson came over and added accompaniments from the buffet table to their plates of kabobs before finding seats at one of the patio tables.

"Is something going on between those two?" asked Ally.

Fern shrugged. "Beats me," she said and excused herself to go to the car. "I almost forgot. We brought cookies that were left over from the petition booth."

The evening was winding down. The grilling and bartending were finished, and Mac and Tim were talking golf. More accurately, Tim was talking and Mac was listening. Most of the guests had left, including Cletus and Daphne and Happy.

Maggie was on her third martini and complaining to her next door neighbor about dog crap left on the nature trails, the roving radar-gun-guy Darrell Dempsey, and HOA President Boggs's latest push to yet again raise dues.

Maggie's neighbor, Jane Haines, a member of the Gallery's board of directors, had some complaining of her own to do. "Emotional support chickens," she huffed, "that's what irks me. And there's nothing we can do."

Jane was talking about the Snodgrass family that had put a

chicken coop in their backyard, an act that was clearly in violation of the homeowners association PRPs: Policies, Rules, and Procedures.

"What a bunch of crap," said Maggie. "How are they allowed to get away with it?"

"Sylvia Snodgrass appeared before the board," said Jane. "She was carrying her red hen and waving paperwork in our faces, stuff she'd gotten online. According to these 'official' papers, Sylvia's red hen, Penny, and Penny's brood were certified as emotional support animals due to Sylvia's supposed 'anxiety'."

Maggie erupted into one of her trademark rants. "So, what does Miss 'Snot'grass do with her emotional support chicken? Put little designer PJs on Henny Penny and take her to bed so they can cuddle and she can de-stress? Jeez!"

"Apparently, these animals don't require any specific training," said Jane. "And, Sylvia smugly told us 'Any animal can be certified'."

Ally and Linc, and Fern and Kyle were standing nearby listening and making faces at each other until Maggie started a new rant, this one about "wackos" and "quackery." The foursome decided to go for a walk. Ally snapped the leash on Bowser and grabbed him a hot dog for the road.

"In all seriousness," said Linc, as they were walking across the 9th hole of the golf course, "I have a good friend, a former marine who served in Afghanistan. Matt has PTSD so severe he can't work, and he wouldn't step foot out of his apartment without his specially-trained service dog. 'Buddy' goes everywhere with him and provides emotional support. And, Buddy's the smartest and most well-behaved dog I've ever seen."

"Hey," said Fern, "that's really cool. But emotional support chickens? That's wild."

"Speaking of dogs," said Ally, "everyone watch your step." She told them about Trojan, the horse-sized dog that was always leaving a small mountain of dog doo in the middle of the paths, and about Security Officer Dempsey. "I met him once while he was on poop patrol," she said. "He was trying to catch the culprit in the act."

The others laughed.

"Just be careful," repeated Ally, "Maggie will have a hissy fit if we come back smelling like dog shit."

Linc pulled out his phone and used the flashlight to illuminate the trail they were now on. Ally told them about the path that led to the rear of Stonewall Mansion and the strange encounter she and Bowser and Officer Dempsey had with Hobart Castlebury the morning after the Sunset Social.

"Actually," said Ally, "I really like Darrell. He's just doing his job in this place with all its hoity-toity HOA rules. He told me he wants to get into the police academy but is having trouble because of his five-foot four-inch height."

Bowser, as usual, was finding lots of good scents to sniff. They took their time and walked in silence, enjoying the warm night and each other's company. But, when they came to a fork in the trail, they decided to turn back. It had been a long day.

Back at the house, Ally let Bowser in, then she and Linc walked Fern and Kyle to their car and said their good-nights. Ally then walked with Linc to his car. Before he got in, he stood and looked at her.

"Do you think we'll be seeing each other again this week?" he asked.

"I'd like to," she said, hoping she didn't sound as eager as she felt at this moment. "I should have more free time this week. Mac has outsourced a lot of the newspaper work to the freelancers so he and Maggie can spend time with my parents while they're here. I'm hoping they're not expecting me to tag along all the time."

Link brushed the hair out of her face and stroked her cheek with the back of his hand. "You are so beautiful," he whispered. "So sweet. I really like being with you."

Ally couldn't speak. She could barely breathe. Linc lifted her chin and kissed her lightly on the lips, then pulled back hesitantly and looked into her eyes. Ally exhaled softly and pressed her body against his chest. They embraced. She lifted her face to his. They kissed again, this time long and passionately.

Thirty-One

It was the morning after the big kiss, and Ally was up early. She was just finishing cleaning up from the cook-out the night before when her parents and the McGuires came into the kitchen.

"Oh, so glad you have the coffee made," Maggie said. "I need a strong jolt to get me going this morning. And, thanks for cleaning up. I wasn't looking forward to that."

"How does everyone feel," asked Mac, "if Maggie and Ally and I go in to the newsroom this morning for a couple of hours?" To Ann and Tim, he added, "And while we're gone you two can plan something fun for us all to do this afternoon."

"Sounds good to me," said Ann. Tim nodded his approval.

"Well," said Ally, "while you guys are having breakfast, I'm going for a walk."

She put on her sneakers, pulled her hair into a pony tail secured with a scrunchy, and said to Bowser, "Come on ole boy, let's go do some sniffin'." The schnauzer jumped up with a bark of approval. He ran over to his leash hanging on a hook by the door, gave it a tug and pulled it down. It was a fun little trick Ally had taught him. She snapped the leash to the dog's harness and he started pulling her to the door.

Ally really wanted some alone time to relive last night and think about how she felt about that kiss. *It was awesome!* she said to herself. *That's how I feel.* While Bowser was taking care of business alongside the trail, Ally pulled out her phone and texted Fern.

Ally: *hey girl r you up?*
Fern: *been up 2 hrs just finished with magic and getting ready for work. What r u doing?*
Ally: *walking bowser. Maggie wanted me to ask you to get Doc J to write a letter of reference to put with the petitions to xplain about magic's condition and progress*
Fern: *ok sure. Fun last nite. I think Linc really likes u*
Ally: *he kissed me!*
Fern: *I knew it! What did u do*
Ally: *kissed him back silly*
Fern: *awesome! r u tingling*
Ally: *lol funny girl*
Ally: *def chemistry*
Ally: *exciting!*
Ally: *cant stop thinking about him*
Fern: *sounds serious! Talk later?*

Ally signaled yes with a thumbs up emoji, and ended the exchange. She was walking along, humming to herself, and stopped at a dog waste receptacle along the trail to deposit the little orange "doggie-doo" bag with Bowser's contribution that she'd been carrying. The dog was looking off in the distance, and let out a low growl. Something out there had raised a few angry hackles along his neck and back. Ally hesitated a moment, full of apprehension. She saw the brush rustling off in the distance and thought it must be an animal, maybe a deer.

When the form of a person emerged Bowser started barking. *Oh gawd*, thought Ally. *Is that Darrell Dempsey rummaging around in the woods again?*

It was a man alright, but not Dempsey. As he stumbled toward her, she was taken aback by his disheveled appearance. His hair was unkempt, his clothes unwashed, his face unshaven. He looked like a vagrant, completely out of place in this affluent, gated community.

His speech was slurred, but Ally could make out that he was pleading for help. As he came closer, he reached his arm out to her. She was having a crossroads moment and needed to make a decision fast. Should she turn and run away or stay and see if she could help him? He didn't look dangerous, just confused and lost.

"Are you lost?" asked Ally.

He mumbled and pointed to her hair. He was trying to say something, but was having trouble articulating. "Rehheah."

"Redhead?" she asked, holding a strand of her hair, which had come loose from the scrunchy.

"Fi-reeee."

"Fiery redhead?" It was starting to click for Ally. "Are you Mr. Castlebury? Hobart?"

He nodded and took ahold of her wrist with a shaky hand. "Bad place."

Ally was trying to put the pieces together. Hobart Castlebury was supposed to be tucked away in some medical facility somewhere. Had George gone and brought him back in the past day? It was possible, she supposed. She hadn't seen George yesterday at any of the Memorial Day events.

"Okay, Hobart, come with me." She took his arm. "I'm going to walk you home."

"No! Bad place!"

Ally figured he was referring to the asylum or wherever he'd been. Maybe that explained why George had brought him back here. "No, not the bad place," she said. "I'm taking you to George." *And,* she thought to herself, *I'm darn well going to find out just what the heck is going on here. This isn't right.*

She linked arms with Hobart and started walking him down

the same trail that she and Officer Darrell Dempsey were on just a few weeks ago. They had to take their time because Hobart was having difficulty maintaining his balance. Ally couldn't believe how rapidly the condition of this man, the captivating Phantom of the Opera of just a few weeks ago, had deteriorated.

When they came to the wooden fence that separated the Gallery from the back yard of Stonewall Mansion, Ally looked for a place to get through. Behind one of the ramshackle outbuildings, she saw that a fence post had fallen and the rails were on the ground. Ally helped Hobart through while Bowser jumped over the rubble.

At the back porch, she tied the dog's leash to the railing then climbed the steps with Hobart and knocked. No response. She tried the door. It was unlocked. She pushed it open and called out for George. Hobart walked in and pulled Ally along. She felt a twinge of apprehension entering this house, but it was, after all, Hobart's house and she was accompanying him.

Hobart ambled over to the narrow servants' staircase and started going up. Ally followed, hesitantly, calling for George as she climbed. At the top, Hobart at first seemed uncertain which way to go. Then, he took Ally by the arm and pulled her into the first room they came to. It was a theatrical dressing room, cluttered with costumes and accessorized with makeup counters along one wall.

Hobart walked over to the closet and pulled out a hanger holding a coat, top hat, and scarf. Holding the costume at arm's length, he started a recitation. His words were slurred and mostly indistinct, but he delivered the monologue perfectly. It was a recitation Ally was familiar with:

> All the world's a stage,
> and all the men and women merely players.
> They have their exits and their entrances;
> And one man in his time plays many parts.

Ally laughed. "Bravo!" she clapped. "If I recall that's a quote from *As You Like It*."

Hobart bowed. "Jaques," he said, identifying the speaker. He seemed much more at ease now, like he was in his comfort zone.

Ally walked over to the closest makeup counter and sifted through the items on top. It looked like a selection of disguises was laid out. There was a beard of well-trimmed short facial hair and a thick dark blond wig. A case holding eye contacts was open. As Ally looked closer, she saw the lenses were all tinted in identical shades of blue. Beside the case was a pair of tortoise shell eyeglasses.

Tortoise shell glasses? Ally experienced a moment of alarm. The wig, the beard, the blue lenses, the glasses...especially the tortoise shell glasses. George Rothman wore tortoise shell glasses. She tried them on. The lenses were clear.

Her heart was pounding. She pulled out her phone and nervously started punching at the screen. Hobart was still delivering his soliloquy, and she didn't hear the movement behind her. The phone was ripped out of her hand and thrown to the floor. She froze.

As she slowly turned around, her eyes widened in fear. The man who had come in behind her looked like he'd just come out of the shower. It was not George. Even with the black hair slicked back and wet, she recognized the dark eyes and the facial features from the photographs.

Ally was staring at Erik Reno.

"What are you doing here?" Reno's face was contorted with rage. "Fuck! Why are you here?"

Ally could barely speak. "George? You're George?" she stammered.

Hobart was cowering in a far corner now, mumbling incoherently.

"Who let him out?" demanded Erik.

"The woods," Ally sputtered. "He was wandering. I was bringing him home to George." She was fighting back tears and telling herself, *Do not show fear. Think, Ally, think.*

Erik was regaining his composure. He walked over to the makeup counter and picked up the wig. "So, you like George, do you? Just so you know, he's my alter ego. I'm the bad boy; he's the good guy I created—Dr. Jekyll and Mr. Hyde in reverse. George comes in handy, wouldn't you say?"

Erik turned to replace the wig on the counter. With his back partially to her, Ally made a run for it, attempting get around him and out the door. But he was quick. He grabbed her from behind and placed her in his trademark rear naked chokehold. In a matter of seconds, she was rendered unconscious.

Thirty-Two

After securing Ally and Hobart, Erik Reno retrieved Ally's phone from the costume room. His first thought was to throw it into the lake, but then he had another thought. *You sneaky rascal*, he said to himself. *A bonafide brilliant bastard, if I do say so myself.* Erik loved the excitement of living on the edge. He decided he'd up the game.

He started out the back door with the phone and saw Bowser tied to the porch railing. *What the hell?* His first instinct was to choke the life out of the mutt. That would get his adrenaline pumping. But once again he thought he could use this to his advantage.

He had put on his purple Patrick Henry Patriots baseball cap and sunglasses, and with the dog on the leash and Ally's phone in his pocket, Erik climbed the wooden fence, pulled Bowser through the rails, and set off down the trail. Just another dogwalker out enjoying a beautiful spring morning. It was good he didn't run into anyone else, especially someone who might recognize the mutt and have to be dealt with. He had his hands full right now. *Enough is enough*, he thought to himself.

When he found a suitable location, Erik took out the phone, then threw it a few yards off the trail. When the phone was found, which was his intent, Erik Reno's prints would be on it. Agent Fuckface and these local goons could search all they wanted. But Erik Reno would no longer exist. With this morning's twist of events, he realized he had to change his plans. He'd be retiring Erik for good and starting a new life. It was time.

He whistled as he dropped Bowser's leash and gave the dog a good kick in the behind. "Get outta here you stupid mutt. Go!" Bowser took off running down the trail in the direction of home, just as Erik hoped he would.

He turned back toward Stonewall Mansion, briskly walking with an exaggerated swinging of the arms. Power walking to the meddling eye of any busybody he might encounter.

Back in the costume room, he put on his George Rothman desguise and bid a fond farewell, for good he hoped, to Levi Eriksson, aka Erik Reno.

Thirty-Three

Mac was getting antsy. It was almost nine o'clock, and he'd expected to be at the *Ledger* by now. Ally had been gone almost an hour.

"Maggie, can you give her a call?" he asked. "Tell her we're heading out and she can meet us at the paper."

Maggie punched in Ally's name and waited. "That's strange," she said. "The phone rang six times, then went to voicemail."

Tim shook his head. "I don't like this," he said.

"I'm going to look for her," said Mac. "She should have been back by now. She may have had an accident."

Tim started putting on his sneakers. "I'm going with you."

The two men set out through the back yard, taking a shortcut to Quail Ridge, which was the trail closest to the house. As they were crossing the 9th hole of the golf course, Bowser came bounding toward them from the trail, dragging his leash.

Mac took the dog home and told Maggie to start calling around. *Tim's right*, he thought. *This is not good.*

Maggie first called the Mean Beans Bistro.

"Hi Susan," she said, "I need to talk to Fern. Tell her it's urgent."

When Fern came to the phone, "Maggie asked if she'd talked

to Ally this morning.

"We texted about an hour ago," said Fern. "She told me you want Doc Johansson to write up a report on Magic. I was going to call him a little later when he should be in his office. Is that what you're calling about?"

"No, Fern, listen…Did she say anything about where she was or where she might be going?"

"She only said she was walking Bowser. What's wrong?"

"Not sure. She hasn't come back yet, and we're getting worried."

"Maggie, if I hear from her or find out anything, I'll let you know right away."

"Thanks, Fern."

Then Maggie called Lincoln Stryker. "Linc, have you heard from Ally this morning?"

"No…Maggie, what's wrong?"

She told him Ally had left to go for a walk over an hour ago. "Bowser just came back dragging his leash, and calls to her phone are going unanswered."

"Has anyone talked to her since she left?"

"She and Fern exchanged texts, but nothing about where Ally might be going."

"Okay, Maggie. I'm on my way over."

Linc, who had just gotten out of the shower, threw on some clothes and headed out of the lodge. He jogged to the Mean Beans and motioned for Fern to come over.

"Maggie said you and Ally were texting this morning. Do you still have it on your phone?"

"Umm…sure. I'll go get it. Linc?" she asked. "What's wrong?"

"She hasn't returned, and Bowser came home without her. Everyone's worried."

Fern retrieved her phone but hesitated before handing it to Linc. "Ally's going to kill me for showing you this," she said. "You know, girl stuff?"

"I promise I won't tell. This is important."

Fern pulled up the text and handed her phone to Linc.

He started to smile as he read the exchange, then got serious. "Mind if I forward this conversation to myself?"

"Ugh!" Fern groaned, then nodded. "Okay, but Linc, will you let me know as soon as you find her?"

"Absolutely, and please let me know right away if you hear from her," he said as he turned to leave.

When Linc arrived at the McGuire residence, Maggie told him that Mac and Tim were still out looking for Ally. Linc turned to Ann with questions about Ally's phone. She confirmed that it was part of their family plan and provided Linc with the necessary login information to access the Cloud.

Linc sat at Maggie's computer and found the three phones that appeared in the Murphys' Devices List. He selected Ally's number and started clicking, dragging the map, zooming in, then out, and changing the grid to get the view he wanted.

"Do you know where this location is?" he asked Maggie, pointing to the screen.

"Quail Ridge Trail. I think I know about where that area is."

Linc loaded the information on his phone. "Let's go," he said.

"I want to come with you," said Ann.

"I'd like you stay here, Ann," Linc said gently, "in case Ally returns or someone calls or comes by the house."

As they were walking across the golf course, following the

same route Mac and Tim had taken earlier, Maggie called her husband and told him they had found the general location of Ally's phone and were heading down Quail Ridge Trail.

"We're on the same trail," said Mac.

"Stay put, we'll meet up with you."

Linc asked Maggie if she'd call the Gallery's guard shack at the front gate and ask if Darrell Dempsey could meet them on Quail Ridge Trail to help search for a missing person who may be injured. Linc gave Maggie the coordinates, which she relayed to the guard at the gate.

They met up with Mac and Tim, who'd been walking up and down the trail, calling for Ally and asking the few hikers and joggers they encountered if they'd seen a female matching Ally's description. No one had.

When the map locater indicated they were in the vicinity of the phone, Linc asked the others to spread out along the trail. He called Ally's number. They all listened for the phone to ring.

"I hear it," called Tim.

Linc called the number again. "Over there," he said, pointing into the brush a short distance off the trail. "Everyone stay here. I don't want to disturb anything."

He carefully made his way toward the sound. When the ringing stopped, he called the number again. Then, he gently moved some dead leaves and small branches. The phone was lying face up, showing an incoming call from "Linc."

He called Chief Hawkins at the police station and explained the situation. "Odell," he said, "how soon can we get a forensics unit over here? I have a bad feeling about this."

"It'll have to come from the sheriff's office in Dominion Mills. I'll get right on it," said the chief.

Linc started calling Ally's name.

Darrell Dempsey came running up, and Maggie held him back to keep him from stepping off the trail.

Linc stuck a twig in the ground beside the phone and carefully walked back through the underbrush to the trail.

"Chief Hawkins is sending over a forensics team. Not sure how long it will take." He turned to Darrell.

"Officer Dempsey, Ally said that one of these trails leads to the rear of Stonewall Mansion. Can you show me the way?"

"Yes, Sir. It's just ahead where Quail Ridge meets Pioneer Trail. You take a right on Pioneer."

Linc told the others to wait there. He started in the direction Darrell had pointed, and the security officer stepped in beside him. As they walked, Darrell told Linc about the strange encounter he and Ally had with Hobart Castlebury the last time they were on this trail.

When they got in view of Stonewall Mansion, Linc said he was going onto the premises. He told Darrell to go back and stay with the others until the forensics team arrived or he returned.

"Don't you want me go with you?" asked Darrell.

"Officer Dempsey, I don't want you stepping outside your jurisdiction." When he saw Darrell's look of disappointment, he added, "I really need you to stay with the others. I don't know what's going on here, but I don't like it."

Linc went over the wooden rail fence and walked along the perimeter of the house. When he got around to the front, he went up the steps and rang the doorbell, which announced his arrival with that annoying Beethoven's Fifth ringtone. George Rothman promptly came to the door.

"Agent Stryker, I mean 'Linc', to what do I owe the pleasure this time?" Rothman smiled.

Linc resisted the urge to wipe that smirk off Rothman's face.

"We're looking for Ally. Have you seen her this morning?"

"I would love to see Ally, but no. I've been here all morning, and no one's come by. What do you mean, you're looking for her? Is she missing?"

"Yes, she was walking the dog and went missing from the trail in back of this house. The dog came back but she hasn't. Do you mind if I have a look around the outbuildings out back?"

"You may certainly do so, and I'll help you if you like. Anything you need, let me know. Do you think something happened to her?"

Linc ignored the question and walked around to the back. God, he detested George Rothman. He poked around the dilapidated buildings, inside and out, and walked around the grounds, calling Ally's name. He found nothing. While walking back to the others, he called his boss, Colin Hynes, in Richmond.

"Colin, we've got a young woman here in Union Gap who went missing this morning in a location near that mansion where one of the murders occurred. Highly suspicious."

"Go on," encouraged Hynes. "I know you're not calling me about a missing person unless you have more."

"We found her phone, and the local police chief is sending a forensics team to retrieve it and scour the area for any other evidence. How soon can we get fingerprint results from the phone?"

"Why? Is there a reason to expedite? You know it could take several days, weeks even, in an ordinary missing person's case."

"I have reason to believe this case may be related to the homicides. I'll explain later. Look, Colin, I'm not asking for full blown fingerprint results, just a comparison against what we have on file for Levi Eriksson, aka Erik Reno, the alleged serial killer."

"Do you think there's a connection?"

"I have my suspicions."

"Is that it?"

"I'd also like a facial comparison analysis of Reno and the strange woman at the press conference from the pictures on file in our office."

"Are you thinking…"

"This guy Reno is a stage actor and skilled in disguise. Yes, I am thinking…"

"Okay, what's the name of the missing woman?"

"Allyson Murphy."

"The girl reporter? Good lord, Stryker. Aren't you supposed to be on leave?"

"I want to cancel my leave to work on this. If I may, that is. I'm more familiar with this case than anyone."

"That's exactly what I am concerned about. You getting emotionally involved."

"I am involved, but you know I'll do my job."

"Okay Stryker, I trust your judgment, but I'm dispatching Dana right away to Union Gap to work with you."

Dana Paladino was Linc's partner at the Richmond field office. He would have preferred to work alone, with the help of the locals, but he wasn't going to argue. "Sure," he said, "Thanks."

"Send the prints directly to the lab in Quantico, and I'll ask them to expedite the check against Eriksson's prints. I'll also get the photos to our Face Services Unit for the comparison analysis. Best case scenario, we may have something within 24 hours."

"Thanks, Colin."

"And, Linc, keep your emotions out of this. You know I won't hesitate to pull you off this case."

"Yes, Sir."

Link thought, *No way in hell can I keep my emotions out of this.*

Thirty-Four

Ally awoke feeling groggy and disoriented. She sat up and looked around, trying to get her bearings. She was in a windowless room with only a single, low watt lightbulb in the ceiling. It was dank, like a cellar or a cave. Definitely someplace underground. Where was she? Why was she here?

A cold shiver went down her spine. She remembered finding Hobart Castlebury, confused and disheveled, wandering in the woods. She'd walked him to Stonewall Mansion. She remembered the room full of costumes and Hobart's little theatrical performance. She remembered the makeup counter with disguises laid out. George Rothman disguises. She remembered staring into the face of Erik Reno. She remembered feeling his arm around her neck, and not being able to breathe.

Erik Reno's choke-hold had rendered Ally unconscious but fell short of strangling the life out of her as he'd done to Ruby Rosa and Gianna Talone. When she'd regained consciousness, her neck was throbbing. She remembered the Erik-monster handing her a glass of water. Her throat had hurt, and she drank it. She remembered feeling unsteady and drowsy almost immediately. Then, she must have blacked out. Drugged? She must have been drugged.

She looked around the room. She was on a cot. Another cot was at the other end of the room. A small wooden table and some folding chairs were set against the opposite wall. There was a sewer-like stench. She got up to see if she could find where it came from. She found a portable toilet, the kind used for camping, in one corner. Beside it was a small wall mount sink. A half-full case of water bottles sat on the floor. That was the extent of the furnishings. She walked over to the door. It was locked. *Of course it's locked,* she thought.

She heard a moan, and recoiled. Someone else was in the room. Incoherent sounds were coming from the far corner. She inched closer. Hobart was lying on the other cot. She went over and knelt on the floor beside him.

"Hobart?" she said. "Hobart, it's me, Ally. You know, 'fiery red-head'." He made some muddled sounds and turned over. "Hobart, please wake up, please talk to me." She started to cry, then told herself to get a grip.

She took a bottle of water from the case and gulped it down, too thirsty to consider if it might be laced with drugs. Then, she realized she was hungry. Starving, actually. She'd left the house this morning without breakfast, thinking she'd pop in at the Mean Beans when they got to town, get a breakfast sandwich, and chat with Fern a bit before going to work. How long ago was that? What time was it now? She had no way of knowing other than her stomach telling her it hadn't been fed in a long time.

She sat back down on her cot and broke into a cold sweat. She was shaking. She had no idea how long she'd been sitting there when she heard a sound outside the door. Her heart started beating rapidly. *Do not show fear,* she told herself. She swallowed deeply and clenched her jaw.

"Hello Sunshine. I hope you had a nice nap and have an appetite. I would've gone over to Creekside and gotten today's specials, but that wouldn't be a good idea given the current state of affairs, wouldn't you agree? But I do have for you a choice of Gourmet Chicken Alfredo Florentine or Pasta with Swedish Meatballs, both fresh out of the microwave."

Disguised as George Rothman, Erik Reno was playing a sick game. He placed the two trays on the table.

"Enjoy." The Erik-monster spread out his hands in a ta-da gesture with open palms.

Despite her reservations, Ally grabbed the closest tray and wolfed down the chicken dish, then grabbed another bottle of water and went over to her cot and sat.

"Now, my dear Ally, we need to chat."

"Okay, first let's chat about Hobart over there." Ally was angry and frightened and trying to sound calm. "What's wrong with him? Not long ago, my friends and I met him here on the front porch at Stonewall Mansion. He was clean, immaculately dressed, completely put together, and quite coherently bouncing Shakespeare quotes off us."

"Dear Ally, as I've told you, Hobart is not well. It's true that when he first came here he was okay in some regards, but if you recall, he was also behaving erratically. There were reports of him posturing on the upstairs balcony with his middle fingers raised to the townspeople and of him jumping in the lake naked. I feel responsible for his reputation so I took it upon myself to make sure he was taking his medications."

"Okay, but just a couple of weeks ago he was charming the townspeople, appearing as the Phantom of the Opera, reciting quotes, line dancing to country music. Now this…" She gestured toward the far wall where Hobart was sleeping.

"Hobart could never have pulled off what you describe."

"What do you mean?"

"Why, his understudy had to step in, of course."

Ally considered this. "You?" She was recalling now that George was supposed to be in New York during the Sunset Social. So, that was all a ruse.

"Is that such a bad thing? I did it for him, for his reputation. I couldn't have it be known that the great Hobart Castlebury was not so great anymore. That wouldn't have served my purpose or his."

"Your purpose?"

"Hobart needed a personal assistant," he continued, "someone to handle his estate after the tragic death of his Ruby. It couldn't be known that he was not of sound mind. You see, Ruby had left a substantial bequest to her beloved surrogate son Erik Reno, but Erik couldn't collect, now could he? He was a wanted man. So, George Rothman stepped in to claim what rightfully belonged to his alter ego."

Ally could scarcely believe what she was hearing. "So, all this time, Erik Reno has been presenting himself around town as George Rothman and, when it suited his fancy, he was Hobart Castlebury in the role of Phantom of the Opera? Incredible! No, beyond incredible!"

"Yes, brilliant, wouldn't you agree?"

"And it was you who had the conversation with Gianna Talone that Maggie overheard?" It was more a statement than a question. Ally was realizing that this Erik-monster was enjoying himself immensely telling her how clever he was. If she could keep him talking, she might be able use it to her advantage.

"And, Hobart's behavior the morning after the Sunset Social when I encountered him on the back porch? Why was he so angry and rude?"

"Unfortunately, I slept late that morning, after my big performance the night before, and was late giving him his meds. His rude behavior, I suspect, was due to the fact that he was furious at me for stealing the stage. But, as I said, I did it for him, to save his reputation."

"So, Hobart knew you were really Erik in disguise?"

"Not actually. He saw Erik in the house and thought there were two of us, George and Erik. But being all doped up he felt helpless. Oh, believe me, he hates Erik but, like you, he's quite fond of George."

"What other aliases does Erik Reno have?"

"Ally, my dear, Erik can be anyone you want him to be. I got the impression you were pretty fond of George, so I thought I'd keep him around. Then, Agent Fuckface showed up."

Ally resisted the urge to slap him. By now, she'd finished her second bottle of water and really, really needed to pee. *No way in hell*, she thought, *am I going to do that with him here.* She sat in discomfort and tried to remain still.

She'd been using every interviewing technique she knew to keep him talking, and was surprised at how much information she was getting. Fat lot of good it was going to do her, she thought ruefully, but she continued because she didn't know what else to do.

"But, why did you say Hobart was admitted to a medical facility, when in fact he's been right here?" She asked.

"He was getting in the way. The authorities, your highfalutin, rootin' tootin', gun-totin' lawman, included, were insisting on talking to him. That nosy 'Linc' as you call him had already been out here poking around. Of course, I could have posed as Hobart, but I've been busy. There's a cache of diamonds stowed somewhere in this house, a million dollars' worth, maybe two million. Ruby was going to turn them over to the authorities. That would have been a real shame, don't you think?"

"That's why you, I mean Erik, killed her?"

"Erik loved Ruby like a mother, but he had no choice, can't you see that?"

"And Gianna?"

"That meddling bitch? She claimed the diamonds were hers by virtue of them being 'family jewels', and she wanted them. She was intent on disrupting my whole search operation if she didn't get them. Believe me Ally, there's no loss there."

"That's why Hobart bought this house? To find the diamonds?"

"Hobart's not interested in the diamonds. He came here planning to open a performing arts center, with George Rothman's help. But, you see, George is preoccupied with the diamonds. Or, he was. Plans have changed now. No time left. We have a trip to plan. And, you my dear will be going with me. Unfortunately, there's no other option. Remember, it was your decision to crash this party. But, it'll all work out. For the better. You'll see."

Ally had a lot more questions, but George patted her on the knee and got up to leave.

"When Hobart wakes up," he said, give him the other gourmet microwave special."

After he walked out, Ally checked the door. It was locked. *Of course it's locked*. She hurried over to the portable toilet and finally peed.

Thirty-Five

Dana Paladino arrived at the LakeView Lodge at quarter after six. As soon as she checked in, she called Linc who'd been sitting in his room thinking and agonizing. "I'm famished," she said. "Let's get something to eat and you can fill me in on what's going on."

Dana was eight years Linc's senior, with short dark hair and a muscular build that she worked relentlessly to maintain. When it came to her job, she was all business and good at what she did. As the senior special agent in her partnership with Lincoln Stryker, she enjoyed taking on a superior role. *Kind of like the way Ally described her "alpha female" roommate Monica,* Linc thought.

"You look like hell, Stryker," Dana said when they were seated in a booth at Jack's Pub.

"It's been a grueling day," he answered.

While she was devouring her burger and washing it down with frequent swigs of Samuel Adams, Linc was responding to text messages and phone calls. Maggie and Fern both wanted to know if he had any news. Chief Hawkins was passing along the forensic results. Linc was trying to find out if the search teams that were formed had found anything. He hadn't touched his food.

"Eat," directed Dana.

Linc picked up a steak fry and went through the motions of chewing without actually tasting. His mind was racing.

"Look, Linc," said Dana, "Hynes said he has reservations about keeping you on this case with your, quote, 'emotional connection', and all. Don't prove him right. You've got to take this down a notch. Eat something and relax a little or you won't be doing anyone any good. Now tell me what's going on."

Linc took a bite of his burger and updated her on the murders, much of which she already knew from the bureau reports. Then he told her about the disappearance of Ally that morning.

"So, what are your thoughts?" she asked. "Hynes said you believe this disappearance may be related to the murders?"

"I'd bet my life on it. That mansion across the lake is at the center of all of it. Ally disappeared from a gated community behind it where the most serious crime seems to be people leaving dog poop in the middle of the trails. Aside from her phone, the forensics team found nothing in the area. No disturbance. No sign of a struggle. Same with the search teams, nothing. Something might have occurred on the trail and the phone got thrown into the brush. Or, maybe the phone was planted there to throw us off."

"What about the search dogs that were brought in?"

"The scent was compromised. Ally walks there all the time. Hell, we were just there last night. The dogs were confused, picking up her scent, then going in circles or back to the house."

"How do you think the mansion fits in? And before you answer, keep eating."

Linc took a drink of beer, then a bite of his burger and continued. "The mansion sits close to the general area where Ally was walking. I've been inside the place and met with the so-called personal assistant to Hobart Castlebury. Both the place and the person make my skin crawl."

"What do you think's going on?"

"Personally, I think our murder suspect Erik Reno is hiding in there. And, I think George Rothman knows something. They may be in this together. The house is a big place. I did a quick inspection, with Rothman's permission, and didn't find anything, but who knows what's in there."

"What's your next move? I mean, *our* next move?"

"Maggie McGuire at the *Lakeside Ledger* may have blueprints of the house for a story she and Ally are working on, and if she doesn't, the historical society does. First thing tomorrow, I want to take a close look at those. Then, hopefully, we'll get some results from the fingerprints and the facial recognition folks. And, maybe there'll be some leads from the missing person's report that went out this afternoon."

"Then?"

"Then, we'll take it from there."

"Okay, Stryker, finish eating, then get some sleep. Looks like we have a big day tomorrow."

Back in his room lying in bed, sleep was eluding him and questions were messing with his mind. *Where was Ally? Was she scared? Being abused? Dead?*

He took out his phone and pulled up the forwarded text messages between her and Fern this morning. By all accounts, these were Ally's last words before she disappeared. He kept reading them over and over.

Ally had told Fern about the kiss and the chemistry. He'd felt it as well. He'd never had these intense feelings of caring and concern before. But, for now, Ally was missing and possibly in grave danger, and that's where he needed to focus his attention. He fell asleep, hoping and praying for insight and a positive outcome to this nightmare.

Thirty-Six

The next morning, Linc and Dana met Maggie in the news-room of the *Lakeside Ledger*. Linc had called earlier to ask if they could see the copies of the Stonewall Mansion blue-prints she'd gotten from the historical society.

"Sure," said Maggie. "So, do you think there's a connection?"

"Maybe," he replied, cryptically.

Mac had decided that the *Ledger* would not be printed that day for the usual Thursday distribution tomorrow. With Ally's disap-pearance, there was no way they could get it ready. But he'd asked the freelancers to continue working on the spread for the Memorial Day celebration.

Maggie had printed out copies of the blueprint photos she'd taken with her phone camera, but the images were too small to make out the detail Linc needed. Zooming in didn't help; it just made them fuzzier.

Maggie called Helen Overington and explained that the FBI needed to see and maybe photocopy the originals as quickly as pos-sible. Helen agreed to meet them in the archives room in the base-ment of the Lake County Court House.

Maggie said she was going along and offered to drive. She needed to feel like she was doing something to help the investiga-tion. She grabbed her Nikon FX camera and its wide angle attach-ment and also gave Linc the pages from Priscilla Jackson's journals that she'd made copies of.

"You and Dana might find something interesting in these from the original owner of Stonewall Mansion if you want to read them on the drive to Dominion Mills," she said.

"Breakfast is served!" Erik Reno, still disguised as George Rothman, entered the dank chamber where Ally and Hobart were being held and plopped three microwavable breakfast entries on the table. "Let's see, we have two orders of three-cheese omelets and a side of organic hash browns, the latter of which, unfortunately, you two guests will have to share. I pray you slept well."

Ally lied, "Yes, fine." Lying awake, she had asked herself what her alpha female roommate Monica would do. She figured her best chance to escape, or at least get out of this room, was to keep playing along, rather than trying to battle this psycho.

She had gotten up sometime during the night to pee and rinse her mouth with water. Hobart was now up and shuffling over to the portable toilet. Ally diverted her eyes. Erik yelled at him. "Make sure you aim and get it in the bowl this time, Hobart. Smells like a sewer in here."

"If you bring me some paper towels and disinfectant," said Ally, "I can clean up some."

"No need," said Erik. "We'll be out of here soon enough. I do apologize for not having your guest room cleaned and readied ahead of time, my dear. But, in my defense, you did drop in unannounced. I wasn't expecting company. Aren't you going to eat?"

Ally pulled the plastic off the top one of the omelets and took a big bite. She opened the other one for Hobart and called him over to sit beside her. She set the side of hash browns in between them. Hobart shambled over, reciting in broken language: *"Things...sweet to taste...prove in digestion...sour."*

Ally ventured a guess. "Shakespeare?" she asked.

"*King Richard II*, Act I, Scene 3, spoken by John Gau..." He trailed off, but raised his arm in the air, index finger extended, in what Ally guessed to be a theatrical gesture.

"Can I ask you a question?" Ally asked Erik.

"Madam, you may ask me anything."

"What day is today?"

"Wednesday, May 31, 9:37 a.m." he said, looking at his phone. Why do you ask?"

"Wednesday...The day the *Lakeside Ledger* goes to press for distribution tomorrow." She wondered if that would happen. She had no idea what was going on in the outside world. She just realized that tomorrow, June 1, was her birthday. *Or, maybe my death day,* she thought ruefully.

"No need to concern yourself with such mundane matters here, dear Ally. We'll be traveling this evening, once it gets dark. Which reminds me, I have to go into town incognito to run an errand. Who do you think I should be? A tourist? A businessman? Maybe an old lady?"

"I personally like the old lady. Where are you taking us?"

Hobart had finished eating and sauntered back to his bed. Erik jumped up off Ally's cot where he'd been sitting, and hurried over. "Time for your meds, big boy," he said, giving Hobart a handful of pills and a bottle of water.

Hobart resisted, shaking his head no.

"Hobart, you know what happens if you don't take your meds."

Hobart glared, but took the pills. Erik watched him go through the motions of plopping them in his mouth and chewing. *"Things sweet to taste prove in digestion sour."* He repeated the phrase he'd recited earlier.

"Now here's your water. Wash them down, please."

"What are you giving him?" asked Ally.

"Meds to keep him docile. For his…umm, disorder. Oh, you were asking about where we're going. We'll be heading to New York. We have paperwork to get in order, and I need to make sure we have sufficient resources. Then, we'll go shopping. Macy's. Saks…We'll go to fine restaurants, Broadway shows…You'll be my princess. And, I'll be anyone you want me to be. Remember when you called me your Prince Charming? You know how good I am. It's going to be wonderful, you'll see. We'll be getting you ready this afternoon, clothing, makeup, wig, the whole enchilada. How do you feel about being a brunette?"

"That's fine. What about Hobart?"

"Regrettably, he will not be going with us. You can see his condition. It just won't work."

"What are you going to do?"

"Not to worry, my dear."

"George, if you do anything to Hobart, anything, I will not be going with you. You'll have to kill me too."

"Ally, you're confused. George does not kill people. Erik kills people. And, Erik I'm afraid would feel compelled to come out of retirement to pay a visit to your family if you don't go along with George."

Ally shuddered. *This person is crazy and batshit dangerous*, she thought. "Will Erik be traveling with us?" She asked.

"That's totally up to you, dear Ally."

"Is there anything in particular you're looking for?" asked

Helen Overington.

Linc and Dana had donned white gloves and were examining the documents from the file labeled "Stonewall Mansion" that Helen brought out from the drawer marked "Historic Blueprints."

"We're trying to figure out if there's some place in the mansion where someone could be hidden," said Linc. "Maybe where slaves hid when it was too dangerous for them to be in the living quarters."

"Hmm...I don't know. I've never really examined the floor plans."

"Helen," said Maggie. "You've read all of Priscilla's journals, right?"

"Well not all, but a good amount."

"Did you come across anything that might suggest a hiding place for the slaves?"

"Not specifically. There are entries referring to 'underground', but it's difficult to know what they mean."

"Such as?"

Helen retrieved one of the diaries. "One of my favorite passages is this," she said. "I think I may have shared it with you when you were here before." Maggie photographed the entry, then Helen read aloud:

From the depths of the well-hidden underground, my heart
overflows with joy at the sound of children's laughter and the
old folks' singing. Safe passage, my friends.

"See what I mean?" said Helen. "It's difficult to decipher Priscilla's meaning. 'From the depths of the well-hidden underground...' Is she referring to the Underground Railroad or perhaps something more literal, closer to home?"

Linc was looking at an updated floor plan, presumably drawn up when certain areas of the house were remodeled. "In this diagram of the new kitchen, next to the servants staircase, there's the word 'Pantry' with a notation 'RC' right beneath. 'RC'? I wonder what that refers to."

Helen went back to the original blueprint. "There's an 'RC' notation here, outside, next to the back porch. Probably 'root cellar'. Old houses had them back then. That's what I'm guessing. That could be a hiding place I suppose. It looks like the outside access has since been sealed off and covered over, though it's possible stairs down were added inside the pantry."

Linc was remembering the bareness of pantry he had peeked in on during his walkthrough at the mansion a few days earlier.

Maggie took photos with her wide-angle lens of the original blueprint and also the updated floor plan for the kitchen renovation. "I think we've got what we need, Helen," said Linc. "Thanks for your help."

Ally was sick of playing games with the Erik-monster, but she sensed he was having fun. Maybe as long as he was in the role of George he wouldn't show his true side, the person capable of murder. Erik Reno was mentally unwell, but Ally could tell he lived for role-playing. She wanted to use that to her advantage.

An elderly lady, just as Ally had suggested, brought lunch. She said she was just back from running errands in town. She had gray-streaked brown hair pulled up in a bun atop her head, wire-rimmed granny glasses sitting low on her nose and attached to a beaded chain. Her dress was boxy and extra baggy, designed to hide a body that had thickened with age. She clonked into the dank room in vintage chunky women's shoes. For show, Ally forced herself to laugh despite her revulsion.

"Special treat, my dears," she said in a contrived wavering voice, setting a carryout box on the table. "Soup and sandwiches from Creekside Café. I even got the senior citizens discount." She laughed at her own joke. "Now eat up. I've a few things to do, but I'll be back soon. And, Ally we'll be going upstairs to get you made up in your travel attire. We have a new set of wheels with plates that can't be traced to us."

"George," said Ally, "Or should I call you Aunt Georgia?"

"Good one, Ally. I like that. You and I are going to have so much fun together."

Over my dead body, Ally thought to herself, then shuddered, realizing those words may prove true.

"Now, no more questions," said the Erik-monster. He went over to Hobart's cot, poured several pills into the actor's hand and watched him chew, swallow and drink water from his bottle.

When he was gone, Hobart said, "He's a monster."

Ally looked at him in surprise. Hobart held out his fisted hand, opened his fingers and revealed a handful of pills. He handed them to Ally and retrieved more from under his pillow.

"Oh my god!" Ally exclaimed, putting the pills in her pocket. "You haven't been swallowing your pills. Can you talk to me? Do you know what's going on here?"

Hobart laughed. "Fiery redhead."

Ally hugged him. "Hobart, we have to get out here. And, for the record, my hair is auburn."

"He's a monster," Hobart repeated. "Bad person, bad place."

Ally started looking around. She needed something to use for a weapon. She looked under her cot. The bed had a metal frame, welded at all connecting points. *Not going to work*, she thought. She went around to the wall mounted sink and portable toilet, looking for something to dislodge. She examined the folding chairs. No way to take them apart. She sat down at the table feeling frustrated, and started to cry. She opened the soup cups and sandwiches. Hobart joined her at the table.

"Hobart," she said through tears, talking more to herself than her companion. "We need something to use as a weapon. Do you understand me?"

Hobart nodded. "Im…per…vise."

"Improvise?"

"Now, my student," he said, "today we will be role playing. Improvised weapons."

"Such as…?"

"A table leg will do well as a club."

Ally didn't know what to make of Hobart's words. He seemed to be talking nonsense. "Okay but…" she said. She got down under the table. It was an inexpensive piece of pressed wood furniture. She examined the wooden legs. They were attached to the table top with wing nuts threaded onto embedded bolts. Ally tried loosening the one closest to the door. It was rusted and wouldn't budge. She took the thumb and forefinger of her right hand, and gripping with all her strength tried but couldn't turn it. Her finger slipped along a jagged edge of the protrusion. It was cut and starting to bleed.

"Shit!" She cried. She went to the sink and rinsed the cut then wrapped it as tightly as she could with toilet paper. She willed her finger to stop bleeding. She knew that the Erik-monster could return at any time. She sat on the floor, frustrated. *Think, Ally,* she said to herself.

She got down again and tried the wing nuts on each of the other three legs. The one in the far corner seemed to give a little, and at least it didn't appear rusted. She tried loosening it with her left hand and felt it turn a bit. Using both hands, she got the wing nut free.

"Hobart," she said, "I think we did it, but now we have to turn the table around."

They cleared the food and containers off and set it all on the floor. Ally removed the leg and laid it aside. After turning the table so that the loosened leg was now on the room side as opposed to being against the wall, she asked Hobart to hold it up while she rested the leg she'd removed in place without securing it.

"Whew!" she said. "High fives!" They performed the hand gesture and reset the table, careful not to bump the leg.

Hobart went over and sat on his cot, and Ally sat beside him. She could sense him fading out.

"Hobart, listen to me," she said. "This is important. When the monster comes back, I'm going to try to make a run for it. I may not make it, but I'm going to try like hell. If I do, I need you to understand that I am not leaving you. I'll come back for you, I promise. Do you understand?"

Hobart mumbled something indiscernible and offered a weak fist bump, which Ally returned. "Now," she said, "let's get rid of those pills, but don't let the monster know. When he comes back, you have to pretend like you're asleep. Can you do that?"

"Of course. I am Master of the Stage... '*One man in his time plays many parts*'."

"Excellent," said Ally as she washed the pills down the drain.

"Fiery redhead," said Hobart.

"It's auburn," said Ally. "Now we wait."

After grabbing a lunch of fast food and eating on the drive back from the historical society, Maggie returned to the *Ledger*. Linc and Dana were camped out in the police station's briefing room along with Chief Odell Hawkins. Their boss, Special Agent in Charge Colin Hynes, was on speaker phone.

"I've gotten some preliminary results back from both the fingerprint and the facial comparisons. Faxing them over now."

"What can you tell us?" asked Linc.

"Both inconclusive without more analysis. Initial findings are the facial comparison shows a possible match. The fingerprints are probable."

"You're saying Ally's phone was 'probably' in the hands of Erik Reno?" A feeling of repulsion came over Linc.

"Not good enough for a warrant linking him to that mansion."

The fax machine in the briefing room was clicking away, and Chief Hawkins went over to retrieve the documents.

Dana took the fingerprint analysis and began reviewing it. Linc was examining the facial recognition report. The photographs of Erik Reno and the woman from the press conference were side-by-side, with distinguishing features and biometrics specified. The analysis found possible similarities, but the comparison was indeterminate due to the heavy makeup.

Linc was staring at the photo of the woman. Something was bugging him. It was the same feeling he'd had after doing the walk-through at Stonewall Mansion. His subconscious was telling him it was something consequential. But, what? He closed his eyes. He'd found that if he focused on something else for a while, the elusive something he was trying to remember would come to mind when he was not expecting it.

Ally was on alert, waiting for the return of the Erik-monster. She was scared. *Who would walk through the door this time? Would she*

be able to make her move? She didn't know how much longer she had, or how much longer she could play along.

Get a grip, she told herself. *Be on guard. Be ready. Be brave.*

She got up to pee, and her legs felt wobbly. *Like gelatin,* she thought. She started taking baby steps, then began pacing, trying to work her legs back to full strength.

Hobart looked like he had fallen back asleep. She wasn't sure if he was pretending. She was worried about him. The Erik-monster had not answered her question about what he was going to do with Hobart, except that he would not be traveling with them.

News for you, Erik, she thought. *I won't be traveling with you either. Not if I can help it.*

She heard the sound of the door opening and cringed. *Showtime,* she thought. George Rothman walked in.

"Hello beautiful," he said. Are you ready for your visit to the wardrobe room? I can't wait to get these grungy clothes off you and slip you into something more comfortable."

Ally recoiled. She had no intention of going upstairs with him. "George, we have a few matters to clear up first."

"Such as?"

"Such as Hobart. I told you I cannot, I will not go with you if you, or Erik rather, do anything to him."

"He can stay here. I'll make sure he has a good dose of meds to keep asleep until we get far enough away. Then it won't matter that he's found. By that time, you and I will have new identities and new looks. I'm a master of deception, you know, and you'll be my partner. I'll teach you everything I know. We'll be the ultimate power couple."

George looked over at Hobart, who was snoring softly.

Ally was eyeing the unlocked door. George stepped up behind her. "You know," he said. "I've loved you since that first moment I saw you in the newsroom. Remember how you were ranting out loud about Hobart calling you a fiery redhead, cheeky and impertinent and all that? Remember the fun we had at the library, laughing? The unsmiling Ethel the Bibliophile? And, her maddening clucking? We had such a good time together, didn't we?"

George was now inching closer into her personal space, and Ally was feeling sick and sweaty. He turned her around to face him. She could feel his breath against her face.

Ally thought, *I don't want to die but I cannot go upstairs with him.*

"Let's go over what we have," said Dana.

Linc started. "We know Ally went missing from the area behind Stonewall Mansion. Her phone was 'probably' handled by Erik Reno. We know the phone was likely 'planted' in the place where we found it. We believe the big house may have a secret hiding space, like an old root cellar. We have reason to believe the strange woman at the press conference might be Erik Reno in disguise since the mansion has a dressing room with makeup and endless costumes."

"Hand me that picture again," he said. "The woman."

"What about it?" asked Dana, sliding it across the table.

"There's something about this picture." He examined the photograph of the strange woman. "That's it!"

"What?" Dana repeated.

"The dress. I saw this dress hanging on a rack in that room."

"Are you sure?"

"I'd bet my life on it. We need a warrant. Now!"

Chief Hawkins spoke up. "Slim chance of that happening here. Look at the evidence. Or lack thereof."

"The chief is right," said Dana. "It's all weak. Nothing solid…"

Linc slammed his hand down on the table. "I'm going in. I can't just sit here and do nothing." He got up and hurried out.

"Linc!" Dana yelled after him. She sat for a moment, gritting her teeth, then got up and went after him. She caught up with him at his car in the parking lot of the lodge. The trunk was open.

"Linc, I can't let you do this. You could jeopardize this whole case, maybe get people killed…You're acting on emotions. Overreacting. Exactly what Hynes warned me about. Not just people's lives, but the reputation of the FBI is on the line here."

Linc stopped and looked at her. "You're right," he said. "I'm going in as off-duty."

"That's ridiculous! You're not off-duty."

"You're pulling me off. I'm emotionally involved, remember?"

"Hynes is going to have your ass."

"Okay, listen…I'm not going to risk jeopardizing this case, but for the record I'm going over there to have another 'friendly chat' with George Rothman. Yesterday when I talked to him, he told me to let him know if there was anything he could do to help in the search. Of course he didn't mean it, but I'm taking him up on it."

"And then what?"

"I'm bringing Ally out." He picked up his Glock, checked the chamber indicator, and stuck it in the holster in the rear waistband of his pants. "Dana, I have to do this."

His partner was glaring at him.

"If anything happens," said Linc, "put it on me. You tried to stop me and I went off on my own."

"Shit! Shit! Shit!" said Dana. She reached in the trunk and removed two walkie talkies, handing one to Linc. "Hawkins and I will be in range. Keep in touch." She wasn't smiling.

As she was walking away, she turned around and called back, "Hynes is going to have both our asses, you bonehead."

Thirty-Seven

Ally was fighting against the repulsion she was feeling while at the same time trying to figure out how to get out of this hellish situation. Making a run for it wasn't an option now. The Erik-monster was right up against her.

She had a flashback: Team Scheme. Happy, Maggie, Fern, and her discussing Milton Grimsley, the resident old geezer with the ogling eyes and wandering hands. Ally had promised him a dance at the Sunset Social in return for his donation of vintage playing cards for their Bridging the Gap project.

"Hopefully," Fern had said, "you won't have to resort to the nuclear option." She was referring to the old standby, "A hard, fast knee to the groin." They'd all laughed and Ally hadn't needed to use it then. But now…she did. She steeled herself, smiled at Erik to keep him off guard, and deployed Fern's nuclear option with every ounce of force she could muster.

"Fucking bitch!" he yelled. "You're dead." His hand went to his genitals, and he tottered but didn't go down.

Ally grabbed the disconnected table leg, and as she pulled it out, the table toppled to the floor. She swung, aiming for Reno's head, but the blow landed on his shoulder. He was now in a rage, and Ally didn't hesitate. She fled through the door. She saw the staircase and scampered up. At the top she came to, not a door but a panel, blocking the passageway.

Reno was right behind her. He grabbed her foot. She started

kicking at him and propelled herself against the panel, which swung inward causing her to fall forward and free from his grip. She heard a yell and glanced back just long enough to see Hobart holding the table leg after taking a swing and making contact with Erik.

Ally had fallen into a pantry and saw that the panel was a swinging wall. She pushed it back in place just as Erik reached the top stair. The panel caught his fingers in the jamb causing another expletive-laced howl.

Ally ran through the kitchen and out the back door. Her eyes tried to adjust to the sunlight as she stumbled down off the porch. She ran in the direction of the wooden rail fence. She jumped on the middle rail, grateful she had on her sneakers from her walk yesterday, and went over, losing her balance and falling to the ground as she landed. The monster was right behind her. He propelled himself over, landing partially on top of her.

Ally found a grapefruit-sized rock and attempted to smash him in the face. He grabbed her hand, forcing her to drop it. She had an adrenaline rush and angrily told herself not to give up. While they were both lying prone and struggling she kicked and hit and managed to get to her feet. So did he.

Ally's vision had adjusted enough for her to see the trail, and she ran, not looking back. Her heart was pounding. She was out of shape and out of breath, but she didn't stop. As she turned off Pioneer Trail and onto her familiar Quail Ridge, she heard the monster's heavy breathing behind her and willed her legs to go faster. She felt him grab her hair. He jerked her to a stop. Her heart sank. No one was around, but she screamed anyway.

"I could have given you the world," he hissed. "You stupid idiot. You're dead."

Ally could feel his spittle on her cheek as his right arm started encircling her neck. She was familiar with Erik Reno's lethal chokehold, which he'd used to kill Ruby Rosa and Gianna Talone and earlier to render her unconscious. She struggled and screamed, determined not to go down quietly.

Erik was having trouble keeping his grip. His right arm had now slipped upward and was across her face. She found flesh and bit into it. Hard. He ripped his arm away, leaving a patch of flesh behind. He slugged her forcefully across the face.

Ally was stunned and staggered before losing her balance and falling face down onto a jagged rock. Her right cheek exploded in pain. She felt weak and defeated. She had no more fight in her.

The monster yanked her up and again wrapped his right arm around her neck from behind, this time grasping his left biceps in a death grip.

"It didn't have to come to this, Ally," he said into her ear. "This is your doing."

She lacked the strength to struggle further. She was gasping for breath, then couldn't breathe at all. His grip was tightening, and she was losing consciousness.

I'm dying, she thought.

Ally heard a popping sound. *Is that the sound of a person's neck being snapped?* she wondered. She felt the pressure on her neck loosen and she slid down to the ground.

Linc left his car on the access road leading to Stonewall Mansion and walked over to the shabby, once-stately old house. He made his way around to the back, crunching below the windows as he crept slowly. He looked through a window of the detached garage and saw a new vehicle inside, not the car he had seen on his walk-around yesterday. He looked over at the back of the house and noticed the screen door swinging open. He took out his Glock and inched up onto the porch. The inner door was ajar. He nudged it.

"George," he yelled. "It's Special Agent Stryker."

He heard someone call back, "Help! Down here."

Linc was making his way into the kitchen and saw the pantry door partially open. He used his gun to nudge the opening wider. The left wall inside the pantry was wide open, and Linc saw a staircase going down. He heard noises below. It sounded like someone mumbling.

"Hello," he called out. "George, I have a few more questions."

Someone hollered back, but Linc couldn't make out what was being said or who was saying it. He headed down cautiously, gun in hand, then looked through a heavy open door into a dank, dimly-lit room. Linc saw the unkempt older man sitting on a cot.

"Who are you?" he asked.

"Hobart Castlebury. But, you may call me Hobart the Great. And, who might you be? Are you going to shoot me?"

Linc holstered his gun. He looked around the room. He saw the other cot outfitted with rumpled bedclothes. He saw the table, broken and collapsed on the floor. He saw the portable toilet.

"Hobart," he said, "do you know Ally? Is she here?"

"Fiery redhead," he replied. "Fair maiden of the phone. Sly little shrew…"

Linc was not sure what to make of this, but Hobart was smiling. "Is she here?" he asked again.

Hobart shook his head no. "Waiting for her to come back," he said. "She promised she's not leaving me."

Linc was getting impatient. "Do you know where she is?" He tried to speak calmly.

Hobart pointed to the collapsed table, and stood up. "Now, my student," he said, "we will be role playing. Improvised weapons…A table leg we will use as a club."

Linc was rubbing his forehead. He didn't want to hear this blather. He demanded, "Is she hurt?"

Hobart was shaking his head. "Don't know. Erik Reno's a monster. He killed my Ruby."

"Where are they? Hobart, tell me what happened. Now!"

Castlebury pointed to the door. *"'Love runs away from those chasing her, / and those who run away, / she throws herself on his neck.'"*

"Did Ally run away?"

Hobart nodded. "As did the monster."

Ally surprised herself when she started gasping and coughing. Her neck was throbbing, her face hurt, and she felt sore all over. She bent over and vomited. *Am I alive?* she wondered.

"Don't make me tase you again!"

A struggle was going on behind her. There was shouting, swearing, grunting. She tried to focus but her vision was blurred. She felt light-headed. Sitting on the ground, she pulled her knees up to her chest and lowered her head. It all seemed surreal.

She heard another pop, and a familiar voice said, "Stop resisting, asshole. You're not going anywhere."

Her vision slowly started coming back. She was now able to focus. She looked behind her. The Erik-monster was lying face down on the trail, and someone was sitting on his back, trying to put zip tie handcuffs on his struggling limbs.

Once Erik Reno was secured on the ground, Security Officer Darrell Dempsey came over to Ally and sat down beside her. "Ally, you're bleeding, but you're going to be okay." He took his handkerchief and gently wiped away a slow rivulet of blood trickling down her cheek from a gash under her eye.

Ally was never so happy to see anyone. She took his hand.

"Darrell," she murmured in a raspy voice broken with sobs, "Hobart Castlebury...captive in Stonewall Mansion...drugged... not well. Can you...get someone over there...please?"

"Ally, I'm going to radio it in now. Do you know this perp?" He nodded toward Reno, lying face down on the trail with his hands bound behind his back. "He kinda looks like that Rothman guy."

Ally shuddered. "It's Erik Reno...in disguise."

Dempsey looked incredulous.

"Pull...wig off," Ally prompted. "You'll see."

Dempsey walked back over to the culprit and jerked on his hair. "Holy shit!" he blurted out, and pulled out his two-way radio.

"We're coming out," Linc radioed to Dana. She was sitting with Hawkins in the chief's police cruiser when she saw Stryker coming toward them with another person. Not Ally. A man.

"Ally's not in there," Linc said. "Neither is Rothman or Reno. It looks like she fled with one of them in pursuit. This is Hobart Castlebury, by the way."

The police radio in the cruiser was crackling. Hawkins spoke over it. "We just got word of a disturbance in the Gallery. An assault on one of the trails. Police and emergency units have been dispatched. We just heard sirens and saw flashing lights coming across the stone bridge."

"Let's go," said Linc.

"What about him?" Hawkins asked.

"We'll have to take him with us." They climbed in the back of the cruiser.

At the entrance to Quail Ridge Trail, two squad cars and a rescue vehicle were parked along the street. Linc had explained on the way over that it looked like Hobart and Ally had been held captive in the old root cellar at Stonewall Mansion. Hobart, it appeared, had been drugged. He kept referring to his pills, which Ally had washed down the drain.

When they pulled up, Hawkins summoned an EMT over to examine Hobart. Linc went over to the emergency vehicle and caught a glimpse of Ally on a stretcher inside. He was stopped when he tried to enter.

"Are you family?" the medical technician asked.

Linc shook his head no. "But I need to see her." He showed his badge.

"Sorry," said the medic. "You'll have to wait until we get to the hospital."

"Is she okay?"

"She's shook up and banged up a good bit, but looks like she's going to be fine."

Linc caught up with Dana and Hawkins who had started walking down the trail. They were met by Darrell Dempsey, who'd been patroling in the woods. He filled them in on what had happened after he heard Ally's screams. "Can you believe it?" Dempsey said. "That perp is Erik Reno, masquerading as George Rothman."

They could see Reno being escorted by two officers, headed their way. Linc stopped them and glared at Reno.

"Ahh," said the perp. "It's Agent Fuckface." He smiled with an evil grin. "Ally and I have had the best time together these past couple of days."

"You piece of shit!" Linc spit out. "I could kill you right here." Dana and Hawkins grabbed him and held him back.

"Get that fiend out of here," Dana ordered the officers holding

Reno. "Or I might help Agent Stryker carry out that threat."

After the rescue squad left, taking both Ally and Hobart to the Lake County Medical Center, Linc, Dana and Chief Hawkins were met by Ally's parents and the McGuires. They had heard the sirens and came out to see what all the commotion was about. Linc told them that Ally had been physically assaulted and was en route to the hospital. They'd have more information as it was available. For now, they all just wanted to get to the hospital.

Linc was dropped off at his car and drove to the medical center. He met up with Ally's parents and the McGuires, who were waiting while she was being examined in the emergency room.

"What can you tell us?" asked Tim.

Linc gave an abbreviated version of what he knew. He told them Ally had been held captive in Stonewall Mansion, along with Hobart Castlebury. That she'd somehow escaped and was chased by Erik Reno. That she was fighting for her life on the trail when Security Officer Dempsey tased Reno and secured him until authorities arrived.

"Darrell Dempsey?" asked Maggie, shaking her head.

Linc nodded.

"But," interjected Mac, "you said Erik Reno. How does he fit into all this?"

"Apparently," said Linc, "Reno was disguised all this time as George Rothman and befriended Ally by claiming to be Hobart Castlebury's personal assistant."

They were all stunned, trying to digest this news when an ER doctor came out with an update. Ally had some scrapes, a bad cut under her eye and some nasty bruises. She was sore, but otherwise in good condition. She was being kept overnight for observation. They could see her as soon as she was set up in her room.

Per after hours hospital rules, no more than two people were permitted in Ally's room. Ann and Tim went in first, while Linc answered questions for Maggie and Mac. He told them about the apparent struggle in the underground room with broken furniture and Hobart's drug-induced state. He asked Maggie to keep this off the record. Too much was unknown or unsubstantiated.

Ally had been sedated, and when Ann and Tim came out, they said she was sleeping. They'd be spending the night in her room, but for now they were going to the cafeteria to eat. Maggie told Linc to go in next. She and Mac were going to walk along with Ann and Tim.

When Linc entered the room, he swallowed hard. Ally was hooked up to an IV, and had an oxygen tube in her nose. The right side of her face was red and swollen, and an ugly gash beneath her eye was being held closed with butterfly strips.

Linc picked up her hand where the intravenous tube was inserted. He bent down and whispered in her ear. "I am so sorry, Ally. So sorry you're going through this." He stood beside her bed, watching her breathe, thankful for each breath she was taking, until Maggie and Mac knocked on the door.

Linc kissed Ally's hand and told her good night. Walking out of the hospital and into the parking lot, he was giving silent thanks that she had survived this nightmare, and he was praying that she would come out of it okay.

Thirty-Eight

The next morning, Linc stopped in the gift shop before heading for Ally's room. Today was her birthday. They had a lot to celebrate, but that would have to wait. For now, he just wanted to show her he remembered.

He checked out the assortment of items: baby gifts, all-occasion gifts, seasonal gifts, flowers, toys, balloons, personal care items, jewelry, perfumes, books, candy and snacks. He looked over the greeting cards and not finding one with a message he liked, bought a pack of Tree-of-Hearts note cards, blank inside, so he could write something personal. As he was heading out, he passed a shelf with a collection of miniature, super-soft, stuffed birthday bears, each in a specific color and with a birthstone pendant to signify the month.

Today was June 1, and Linc found a light purple June bear with a faux teardrop pearl hanging from a delicate gold chain around its neck. It was cute. He hoped it might make her smile.

The hospital lobby had a kiosk with hot beverages and a few small scattered round tables with chairs. He bought a cup of black coffee and found a place to sit down. Setting the birthday bear on the table for inspiration, he opened a note card and started to write. When he finished, he reread it. Hopefully, she wouldn't think it too mushy or corny or gooey or sappy or whatever term was being thrown around these days for displays of affection. He was expressing what he felt.

June 1, 2017

Dear Ally,

I'm sending you a warm bear hug to let you know how special you are and how proud of you I am. Happy Birthday! I hope we can celebrate when you're up to it. Please know that I am here for you, and if you'll let me, I'd like to help you on your journey toward a strong and steady recovery. In your own time and on your terms, I look forward to picking up where we left off. You are amazing and in my thoughts always.

Linc

When he got to Ally's room, a "Do Not Disturb" sign was on the closed door. He walked down the hall to the waiting area and found Ann, Tim, and Maggie.

"The local guys are interviewing her," said Tim. "We got kicked out."

"What's the news on her condition?" asked Linc.

"She's supposed to be discharged this morning," said Ann. "Everything looks good."

Tim asked, "Are you going to have to do this?" He nodded toward her room. "Question her? She was pretty upset, being left alone with them."

"Unfortunately, yes, we'll need her statement. But Dana agreed it can wait until she's released and we can do it at the house where she'll be more comfortable. If that's okay with Maggie."

"Of course it is," said Maggie.

"Thank you," said Ann. "Can Tim and I sit in?"

"I have no problem as long as you're just observers and keep it all confidential. But, the decision is Ally's. There may be details she would feel more comfortable discussing in private."

"Are you saying...?" asked Tim. He was clenching his jaw and his lips tightened in an expression of anger. "I'll kill him."

Linc held up his hands. "Tim, I'm not saying anything. I don't know what to expect." He was remembering Reno's smirk and taunting comment yesterday when they met on the trail: *Ally and I have had the best time together these past couple of days.* Linc's stomach roiled.

"Include me too," said Maggie, "if Ally's okay with it. By the way, I stopped at the nurses' station and found out Hobart is in a room down at the end of this hall, alive and kicking and being his usual pain in the butt self." She shook her head. "Those poor hospital workers who have to deal with him."

Linc laughed. "That's good news, I guess, considering the condition he was in when I found him."

"They want to discharge him as soon as possible, but there's a problem. He has no place to go. The mansion has been cordoned off, and he also needs someone to look after him. I'm working on a solution but it's all on the q.t. for now."

They saw two detectives, one from the Lake County Sheriff's Department and one from Union Gap Police Department, coming out of the room.

"About time," said Maggie. "Mac went in to the *Ledger* early this morning to see if we can get a paper out this week. I told him I'd be in to help after I check on our girl."

Ally was sitting up in bed, her battered face ashen and her expression unsmiling. The bruising had spread and more swelling had set in on her right cheek.

Linc gave her a cheery smile despite his anger at Erik Reno for doing this to her. "How are you doing?" he asked.

"The questioning was draining," she said in a raspy voice.

A nurse came in to take her vitals. She said the doctor wanted her up and walking. He'd be in shortly to sign off on her discharge.

"Maggie found out that Hobart's in a room down the hall," said Linc. "You might be able to pop in and see him if you're up to it."

Ally's face lit up. "Sure," she said. "Will you walk with me?"

They heard him before they saw him.

"Stop! At once! You have entered my chambers once again, uninvited. Poking, probing. Begone with you, wench!"

"Mr. Castlebury, please. You're in a hospital, and I'm doing my job."

"Come no closer. And, if you please, call me 'Hobart' or call me 'Hobart the Great'. I am a brilliant master of the stage, as you should well know."

"And I am the dour head nurse on this floor."

Ally and Linc had been standing outside the door, listening. Ally tried to suppress a laugh. She stuck her head in the door. "I'm so glad to see you're back to your normal brash self, oh 'brilliant master of the stage'."

Hobart turned toward her and grinned. "Aha! My fiery redhead! Cheeky and impertinent as ever. Come over here."

Ally looked at the nurse. "May I have a couple of minutes with him?"

"Sweetie, you may have all day with him...Please." She walked out.

Ally walked over to the bed and took his hand. "How are you doing?" she asked

"Better than you, I can see."

"Yeah, that," she said, touching her cheek.

"Erik Reno...my would-be son. Foulest of the foul."

"I know."

"He was drugging me, you know. All along."

Ally nodded and took the chair beside his bed. They talked until Maggie finally came in. "The doctor's ready to examine you," she said.

"Hobart, I'd love to stay and visit longer, but I have to go. Hopefully, when we're both out of here, we can get together again. Oh, and try to be kind to the nurses and doctors while you're here. You've already earned a reputation on this floor as the patient from hell."

He laughed. "That's the reputation I have to maintain. These nurses love it," he said. "Let's negotiate."

"Negotiate?"

"Come here," he said. Motioning for Ally to lower her head, he whispered, "If you can get me another of those secret-recipe Caribbean key lime pies, I will be the lapdog for that ill-tempered head shrew of this floor."

"Deal," said Ally. "My best friend happens to be owner of the bistro from which that pie came. But, if you get a bad report, the deal is off."

As she was walking away, she turned back and added, "You might fool others with that crusty exterior, but I know who you are inside."

Ally was in bed when Linc and Dana arrived at the McGuire house at two o'clock to get her statement.

"As soon as she got home, she got in the shower," said Ann. "Must have been in there for forty-five minutes. I got her to eat some scrambled eggs and toast, then she went to bed and she's been there ever since. I tried to get her up, but…The hospital said she might be groggy from the meds but all that should have worn off by now."

"Do you mind if I go in and talk to her?" asked Linc. " I have a few things to go over with her anyway before we start."

Ann led him to the bedroom, then left them alone. Ally was under the covers with her back to the door.

"Ally?" Linc spoke softly from the doorway. When she didn't respond, he went over and sat on the edge of her bed. He'd brought her phone and saw the charger on her nightstand. He reached over to plug it in and noticed the little purple bear he'd left on her tray at the hospital. His card was standing open beside it. He smiled.

"Hey," he whispered, touching Ally's shoulder.

She slowly rolled over toward him, exposing the right side of her face, which was even more swollen and redder than earlier. "Hey," she said back.

"Ouch," he said, getting a close up look at her cheek. "Does it hurt?"

"Yeah. The pain pills are wearing off. I'm trying not to take more. Especially after seeing what they did to Hobart."

"You know what I think?" asked Linc.

"What?"

"I think you need a hug. Come here," he said, patting the space beside him on the edge of the bed.

Ally groaned but eased herself up into a sitting position and slid over. Linc wrapped his arm around her. "Seriously, how are you doing?" he asked.

She shook her head back and forth. "How could I be so stupid, Linc?"

"Ally, you're not stupid. Why would you think that?"

"I thought George was a nice person. He wasn't even George. He was Erik Reno, a murderer, and I walked right into his lair. You said you didn't trust him, and I didn't listen to you. I'm sorry."

"Nothing to be sorry about. Erik Reno is a brilliant actor. He was trained by one of the great masters of the stage, Hobart Castlebury himself. He fooled a lot of people."

"But not you."

"Ally, you were brave," said Linc. "I can't tell you how proud I am of you. I heard that you put up a real fight. Reno has battle scars to show for it."

Ally grinned. "I was in survival mode."

"And, Officer Dempsey said your first words to him were your concerns for Hobart back at the mansion. Do you know, when I went in, I found him sitting on his cot in that cellar room waiting for you because you told him you'd be back for him."

Ally teared up. "I wanted him to know I wasn't leaving him."

Linc turned sideways, facing her. "Now, before we go out there," he said, "your parents want to know if they can sit in. It's up to you. If there are details you wouldn't feel comfortable talking about in front of them, we can do this in private."

"You mean like, was I...? You mean did he...?" She trailed off.

Linc couldn't bring himself to ask. He continued looking at her and waited.

She cast her eyes down and spoke softly. "He had his hands on me and his face was inches from mine. He was saying he loved me." She shuddered. "He had come to take me upstairs. I knew what that meant, and I wasn't going to let it happen." She looked at Linc. "I would rather have died. That's when I kneed him in the groin and whacked him with the table leg and made a run for it."

Linc smiled slightly and patted her on the knee. "I am so proud of you," he told her again. "Now, come on, let's get up and get this over with. I hear your parents and Maggie and Mac are planning a birthday dinner in your honor tonight."

"Oh no," she objected, shaking her head. "I don't want to see anyone."

"Just family, they said."

"Will you be here?"

"Maggie invited me, but it's up to you. If you want me to be here, I will."

Ally squeezed his hand. "I do," she said.

Linc arrived at six o'clock for Ally's birthday dinner carrying a dozen red roses in a vase from Dockside Station. He hadn't had time to shop for the birthday gift he had in mind, but he didn't want to arrive empty-handed.

Mac was grilling ribeyes on the patio and Tim was standing beside him talking golf. Maggie and Ann were working in the kitchen, and Ally was curled up in one of the oversized wicker chairs on the veranda. Linc set the flowers on the outdoor dining table and took the chair next to her.

"Doin' okay?" he asked.

"Just tired," she replied. "Having to relive that nightmare today to answer all those questions...I know you and Dana and the others are just doing your jobs, but it's tough. Now that I'm decompressing, it seems more frightening than when it was happening. Does that make sense?"

"You did great. And what your describing is a very natural response. "

Tim walked past and into the kitchen to grab another beer. "Ann," they heard him say to his wife, "can't you ask Ally to put on something more appropriate. I don't think she should be parading around in mixed company with her bed clothes on."

"She's fine," Ann responded. "She comfortable, and I don't want to embarrass her."

"Good grief," huffed Ally, who was wearing her black lounging pants and a snug-fitting gold VCU Rams T-shirt, the outfit that she'd had on all day.

Linc leaned across from his chair to hers and whispered, "I think you look adorable in that outfit."

She smiled. "Are you flirting with me, Agent Stryker?"

He nodded and smiled back. "Guilty," he admitted.

At the dinner table, Mac popped open a bottle of champagne. "Before we celebrate, however, let's give a prayer of thanks." While they held hands around the table, Mac expressed gratitude for the resolution to the nightmare they'd been through, for Ally's safe return, and for an end to the presence of evil that had been lurking in their midst.

They all chimed in with "Amen," and Mac said, "Now let's celebrate."

Over dinner of shrimp cocktail, fresh garden salad, baked potatoes with chive butter, and Mac's grilled steaks, Ally told them about her conversation with Hobart that morning.

"What's going to happen to him?" she asked. He told me he wants to go back to tutoring and mentoring young people in the performing arts."

"I'm working on something," said Maggie. They all looked at her. "Don't ask," she said. "I don't have the details ironed out yet."

Earlier in the day, Fern had sent over a Jamaican Rum Cake that Clover had baked especially for the occasion. While they ate dessert, Ally thought about the other birthday gifts she'd received earlier that day. The McGuires had given her a Nikon FX camera like the one Maggie used, a top choice of many photojournalists. Her parents were giving her Ann's two-year-old Volvo because Ann wanted a new model.

Ally thought of the little plush bear and hand-written card Linc had given her when she knew he had no opportunity to go shopping and smiled. The personal message that came from his heart meant as much to her, or maybe more than, anything else.

After dinner as the others were going inside, Ally said she'd be in shortly. When she and Linc were alone on the veranda, he invited her over to sit beside him in the double wicker chair. Curling up and laying her head on his shoulder, Ally felt safe, truly safe, for the first time since being rescued. They sat quietly for a long time.

Linc broke the silence. "I know you're processing a lot," he said "If you want to talk, I'm a good listener."

"I was thinking about that night," she said, "when I was lying on my cot in that windowless, dank, smelly room. I thought it was the end for me."

"I'm so sorry that you had to go through that," said Linc. "I can't even imagine how scared you must have been."

"Scared, but also sad. I felt terrible that my parents were going through this. I thought about my future, my family and friends, my career, the life I wouldn't have. I thought about you."

Linc gave her a squeeze.

"I didn't expect to come out of this alive, Linc. That Erik-monster, whoever he is, talked about taking me away with him. He told me he would be anyone I wanted him to be. He would give me anything I wanted. The thought of him touching me was so repulsive I knew I'd rather be dead."

Linc kissed the top of her head.

"I was really afraid he was going to kill Hobart. He said we couldn't take him with us. I played along and told him if he did anything to Hobart, he'd have to kill me too. But I also knew I'd never voluntarily go with him, regardless. If I had the chance, and I prayed I would, I'd run for it, I'd fight like hell, I wouldn't go down quietly…But, honestly, Linc, I didn't think I had much of a chance."

Ally was making doodling motions on Linc's chest with her index finger while she talked. "Can I tell you a secret?" she asked.

"Of course."

"I mean a real personal secret?"

"I'm good at keeping secrets. You can tell me anything."

"When I was in that place…thinking of you and our kiss the night before, our first kiss…" She paused. "I was thinking…" She choked back tears. "I was thinking, life could be so unfair…" Tears started running down her cheeks. Linc gently wiped them away. "I was thinking…" she sniffled. "I thought I'd never get to know where that kiss might take us. I would never get to experience our romance, or maybe love-making, or even if it was meant to be."

Linc lifted Ally's face to his and they kissed. Unlike their first kiss, which had been exciting and full of promise, this one was emotionally-charged in a different way. With her face bruised and swollen and taped together and with nightmarish thoughts, she felt broken and insecure. She pressed her body against his and clung to the safety of his embrace.

Linc's own raw emotions were hitting him in the gut. Since seeing Ally in the hospital, he'd felt an intense hatred and anger toward that lowlife Reno who'd done this to her. He felt Ally's heart beating against his chest and heard her low sobs. All he could do right now was hold her against the demons she was battling.

It was a sobering moment.

It was almost midnight. When he'd first got back to the lodge an hour ago, Linc had walked along the lakefront and past the campgrounds. Thinking. Now back in his room, he sat in the arm-chair looking out the window at the lake. Still thinking. Processing all that had happened.

It was complicated. Some might see him as a tough crime fight-er, but deep down he was a romantic. When Ally went missing, he was crazy, over-the-top, out of his mind, worried about her. He had feelings he'd never experienced before. He'd acted recklessly, pre-pared to break all the rules and possibly jeopardize the case he'd been working on. He didn't need to ask himself why. He knew why. Because she meant that much to him.

Ally was so genuine. She had poured her heart out to him to-night, speaking of her private and most deeply felt emotions, her anticipation of their love-making. When it happened, and he knew it would because the mutual attraction was too strong and the de-sire for intimacy too intense for it not to, he wanted it to be the ex-perience she had dreamed about when she was lying on that filthy cot in that gawdawful, smelly root cellar believing she was going to die. He wanted it to be an occasion that would restore her belief that goodness and beauty still existed in the world.

He reread Ally's text to Fern. Before all this she was so happy, so alive, so full of expectation. He wanted to show her that she had a right to "tingle" with excitement when she was touched, not cower in fear or cringe with revulsion. She deserved nothing less.

Linc picked up his phone and texted Ally. *Are you awake?*

He waited until he saw the familiar balloon with three wavy dots, indicating someone was typing. *Yes* was the reply. He called her phone, and she immediately answered.

"Linc?" she asked. "Are you okay?"

"I'm good."

"Is anything wrong?"

Linc laughed. "Ally, everything's fine. I'm just sitting here thinking about you, and I wanted to hear your voice. I think about you all the time, you know. I'm surprised you're awake."

"Can I tell you about something? Just between you and me?"

"Of course. Are *you* all right?"

"Not really. I've been lying awake because when I close my eyes, this darkness comes over me, like an intense wave of fear. I can feel my heart pounding, and I start trembling."

"It sounds like you're having a panic attack. I'm not surprised."

"But, I can't talk to my parents about it. My father is so hyper-protective. I know he cares about me, but he wants me to go back to Roanoke with them, get therapy, and spend my summer sitting beside the pool at the country club doing nothing. That's not who I am. I don't want to go to Roanoke, and I'm afraid if they find out I'm having panic attacks, they're not going to let me out of their sight."

"What do *you* want?"

"I don't know. That's the problem. I wish I could stay here. I love working at the *Ledger*, but I'd be an object of curiosity and gossip around town and a pain in the butt to Maggie and Mac with my problems."

"You're being too hard on yourself, Ally. Maggie and Mac love you. I don't think they'd ever see you as a problem. But, just a couple of thoughts...First, therapy sounds like a good idea. It's not a sign of weakness. You've already taken the first step by admitting to yourself and to me that you're not okay. Second, I think getting away from Union Gap may be what you need. But do you know what else you need?"

"What?"

"You need to know, I love the darn heck out of you."

"I feel that way too."

"So, here's another option. Come back to Richmond. You have an apartment there. If you feel like it, you can take summer classes at VCU, get a jump start on fall. Or, if you prefer, I have a spare bedroom you're welcome to. You can spend your summer sitting beside the pool at my apartment complex."

"Very funny."

"I'm not asking for a commitment. I'd just like to have you close by. I want to spend time with you. Isn't that what you want?"

"I did before this."

"Before what?"

"Before I got messed up."

"I'm not thinking in those terms. My feelings haven't changed because of what happened to you. But, it's your decision. No pressure. Just give it some thought."

Thirty-Nine

riday morning Maggie and Mac were at the breakfast table looking over their copies of the *Lakeside Ledger*, which had just been delivered. For the first time since they'd started the weekly paper, it was a day late. They'd debated how to report the big events of the week.

Before Maggie left the hospital the previous morning, Ally had asked her if she could be kept out of the news. But, keeping her name out was not an option. From the earlier accounts of her being reported missing, then of her being held captive in the old root cellar of Stonewall Mansion, and finally her assault on the trail, Ally was central to the arrest of alleged serial killer Erik Reno. Maggie made the decision that to the extent she was able, she would stick to the original police reports in her story, with the least mention of Ally as possible. Her lead paragraph read:

> *Darrell Dempsey, a Security Officer at The Gallery at Union Gap, is being hailed as a hometown hero this morning. Dempsey was instrumental in apprehending Erik Reno, aka Levi Eriksson, during an attack by the alleged serial killer on a local woman in the gated community. He restrained Reno and held him until authorities arrived.*

Maggie went on to identify the woman as the missing Allyson Murphy, an intern at the *Lakeside Ledger* and houseguest of Gallery residents and owners of the paper, Mac and Maggie McGuire. She mentioned that Ally had been held by Reno for thirty-two hours in Stonewall Mansion, along with the mansion's owner Hobart Castlebury. Beyond that, the article focused on the arrest and a re-cap of the two murders. Reno had been charged with two counts of murder in the deaths of Ruby Rosa and Gianna Talone, and charges were also pending in connection with holding Hobart Castlebury captive and the kidnapping of and later assault on Ally.

Other news media were sensationalizing the story, playing loosely with the facts about what had been going on in the big house and the role of Erik Reno in disguise as George Rothman.

For a hard-hitting investigative reporter like Maggie, getting the inside scoop on a major news story and having her own news-paper to report it would have once been a no-brainer. She would have run with it with little regard for who she was trampling on. But, having the story dropped on her doorstep within her personal orbit, it took on a new dimension. Ally's wishes were more import-ant than any story.

Ally was humbled by the outpouring of support she was re-ceiving. Cards and flowers, emails and texts had been arriving con-tinuously. Now, she was propped up in bed, reading her copy of the *Ledger*, which Maggie had brought in to her along with a cup of Mountain Mama Blend.

She'd only scanned the front page story. The photo of Erik Reno, handcuffed and being escorted into the Lake County Sheriff's Department, sickened her. The picture of Darrell Dempsey with the caption "Hometown Hero" made her smile. She said a silent prayer of thanks for this under-appreciated guy who'd saved her life.

She turned to the editorial page and read Mac's weekly com-mentary, which he'd titled "A Day of Thanks."

In the days and weeks ahead, we will have time to reflect on and analyze the bizarre series of events that have taken place in Union Gap. Today we pause. Here at the Lakeside Ledger, *we are simply thankful. The alleged serial killer Erik Reno is now in custody, and our Ally has been safely returned to her family and our community.*

We owe a tremendous debt of gratitude to Darrell Dempsey, a security officer in the Gallery, for his heroic role in this. We offer our sincere thanks to you, our readers and residents of Union Gap, for your tips, prayers, and well-wishes.

And on a final note, we offer our apologies and appreciate your understanding for the delay in getting our hometown newspaper out this week.

Ally closed the paper and started to lay it aside when she saw the picture at the bottom of Page One. The cutline read, "It's a Betty!" Bumper Presgraves was holding Union Gap's new mascot, flanked by Merle Smirkley, and JD Stockman.

Ally reopened the paper and went to the inside spread. The freelancers and Sarah Sanderson had done a good job putting the Memorial Day celebration together. The photos were great, the captions were clever, and the recaps of the events were well-written.

Memorial Day, thought Ally. *That seems like eons ago.*

Linc and Dana were in the briefing room at the Union Gap Police Station for a one o'clock conference call with their boss, Colin Hynes. Linc had gone off on a personal errand earlier, after which he and his partner grabbed a quick lunch at Jack's Pub.

"You know, don't you, Stryker," said Dana, "you could have jeopardized this whole case?"

"I know." Linc looked at his partner. "What are you going to put in your report?"

"The facts."

"There are facts, and there are extenuating circumstances... Give me a heads up of what to expect."

"Just the facts," said Dana. "Our missing person, Ally, escaped after being held captive in that mansion. She was being pursued by alleged serial killer Erik Reno, who was brought down by the security officer Darrell Dempsey."

"Right," said Linc. "No FBI involvement there."

"We had new, but inconclusive, information that Ally might be in the big house. You decided to go over and have a 'friendly chat' with George Rothman. You found the back door open and heard calls for help coming from inside. You went in and found a drugged Hobart Castlebury in an underground room that once served as a root cellar where he was being held against his will and where Ally had been held captive."

"That's it?"

"What? You want more?"

"No," Linc said. "That pretty much covers it."

"But...you and I both know there's this matter of emotions. Your emotions. With the capture of Reno, and the information we got from Ally to help with our case, I'm good. This time."

"Thanks, Dana."

"Looks like the FBI was outmaneuvered by that little security guard."

"No regrets here. I know that if I'd gone in earlier and found Ally and encountered Reno, I would have given him a lot more than a tasing. I know this could have ended badly."

"Linc?"

"Yeah?"

"Ally's special. I can understand why you feel about her the way you do."

Linc nodded. "When are you heading back to Richmond?"

"This evening. Right after the recognition ceremony for Dempsey and the press conference. Val and I have plans this weekend with Ava."

Valerie was Dana's wife, and Ava was their adopted daughter. Dana pulled out her phone and passed it to Linc with her photo gallery open.

"Ava's in Toddler Tumbling, and tomorrow's parents' day. We get to watch a performance."

Linc was scrolling through the pictures, smiling at the shots of the little girl with curly blond hair. Val was a veterinarian, specializing in livestock, and they lived on a small farm outside the city. The pictures showed Ava out and about on the farm. She was sitting in the straw holding a baby goat, feeding it from a bottle. She was in the chicken coop wearing knee-high rubber boots, dropping handfuls of feed from a bucket and laughing at the chickens as they followed her. She was in the saddle on her miniature horse with a cowgirl hat on.

"She's such a sweetheart," said Linc. "I'm envious."

"Her birthday party's in two weeks. She's going to be two. You'll have to come."

"I wouldn't miss it."

The conference table phone rang, and Dana put it on speaker.

"I've seen your reports," said Hynes. "Nice work. The question I have is, when are you two coming back to the office? Stryker, are you still on leave, or back on leave, or not on leave, or what?"

Linc spoke up. "I'll be back in the office Monday and get all this leave business worked out."

Forty

The mayor had scheduled a ceremony at four o'clock to honor Darrell Dempsey for his heroics in the capture of Erik Reno. Of course Ally was going to attend. But, that meant she had to change from her comfortable lounging clothes that her father deemed inappropriate for mixed company into something more presentable. She looked through her "cute little short sundresses," as Maggie referred to them, and selected one that was a favorite because the vivid Kelly green color matched her eyes.

She showered, washed her hair, and sat down in front of her makeup mirror. The face that looked back at her was blotched with the ugly bruising and swelling on her right cheek and the cut under her eye. She tried covering the bruise with foundation, but it just looked like a feeble attempt to hide a big ugly bruise with makeup. *The heck with it*, she thought, and washed the makeup off. This was what that monster, Erik Reno, did to her. She couldn't make it go away with makeup.

Arriving with her parents and Maggie and Mac, Ally met up with Linc and Dana outside the town hall. The ceremony for Darrell was being held in the media room, and would be followed by a press conference for only a limited number of journalists and photographers due to the size of the room.

They were a little early. Ally wanted to stop by the fish tank and show her parents the new town mascot. Most people she knew would think it silly to keep a largemouth bass as a mascot, but Ally thought it captured the character of Union Gap and the spirit of the people perfectly.

She'd proofread Happy's article about the largemouth bass mascot contest and now knew all about keeping "Big Mouth Betty" in an aquarium. She started telling her parents about all the regulations. As people started filing into the media room Ann suggested perhaps they should go in now. Ally figured she was boring her parents talking about the feeding of largemouth bass and cleaning the massive amounts of waste they produced in the tanks.

Seats had been reserved for them in the front row, just in front of the stage. As they entered the room, Ally walked close to Linc and kept her head down, avoiding eye contact with everyone.

Mayor Mervil Turnbull was at the podium checking the microphone. People started taking seats on the stage behind him. Ally recognized Lake County Sheriff Linwood Farley and Union Gap Police Chief Odell Hawkins. Darrell Dempsey was in his security officer uniform. He glanced at her and gave a slight nod. She smiled in return.

The mayor, who preferred that everyone call him Mayor Merv, was his usual jovial self. Ally could see he intended to make this a celebratory occasion. After a hearty welcome and a few introductory remarks about unsung heroes, he asked Darrell Dempsey to step forward. Another man, who had been introduced as Harley Larson, President of Allegheny Security Services and Darrell's supervisor, jumped from his seat and accompanied his employee to the podium. While Darrell stood erect and serious, Larson grinned broadly at the cameras.

"This young man," Mayor Merv began, "performed an act of

great bravery." He gave the account of how Darrell, after hearing the screams then seeing an assault in progress on the trail where he was patrolling, jumped into action and restrained the perpetrator, not knowing that the culprit was Erik Reno, wanted for two homicides in Union Gap.

"At this time it is my great pleasure to present Officer Dempsey with the Mayor's Award for Heroism." He stepped behind Darrell and hung a medal attached to a red, white, and blue ribbon around his neck. He handed Darrell a gold trophy in the shape of a star, and shook his hand. He said he was having a plate engraved, which would be attached to the trophy as soon as it was ready.

"Now, I believe our police chief has a few words to say. Odell, would you come forward?"

Hawkins told how Darrell had for some time expressed interest in becoming a police officer and had talked to him about the challenges he was facing getting into the police academy because of his height.

"I've been working with him," said Hawkins, "letting him know that qualities like courage and character are more important than size. I'm proud to say he's been working hard on developing those characteristics. I believe I can now say with absolute authority that Officer Dempsey has displayed the necessary grit, and I intend to write a glowing letter of recommendation to the academy on his behalf."

The audience clapped and rose for a standing ovation. Darrell puffed his chest out and held his head high.

"Now," said Mayor Merv, "I wonder if Ms. Murphy would like to say a few words." He looked at her in the front row. "Ally?"

Ally was caught off guard, suddenly dreading getting up in front of this crowd. She shook her head no, and turned her face toward Linc, eyes down.

He put his arm around her. "It's okay," he whispered.

Mac rose from his seat and held up an index finger, signaling to the mayor to give him a minute. He knelt in front of Ally and they whispered to each other.

Mac went up on the stage and took the mic. "Ally is still recovering from her injuries," he said, "and a bit camera shy." He looked at Ally in the front row and winked. She offered a weak smile in return. "She and Officer Dempsey are old pals on the trail, and she has said all along that he will make a terrific police officer. She's thrilled that now he's being given the chance to prove it and asked me to extend her best wishes to him. In our eyes, he's already proven it. There's no downplaying the fact that Officer Dempsey saved Ally's life, and we can't thank him enough for giving her back to us." Mac's voice was cracking and he handed the mic back to the mayor then turned to Darrell and gave the security officer a hug and pat on the back.

Mayor Merv said it was time to move on. "I know the media have questions."

"Mr. Mayor?" Harley Larson, still standing beside Darrell, was asking to be recognized. "I'd like to say a few words about this fine employee of mine."

"Umm, okay, sure, I guess," said the mayor, unprepared for this ad hoc change to his agenda.

Larson took the mic. "At Allegheny Security Services, we hire only the best and the brightest, just like Officer Dempsey here." He began tooting his own horn and talking about his company's achievements in what sounded like a commercial endorsement.

The mayor was perturbed. The audience was looking bored and tuning out this self-absorbed speaker. Mayor Merv looked at his watch. He interrupted Larson and said that due to time constraints they would need to move on to taking questions.

During a five minute break after the recognition ceremony, Ally told her companions she didn't want to stay for the press conference. She wanted to stop in and see Fern, Kyle, and Happy before going home. They decided they'd all go. Maggie was pleased to see their freelance photographer Bradley taking pictures. She handed him her tape recorder and asked him to record the session for her.

It had been agreed beforehand that Dana would be the one to answer questions, if any, on behalf of the FBI. She walked outside with them to say good bye because she'd be heading back to Richmond right afterward. On the sidewalk, they were immediately confronted by a gaggle of reporters. Ally hid her face in Linc's chest, trying to avoid their looks and deflect their questions.

"No cameras," shouted Dana, flashing her badge. Some of them ignored her, and reporters started calling out to Ally.

"Ms. Murphy, can you comment?"

"Ally, what was it like being held captive in that old house?"

"Were you in a relationship with Erik Reno?"

Dana went back inside, and the others continued on along the Lakewalk ignoring the reporters and photographers dogging their steps. At the Mean Beans Bistro, the entourage tried to follow them inside. Mac attempted to block their entrance.

Fern, who was just setting up for the evening's five o'clock Wined Down, saw the commotion and went to the door and announced, "Sorry, we're closed." After she herded them out of the entryway, she locked the door, then flipped the sign to "Closed" and pulled down the window shades. She approached Ally, and the two embraced. "I've been so worried about you," said Fern. "Oh my god, your beautiful face. He did this to you?" She teared up.

With a spur-of-the-moment decision that Wined Down would

be canceled, Fern invited everyone to help themselves to the wine and the cheese platters she'd set out. Maggie went through the adjoining door to Books Galore to ask if Happy and Kyle might like to close up and come over. "Of course we would," Happy replied.

When they entered the Mean Beans, with the little terrier Pippy barking and wagging excitedly, Happy hugged Ally. Then she looked around. Seeing everyone assembled, she loudly announced, "We have a surprise!" She went back to the bookstore and returned with Hobart Castlebury, who waltzed in beside her. He was missing the Phantom mask and costume, but he knew the words: *"Why so silent, good monsieurs? / Did you think that I had left you for good? / Have you missed me, good monsieurs?"*

Hobart took a bow and everyone clapped. For those who didn't know all the details, Maggie explained how Erik Reno had commandeered the performance of the Phantom from Hobart and stolen the stage at the Sunset Social through trickery and deceit.

Ally couldn't believe Hobart's transformation now that he was free from the influence of the drugs. He wasn't the walking zombie she'd encountered along the trail and spent thirty-two hours locked up with. She asked, "Hobart are you staying here in Union Gap?"

Hobart looked at Happy. She cleared her throat. "Maggie came to me yesterday and told me of Hobart's dilemma. Stonewall Mansion is closed off, for how long we don't know. Maggie suggested that perhaps I may be able to help out."

Happy had a small efficiency apartment the O'Hurleys had added on as nurse's quarters when Liam's ALS was advancing and he needed around-the-clock in-home care and where Kyle had stayed before he got his own place.

"I've agreed that we'll give it a go. Hobart can stay there while Stonewall Mansion is cordoned off, then we'll see. I'm looking forward to having his company and picking this man's brilliant mind about Shakespeare, Hamlet, McBeth, and anything else if he feels inclined to enlighten me."

Ally asked, "Hobart, are you planning to return to Stonewall Mansion when you're able to?"

"Not just return, my fair maiden. Perhaps you've not seen the glorious ballroom or the massive dining room sitting empty and collecting dust. Imagine, if you will, acting classes, recitals, community performances. That was my intent before…well, you know. And is now, more than ever."

Ally took both his hands in hers and smiled. "I've not seen those rooms, but I can envision it, all of it. And, Hobart…thanks for not referring to me as the 'fiery redhead'."

"I'm on my best behavior, remember?"

Fern disappeared into the kitchen and returned with a gift for Hobart.

"Is that what I hope it is?" he asked.

"Yep. Clover's award winning Caribbean Key Lime Pie with coconut crust and all her secret ingredients."

"Fern" said Ally, "how did you know about this little agreement between me and Hobart?"

"Oh, I heard it through the grapevine. Hobart told you, you told Maggie, Maggie told Happy, Happy told Kyle, Kyle told me, I told Clover…And, Voila! Small town, isn't it?"

"Well, Hobart," said Ally, "I guess this means you've been behaving yourself."

"Yes ma'am. All that brusque behavior? Just for show."

They all laughed.

"Hobart," said Fern, "that pie is all yours. You don't have to share it."

"Not a chance of that."

Ally announced she had something to say. "While we're all

together, I might as well tell you now. This is something I've not told anyone yet. Actually, I only just decided it for sure myself."

They all waited.

"As much as I'd like to," Ally began, "I can't stay here in Union Gap. The stares, the questions, the cameras, the hounding...like what we just experienced walking over here."

Fern brought her a glass of white wine, and she took a sip.

"I never wanted to be the news. I want to be the reporter covering the stories. Now I am the story. I've decided to go back home to Roanoke for a few days with my parents, then return to Richmond. If I take summer classes I should be able to ease up on my coursework next semester and finish out my senior year with the credits I need to graduate at the end of the fall semester."

She looked at the McGuires. "I know I'm cutting my internship short, but Maggie, I'm hoping you'll give me a good report for the credits I need. I can't thank you and Mac enough for the opportunity and guidance you've given me, working at the *Ledger*. And, I still plan to write that article for your feature on Stonewall Mansion. My roommate Monica won't be back until fall, and I'll have our apartment to myself to work without interruption this summer."

She looked around. "Gosh, I'm going to miss all of you. Happy...Thank you for including me as a member of the team for all our escapades: 'Team Scheme', 'Bridging the Gap', the Sunset Social...I hope you do decide to run for mayor. You'll be perfect."

She turned to Fern. "Saying good-bye to you is probably the hardest. You're like the sister I've always wanted, someone I can laugh with and talk to about silly girl stuff and about serious stuff. I'm going to miss the time I've spent with you and Kyle."

Fern had tears running down her face. "I'm going to miss you too. Thank you for all you've done, especially helping with Magic. I hope we'll always be 'sisters'."

"Absolutely," Ally promised.

She looked around. "I'm not saying good-bye, because I'll be back. I love you all."

Maggie spoke up. "Ally, you know Mac and I have a room for you whenever you decide to come back for a visit. I want to say something, though, reporter-to-reporter."

Ally looked at her and waited.

"Of course," Maggie began, "I respect your decision to leave. I understand that you don't want to be the story. But, I hope you'll consider writing a first-person account of all that's happened."

Ally started to protest.

"Just hear me out," Maggie continued. "I'm not going into details here, because I agreed not to disclose anything that was said in your interview with Linc and Dana yesterday. But, it was nothing less than remarkable, the way you got Erik Reno to open up to you. You used all of your skills as a reporter. And, you got the scoop."

"Yeah, but..."

"Ally, eventually that story, or pieces of it, is going to leak out. It may be accurately reported, maybe not. You'll be portrayed any way the media chooses. Usually, that means whatever gets the highest ratings. Ally, this is your story. It should be told by you. Don't let some ruthless reporter, like me, take the credit for 'Breaking News'. You were there. You did the interview. You got into that monster's head. You're a damn good reporter and an excellent writer. If you want to be a journalist, you can do this."

"I hadn't thought of it that way."

"But, you will? Consider it?"

"I will. Thanks."

When he found a corner and a moment to be alone with his daughter, Tim had a few comments of his own to deliver.

"Ally, I thought we agreed that you'd spend the summer with us. With the trauma you've been through, I don't think you're ready to be alone in your apartment. You need time off, away from work and school and the bad memories."

"Dad, if I did that, I would be spending the summer with nothing to do, nothing except relive the bad memories. I've thought about this. You and Mom both work full time, you have your friends and your lives in Roanoke. I need to work on my life, finishing college and starting my career and putting this episode behind me. And, I won't be alone. Linc will be there."

"That's another matter I wanted to talk to you about. We've all seen how dependent on him you've become. You're very vulnerable now. I'm concerned this may be a rebound relationship and…"

"Dad, stop right there! Linc and I have a special connection, and we're going to be spending time together."

"Do you know how worried your mother and I have been about you? Don't you care how we feel?"

"I'm sorry you feel the way you do. But I'm not going to be your pampered pet. I'm not trying to hurt you. It's about what I need for myself. I was hoping you'd be happy for me."

"You're making a big mistake. You're the one who's going to get hurt."

Ally threw up her hands and walked away.

Forty-One

The horde outside the Mean Beans had dissipated. Ally told her parents that she was going to stay on the Lakewalk for a while with Linc. After they left she stood outside, staring across the water at Stonewall Mansion. It was dark and looked desolate. She shivered. Linc took her hand and turned her away. They walked along the waterfront.

"So," said Ally, "about my decision…I didn't intend to catch you off guard. I'd been thinking about what you asked me to consider about Richmond. But I only just decided after the way we were mobbed on our walk over here."

"I'm glad that you're going to be back in Richmond. I like the idea of you being close by. I want to spend time with you, a lot of time."

She squeezed his hand. "Okay, but just so you know, I want to stay in my own apartment. I need to be self-sufficient."

"I get it. But I'm also concerned about you being alone. You're a survivor of a serious trauma, and I can tell you're not completely okay."

"You're right. I'm damaged and broken, inside and out. Look at me."

"What I see is a spunky fighter with a big heart and dreams and determination. You're not damaged and broken, but those feelings are normal. PTSD is real. When you get to Richmond, I hope you'll be open to therapy and not close yourself off from others."

"I just don't want to be coddled. I want to be whole again. If you and I are going to have a relationship, I want us to be equal partners."

"I know you think you're not. I don't see you that way. I just hope you'll let me help you heal." He squeezed her hand. "You're special. We'll get through this. Let's just not force it. Let it evolve."

"Agreed."

"Different subject...I have your birthday present."

Ally gave him a questioning look. "Another one? Linc?"

"Um-hum. It's in my room. Shall we go get it?"

He waited for her response. She didn't say anything but squeezed his hand, and they walked to the lodge.

Linc had gone to Goldman's Jewelers in Dominion Mills that morning. In his room, he handed Ally a small box, wrapped in pale blue iridescent foil and tied with a bow of silver ribbon. She opened the box and took out a necklace with a delicate gold heart pendant encircling a white freshwater pearl.

"My birthstone. It's beautiful, Linc." She put her arms around his neck. "Thank you." She lifted her face to his. They met with a gentle, soft touching of lips. Then Linc pulled back.

"Ally," he said, "do you trust me?"

Ally looked at him. "Should I not?"

"After what you experienced, I can understand you having issues with trust. I would never hurt you. You have to believe that."

"I do. I know you're not him, not like him."

"Do you remember what you told me about our first kiss? How you were afraid you'd never get to find out where it might take us?"

Ally nodded.

"Are you ready to find out?" he asked.

"I want that more than anything."

Linc took the necklace from her hand and turned her around

to face the mirror. From behind, he slipped it around her neck and clasped it in the back, pulling her long auburn hair out from beneath the chain. He stood in back of her as she touched it, admiring it in the mirror.

Then her hand went from the pendant to the gash beneath her eye and the unsightly bruise covering her right cheek where Erik had hit her. What was reddish yesterday was now turning a hideous shade of blackish blue.

Linc gently took her hand and held it away from her face. He put his own face against hers and looked at her in the mirror.

"You're beautiful," he said softly.

Ally started to protest, but as she looked back at him in the mirror, she was mesmerized by his hazel eyes as they stared so intently into her own. She hadn't noticed before that they were spangled with green flecks that seemed to dance. She felt an instant connection.

"Do you know..." he whispered in her ear. "According to mythology, pearls are considered dewdrops from heaven that fall into the sea. They're caught by shellfish in the first rays of the rising sun during a period of full moon. And...they represent a new beginning."

As he was talking, Linc was slowly unzipping Ally's dress in the back.

She closed her eyes, held her breath, and savored the moment.

Linc kissed her neck as he slipped the dress off her shoulders and let it fall to the floor.

Every nerve in Ally's body was tingling with excitement.

PART II
Six Months Later
December 2017

Forty-Two

A lly took Linc's hand as they pulled up in front of the gaze-bo at Union Square. "This is so exciting," she said. Beneath the permanent sign of "Welcome to Union Gap" with its trademark largemouth bass logo, a banner was suspended:

An Old Virginia Christmas
HMN Original Movie Premiere December 16, 2017

Before they turned left into the entrance of the LakeView Lodge, they sat for a few moments to let it all sink in. It was a big deal for the little town.

When Ally and Linc left Union Gap six months before in the wake of the "Erik-monster nightmare," as Ally referred to it, the screenplay was in the works but had been largely forgotten by the people in town.

"So," Linc had said when they were driving from Richmond today, "refresh my memory about the origins of the movie and the local connection."

"It's a pretty amazing story," said Ally. "It started with 'An Old Virginia Christmas', a song written by a Virginia couple. Apparently, they were high school sweethearts, and the song is based on their experience of growing up in a small town, not unlike Union Gap, then each going their own way but always nostalgic for their home-town at Christmas."

"And, how does Hobart Castlebury fit into all this?"

Ally continued: "Somewhere along the way, the couple, I can't remember their names, showed their song to Hobart and Ruby, who loved it. So, along with Erik Reno—sorry I have to bring him into this conversation—they wrote an award-winning Broadway play based on the lyrics. Then, a Los Angeles screenwriter approached them about turning it into a film for the Holiday Movie Network."

"And what's the local connection?"

"Ruby and Erik were working on the screenplay, and had rented Stonewall Mansion as a quiet place to work while Hobart stayed in New York taking care of business. That's when Ruby was found dead and Erik disappeared."

"But," Linc asked, "the movie plans continued?"

"Right. HMN continued production of the movie, *An Old Virginia Christmas*, after the death of Ruby and later the arrest of Erik for her murder. From what Happy told me, at some point after we left town, the producer and a team came to Union Gap to meet with Hobart and found the setting perfect for some of the movie's outdoor scenes."

The town was going all out to make the local showing of the movie a large scale celebration, coinciding with the Union Gap's annual Christmas events. This wasn't surprising considering that Happy O'Hurley was now acting mayor because Mervil Turnbull was recovering from open heart surgery. Happy was the quintessential events coordinator.

A special viewing of the Saturday afternoon premier was by invitation only in the downstairs theater room of the civic center, which had an 85-inch flat screen television and seating for 60.

This would be followed by a series of events. A black tie gala was being hosted by Hobart Castlebury at Stonewall Mansion with a grand buffet in the massive dining room and musical performances and dancing in the newly refurbished formal ballroom. For those not lucky enough to get invitations to that event, an informal reception, open to all, was being held at the civic center.

On Friday, the eve of the premiere, there'd be the annual flotilla of decorated boats, Union Gap's version of a Christmas parade, followed by the community tree lighting ceremony at the gazebo.

Ally and Linc's arrival on Tuesday, three days before the celebrations, was planned to allow time for visiting. Ally was looking forward to that as much as the festivities.

Now as they pulled into a space in the parking lot, Ally caught Linc staring at the lodge and asked, "What are you thinking about?"

Before he could respond, she added, "Wait, don't tell me. Let me guess. I think we're both remembering the last time we were at this lodge. Am I right?"

"How could we not?" he asked, taking her hand and kissing it.

From the moment Linc had slipped the pearl pendant around Ally's neck six months ago, signifying a new beginning, it had been a magical, sensual evening, everything Ally had dreamed about and an experience that left both of them breathless. It felt right.

That night, lying with her head on his chest, Ally was thinking about the way Linc looked at her, the excitement of his touch, and how he made her feel special and protected and...

"Linc?" she'd asked softly.

"Yes?"

"Is this what it feels like to be in love?"

He didn't hesitate. "It is for me."

In that moment a new reality sank in for Ally. She was alive and in love, and she knew her life would be forever changed.

Now, before they went into the lodge, Linc asked, "Are you still sure you're okay with this? I mean coming back here?"

"I'm sure. Looking forward to it, in fact."

"And you're okay with not taking Maggie and Mac up on their invitation to stay at their house?"

Ally nodded.

When Maggie found out they were coming to town, she and Mac of course invited Ally and Linc to stay with them. Ally politely declined when she learned her parents would also be houseguests of the McGuires. Her father hadn't been supportive of her decision last June to return to Richmond with Linc instead of spending a leisurely summer in Roanoke with her family to recover from the physical and emotional trauma of her kidnapping and assault by Erik Reno.

Then, last month, when Ally and Linc spent Thanksgiving with Ally's parents, things hadn't gone well. Tim again wasn't happy with his daughter when he learned she wouldn't be going to graduate school. Instead, she had interviewed for a job with *The Washington Post*, and it looked promising. An atmosphere of friction hung over the holiday. Words were exchanged between Ally and her father, and she and Linc had cut their visit short.

Ally knew that she'd be seeing her parents during this trip, but because the tensions still remained, she felt it would be better for everyone if she and Linc didn't stay under the same roof with her parents, thus risking another confrontation.

As they walked into the lodge, the lobby was bustling with activity. In the center of the room, a 16-foot Douglas fir had been put up and was being decorated. Elsewhere, the decorating crew was assembling displays of poinsettias, wreaths, garland, and holly. Just inside the lobby entrance, a double wing easel held a display board with a personalized message welcoming members of the cast and crew and special guests to the movie premiere of *An Old Virginia Christmas*.

In an email a few days ago, Happy had told Ally of some of the changes to expect in and around the town, including the addition of a full-service restaurant in the lodge. Ally pointed to the far side of the lobby where an overhead sign for the new BB's Restaurant and Bar, with Union Gap's signature largemouth bass logo, hung over the doorway. Happy had explained that the two Bs in the restaurant name were derived from the town's yearly tradition of keeping "Billys" and "Bettys" as mascots.

With six days' worth of luggage, including outfits for all the special events, Linc had recommended they splurge and upgrade to a suite at the lodge. Opening their door and stepping inside, Ally was glad they did. The suite's spacious sitting room was tastefully furnished. There was a small kitchenette, and on the far side of the room a two-sided gas fireplace was built into the wall, the other side of which was a separate bedroom.

"Perfect," said Ally, "in case we want to invite people over."

On a table just inside the door was a floral arrangement of mini red carnations, red spray roses, white carnations, and branches of holly in a green glass bowl with a holiday bow. Beside it, a bottle of champagne was chilling in a silver ice bucket. A "Welcome Back" card read: *"We have missed you both so much! —Maggie and Mac."*

A swag bag was also on the table, a welcome gift from the town of Union Gap that had been placed in all the suites. The canvas tote was embroidered with the words "Union Gap, Virginia" above the town's largemouth bass logo, and *"An Old Virginia Christmas* 2017" below. Ally rifled through the bag and pulled out an assortment of gifts from local merchants, and promotional coupons with discounts and giveaways at various businesses around town.

Ally recalled the swag basket Team Scheme had put together and delivered to Hobart Castlebury as a welcome gift last spring after he'd moved into Stonewall Mansion. They'd called it "Stuff We All Give." The team's Bridging the Gap project had been fun and Ally now looked back on it as one of her happier times in Union Gap.

As she was telling Linc about it, her thoughts returned to the dark goings-on at Stonewall Mansion. She quickly scooped up all the freebies, put them back in the bag and set it aside. She wasn't going to dwell on those memories.

There was a raw December chill in the air. Linc had started the fireplace and was watching the glow of the natural-looking flames as warmth filled the room. Ally walked up behind him and wrapped her arms around his waist.

"It's almost five o'clock," said Linc. "Do you still want to walk down to the Mean Beans and see Fern? Or...we could just stay here and find something to do."

"Hmm...Find something to do? Hold that thought. Right now, I'm excited to see Fern and confirm our plans for tomorrow."

They grabbed their coats and went down to the lobby where the decorating activity had stopped for the day. The holiday atmosphere was inviting with the festive scenes, scents of cinnamon and pine filling the air, and Christmas music playing softly.

Incoming guests were lining up to check in. By the weekend, the lodge would be full. Linc was glad they had made reservations early for one of the third-floor suites and that they'd arrived ahead of the crowd. He'd been reluctant at first to return to the scene of Ally's nightmare with her, but so far she seemed fine. He started to relax and look forward to the days ahead.

Before heading out, they stopped in at BB's to make dinner reservations. Once outside, Linc pulled Ally close to shield her against the icy wind blowing off the lake. They crossed Union Square, where a ten-foot Scotch pine was being placed in the gazebo in preparation for Friday's tree lighting ceremony.

The shops along the Lakewalk were lit up and holiday displays filled the bay windows. Shoppers loaded with bags were bustling in and out of the stores. In front of the Generation Gap, Milton Grimsley was setting up an outside display. Ally gave him a cheery "Merry Christmas, Mr. Grimsley."

He looked up, saw who it was, and growled, "You! You still owe me. I've not forgotten."

Linc returned his ominous look, and he hustled back inside the store. Ally laughed as she told Linc about the "Grimm episode" at the Sunset Social and how she was rescued from his clutches by the Phantom of the Opera. Now, recalling that the Phantom was actually Erik Reno and not Hobart Castlebury, she shuddered.

"It's not really so funny when I think of it that way," she said.

They passed Waterside Treasures as an older bespectacled woman was exiting. Ally thought she looked familiar. When the woman looked right at her with a scowl on her face, Ally remembered where she'd seen her.

"That woman..." she said to Linc when they were out of her earshot. "That's Ethel, the old sourpuss librarian, who was always tsk-tsking. She made me feel like a guilty teenager." Then Ally remembered she'd been accompanied on that library visit by George Rothman who, she now knew was Erik Reno in disguise. Again, she shuddered. So many memories. Erik Reno was everywhere.

"Are you okay?" Linc asked.

"I'm fine," she said. She thought to herself, *Six months of therapy, two times every week, I damn well am going to be okay.*

Nearing the Mean Beans, Ally ventured a glance across the lake at Stonewall Mansion. It was all lit up, not dark, deserted, and dismal like the last time she'd seen it. In fact, it had undergone a serious transformation. It actually looked inviting, exactly how a stately house such as this should look.

I am not going to dwell on Erik Reno, she thought.

The small dining room inside the Mean Beans was nearly full as holiday shoppers were taking a break for Wined Down. Fern was just coming out of the kitchen with a platter of assorted cheeses and crackers when she saw Ally and Linc. She set the tray on the counter and rushed over, giving Ally a welcome hug and smiling at Linc.

"You made it," she said enthusiastically. "Ally, you look great… You do too Linc, but I'm remembering the last time I saw Ally. It broke my heart seeing your beautiful face all bruised and swollen," she said to her friend.

"Yeah, I still have this scar under my eye," said Ally, touching her right cheek. "Probably always will since I'm not a fan of cosmetic surgery."

Linc put his arm around her shoulders and gave her a squeeze.

"Hey guys," said Fern, "I'd love to chat, but I'm short staffed tonight and really busy right now. You're still coming out to the farm in the morning, right? So many changes there I want to show you and tell you about. Kyle and I are both off all day. Kyle has some 'secret mission' he wants to enlist Linc's help with when they go pick up their tuxes for Saturday's gala." Fern emphasized *secret mission* with air quotes and rolled her eyes.

"Absolutely," said Ally. "Around tenish?"

"Great. Go ahead and help yourselves to wine and cheese, and we'll see you in the morning."

Back at the lodge, Ally and Linc were early for their seven o'clock dinner reservations and decided to hang out in the lobby. The area was filling up with guests, and more new arrivals were checking in. A bar had been set up in the corner near the fireplace. Linc ordered two of the evening's special cocktail: Jingle Bell Julep, a blended concoction of crushed cranberries, bourbon, and a simple syrup, and garnished with mint leaves.

While they were sitting, sipping their drinks, and waiting for their table, Ally asked, "Remember the microwave 'gourmet delights' you managed to scrounge up for dinner the last time we were here?"

Linc shook his head. "About all I remember is my gorgeous dinner partner wearing my favorite shirt and nothing else." He winked.

Ally giggled. "Shameless," she teased. She remembered how it had been getting late that night, and they were both famished. Linc had asked her if she wanted to go over to Jack's Pub to grab a bite to eat. She had shaken her head no, so he'd gone down to the lobby in search of something from the refrigerated display cases he'd seen in the mini-mart section of the gift shop.

While he was gone, Ally had checked out his closet and found a blue denim button-down shirt. She'd put it on and rolled up the sleeves. Checking herself out in the full length mirror, her hand went to her cheek, all bruised and battered. Linc had called her beautiful in spite of how she looked. He made her feel special and she hoped she could make him as happy as he was making her.

Linc had returned with three microwaveable entrees. As he'd entered the room and saw her in his shirt, he laughed. "Cute, Ally," he commented. "That's my favorite shirt."

She gave him an alluring look. "I'm rather fond of this shirt myself," she teased. "If you want it back, I think you're going to have to take it. Or try to."

"Scallywag," he teased back. He set down the entrees and playfully pulled her toward him.

"Wait." She'd laughed, wiggling loose from his hold. "Can we eat first?" He loved seeing her laugh. It warmed his heart to see her forgetting about the nightmare she had just been through, if even for this short time.

They heated the stir-fry dinners one at a time in the small microwave and shared them at the little table in the room. They laughingly called their entrees "gourmet delights" and the bottled water they drank out of plastic cups "fine white wine."

Neither had wanted the evening to end. At midnight Linc pulled himself away. "I better get you home," he said with a sigh, "before you turn into a pumpkin."

He had gone into the bathroom and when he returned, Ally was on her phone. "Hey," he said, "are you going to get ready?"

Ally shook her head. "Nope," she said and handed him her phone to read a group text she had just sent to "Dad", "Mom", "Maggie", and "Mac": *Please don't wait up for me and please don't worry. Everything is fine. Its late and I'm staying with Linc tonight.*

Linc smiled, then wrinkled his forehead. "That's pretty bold, isn't it?" he asked.

"It's liberating," she responded. "Unless...Maybe you don't want me to stay."

"Silly girl. Of course I want you to stay. Tonight, tomorrow, the next day, the rest of our lives..."

Now, back in their suite after a quiet dinner by candlelight in BB's restaurant, they found that housekeeping had turned down

the bed and refreshed the ice in the bucket. Ally went into the bedroom to "slip into something comfortable" while Linc opened the
bottle of champagne from Maggie and Mac and poured two glasses.

When Ally came out, Linc looked at her and laughed. She was
wearing his blue denim button-down shirt, the same shirt she had
slipped on six months before, when they'd shared his room in this
lodge.

"Still a scallywag, aren't you?" he said, playfully grabbing her
and wrapping her in a hug.

"I'll take that as a compliment," she responded.

"I love you so much," he said, lifting her chin and meeting her
lips with his.

This kiss, she thought. It was *the kiss* that still caused her to tingle all over with excitement. *Every time.*

"Are you going to take your shirt back?" she teased.

"Are you daring me?" he teased back.

Ally nodded. "Uh-huh."

Forty-Three

Fern was in the saddle putting Magic through his gaits in the paddock when Ally and Linc pulled up Wednesday morning. They parked nearby and walked over to join Kyle, who was leaning over the wooden fence watching admiringly.

Fern was demonstrating the running walk, one of the natural gaits a Tennessee Walking Horse is noted for, unlike a man-made showring gait created with the pain of heavy shoes or soring. In a smooth overstride motion, Magic's back feet effortlessly glided forward, overstepping the footprints left by his front feet. His head and neck bobbed up and down and his ears flicked forward and backward, all in rhythmical fashion with the rise and fall of his feet.

Fern rode over to the paddock gate and dismounted.

"Very impressive," shouted Ally as Fern began walking toward them. "You're a natural in the saddle, and Magic is a beautiful horse."

"I know," said Fern. "I can't understand why anyone would want to subject a graceful creature like Magic to the pain of chemicals and chains when his inbred ability is so amazing. The overstride you saw, his smooth moves and sure-footedness, his head nodding and ears flicking, those are all characteristics of this breed."

Magic came toward them, stood behind Fern and put his head over her shoulder, just like Ally remembered him doing when she was here working on the story for the *Ledger*. "And," said Fern, "he has such a calm disposition, as you can see."

"He's waiting for Fern to stroke his neck and muzzle," said Kyle. "That's his reward after a workout."

"He's a real sweetheart," agreed Linc. "I've never been around horses much, but I could spend all day watching these two work together."

Fern beamed. "I still can't believe I was able to adopt him," she said. "You know, Ally, I owe so much to you and Maggie, and everyone who had a hand in that."

"I'm just glad it all worked out," said Ally. "Magic is exactly where he belongs."

Fern had emailed Ally after she received the news that her application for adoption was approved. The process had been put on hold and marked "For Additional Review" after the Tennessee Walker Equine Rescue, "TWER," received the package from Maggie containing the letters of reference, the veterinarian's report from Dr. Johansson, the newspaper clipping, photographs, and the signed petitions.

But, the deciding factor in Fern's favor came when a big-name TWER donor threatened to cut off funding to the rescue group. The wealthy owner of a prestigious horse farm in Virginia's Hunt Country and a long-time critic of the practice of soring, issued the ultimatum after seeing the story about Fern and Magic on the local news.

Ally looked around the farm. "Boy," she said, "you weren't kidding when you told us there were changes here." She pointed first to the old farmhouse, which had received an impressive make-over since she last saw it.

"Yeah, pretty amazing, isn't it?" said Fern. "New roof, new windows, red shutters, and Dutch lap siding to replace the severely weathered original wood. Dad and I had started restoring the old homestead, then the movie people came to town scouting out a place to shoot some outdoor farm scenes. Our place was close to what they were looking for, but they wanted more eye-appeal. So, the producer offered to finance some additional improvements in return for us allowing them to film here."

"And, the barn," said Ally, noticing a fresh coat of red paint and a new tin roof. "This place looks like a picture postcard."

"We're not sure what to expect in the final cut of the movie," Fern continued, "but they shot quite a few outdoor scenes around the house and barn. And Magic and Misty were filmed in scenes with the two stars, Staci Upton and Luke LeMere."

The door to the farmhouse opened and Cletus came out, accompanied by a border collie.

"This isn't Molly," Ally commented as the dog came running over to check out the visitors.

"Nope," said Kyle. "This is Jesse."

"We lost Molly last summer," Fern offered. "I found her one morning curled up in the straw in Misty's stall. She looked like she had died peacefully in her sleep."

"I'm so sorry," said Ally.

"She lived a good life, and she went out on her own terms. I'm grateful we had sixteen good years with her and she didn't suffer."

"What's Jesse's story?" asked Linc. "She's not a youngster."

"Dad and I were looking at rescues, right Dad?" Cletus had just walked over and Fern wanted to include him in the conversation.

"A farm's not a farm without a dog," said Cletus.

"We were hoping to adopt a dog that needed a good home and would be a good fit for the farm. I found Jesse online. She was with a group that rescues and rehomes older dogs from puppy mills once they're no longer able to reproduce. Jesse had lived for ten years in a crate as a breeder mom, producing litter after litter to be sold for commercial purposes."

"That's sad," said Ally.

"Fortunately, there are some dedicated rescue groups like the one where we got Jesse. I've joined them in advocating to end puppy mills."

"Of course you have," said Ally. "That's so you. And, I guess if we look at it from that perspective, Jesse is one of those lucky ones. At least she'll get to spend the remaining years of her life loved and cared for."

As though she knew they were talking about her, the dog came up to Fern, sat down and lifted her paw. Fern took it and stroked affectionately. Ally bent down and scratched behind her ears.

"Fern, you're amazing," said Ally. "I suspect the next time we come here, you'll have a whole farm full of rescued critters."

Fern, Kyle, and Cletus all laughed.

"What?" asked Ally.

"You may as well tell them," said Cletus.

Fern turned, faced south, and spread out her arms. "A hundred and twenty acres," she said. "All being turned into lush grazing land."

Ally and Linc both looked at her, waiting to hear more.

"Let's go inside," said Fern. "Dad and I'll tell you over a cup of coffee."

"I'll take care of Magic," said Kyle, leading the horse into the barn.

Sitting around the dining room table with a fresh pot of Mountain Mama Blend and a cinnamon-streusel coffee cake from the Mean Beans, Fern and Cletus took turns telling Ally and Linc about the conversations they'd finally gotten around to having about the settlement money from the wrongful death of Fern's mother, Willa Dean. The two million dollars they'd received had barely been touched in more than a decade, and with the investments made by their accountant, the amount had grown substantially over the years.

"Dad always felt," said Fern, "that we'd be capitalizing on Mom's death if we spent the money needlessly or extravagantly or for enjoyment. Neither of us has ever been particularly concerned with material things beyond what we need to live comfortably."

"Fern wanted to do something good with the money as a tribute to her mom," said Cletus.

"And, Dad, it was your idea, right?"

"I was pretty sure you'd go along with it."

Fern had become concerned about her father continuing to work the fields. He was having problems with his back, and she could see the strain farming was putting on him as he got older. She had talked to him about selling off most of the land, but Cletus wasn't about to part with the property that had been in the family for generations.

"Then," said Fern, "Dad suggested turning the acreage into a sanctuary and maybe a rescue for abused, neglected, and otherwise needy horses. Can you believe it was his idea, not mine?"

"That sounds absolutely perfect for you guys," Ally said.

"We're working with our lawyer, Henry Livermore, and his son, Henry Junior, who's a CPA, to get all the paperwork in order, and I've been researching how to go about this, what to expect, and what we'll need. To do it right we have to set it up as a business, possibly a non-profit. There are specific requirements like the number of acres needed per horse for grazing and roaming, separate accommodations for quarantining new arrivals, providing shelter and medical care. We plan to start small. And, guess what we're going to call it?"

"What?" asked Ally. "Don't keep us guessing."

"Dad, you tell them," said Fern.

Cletus beamed. "Willa Dean Acres," he said proudly, "in honor of Fern's mom."

"Wow!" Exclaimed Ally. "I love it."

"That has a nice ring to it,"agreed Linc. "And, this sounds so much like you, Fern. Exactly what you're cut out for. But, what about the bistro? Will you still have time for it?"

"I've been considering that too," responded Fern, "and I'm working with Phoebe to take over as general manager. She's been with us from the start and as she takes on more responsibilities, I'll be stepping back with much less of a hands-on role."

It was almost noon as they walked back outside and met up with Kyle, who was just finishing with Magic's post-workout routine. He and Linc were getting ready to drive to Dominion Mills to pick up their tux rentals for Saturday's black-tie gala at Stonewall Mansion.

Ally caught sight of Kyle and Linc talking quietly and remembered Fern's curious comment about some "secret mission" Kyle wanted Linc's help with.

As they were getting ready to leave, Linc pointed to a concrete foundation that had been poured alongside the gravel drive from the road to the house. "What's that going to be?" he asked.

"That," said Kyle, proudly putting his arm around Fern, "is going to be our new house."

"Wow!" said Linc. "You all are full of surprises."

After the guys left, Fern asked Ally what she wanted to do since she had the rest of the day off.

"I just want to spend time with you," said Ally. "How do you feel about going to the lodge. We can have lunch in the new restaurant and hang out in our suite. We've got so much to catch up on."

"I like that idea," said Fern.

The lobby at the lodge was teeming with guests. BB's Restaurant was crowded and had a waiting list. Ally suggested they go up to the suite and order room service. They decided to share a smoked turkey club sandwich and chopped broccoli slaw. Ally called in the order, then started the fireplace.

"Okay, girlfriend," she said, "what's going on? I'm not talking about the farm or the movie or the rescues. I mean with you and Kyle." She opened the small refrigerator in the kitchenette and took out two diet sodas.

"You mean the house we're building?"

"Yeah, that's a pretty big step."

"With Kyle's student teaching over," said Fern, "he's been offered a job with the Lake County Public School System, starting after Christmas break. He's not sure yet where he'll be assigned, but there are several openings, positions they've been filling with subs."

"That's awesome," said Ally.

"Kyle wants to get married. I told him I could never leave my dad, and he's cool with that. He's come to love the farm and sees us having a bunch of kids. 'To help with the chores', he jokes."

"Sounds like a great arrangement," said Ally. "But, what's this 'secret mission' he and Linc are off on?"

"He's so transparent. I know exactly what Kyle's up to. He wants to give me an engagement ring and wanted me to pick it out. I told him to surprise me, just nothing big. That was my only stipulation. I'm used to working on the farm and in the kitchen at the

Mean Beans. I've never worn jewelry."

"So, you think he's drafted Linc to help him pick out a ring while they're in Dominion Mills getting their tuxes?"

"Oh, yeah. And, Ally, about Saturday night…I have a favor to ask you. Will you go with me, maybe tomorrow, to get a dress? I don't have anything to wear to something like that."

"Sure, we can go tomorrow if you want. But…" she had a thought, but before she could explain, there was a knock at the door. "That must be room service," she said.

As they ate lunch, Fern said, "You started to say something when we got interrupted."

"I have an idea, something I want to show you and see how you feel, but let's finish eating first."

"Okay, but now it's your turn to tell me about you and Linc."

Ally wasn't sure where to start or how much to share. "Fern, I love him to pieces, but it hasn't been 'happily ever after' since we left Union Gap. Linc's been through a lot with me."

Ally told Fern that six months ago, after the arrest of Erik Reno, she'd left Mac and Maggie's house to spend a few days in Roanoke with her parents. She and her father had argued about her plan to return to Richmond.

"He wanted me to stay and thought he had a perfect incentive to keep me there. The son of some friends from the country club was home from college, and Dad wanted me to go out with him."

"Your father knew about you and Linc, right?"

"He's been in denial. I think he had the idea that if I went out with this privileged, preppy, 'Miles Beckett Harrison the third', I would forget all about Linc. But, Fern, even beyond the fact that

I told him Linc and I were in love, you remember what my face looked like. I didn't want anyone to see me, and I certainly didn't want to be put in a position of having to talk about it."

"What'd you do?"

"I packed and left, couldn't wait to get to Richmond and be with Linc. I've never had to feel self-conscious around him. He'd seen me at my worst and he knew the story. Hell, he was part of the story. He'd been through that nightmare with me. In a different way, but he got it. And he's shown me in so many ways that he cares about me."

"I can see how much he cares," said Fern.

"I don't know if you saw the news reports after that nightmare. The media all wanted to talk to me, and because I refused every request to be interviewed, they took it upon themselves to analyze me from their studio seats. They speculated why I was in the mansion, whether I was romantically involved with Erik Reno, was I actually planning to run away with him…It made me sick. I knew Linc would never believe any of that. I really didn't trust anyone else outside our little circle of family and friends. I still don't, and that might be a good thing."

"Why do you say that?"

"I was so stupid to trust George Rothman. Linc didn't trust him and I didn't listen. He's never said 'I told you so' or in any way acted like I brought all that on myself, but I know he must think it."

"Ally, you didn't do anything wrong," said Fern. "How are you doing now? I mean emotionally."

Ally told Fern that she had spent her first couple of days in Richmond with Linc then intended to stay in her own apartment, which was close to the university where she planned to enroll in summer classes.

"But, the first night I was alone," she said, "I was terrified. I tried to go to sleep, but every time I closed my eyes, it was like dark waves were rolling over me, suffocating me. I turned on the TV and every light in the apartment, but my heart kept pounding and I had a feeling of...doom."

Fern was on the verge of tears. "Oh, Ally, I'm so sorry. What did you do?"

"I know I probably shouldn't have, but I drove across town and let myself in Linc's apartment with the key he'd given me. I just wanted to climb in bed next to him. That was the one place I always felt safe. I didn't expect to scare the crap out of him. But I did. In like five seconds, he was out of bed, the light was on, and I had a gun pointed at my head."

"Oh my god, Ally!"

"I think it scared him more than it did me. He was rattled. He yelled at me, something he never does, and told me I could have gotten myself killed. Anyway, after he calmed down, he apologized. The next morning, he said if I was going to stay in Richmond, two things needed to happen. One, I would get professional counseling for my panic attacks, and two, I would be not be spending any more nights alone."

"What did you say."

"I agreed. It's been a slow process, but I've made progress. This trip will be a test. So many memories. Linc's been concerned about my coming back here, but I have to face this town again if I'm going to move on."

Ally wanted to change the subject back to Fern, but suggested they go down to the lobby first and get something to drink.

"You have to try a Jingle Bell Julep. Very Christmassy. Linc and I are hooked."

The lobby was even more crowded than before, with guests milling around, chatting, laughing, and drinking. The drink of the day was a Cran-Merry Mimosa garnished with rosemary sprigs.

"Yum!" said Ally. "That sounds good too."

"I want to try the one that you were raving about," said Fern.

Ally ordered a Jingle Bell Julep for Fern and the festive mimosa for herself. Waiting for their drinks, a guy with slicked back hair came over and flashed a smile that said, "I'm pretty cool." He was wearing a black turtleneck, tight jeans, and loafers with no socks. *Very California*, thought Ally. *Or, trying to be.*

"You look familiar," he said to Ally.

Oh god, she thought. She replied, flippantly, "That's so cliché. And no, I don't think so."

"Didn't I see you in some movie?"

"Oh, you mean *Children of the Bog*?" The film had been all the rage the previous year.

"You were in it?"

"Remember the scene where the swamp creature rises up out of the water with pond scum hanging from its teeth and fingers?"

"Yeah. Pretty gruesome."

Ally raised her arms and twisted her fingers into claws. She made a face at the stranger, baring her teeth. She picked up two peppermint flavored swivel sticks from the bar and stuck them under her upper lip, letting them hang down like fangs.

"You're weird," he said.

"And you're not in California anymore," Ally replied.

The bartender set down the two drinks and Ally quickly signed for them. "Let's get out of here," she said to Fern.

"Nice meeting you," she said to the stranger as she and Fern left.

Back in the suite with their drinks, Fern and Ally laughed until they both doubled over.

"What a creep," said Ally. "You could tell he wasn't from around here. Probably rolled in with the early California crowd. Anyway, I hope I don't run into him again. Or if he sees me, maybe he'll think I'm a kook and run in the opposite direction. I'm in a goofy mood, and it feels good."

Fern was amazed that Ally didn't even realize she was a magnet, attracting men like flies to honey. "You handled that well," she said. "You're so cool around guys. You make it look easy. In high school, and even afterwards, until I met Kyle, I was so shy I didn't know how to act, and boys were so annoying I didn't really try. I never even dated."

"That whole teenage dating business is overrated," said Ally. "You've heard the saying, 'You have to kiss a lot of frogs before you meet your prince'. Well, I kissed my share of those annoying frogs. That just makes me appreciate Linc all the more. We don't talk about our pasts, but I'm sure he's kissed his share of frogettes."

"Frogettes?" Fern started giggling.

"Anyway…" Ally was now laughing too and starting to feel giddy from the drink. "I admire you, Fern, the way you bypassed all that and went right for your prince. I've seen the way Kyle looks at you. He adores you."

They sat in front of the fire and sipped their drinks for a few minutes. "Now, back to you and Kyle," said Ally. "When are you getting married?"

"If everything goes as planned, sometime next year. I just want a small wedding, probably at the farm. Hopefully, his mom will come from Chicago. Kyle doesn't like to talk about her, so I'm guessing they don't have a close relationship."

"Fern, I am so happy for you and Kyle. I certainly hope Linc and I are invited."

"Absolutely!"

"Oh, I almost forgot," said Ally.

"What?"

"I want to show you something. Wait here." She got up and went into the bedroom, then called Fern to come in. Spread out on the bed were two evening gowns. One was an emerald green sleeveless A-line with a deep v-neck and cut-in shoulders. The other was black, sleeveless, with a halter top, silver lace appliqués on the bodice, and a flowing chiffon skirt.

"I brought both because I couldn't decide which to wear to the gala. Last night I asked Linc, and he chose the green one because it matches my eyes. So, that's decided."

She looked at Fern. "You and I are about the same size. If you like the black dress and it fits, you're welcome to borrow it. You don't have to. If you have something else in mind and you'd rather go shopping, I'll go with you. But, why don't you try this one on?"

"Oh my god," said Fern, eyes wide. "It's way more beautiful than anything I was hoping for."

Ally helped Fern into the dress, told her to close her eyes, and walked her to the full length mirror on the closet door. She was smiling when she told Fern to open her eyes.

Fern gasped. "Ally, I've never worn anything like this," she said.

Standing behind her, Ally ran her fingers through Fern's long light brown hair. She pulled it back off her face, scrunching it loosely on top of Fern's head.

"We need to do something like this with your hair," said Ally. "Show off your delicate facial features. I wish I had perfect bone structure like you. Do you know any hair dressers where we might get an appointment Saturday morning?" Ally pointed to her own straight auburn tresses. "I'm thinking I'd like some curls myself."

"I have a high school classmate, Kelly, who owns a shop a few blocks over."

"Can you call her? That'll be fun if we can get in."

They heard the door open and a voice call out, "Hello?"

"In here," Ally called. "Come on back."

Linc and Kyle walked into the bedroom. Kyle did a double-take, smiling admiringly. "Wow!" He whistled. "Just wow! My date is going to be the belle of the ball."

Linc added, "Fern, you look beautiful."

Fern was beaming. "I guess it's decided. I'll be wearing this dress, Ally," she said. "Thanks for letting me borrow it."

"My pleasure."

On the way back from Dominion Mills, Linc and Kyle had decided that the four of them should go out to an early dinner. Kyle suggested a new Thai restaurant that had opened in town. Small and nothing fancy, but it was just a short walk from the lodge.

On their way out, the concierge informed them that the movie producer would have two limos to shuttle guests back and forth between the lodge and Stonewall Mansion for the gala Saturday night.

Ally turned to Fern and Kyle. "You guys will have to come over here and go with us. We can all ride together and make our appearance Hollywood style."

"I wonder," said Linc, as they were walking to the restaurant, "if Hobart will roll out a red carpet on the front walkway."

"This is going to be so much fun," said Fern.

"I'm glad we came," Ally told Linc.

Forty-Four

After a light breakfast Thursday morning from the buffet in BB's Restaurant, Ally stayed downstairs in the lobby to meet her mother who was on her way over. Her parents had arrived the night before, and Ann wanted her daughter to go Christmas shopping with her. There was a four-day Christmas Crafts Fair at the Historic Harrison House in Dominion Mills that Ann wanted to check out. And she wanted to get an early start. Ally and Linc were coming over for dinner at the McGuires, and Ann wanted to get back to help Maggie get ready.

"I'd like to find a few things myself," Ally told Linc, "to take to Cambridge next week." They were spending Christmas with Linc's family, who she hadn't yet met. She was nervous about that trip but relieved that they weren't expected to be at her parents' house. Ann and Tim were heading out on a Christmas cruise with some friends next week. Ally thought they probably planned it this way after the Thanksgiving fiasco in Roanoke.

Back upstairs in the suite, Linc was taking advantage of the time alone to catch up on some work. He sat at his computer and scanned the growing list of emails in his inbox. He got up and was fixing a cup of coffee when the room phone rang.

It was Tim Murphy. "With the girls gone, I thought maybe we could meet for breakfast, get to know each other better," he said.

"Thanks for the invite, Tim, but I've already eaten. I'm staying in this morning to catch up on some work, but you're welcome to stop by here if you want."

Tim said he'd be there in about an hour.

Linc closed his computer and stepped out onto the balcony. He was feeling a little uncomfortable meeting with Ally's father while she was away. He started thinking about all that had happened in the six months since they left Union Gap. There were many happy times but also times he wanted to forget forever. Only he and Ally and maybe her therapist knew the extent of the inner demons Ally was battling. As much as he loved having her close by in Richmond, he hadn't anticipated how fragile she was after the Erik Reno ordeal.

He was remembering the night he awoke and grabbed his pistol, realizing someone was in his bedroom, only to discover it was Ally, who'd been terrified being alone in her apartment. Stunned, he'd sat on the side of the bed for a few minutes to decompress, then got up and found her on the living room floor, hugging her knees to her chest, shaking.

After that, they'd agreed she'd spend her nights with him. Those were times he'd looked forward to, romantic evenings filled with playful exchanges and moments of intense passion. Ally's touch was electrifying, and when they kissed their special kiss, no words were necessary. Her body language said it all.

Soon, Ally had pretty much moved in with him full time, and their life together was uncomplicated, times of simple pleasures. He'd come home and find Ally working on a class assignment or trying out a new recipe. She was determined to learn how to cook.

Dinner was always a time for easy, sometimes silly, conversation. Often, Linc would lead off with, "So, how was your day?" Ally might tell him about a class she'd attended or an assignment she was working on or a funny incident at the gym or the grocery store. Linc loved hearing Ally's stories, and he treasured these times of normalcy.

Ally's face would always light up when he shared a story about Ava, the two-year-old daughter of his work partner Dana and Dana's wife Val. He and Ally had visited the farm where the little girl would take them both by the hand and show them around.

One evening at dinner, just back from a visit to the farm, they'd talked about having kids, much like any ordinary young couple in love envisioning their future together. But, he knew they were not like other people. Ally felt damaged and it made her sad to talk about a normal life that she thought she may never have.

Linc worried about Ally having a panic attack while away from home. Yet, so strong was her desire to be self-sufficient that she would brush off his concerns. Like the time she got home an hour later than expected because she'd run out of gas.

He wanted to be mad at her for letting her tank get down to empty after he'd warned her more than once about running on near empty. He wanted to be mad at her for calling a service truck instead of him. Most of all, he wanted to be mad at her for not letting him know what was going on. But then she said, "I'm sorry" and wrapped her arms around his neck and kissed him. And, he melted.

It was impossible for him to stay mad at her. At times like that, he'd remember how close they came to losing her. He didn't want to waste precious moments being mad. He was relieved that she was home, and what mattered was that she was okay.

Then there were the panic attacks that came mostly at night. Ally would awaken suddenly in a state of fear. He'd wrap his arms around her and hold her, telling her she was safe, until the terror subsided. Or they might be watching a movie in the evening, lying together on the sofa. He'd feel her heart pounding against his chest and her body trembling, and she'd have a distant look in her eyes.

But, the worst were the dark episodes when something would trigger a flashback and Ally responded in fear, reliving the nightmare she'd experienced. Like the time he came up behind her in the kitchen and she didn't hear him because she was running the blender, making Margaritas to go with a special Friday night Mexican dinner. He'd playfully wrapped his arm around her shoulders from behind to nuzzle her neck. She'd panicked. On reflex, she started clawing at his arm and pulling away. Then, she slid down to the floor, gagging and holding her throat.

The episode ended when she realized where she was and who she was with. But for Linc, it released a repressed inner struggle of his own. Throughout the evening, a slow rage was building inside him. Later, after Ally was in bed asleep, he'd gotten up. He rarely got angry, but now he was consumed with loathing for Erik Reno, the monster who'd done this to her. He saw the bottle of tequila on the kitchen counter and started downing straight shots. The alcohol hit him hard. He began shouting, "I'm not him, Ally!" "I would never hurt you, Ally!"

She'd gotten up and was standing in the bedroom doorway. He looked at her and poured himself another shot. "He's everywhere, Ally. He's in our home. He's in your head. He's messing with my mind. I would never hurt you!"

Ally had never seen him like this before.

"Now, am I supposed to be afraid to touch you?" He threw his glass against the hearth, where it shattered, splattering tequila and scattering broken glass.

Ally had ducked back into the bedroom and locked the door as he continued to yell, "I'm not him, Ally. This is what he wants, Ally. He wants me to be afraid to touch you."

Now, standing on the balcony Linc was brought back to the

present by an icy wind blowing off the lake, giving him a chill. He went back inside and started the fireplace. Sitting across from it, staring into the flames, his thoughts went back to that incident, remembering how it nearly destroyed their relationship.

When Ally had come out of the bedroom the next morning, he'd sobered up, cleaned up the mess from the broken glass, and was sitting at the table with a cup of coffee. He was holding his head.

Ally had poured herself a cup of coffee and sat across from him. Neither said anything for several moments, then she spoke softly. "I'm going back to my apartment," she said.

"I don't want you to go," he'd responded, almost in a whisper.

"I can't stay with you. You said...You're afraid to touch me?"

"Come here." He'd held out his hand, across the table.

She shook her head no. "You're afraid to touch me?"

"Please come over here."

"No. I know I'm broken, Linc, but you don't get to say that. You're afraid to touch me?" Her voice was now raised and filled with hurt. She slammed down her cup. Coffee slopped out. She got up and stomped into the living room where she'd left her bag, packed and ready to go.

"Ally!"

"Screw you!" She put her hands over her ears.

"Ally!" There was anguish in his voice.

She'd dropped to the floor in her familiar protective pose, head down, hugging her knees, trying to shut out the world.

He went over and sat in front of her. He tried to take her hand, but she shook him off.

"Ally, look at me. Please."

She shook her head no.

"Then just listen...Ally, you're not broken, and I'm not afraid to touch you. I was a jerk last night, I screwed up, I lost control. I'm sorry. Sometimes I feel so much hatred toward that monster who did this to you that I want to kill him. It's not you, it's my own inner demons I'm battling."

She didn't move.

"Ally, I love you. I want to spend my life with you. I want you to be my wife. I want us to be a family. *Our* family with kids. And a dog." As an afterthought, he said, "I've never had a dog."

Ally smiled at that, then lifted her head and tried not to laugh. "You've never had a dog, even as a kid?"

"No."

"That's sad. I want all that too, Linc. But, look at us…How can we ever have that?"

"Ally, just stay with me. Please. We'll get past this. Both of us. We can't let *him* win."

They made up, but the fact that the incident almost ruined what they had scared him, more than he wanted to admit.

Linc got up to make himself another cup of coffee, now taken back to another incident, that early-November Friday when things seemed to go to pieces.

It had started out pleasantly enough. He was in his office and Ally was attending a morning class. Just before noon, she texted him that her class was over and she was going to the gym, then to the store to pick up a few things for dinner. *"Such a warm day. How do you feel about grilling swordfish steaks tonight?"*

He responded, *"Sure. Sounds good,"* then signed off, *"I love you."*

Then she signed off with a red heart emoji and *"xoxo."*

He was feeling good about how normal their day-to-day lives

were becoming. Ally's panic attacks were less frequent, and she'd learned techniques to defuse them when she felt them coming on. Their time together was filled with lots of love and laughter.

But that afternoon, while he was in his weekly Friday staff meeting, his phone vibrated. He saw it was Ally and at once felt uneasy. Ally would often text him during the day, like she's done earlier, but she never called him at work. He swallowed hard. This was not going to be good. "I have to take this," he said, getting up and walking out of the conference room.

"Ally?" he said, "Are you okay?"

Her voice was so low he could barely hear her. Plus, she was babbling. "Can you come? Please? I'm so scared…I just want to go home…I'm not a criminal…"

She was in custody at the police station. Linc found her alone in a small room with a table and two chairs. "What happened?" he asked, taking a seat across from her and reaching for her hand.

She told him she'd been on a treadmill at the gym and was spooked by the sudden loud sound of large weights that dropped behind her. She lost her footing, went off the back of the machine, and fell onto the floor. Then, a strange man was standing over her. She felt his hands on her. Suddenly, she was back on the trail mentally, being grabbed and choked. She panicked.

"Everything after that's a blur," she said. "I know what they said, but I didn't mean to do anything. I freaked out."

Linc squeezed her hand and got up. "I'll be back," he said.

According to the police report, Ally had started acting erratically when another customer at the gym tried to help her to her feet. She was yelling "Don't touch me," then started kicking, hitting, clawing at the man, and making choking sounds. After she was subdued by the gym manager, she sat on the floor hugging her knees to her chest and wouldn't talk. The customer was badly shaken. The gym manager claimed Ally was "disorderly" and "appeared to be intoxicated or high on drugs."

Linc met with the arresting officer and the gym manager, then went to get Ally. "C'mon," he said. "Let's go home."

In the car, she asked, "Am I being arrested?"

"Nope," said Linc. "It was a misunderstanding, and no one's pressing charges. "However..." He glanced over at her.

"What?" She squirmed.

"I'm afraid you've been banned for life from that gym." He said it with a slight grin, trying to make light of the situation.

Ally groaned. She wasn't laughing.

Once home from the police station, Ally told him she was going to lie down and just needed to be alone for a while. "Thank you for bailing me out," she said. "I guess my father was right after all. I'll be going back to Roanoke. I never wanted to be a burden to you."

He pulled her into a hug and kissed the top of her head. "Just try to relax and unwind," he said. "We'll talk later."

He took a beer from the refrigerator, and went out onto the balcony. It was an unseasonably warm November day, and he had some unwinding of his own to do.

He'd been able to defuse the gym situation by explaining that Ally was neither drunk nor drugged. He described the trauma she had experienced and the PTSD she was being treated for and that she was a key witness in a high-profile murder case.

But, in all seriousness, he realized this *was* a real problem. His mind was flooded with questions: *Was she a danger to herself? To others? Would it be better for her to go back to her parents in Roanoke? Better for whom?*

Linc knew that Ally could go back to her family's upper middle-class neighborhood in Roanoke with its large houses, perfectly manicured lawns, and expensive cars. She could easily marry into a well-to-do family and live a life of relative leisure. But, he also knew that she wanted no part of that. He knew she'd always be haunted by the life she left behind. She was weeks away from graduating with honors, and she was being considered for a job at *The Washington Post*. Her dream job. Ally had ambitions.

If she felt broken before, maybe she was beyond repair now. But, he knew he wasn't going to give up on her.

That night, after the gym incident, Ally had reluctantly gotten up and come to the table when Linc went to get her for dinner. "So…" he'd said after setting plates of spicy shrimp stir fry in front of them and sitting down. "How was your day?" It was an intentionally ridiculous question, intended to get a smile.

Ally looked at him and groaned. "Not funny," she'd said, but then she smiled in spite of herself.

Linc could see that she was devastated. "Ally," he'd said, "you don't deserve this, and it breaks my heart to see you hurting this way. Right now you might feel like throwing in the towel. But, ask yourself, could you really go on with life knowing you gave up everything you've worked for because Erik Reno beat you down?"

"I don't want to give up on my career or what you and I have, but how can we ever have a normal life? You deserve better."

"What's normal? You think you can leave and I can just trade you in for a 'normal' model? I don't want a replacement. I love you."

"But what if this happens again?"

"Ally, this isn't the end of the road unless you decide it's going to be. Today was just another bump in the road of life. Regardless what path you take, there'll always be obstacles to overcome, disappointments, pain…"

"But I'm scared."

"I know. But, the worst thing we can do is let Erik Reno win. You're not alone. I'm in this with you. We can put today behind us, pick ourselves up, and move on. Can't we?"

"I want to." She gave him a weak smile.

They got up and started clearing the table. "Sweetheart," said Linc, "what happened today doesn't define you. Look at all you've done. Look at all the people whose lives are better because of you. I'm one of them."

Big tears started rolling down her cheeks.

"Come here." He pulled her into a hug. "It's going to be okay."

Ally sobbed against his chest.

Linc had accepted these dark moments as a part of their life together, at least for now. Before Ally, he'd always felt an emptiness in his life. The women he'd dated were bright and accomplished, but opinionated and competitive, and relationships had left him unfulfilled. Ally was a breath of fresh air. She was genuine and expressed her emotions openly, her fears and her feelings. She didn't try to hide her weaknesses or secrets. He felt completely comfortable around her and loved being with her.

To love Ally, he realized, was to accept the whole package. And he did. He couldn't imagine life without her.

Forty-Five

Linc and Tim were in the sitting room of the suite with a fire in the fireplace and fresh cups of coffee. Tim wanted to talk about Ally having been notified by *The Washington Post* to expect a job offer after the first of the year.

"As you probably know," he said to Linc, "I'm having a difficult time talking to Ally these days. I'm hoping you can help me convince her that this plan to move to Washington is a bad idea."

"Tim," said Linc, "I'm not comfortable getting in the middle of this."

"But, she'll listen to you. Ally won't fit in with the cut-throat competition and all those self-important jerks. My experience with D.C. is it's a city of transplants, people who've moved there for careers, no real sense of community. That's not who Ally is. Do you think she's ready to move there by herself and take that on?"

Linc said, "I've put in for a transfer back to FBI Headquarters in D.C. I started my career there in the Legal Division before becoming a special agent. I'd be returning as an attorney-agent. I also have my sights on other positions within the DOJ. If Ally gets the job, my plan is to move there with her.

"I didn't know you had a law degree, Linc. Where'd you go to law school?"

Linc hesitated before answering and prefaced his remarks with a little of his family history. "My parents both teach at Harvard. My sister and I were both prepped for Harvard from a young age."

Tim cut in. "Wait. You went to Harvard Law School?"

"My sister, Lauryn, went to Harvard Medical School, and yes, I went to Harvard Law."

"Well," said Tim, "that's impressive. Why in the world would you want to work for the FBI when so many doors could be open for you with a Harvard Law degree?"

This was the reason Linc had hesitated before answering Tim's question. "It's a long story, Tim, but it's the career path I felt I needed to take at the time." He didn't want to get into his family roots with Tim or the story he'd shared with Ally and her friends about why he went into law enforcement.

"Okay," said Tim, "but let me ask you something. Are you agreeing that Ally's not ready to go off on her own, that you need to go with her?"

"Tim, I can understand you're upset with this turn of events. Ally's your daughter, and you want her to be safe. I share those feelings. Ally means the world to me too, and I would never do anything to put her in harm's way. But, she's going regardless. If I tried to stop her, she'd resent me. This is her dream job, and she's laser focused on starting her career. She's worked hard for this, and she's earned it. I know she'll be good at it. My only decision is whether I go with her or not."

"And why are you? Going with her?"

"Truthfully, I'm ready to go back to Washington. Working in a field office, being on the front lines as a special agent has been a great experience for me personally as a single guy in my twenties, and it's good for my career. But, I'm in a different place now. I won't miss the midnight raids, the travel on a moment's notice, the possibility of being transferred. With Ally in my life now, I want stability. This move will open up new opportunities for me as well as for her. I want to be there to share this new chapter in both our lives. I love

Ally. You should know that by now."

"Well, I'm worried sick about this. She doesn't have to do this. Now that she's got her degree, our plans—her mother's and mine— have always been that she'd go on to graduate school. I mean, I'm her father. I should have some say in this. I've given her everything: a good education, her apartment, a nice car, bank account, credit cards…"

"You and Ann have done a wonderful job raising Ally, and it shows. You should be proud. She's remarkable. But, she's also determined. We all want what's best for her, but it's her life. When I think of how close we came to losing her…I just want her to be happy and not be afraid of life because of what happened."

"But, come on, Washington?"

"It's a great opportunity for Ally to start her career."

"What about her emotional state? It's been six months now since that Erik Reno incident. I know Ally's been in therapy all this time because I get the insurance statements."

"What has she told you about that?"

"Only that she was having nightmares. I feel like she should be moving past that, but when I try to talk to her, she shuts me out."

"Tim, listen. The 'incident', you refer to was a kidnapping and a deadly assault. Ally had a violent near-death experience. You don't just get over something like that."

"Do you think she'll ever be cured?"

Linc shook his head. "Ally's 'nightmares', as she describes them, are post-traumatic stress. I'm not an expert, but I don't think there's a cure for PTSD. I have a good friend who lives a couple doors down in my apartment complex. He's an ex-marine, served in Afghanistan and experienced some unbelievably shocking events. He suffers from stress so severe that he can't work and has a specially-trained service dog that goes everywhere with him for emotional support."

"Okay, I get that. But Linc, Ally's not been in a war zone, and she doesn't have a debilitating condition like your friend."

"You're right, Ally's situation is different and not nearly as severe, thankfully. I think it could be worse but for the fact that she's so determined to overcome the fallout from her experience."

They chatted some more about Ally's progress and her accomplishments at VCU, graduating with honors. Then, Tim sighed and got up to leave. "I'm glad we had this talk. I feel better now. You know, Linc, I really didn't like you at first. I thought you were moving in on Ally and taking advantage of her vulnerable condition."

"I can understand that you might have felt that way. I hope you know now that's not the case.

"I see now that you care deeply about Ally. "

"We may never see eye-to-eye, Tim, but when it comes to Ally, we're on the same side. We both want what's best for her. And, I'm glad you stopped by."

"Welcome back you two," said Maggie.

"It's been too long," added Mac.

Ally and Linc arrived at the McGuire house in time for an early happy hour as Maggie had requested. They were greeted with hugs and the spicy aroma of mulled wine that was being kept warm in a slow cooker. Linc handed Mac two bottles of special holiday wine, Merry Berry Red and Snowfall White, which they had picked up at the Virgin Glen Vineyards Outlet on the Lakewalk. Ally gave Maggie a gift box in which she'd packed a set of six Christmas wine glasses, hand-painted with green holly and red berry vines.

Bowser came running up and started doing his dog dance

around Ally, excited to see her. He ran to his leash hanging on the hook beside the back door and pulled it down, wagging his tail expectantly."

"Aww, he remembers me," said Ally. "Sorry, Bowser, no walks along the trail today." She shuddered, remembering their last walk together.

Tim Murphy hugged his daughter and gave Linc a pat on the shoulder. The atmosphere was cheerful. Ally and Linc both hoped it would remain that way.

Maggie was admiring the wine glasses as she unpacked and handed them one at a time to Ann to wash. "I love these," she said. "We'll use them for dinner with the holiday wines you brought."

Ally had bought the glasses that morning during her shopping trip with her mom to the Christmas Craft Fair in Dominion Mills. She'd spent most of her time there browsing the displays of Virginia handblown and hand-painted glass and the handmade pottery. In addition to the wine glasses, she'd bought Christmas gifts for Linc's family: an amethyst crackle glass pitcher and set of long stem water goblets for his parents and a set of rustic-looking stoneware ramekins and matching serving bowls for his sister and her family.

"Mom and I had a nice time together and I would say a successful shopping trip," she told Maggie, giving her mother a hug around the waist.

"Ally took me to lunch at a lovely inn along the river. What was the name of it, dear?"

"The Old Gristmill Inn," said Ally. "Just opened. The concierge at the lodge recommended it. It's worth a trip. We sat in the oyster bar. You know how much I love Oysters Rockefeller, and they didn't disappoint."

"The fried oysters are great too," added Ann.

In fact, Ally had slipped away during lunch and bought a

restaurant gift certificate for her parents to use on a future visit. They'd agreed not to exchange gifts this year because Ann and Tim would be gone over Christmas and the fact that they'd already made a substantial deposit to Ally's bank account as a gift for graduating with honors. Ally intended to mail the gift certificate to them as a good-will gesture, along with a heartfelt letter she was planning to write in an attempt to smooth things over. She wanted more than anything to have her parents, especially her father, accept her and the choices she made. Working on that would be her New Year's resolution.

"How did you spend your morning, Linc?" asked Mac.

"Catching up on work from the office," he said. "And Tim stopped by for a chat."

Ally glared at her farther.

Tim held up his hands in a show of surrender. "Everything's good," he said. "Just trying to get better acquainted. Right, Linc?"

"Well," said Maggie, thinking this situation might need diffusing, "we all have a lot of catching up to do too. Let's grab drinks and go into the living room. I want everyone to try the mulled wine and let me know what you think."

As a rule, Maggie and Mac weren't much on decorating for Christmas, but this year they'd put up their Martha Stewart pre-lit Alexander pine, hung a wreath on the front door, and put tiny Santa hats on Mac's four hand-carved wooden duck decoys that sat on the fireplace mantle. Maggie brought out a tray of appetizers and set it on the coffee table while Mac started a fire.

"The mulled wine is really good," commented Ally as she and Linc settled onto the sofa.

"It's Maggie's special recipe," said Mac.

"Not really all that special," corrected Maggie, "just my own creation. I've experimented with various red wines and different combinations of spices."

"I can taste the orange and cinnamon," said Ally.

"Well, that's two out of Maggie's twelve magic ingredients," said Mac.

"It's heavy on cloves," offered Ann, sipping hers.

"Definitely a nice touch of brandy," commented Linc.

"Well," said Tim, "I can state with authority that the red wine is Zinfandel. That's my educated contribution to this guessing game."

"Yeah, but you're cheating," Maggie scolded. "You saw the bottle sitting out by the stove."

"Guilty," he admitted. "But still delicious, Maggie. Mind if I go help myself to seconds?" He stood. "Anyone else, while I'm up?"

After Maggie rattled off the rest of the ingredients, then joked that they would all be quizzed on them later, she left to put the baked ziti casserole in the oven.

When she returned, Ally asked, "What's going on at the *Ledger* these days?"

Maggie responded, "You mean, since we don't have you to keep us straight anymore?"

"Ha ha," said Ally, "Actually, I meant since you don't have me to *kick around* anymore."

Everyone laughed.

"Well," Mac said to Ally, "you're a tough act to follow. Especially when it comes to processing obituaries."

"Very funny, Mac," retorted Ally. "So, who have you horn-swoggled into doing that now?"

"Actually," explained Maggie, "we've partnered with the high school to work with journalism students through *Quill and Scroll*."

"Quill and Scroll?" asked Linc.

Ally explained: "It's the international high school honor society that promotes journalism."

"Ally was president," bragged Ann.

"As well as editor of the school paper," added Tim.

"Stop it you guys," said Ally, "You're embarrassing me. So, what will the students be doing?"

"Mac and I like to call it *work release*," said Maggie. "The best and brightest get to cut classes and come to the paper for some on-the-job training. And, yes, that includes obituaries. Eventually, we'll be bringing someone on full time. But, enough about us. We want to hear about your job offer with *The Washington Post*."

"Well," said Ally, "technically no job yet, but I was told to expect an offer after the first of the year."

"I've been trying to tell her," said Tim, "that this is not a good idea. She should go graduate school. It would give her more of an advantage instead of rushing out to get a job now and starting at the bottom."

"I'm not opposed to starting at the bottom," responded Ally, "and working my way up. And, I do intend to work on my master's, just not as a full-time student. For now, getting a job is what I need to do. I don't fit in with that college scene anymore."

"What's wrong with the college scene?" asked Tim.

"Dad, I'm not the same person I used to be. The truth is I feel like a freak around people who know, or think they know, what happened to me. Even Monica, my roommate...She came back to Richmond early last August so I'd have someone to stay with when Linc had to go to Charlottesville for those riots. I went with her to our old hangout, the Pizza Pit, and she was parading me around like it was cool to be kidnapped by a serial killer."

Ally continued: "At least in D.C. I'll be a little fish in a big pond. If everyone there is so wrapped up in their own egos, as you keep telling me, Dad, nobody will care about my 'cool adventure' with Erik Reno." She used air quotes to emphasize cool adventure.

The agitation in her voice was starting to show.

"Okay, look," said Tim, "I'm sorry. I don't want to put a damper on this evening. I just care about you. That's all."

When dinner was ready, Maggie and Ann carried in plates of baked ziti, a basket of garlic bread to pass around, and a bowl of Caesar salad, which Maggie tossed tableside with anchovy dressing and dished into salad bowls. Mac opened the holiday wines from Ally and Linc and poured them into the new Christmas glasses. "Farewell to 2017," he said. "The good, the bad, and the ugly."

"To 2017," they all repeated, clinking their glasses together.

"That covers a lot," said Ally.

"All good now, gathering at this table," said Linc.

"How about to 2018 and a kinder, gentler new year?" said Ally. They clinked again.

Maggie said, "Now, I for one want to talk about the personal essay Ally wrote about her experience. It was powerful, Ally."

"Thanks, but definitely out of my comfort zone," said Ally. "I struggled with it. Linc helped because I wasn't sure how much I could say without jeopardizing the case."

"Good point," said Mac. "And where exactly does the case stand now?"

Linc said, "Reno remains in custody and is undergoing a court-ordered psychological assessment for 'personality disorders'. Ally's been notified to be available to appear at any time for depositions or as a witness at trial. But so far that's not happened."

"The wheels of justice turn slowly," said Tim.

"That's fine," said Linc, "as long as he stays locked up."

"Ally," said Maggie, "you were with him. Do you think Erik

Reno really has split personalities?"

"Well, all I know is he could be very convincing in his disguises. Such as the charming George Rothman or the Phantom of the Opera. Maybe he was just a masterful actor pretending to be charming. But, there were times where I think he actually believed he was that other persona."

"What do you mean?"

"Like when he came into the cellar room disguised as George Rothman and I asked him if he was going to kill Hobart. He said, 'Ally, you're confused. George doesn't kill people. Erik kills people.' Then he added something chilling, something to the effect that if I didn't go along with George, Erik would come out of retirement and pay a visit to my family. And when I asked him if Erik would be traveling with us, he said that was up to me."

Ally talked matter-of-factly. She'd relived it all so many times that by now she was undaunted describing what happened. But, her parents were still shocked.

"Chilling," said Ann. "It makes my blood run cold."

"Chilling doesn't begin to describe it," added Tim.

"Yeah, but does that make him crazy?" asked Mac. "Not guilty of his crimes by reason of insanity?"

"That's not for us to decide," said Linc. "He may have had other disguises, but Erik Reno committed the crimes, and Erik Reno's the one who has to answer for them."

"I just hope he never gets out," said Ally.

"Amen to that," said Ann.

"I'd like to give him a dose of his own medicine," said Tim.

"I hope he rots in hell," said Maggie. "Now, back to that piece you wrote..."

"Maggie," said Ally, "it was just like you predicted. I wouldn't talk to the media so they played loosely with the facts, theorizing why I was in the mansion and speculating that I was in a relationship with Erik Reno, maybe even his accomplice, because I'd been spotted around town with him when he was disguised as George Rothman."

"Victim-shaming," said Maggie. "Good for ratings, but a shitty business, if I do say so myself."

"It was tough," said Ally. "Bad enough being the story, but worse being the subject of fake news. Then, it spilled over to social media, and those attacks were even more brutal."

As Maggie had suggested, Ally had started writing the first-person account of her experience to set the record straight. She started it off with, "I never wanted to be the story…" then described in honest and unpretentious detail her experience with George Rothman, how she was kidnapped, what it was like during her 32 hours in captivity along with Hobart Castlebury, her conversations with serial killer Erik Reno, her escape, and personal facts about how the nightmare affected her in the aftermath of her experience. She made special mention of Security Officer Darrell Dempsey and his heroic role in saving her life and apprehending Reno.

She concluded her account by expressing the frustration and anger she felt with the media. "As an aspiring journalist," she wrote, "I've learned an important lesson. I now understand, first-hand, the consequences of sensationalizing a story at the expense of accuracy. I hope it serves to make me a better reporter, one who is fair, objective, and factual. Those are my goals."

Maggie and Mac had kept Ally in internship status, working remotely to finish out the credits she needed. They ran "Ally's Story" as the last segment in a four part *Lakeside Ledger* series entitled, "The Erik Reno Affair: A Small Town With Big Secrets." Maggie had started the series off with her history of Stonewall Mansion, the once secret Underground Railroad "safe house" that centuries later became the secret hideout for Erik Reno. Then, they ran Ally's article that covered the romance of Hobart Castlebury and Ruby Rosa, the Talone Crime family, the entrance of Reno into their lives, the movie script that brought them to Stonewall Mansion, and the mystery of the missing family jewels. Next, Maggie covered the murders of Ruby Rosa and Gianna Talone, the search for alleged killer Erik Reno, and finally his apprehension.

Both Maggie and Mac agreed that Ally's personal account, getting inside the head of the Erik-monster, as she called him, was the crowning touch, the final flourish that took the series from "good" to "award-worthy."

Ally had included copies of the series and other work samples to *The Washington Post* along with her resume.

"I think," she said, "my personal story piqued their interest enough to get me the job interview. They asked a lot of questions about my experience based on what I wrote."

"I hope you told them," said Maggie, "that you're in high demand."

"That might be pushing it," laughed Ally, "considering this was my first, and so far only, job application. I'm putting all my eggs all in one basket here."

They all laughed.

Except Tim.

Forty-Six

The breakfast crowd at BB's Restaurant Friday morning filled every seat in the dining room, and there was a line waiting for tables. Ally suggested they walk down to the Mean Beans. "I could really go for a butter almond bear claw," she said.

Linc shook his head. "And, you've been doing so well sticking to your morning oatmeal," he chided with a smile.

"Exactly why I deserve a bear claw," she replied. "But first, I want to go over and see Happy at Town Hall. We've been so busy, I feel bad we haven't already stopped in to say hello to the acting mayor."

❖ ❖ ❖ ❖ ❖

"Hi Dee," said Ally as they stopped at the reception desk. "We're hoping we can pop in and say hello to Happy."

The mayor's secretary looked up and smiled. "Ally," she said brightly. "Welcome back to Union Gap. You too Agent Stryker. Happy will love to see you. Go on back. She's in her element, getting everything ready for all that's going on today and tomorrow. And loving every minute of it."

"Well, we won't keep her."

Happy was at her computer when Ally gave two short knocks and opened the door without waiting for a response.

"Well I'll be. Look who the cat dragged in," said Happy. "Come on in, have a seat."

Happy's little terrier-mix Pippy came bounding out from under the desk. He bounced about, wagging his stump of a tail excitedly. Ally picked him up.

"We know you're busy, Madam Mayor..." Ally giggled, trying to hold Pippy back as he wiggled and licked at her face.

"Not for you two."

"How's Mayor Merv doing?" asked Ally.

"Recovering nicely from his heart surgery. He plans to ride in the flotilla this afternoon. You know him, nobody can play Santa Claus like he can."

They spent a few minutes chatting about Fern and Kyle and how everything seemed to be going so well for them now. "Looks like we'll be having wedding bells next year," said Happy.

"That's so exciting," said Ally. "And wow, the changes at Finfrock Farm."

"Lots of changes around here. And, now this movie..."

"The lodge is completely full," said Linc.

"Mostly California types, I think," added Ally. "I'll have to tell you about the encounter Fern and I had in the lobby with an out-of-towner who fancied himself to be a super cool hustler dude."

Linc chuckled, recalling Fern's telling of the story over dinner at the Thai restaurant. "I got a kick out of Fern's take on it," he said.

"Yeah," said Ally, "I can't wait to see how she reacts tomorrow at the big shindig."

"We're all pretty excited," said Happy. "Hobart has some surprises in store."

"We've seen Stonewall Mansion from across the lake and it's not the same place I remember. It looks like the stately manor it was intended to be."

Happy told them about Hobart's miraculous transformation

after Erik Reno was "carted away" and Hobart was free from the drugs that had left him in a zombie-like state.

"He's back to his old eccentric self, but not quite as cranky," she chuckled. "Once he got back in Stonewall Mansion, he began carrying out his original plans. I helped him find a new personal assistant. And, this time I made sure she was who she claimed to be."

"She?" asked Ally.

"Audry Emmerson, really nice lady, and super smart."

Ally was remembering the day "George Rothman" came into the newsroom at the *Lakeside Ledger* and identified himself as Hobart Castlebury's personal assistant. She shuddered.

Happy continued: "He got his finances back in order after the so-called 'George Rothman' tried, but fortunately failed, to channel most of Hobart's money to offshore accounts. Hobart started making upgrades to the mansion right away. One of the biggest changes," she said, "was hiring Sonja and Geoffrey Kirkpatrick."

"Who are they?" asked Ally.

"Sonja was one of Hobart's most promising students at the Ruby Slipper Center for the Performing Arts in New York. Geoffrey, her husband, is a music instructor, a graduate of Iverson Barclay Conservatory of Music. They've moved to the Gallery and live in one of the smaller cottages."

Happy told them how the Kirkpatricks, together with Hobart, turned the big formal ballroom into the Stonewall Studio for the Performing Arts. "Dance and acting classes, voice and music lessons," said Happy. "Plus, there's a free clinic two Saturdays a month for kids whose parents can't afford to pay."

The phone on Happy's desk rang. "Yes, Dee?" She listened, then told her secretary to take a message and hold her calls.

Ally said, "We know you're busy, so we'll let you get back to work. But, one last question…We were wondering, what's going on at Books Galore these days? Who's minding the store?"

Happy told them about Lucia Flores. "You may remember, she did cleaning for businesses up and down the Lakewalk and for several households. She always had little Carlos with her."

"I do remember Lucia and Carlos," said Ally. "Carlos was so well behaved. He'd sit quietly, reading a book while she worked."

"Lucia's a single mom, and she's struggled to provide a decent home for Carlos. I started teaching her the bookstore business after Kyle began student teaching, and writing his novel, and playing house with Fern in that little cabin..."

Ally laughed.

"Lucia was an eager student and a fast learner," continued Happy. "She's worked out real well at the store, and she's been a lifesaver since I've stepped in as acting mayor."

"What about Carlos?"

"He started third grade this year, and guess what? Kyle is his Big Brother, kind of filling in as a father-figure. Kyle was fatherless growing up, and now he wants a whole house full of kids."

"A whole house full of farm hands is what my people are saying," said Ally as she and Linc got up to leave.

"Oh," said Happy, "Before you go, I'm inviting you both to the 'Producer's Reception' tonight after the tree lighting ceremony. It's in the Allegheny Room at the lodge."

"Wow!" said Ally, elbowing Linc. "How cool is that?"

Happy winked and pulled out two gold tickets from her desk drawer. "Being mayor has its privileges," she said.

As they were leaving the town hall, Ally wanted to check on Betty, Union Gap's reigning largemouth bass mascot.

"She doesn't look happy," Ally told Linc.

"I'm not sure how to tell," offered Linc. "But I guess it could be worse. She could end up in someone's frying pan."

"That's true," Ally sighed. To the fish, she said, "Hang in there, Betty. It won't be too much longer, you'll be at the sanctuary, and you and Billy will be spawning a whole village of little Bettys and Billys."

"You're silly," said Linc.

At the Mean Beans Bistro, Fern and Phoebe were seated at a table with an open binder between them.

"Hi guys," Fern called out when Ally and Linc walked in. "Glad you stopped in. I have something for you."

"I just hope you have bear claws," said Linc. "That's all Ally's been talking about."

Fern laughed. "Sorry Ally, no bear claws today, but we have fresh baked caramel pecan sticky rolls."

"Yes, please," said Ally.

"And," added Fern, our Sunrise Special today is a poached egg on avocado toast, served with roasted cherry tomatoes."

"That sounds good to me," said Linc.

"Make that two," said Ally.

While Fern went to turn in their breakfast order, Ally asked Phoebe, "How's it going? The manager training?"

"It's a lot," said Phoebe. "I always thought Clover made up the weekly menus, and all the ingredients and supplies just magically appeared." She pointed to the binder. "Inventory, vendors, finances, budget...Whew!"

"This is for you guys," said Fern, returning with a bag. "Go ahead and peek while I get your coffee."

Ally took out two T-shirts in light gray with a logo of two angry-looking coffee beans, each with a coffee cup in one hand and a closed fist in the other. The shirts were inscribed with "The Mean Beans" above the logo and "Home of Mountain Mama Blend" below. The bag also contained two coffee mugs with the same design and a gift pack of Mountain Mama Blend coffee pods.

"Love it all!" said Ally. "And, if you're selling these, I'd like to buy four more of the mugs and two gift packs of the coffee." Turning to Linc, she said, "To take to Cambridge next week."

"Great idea," he said.

Fern went back to the kitchen and returned with their breakfasts. "Ally," she said, "I was going to call you. We have hair appointments tomorrow morning at nine. Kelly had planned to take the day off but agreed to come in just for us." Fern gave the address to Ally, and they made plans to meet there.

"Well," said Linc, "What should I expect?"

They laughed. "We'll see," said Ally. "I may come back and wash it out, but it'll be an adventure."

"And," added Fern, "this is a big deal. I'm a nervous wreck."

"I hear you," said Ally. "I'm going to need another caramel pecan sticky roll."

Linc gave her a quizzical look.

"What?" she asked. "It's nerves."

Back outside, Ally said she wanted to pick up a few more Christmas gifts from the stores along the Lakewalk. Linc said he was going back to the suite and try to get some more work done.

"That reminds me," said Ally. "What did my father want to, quote, 'chat' about when he stopped by yesterday."

"Oh, you can probably imagine. He wanted me to help talk you out of going to D.C. and instead go to graduate school like your parents intended."

"What did you tell him?"

"That it's your decision, and I'll support you, whatever you decide."

"You didn't talk about, you know, the 'incident' at the gym?"

"Of course not. It's not my place, but at some point you may want to think about telling him yourself. He thinks you should be, quote, 'cured' by now."

"Maybe sometime I'll have a sit down with him, but not now. There's too much going on."

Ally handed Linc the bags from Fern to take back to the room. He gave her a peck on the cheek, and turned to walk away. "Happy shopping," he said over his shoulder.

Ally walked over to Books Galore Bookstore and was greeted by Lucia. "Ally," she said, "welcome back to town. Happy said you were coming."

"Happy told me you're working here," said Ally. "How's Carlos?"

"He's great. Kyle's a wonderful 'Big Brother' to him, and Hobart's been giving him acting lessons. And, now with this job..." She started to tear up, "We're blessed. Oh, don't mind me. Can I help you with something."

"I'd like a copy of *The Lake at Union Gap* by Professor O'Hurley if you still have any left." Linc had told her that his father had a large library at home with books numbering in the hundreds. She thought he could add this one to his collection.

"Oh believe me," said Lucia, "Happy never lets that shelf go bare. Let me get you one."

As she was ringing it up, Lucia asked, "Are you going to the flotilla this afternoon?"

"Linc and I intend to," said Ally.

"Carlos will be on a boat with Hobart for the Stonewall Studio for the Performing Arts. Not sure what theme they have planned. Carlos said it's a secret."

"Well, I'll certainly be looking forward to that."

Ally continued down the Lakewalk, stopping at Virgin Glen Vineyards Outlet for four bottles of the special holiday wines and at Mandie's Candies for gift boxes of Mandie's Passion, the champagne and white chocolate earth-balls.

She was ready to head back to the lodge, but then decided to stop in at Daphne's Waterside Treasures. If Fern was getting her hair done in some off-the-face style, she would need a pair of earrings.

"Well, helloooo, Ally." Daphne started talking non-stop, as was her custom, about Fern and Kyle, about the makeover at Finfrock Farm, about the plans for the horse sanctuary, and about Cletus.

"Are you going to the big event tomorrow," Ally asked.

"Oh my, yes indeedy. And believe it or not, we're getting Cletus into a monkey suit."

Ally laughed. "That'll be a sight to see. About the gala, I'm thinking Fern might need a pair of earrings."

"You know I have earrings...And earrings...And earrings." Daphne touched the long dangling hoops hanging from her lobes. "Let's go have a look."

Ally was looking for something to match the brocade appliqués on the gown Fern would be wearing. "I think these will be perfect," she said, holding up a pair of sterling silver teardrop dangles. "Can you gift wrap?"

While she rang up and wrapped, Daphne talked. And talked. Ally was relieved when other customers came into the store. She wanted to make a hasty exit as soon as Daphne finished.

As she was passing the Generation Gap, she noticed a collection of vintage train sets in the window. They didn't have a Christmas present for Neel, Linc's four-year-old nephew. Ally wanted to go in and check the sets out, but, there was Milton Grimsley, looking out the window. *No way,* she told herself and hurried past. She decided to see what Linc thought, and maybe she could send him over.

Thinking of Neel, she remembered seeing some special kids items of clothing in the window at Tee Time Lake Apparel, which she passed a few doors back. She backtracked and purchased a child's Union Gap T-shirt with two largemouth bass snap-ons as a gift for the four-year-old.

"Ally," laughed Linc. "We're going to need a U-Haul. You're going to spoil my family."

Ally was laying out all the items she had purchased. She was relieved Linc was laughing. She'd been afraid he'd rag her about her binge-buying. It was her way of coping with the nervousness she felt about meeting his family.

"These are mostly just little parts of Union Gap," she said. "Conversation pieces. I want to make a good impression."

"My family's going to love you. How could they not? You're very lovable."

"Seriously, Linc. How much does your family know about me? I don't want to be blindsided."

"They know about the Erik Reno episode, if that's what you're asking. It was all over the news. They had lots of questions, and I'm sure they'll have more for you, so be prepared and don't let it upset you. They also know how much you mean to me."

"What about the panic attacks and flashbacks? Do they know about those?"

"Not so much, but please don't worry, it's going to be fine."

Stressful is more like it, thought Ally.

Forty-Seven

For Ally and Linc, walking into the Allegheny Room at the LakeView Lodge that evening for the producer's reception was like stepping into an alternate universe. They were greeted at the door by a male mime. *A mime!* It took Ally a moment to let that sink in. He was wearing a white shirt with black horizontal stripes, black pants with red suspenders, a red scarf and beret, black patent leather shoes, and white gloves. His face was painted white with black high-arched eyebrows and star-designs around his eyes, and he had a red-tipped nose and red lips. With exaggerated facial expressions and body movements, he picked up Ally's hand and mock-kissed the back of it. He then spread his arms wide in a welcoming gesture.

A female mime appeared at Linc's side. Instead of the black pants worn by her male counterpart she had on a short black ruffled skirt and wore striped over-the-knee stockings with square-toe chunky-heeled patent leather Mary Jane pumps on her feet. A black teardrop appeared on her cheek below her right eye, and a black heart was in the center of her crimson lips. She batted her extra-long false eyelashes in Linc's face and pursed her lips. She blew him a kiss and placed it an inch from his lips with a white-gloved hand.

Linc whispered to Ally, "I don't think we're in Virginia anymore."

Earlier in the day, they'd attended the town's small Christmas celebration. The flotilla of decorated pontoon boats cruised along the waterfront in Union Gap's version of a Christmas parade. Leading the procession in the first boat were Mayor Mervil Turnbull as Santa Claus and Acting Mayor Happy O'Hurley as Mrs. Claus. A group of young children dressed as elves appeared to be busy at work, hammering and sawing, making toys.

Next came the town's Lake Patrol boat with Chief of Police Odell Hawkins at the helm and the town's newest police recruit and hometown hero Darrell Dempsey as first mate.

Ally smiled, recalling that she'd accidentally run into Darrell yesterday in Dominion Mills. She had thought of a little gift she wanted to surprise Linc with for his tuxedo, and she and her mom encountered Darrell at Michael's Menswear. It was an unexpected pleasure.

"Darrell," said Ally, "I was hoping I'd get to see you this week. Are you going to the gala at Stonewall Mansion?" She pointed to the tux rental he had just picked up.

"Yeah," he said, sheepishly. "Mayor O'Hurley put me and my girlfriend on the guest list. Not something I feel comfortable about but my girlfriend's really excited."

"That makes two of us," said Ally, reassuringly.

They'd spent several minutes chatting. Darrell told Ally about his new job as police recruit, meaning he was a non-sworn employee of the Union Gap Police Department while completing training at the police academy in Roanoke.

"Yep, I got accepted with the help of Chief Hawkins," he said.

"Well," said Ally, "you deserve it. I am so happy for you, Darrell. And, looking forward to seeing you, and meeting your girlfriend, at the big event Saturday."

The flotilla continued with a boatload of town councilors,

waving and flashing their campaign smiles. Then came the Stonewall Studio for the Performing Arts boat. Hobart Castlebury appeared as Ebenezer Scrooge, with Lucia's young son Carlos as Tiny Tim on his lap. A boat with carolers dressed in vintage costumes in the style of *A Christmas Carol* floated by singing "Good King Wenceslas." *Riverdance* performers from the Stonewall Studio were demonstrating traditional Irish dance steps. Finally, members of the cast and crew in town for the premiere of *An Old Virginia Christmas*, the movie, were singing "An Old Virginia Christmas," the song.

As the boats approached the town's Union Square, the parade participants disembarked and gathered around the gazebo for the annual tree lighting ceremony. Copies of sheet music and candles were handed out so everyone could join in caroling.

Happy said a few words, then introduced Carlos, dressed as Tiny Tim, who flipped the switch. The ten-foot Scotch pine came alive with a thousand lights that illuminated an assortment of plush miniature gnomes wearing elf costumes. The elf-gnomes had been positioned at intervals to appear as though they were climbing toward the treetop where a 3D rotating star projected snowflakes on the ceiling of the gazebo. A string of red and white candy canes that had been set up along the Lakewalk wall were now glowing brightly.

Ally told Linc she didn't want to stay for the caroling. She was agonizing over what they should wear to the producer's reception and regretted not thinking to ask Happy what the dress code was.

Now, as they stepped into the room, they saw two servers on stilts towering over the guests. *Servers on stilts!* Ally shook her head in amazement. One was carrying a tray of champagne flutes. The second was balancing a platter of hors d'oeuvres above his head. They wore white shirts and tailored black vests, bow ties and above-the-elbow arm bands.

Everywhere, they saw beautiful, smartly-dressed people. Ally was feeling self-conscious being in this crowd. She was glad that at least she and Linc were color coordinated and seemed to fit in well enough. She had on a sleek black jumpsuit with wide legs, spaghetti straps at the shoulders, and an open back. She left the matching bolero jacket back in the suite. Linc wore a black short sleeved ribbed mock neck shirt and black slacks.

A stilt walker appeared next to them and lowered a tray. Linc took two flutes of champagne, handing one to Ally, who was looking anxiously around, hoping to see Happy or any other familiar faces they could mingle with.

"Well, well," she heard someone behind her say. "If it isn't the swamp lady."

"Oh, good lord," Ally whispered to Linc.

She turned to the man behind the voice. "And, if it isn't the California hustler with the worn out pick-up line."

"Ouch," he said, pretending to be offended. "Honestly, you really do look familiar."

Linc was enjoying this exchange. He turned to the stranger. "And you are?" he asked.

"Deke Saxton." He extended his hand and he and Linc shook.

"Mr. Saxton," said Ally, "was in the lobby when Fern and I were getting our drinks. And we had a little chat." She introduced herself to Deke. "I'm Ally Murphy," she said, "and this is my husband-to-be, Linc Stryker."

"Mr. Saxton," asked Linc, "are you here with the movie?"

"Please call me Deke. And yes, in a sense. I'm Ezra Silverstein's production assistant."

"Ezra Silverstein?" Ally gasped. "He's the producer."

"Bingo! I'm part of the advance team that gets sent ahead to handle preparations and ensure everything runs smoothly."

"You mean like this reception? And the limos for tomorrow? That kind of preparations?"

"Yep. Usually, we have an endless list of special requests: room arrangements, foods, quirky demands, incessant complaints…" Deke threw up his hands in a "Whatcha gonna do?" gesture. "But this trip's a welcome relief. Only two actors and both are pretty low maintenance."

An attractive young woman slipped her arms around Saxton. "You love us, Deke," she said. "You know you do."

"Ally, Linc," said Deke, "this is Staci Upton, co-star of *An Old Virginia Christmas*. Staci, you're the best."

"You say that to all the actresses."

"Not so. Only the cute ones. By the way, when are you going out with me?"

"In your dreams, Sneaky-Dekey."

Turning to Ally and Linc, Deke said, "See what I have to put up with? By the way, what do you guys do?"

"I'm a reporter for *The Washington Post*," said Ally, wishfully, "and Linc is a special agent for the FBI."

"Whoa!" Deke held up his hands. To Linc he said, "I didn't do it." Turning to Ally, he added, "And everything I've said or might say is off the record."

Ally didn't bother to tell him you can't call off-the-record after the fact. Anyway, she wasn't actually a reporter for the *Post*, at least not yet.

"Oh look," said Staci, "There's that Hobart Castlebury guy. I want to meet him."

"I can introduce you, Staci," said Ally, thankful for something to do except stand around. "I want to go over and say hi myself."

"You know him?" asked Deke. "Mind if I tag along?"

As they made their way across the room, Linc whispered to Ally, "You were kind of stretching it back there, weren't you?"

"Maybe a little bit. I just wanted to send a clear message to Deke."

"I liked the part where you called me your husband-to-be."

"I thought 'boyfriend' was too, you know, 'juvenile-ish'."

"You're missing my point."

Ally pretended not to hear. Instead, she laughed at something Hobart had just said.

The actor was dressed in a vintage 1920's director's outfit with a belted jacket, knickers that ballooned at the thighs, a beret and monocle. He held a megaphone into which he was belting out mock insults at the small crowd that had gathered around him.

"What have I to cope with here? Vagabonds, rascals, runaways…A sorry lot of lackeys you are, whom your o'er-cloyed Hollywood vomits forth."

Ally clapped. "Bravo," she shouted. "Belligerent as ever, I see."

"Aha!" bellowed Hobart. "It's my fiery redhead. Come forth, my dear."

"That's a switch," Ally said to him as she stepped out of the crowd and walked toward him. Turning to the group that had gathered, she added, "This crusty old curmudgeon usually tells me, 'Begone, wench!'"

There was a chorus of laughs from the audience.

"Cheeky and impertinent as ever, I see," retorted Hobart.

"Careful now," said Ally, "Remember our deal."

Hobart laughed, and Ally kissed him on the cheek. "Someone wants to meet you," she said, motioning for Staci Upton to come over so she could introduce her to "Hobart the Great."

"And a fair maiden she is," said Hobart.

Staci called over to Saxton. "Deke, come take our picture."

"Do you mind, Hobart?" asked Ally.

"Not at all."

Then others started moving up, wanting to be photographed with the brilliant master of the stage. While Hobart graciously acquiesced, Ally returned to Linc, who had just spotted Happy, across the room, talking to a couple. They made their way over.

"Hobart is making quite a hit with the crowd," said Happy. "And I loved your comeback when he said 'Come forth'."

"I'm just so happy to see him enjoying himself. He seems to be in his element."

Happy nodded and said, "I'm glad to see you doing likewise." Then she introduced her companions.

"This is Anne Martin and Ryan Marks. They wrote the song 'An Old Virginia Christmas'."

"That's so amazing," said Ally. "I heard you guys aren't really song-writers, that you just wrote this on a lark, so to speak."

Anne and Ryan took turns telling their story. They were high school sweethearts in a little town in central Virginia called Squall Falls. After graduation, they went their separate ways, first to college, then on to their individual careers.

"We were both seeking fame and fortune," said Anne. "Ryan went on to New York and Wall Street, and I ended up in Los Angeles, doing public relations work, waitressing when I had to, and grabbing acting roles wherever I could."

"Did you keep in touch?" asked Linc. "The two of you?"

"We always returned to Squall Falls," said Ryan, "to spend Christmas with our families. Usually, Anne and I got together."

"Then," added Anne, "we decided to try a long-distance

romance. We were both so busy with our careers that neither of us had married. We both left a trail of failed relationships."

So, they explained, they'd fly cross country when they could, and kept in touch daily with phone calls and email.

"That was when Ryan had this idea to write a song," Anne said. "He'd write a verse, then email it to me, and I'd write a verse and send it back. The song made many journeys back and forth across the continent, and…"

"…We squabbled over the lyrics before we both signed off on it," said Ryan, completing Anne's thought. "It's based kind of loosely on our experience."

Anne added, "I tried shopping it around L.A. but no one seemed interested."

"Then what?" asked Ally.

"Our careers had reached the point where we were both tired of the rat race," said Ryan. "And after Nine Eleven…"

"…He lost several friends."

"So, we made a joint decision to move back to Virginia and a simpler life. I got an accounting job, and Anne works in public relations at the local community college. And…"

"…We settled down outside of Winchester in the Shenandoah Valley," said Anne.

"And, what about the song," asked Linc.

"We'd pretty much forgotten about it," said Ryan. "Then, we met Hobart after seeing one of his Ruby Slipper musicals during a visit to New York City…"

"…And," continued Anne, "on a whim, Ryan asked Hobart if he might be interested in seeing our song."

"The rest is history," said Ryan. "We emailed a copy to Hobart, and he and Ruby Rosa and that Erik Reno guy turned it into a play…"

"…And then Lyon Lenning, he's the screenwriter, worked his magic and turned it into the movie," said Anne.

Ally was loving the way these two had a way of completing each other's sentences, almost like a couple of identical twins she knew from high school.

"What a fascinating story," said Ally. She was thinking it would make a great feature for *The Washington Post*, when, or if, she actually got the job.

"Hey, that would make a great story," said Deke, who had joined the conversation. "Ally works for *The Washington Post*. Maybe she can…"

An announcement was being made, saving Ally from the questioning look Happy was giving her and the embarrassment of having to explain to Deke and the others that she didn't actually work for the *Post*. Not yet, anyway.

The wall-mounted large screen TV had been turned on, and, standing below it, a thirty-something man had taken the microphone. He was wearing denim jeans with tears, holes, and frays in multiple places and a black T-shirt with the words, "Beat…Repeat… Beat Beat…Repeat." He wore a vintage fedora hat, and his face had the trendy scruffy look of three-day stubble.

"That's Alex Manning," said Deke, "the music producer."

"Does he always look like that?" asked Ally.

"Alex likes to go for that unkempt look, and he gets away with it 'cause he's so good at what he does. All the ladies love him. Staci calls him sexy."

"Maybe the British accent has something to do with that," said Ally, as Alex started to speak. "Many American women find it charming."

Manning was announcing the start of his music video, *An Old Virginia Christmas*. As the song played, Staci Upton, in character as Anne Merritt, and Luke LeMere, as Ryan Monroe, appeared on screen. First, Monroe was looking down from his penthouse on the busy New York street below. Then Merritt, from her beach house in Malibu, was looking out across the ocean. Both were remembering Christmases in back in Virginia with family traditions and simple pleasures.

> "It's an old Virginia Christmas, a back-to-basics Christmas,
> A simple pleasures Christmas; the family's coming home."

There were shots of the mountains and scenes of families trimming trees, singing, gathered around dinner tables, celebrating bountiful harvests and togetherness.

> "The mountains ring with music, the valleys echo laughter
> The house is filled with stories of places where we've roamed."

"Oh look," said Ally, excitedly. The character Anne Merritt was in a scene with Fern's horse Magic in the paddock at Finfrock Farm.

As the video ended and the screen went black, Staci and Luke, in person, took mics and continued singing to each other and to the crowd and as they worked their way through the room.

"Now," said Ally, "I can't wait to see the movie. And we've got to get copies of this music video."

Forty-Eight

On Saturday morning of what they referred to as "The Big Day," Ally rolled out of bed, slipped on some comfortable clothes, and kissed Linc good-bye. "I'm off to meet Fern for our hair appointments," she said.

"Have fun," said Linc.

I don't know about that," said Ally. "Wish me luck."

"Do you want me to make reservations at BB's for an early lunch before the movie premiere?"

"Yeah, I guess so, but I'll probably be too excited to eat."

❖ ❖ ❖ ❖ ❖

As they sat in salon styling chairs side-by-side, Ally was telling Fern about last night's producer's reception at the lodge.

"That sounds really wild," said Fern. Mimes greeting guests and stilt walkers balancing trays of champagne."

"Yeah, but the best part was seeing the music video based on the soundtrack. There was a scene of Staci Upton—she plays Anne Merritt—in your paddock with Magic. I'm trying to get copies. Especially one for you."

"That's cool. I can't wait to see what they do in the movie."

Fern's classmate Kelly, their hair stylist, chimed in. "I've set my recording on HMN and I'll be watching for sure." Kelly was a cute, petite blonde with dimples and a bubbly personality. Now what are we doing with this?" she asked, holding Fern's hair, which she'd washed and just finished blow drying.

"Ally, you tell her," said Fern.

Ally was looking over a display of hair clips and barrettes. "I'm thinking an updo," she said, "something off her face, maybe one of those, what do you call them, 'chignon' styles? And, how about a couple of these silver hair pins for accent? We're going formal tonight, to the big gala at Stonewall Mansion, so don't be afraid to make it fancy."

"It's all so exciting," said Kelly. "I'm going too, with my boyfriend. I can't wait."

"That's so awesome!" said Fern. "But, who's your boyfriend? Someone from high school?"

"No, but he works in Union Gap. He's training to be a police officer."

Ally perked up. "Wait a minute. Your boyfriend wouldn't happen to be Darrell, would he?"

"Yes! Darrell Dempsey. Do you know him?"

"I knew him when he was a security officer at the Gallery. Darrell's a great guy." Ally didn't want to get into the specifics and hoped Fern wouldn't say anything. She was relieved when Fern changed the subject.

"What are you doing with your hair?" she asked Ally.

"Ugh, it's so thick and so straight. Kelly, do you think you can do some cascading curls, maybe swept to one side with one of these fancy hair clips?"

"Wow!" said Linc when Ally returned. "I feel like whistling."

"Except, you can't whistle," Ally reminded him.

"Good point."

"Do you think it's too much?"

"I think," said Linc, pulling her in for an embrace, "you're beautiful."

"You'd say that regardless. Just don't muss it up," she teased.

"Spoilsport," he joked back. "Anyway, look what I found when I went down to the lobby earlier to get a bite to eat." Linc held up four music video DVDs. "That Alex guy with the British accent girls find so charming, had a table set up and was selling these. *An Old Virginia Christmas* is on it."

"Wow! That's great! I was just telling Fern I really wanted to find a copy for her. And I want one for us. And one to show your family. Maybe one for my parents…No, scratch that, they won't be impressed. I'll give the last one to Maggie and Mac, they'll appreciate it more."

The movie, as they already knew, was about the long-distance romance between two high school sweethearts who went off to seek fame and fortune, but were always nostalgic for the traditional family Christmases they'd grown up with. It was a cute story, but Ally and Fern, sitting side-by-side in the downstairs theater room of the Civic Center, were more interested in the local scenes.

Several outdoor scenes were filmed around Finfrock Farm, which was the setting for the family home of the female lead character, Anne Merritt. Another Union Gap residence, a riverfront log house with a large wrap-around front porch, was the childhood home of the male lead, Ryan Monroe. Shots of the Allegheny Mountains, the Dominion River, Big Gap Lake and the quaint shops along the Lakewalk were prominently featured. All of the indoor filming had been done in Los Angeles.

The movie ended with the sweethearts returning to their home-town of River Rapids and settling into a simpler life. Remembering the conversation from last night with the song writers, Anne Martin and Ryan Marks, Ally was struck by how closely the movie script followed the couple's real life stories.

"What did you think?" she asked Fern afterward.

"What a great love story," Fern answered, "and of course I loved seeing all the local footage. It's just amazing that our little farm got so much camera time."

"And now on to our big night. Feel free to come by early. I'd like to get pictures of all of us before we go. It's not every day we get all fancied up."

"I never have," confessed Fern.

Ally sat at the dressing table in the bedroom of their suite, ap-plying the finishing touches to her makeup. She had slipped into her emerald green evening gown. Linc now stood behind her, dressed in his tuxedo, and zipped her up. Ally's mouth dropped open.

"You look so…" She searched for the right word. "Dashing."

"And my darling date is gorgeous. Oops! I meant to say 'my darling *wife-to-be*'."

"You're funny, Linc," said Ally.

"I was being serious."

Ally changed the subject. "I have something for you," she said. She opened the drawer of the dressing table and removed a thin box tied red and green ribbons.

Linc opened the box and removed a rectangle of emerald green mulberry silk. He looked at her, confused.

"It's a pocket square. I picked it up when Mom and I were in Dominion Mills. It's to accessorize your look and color coordinate us. Let me show you."

She took the cloth and began wrapping it into a classic fold as she had been instructed to do at Michael's Menswear where she'd bought it. Then she tucked it into the chest pocket of Linc's tuxedo.

"I like it," he said. "A perfect complement to your dress. Speaking of which…" He reached in his pocket, then handed her a small box wrapped in gold iridescent foil with a matching gold bow. "An early Christmas present."

She opened the box and took out a solitaire emerald pendant in a gold bezel setting. The stone appeared to be floating on the necklace's thin chain.

Ally's mouth dropped open. "It's beautiful," she said. "Simple. Elegant. Perfect!"

"The stone of eternal love," said Linc as he took the necklace and from behind, slipped it around her neck, and clasped it in the back, pulling her long auburn curls out from beneath the chain. The pendant hung perfectly in the v-neckline of her evening gown.

"You have great taste," said Ally. "Now, isn't this the part where you rip my clothes off and seduce me with your hot passionate kisses?" She was reminding him of the first night they'd spent together when he slipped the pearl pendant around her neck.

Linc laughed. "That's not quite the way I remember it. Besides, I don't want to get in trouble for mussing up your hair."

There was a knock at the door.

"Saved by the bell," joked Ally.

"Guess that part will have to wait for tonight's Act II."

They went to the door together and welcomed Fern and Kyle, and Cletus and Daphne.

Ally told Cletus he looked dapper in his tuxedo, but she

could see he felt very uncomfortable. Daphne wore a long colorful peasant style dress, with jeweled sandals and assorted pieces of wood jewelry.

Ally still couldn't figure out the connection between Cletus and Daphne. Whenever she asked, neither could Fern. "I don't know what their story is," Fern would say, "but I think they're good for each other. She talks and he listens. Just the way they like it."

Fern was dressed in Ally's black and silver gown, and with her hair styled in an updo and wearing light makeup Daphne had helped her with, she looked radiant. She was glowing as she showed Ally her engagement ring, which Kyle had given her earlier.

"He wanted me to have it tonight so I can show it off at the gala," she said, smiling broadly.

The design was perfect for Fern's slim finger and hands-on life-style, thought Ally, admiring the ultra-delicate marquise diamond in an east-west setting. Exactly in line with what Fern had described she wanted.

Kyle was beaming. "Linc helped me pick it out," he said.

Ally and Fern exchanged knowing grins. "It's beautiful," said Ally.

"And so is the bride-to-be," added Linc. "Congratulations!"

"I'm so happy for you guys," said Ally. She hugged Fern and smiled at Kyle. "Now for the finishing touch." She gave Fern the wrapped box containing the earrings she had purchased with the help of Daphne.

"Doesn't she look amazing?" Kyle asked, as Fern added the earrings.

"You're a lucky man," said Linc.

"And, I'm one proud papa," Cletus chimed in.

Forty-Nine

The ride to Stonewall Mansion in the limo. The walk up the steps on the red carpet. The festive atmosphere inside the grand ballroom. The elaborately laden long table in the dining hall. The beautiful, elegantly dressed people.

"Ally," said Fern, looking around, "pinch me. I have to be dreaming."

"Hobart Castlebury knows how to throw a party," replied Ally. "That's for sure."

"Speaking of which," said Linc, "Here he comes now."

Hobart approached with his arms outspread in a welcoming gesture. He gathered both Ally and Fern into a hug, then shook hands with Linc and Kyle. He was dressed in black trousers, a black button-down shirt, a green paisley puff tie, and a green velvet notch-collar vest with traditional Celtic knotwork.

"Irish?" Ally asked.

"You'll see," laughed Hobart, patting Ally on the arm, then moving on to greet other guests.

"I guess we're all-out Irish tonight," said Linc, looking over the array of foods spread out on the extra-long Windsor Court style dining table. The appetizers were labeled, all with an Irish theme: smoked Irish salmon, cheesy Irish potato skins, Reuben spread, Colcannon puffs, corned beef cheese balls, Irish egg rolls, cabbage chips, soda bread, and Irish brown bread. A side table held desserts: miniature mince pies, traditional Irish Christmas cake, plum pudding, Tea Brack, and Spotted Dog.

"I want to try it all," said Fern.

"Where do we start?" asked Ally.

"How about starting with a cocktail?" suggested Linc. Several bars had been set up, and he pointed to one in the corner of the adjoining ballroom.

"Sounds good to me," said Kyle.

As they made their way across the ballroom floor, Ally took in the sights and smells of evergreens and holly, mistletoe suspended from the ceiling, and candles in the windows and on the hearth.

She stopped to check out the huge fir tree, decorated with pomander balls. Some were hung as ornaments and others were strung as garlands. The firm oranges were decorated with cloves in patterns of diamonds, circles, stripes, stars, and Christmas designs.

"The pomanders were made by the children in our free clinic," a female voice was saying.

Ally turned to see a pretty young woman with delicate facial features, long slim legs and arms, and strawberry blond hair that fell to her shoulders in soft curls. In keeping with the event's Irish theme, she was wearing a short brightly-colored dress designed with intricate Celtic knotwork.

"Oh, hi," said Ally. "I was just admiring them. Now, I'm even more impressed, knowing they were made by the children."

The woman gave her a warm, friendly smile and introduced herself. "I'm Sonja Kirkpatrick, dance instructor here at the Stonewall Studio."

"I'm Ally Murphy, a friend of Hobart. I've heard good things about you and the work you and your husband are doing here."

"And I've heard good things about you, Ally. Hobart thinks the world of you."

"He's a sweetheart."

"Hope you're sticking around for a while," said Sonja. "We have some pretty exciting entertainment planned."

"So I've heard," said Ally. "I wouldn't miss it." She gave Sonja a small wave as she turned to catch up with her friends.

"I have no idea what to order," said Kyle, looking over the beverage list at the bar. "It's all Irish to me."

"It's supposed to be," laughed Linc.

Ally was also looking over the list. "Lots of whiskey," she said. "Irish Old Fashioned, Irish Whiskey Sour, Hot Whiskey…"

"They also have beer," said Kyle. "I'll have a Guinness. That sounds pretty safe."

"The 'Irish Bubbles' looks interesting," said Ally. "Is it champagne?" she asked the bartender.

"Champagne cocktail," he responded, "with Black Barrel—that's whiskey—rhubarb liqueur, and fresh lemon, served in a champagne flute."

"I feel adventurous," said Ally. "I'll try it. How about you, Fern?"

"I don't know," her friend responded. "What's the 'Bloody Thyme'?"

"It's a variation of Bloody Mary but muddled with sprigs of thyme and lime wedges," said the bartender.

"I'm not sure about that. I'll have what she's having." Fern pointed to Ally.

Linc asked, "Can I just get an Irish whiskey straight, over ice?"

"Oh look," said Fern. "There's Happy, and she's wearing a female version of Hobart's Irish dance outfit. Let's go over."

Linc said, "You all go. I'll join you in a minute. I want to sit and listen to this music." Two violinists and a piano player in the far corner were playing slow dance music.

"Okay, Happy," said Fern, "What's with the Irish dance out-fit?"

"You'll see," laughed Happy.

"That's what Hobart said."

"Well, stick around and you'll find out." To Fern, she asked, "What are you drinking?"

"I don't know," said Fern, "but it's pretty good. We're headed over to check out the food."

"I'm starving," said Ally.

They were circling the dining table, sampling appetizers as they went and giving each food item a rating of one to five.

"Who made you all food critics?"

Ally turned to see that Deke Saxton had joined them. Fern groaned, remembering the incident in the lodge a few days before.

Ally introduced Ezra Silverstein's production assistant and said to Fern, "Deke and I have moved past that episode. Right Deke?"

"I'm keeping a low profile," he said, "now that I know you're a hot shot reporter with a federal agent boyfriend. Where is he by the way?"

"Husband-to-be," corrected Ally. "And he's right over…" She stared over at the bar. "What the…?"

Fern put her hand over her mouth.

Kyle looked over and shook his head.

"I'll be right back." Ally set down her plate and her drink and started across the ballroom floor.

"Uh-oh," said Deke. "There may be fireworks."

"Who's the bleached blonde with the cleavage?" asked Kyle.

"That's Tiffany. She's a member of our advance team. A notorious flirt, to put it mildly."

"The female version of you?" asked Fern.

Ally walked over and stood beside Linc, who was sitting on a bar stool. "Hi, I'm Ally," she said, casting a fake smile at the woman on the other side of Linc, the woman with her hand on his thigh.

The woman looked at her but didn't respond.

Ally picked up Linc's arm and wrapped it around her waist. She held the smile and stared at the other woman. The other woman stared back, unsmiling. When the stare-down got nowhere, Ally reached over and picked up the other woman's hand and dropped it from Linc's thigh.

"What the hell!" she huffed. "Keep your hands off me."

"You don't get to touch him," said Ally, still smiling.

Linc got off the stool, took Ally by the hand and pulled her onto the dance floor.

As she was being lead away, Ally turned back to the woman. "Nice meeting you," she said.

"Okay, what was that all about?" Linc asked when they were slow dancing.

"She was hitting on you."

"I was just trying to be friendly."

"Yeah, with her hand on your thigh and her silicone boobs in your face?"

Linc spun her around in a half turn. With her back to him he pulled her in and whispered in her ear. "You know, you're awfully cute when you're jealous."

She pulled away and spun herself the rest of the way around, facing him. "I'm not jealous. And, keep smiling. I don't want her to have the satisfaction of thinking we're fighting because of her."

"Are we? Fighting?"

"She doesn't get to touch you. And, I'm not jealous. I'm possessive. Now keep smiling." She put her arms around his neck for show.

He spun her half way around again and whispered in her ear, "I wasn't touching her back. You're the only person I touch."

The music stopped, and one of the violinists announced there'd be a short break. Ally and Linc walked back to Fern and Kyle in the dining room.

"You know," said Ally, "you could at least give me some credit for rescuing you from a bad situation. It didn't look good."

"I didn't carry on this way about your friend Deke trying to pick you up."

"I wasn't trying to pick her up," said Deke, who'd been listening to the heated exchange.

"People, what's going on here?" Maggie asked. She and Mac and Ally's parents had just joined them. "What are you guys fighting about?"

"Nothing," Ally said quickly. "Everything's fine. We're not fighting."

"I want to know," said Fern, "what Deke meant about you being a 'hot shot' reporter and you referring to Linc as your 'husband-to-be'."

Someone was making an announcement. Ally was relieved when everyone began wandering over toward the ballroom.

"Are we good?" Linc asked.

"Of course we are," said Ally. "Just keep smiling."

The guests were gathered around the outer walls of the ballroom, waiting for a dance performance to start. A fiddler had joined the two violinists and pianist. They started playing a tune from *Riverdance.* Then dancers in black and green Irish outfits filed in and made two lines, one on each side of the dance floor.

The dancers performed an Irish step dance with stiff upper bodies and energetic foot movements. Then, a couple came out and began tapping their feet and shuffling, hopping, and spinning their way down the passageway between the two lines. They seemed to be gliding along as they danced.

"That's Hobart and Happy," Ally squealed excitedly. The crowd clapped and cheered. When they reached the end of the passageway, they each joined a row, and the female dancers began weaving between the males. Then the two lines moved toward each other, and dancers from each line moved between the dancers of the opposite line then back to their original positions.

They performed a few more routines, then the dancers moved into the crowd, selecting partners from among the guests. After they were paired, the dancers began teaching the basic steps to their partners. Soon, other guests joined in and before long the entire floor was awash with dancers. There were wannabe Irish step dancers with their arms plastered to their sides, attempting to move their feet in step with their teachers. And there were dancers who had given up on that and were moving to their own beat.

Ally was grabbed and whisked onto the dance floor by Luke LeMere. She found herself in a conga line, which began weaving its way through the dancers with a series of repeated step, step, step, kick…step, step, step, kick.

Linc had been holding his breath and was relieved to see that

Ally didn't flinch; in fact she didn't react adversely at all to being grabbed and maneuvered about. She looked like she was having fun.

As the conga line was snaking through the dancers, Ally saw Linc in a group that was doing something more like a polka than an Irish step dance. Paired couples were hop-stepping and rotating partners as they traveled around in a circle.

She saw Darrell Dempsey, looking certifiably awkward, and his dimpled girlfriend Kelly, looking star-struck, slow dancing. *Very slow dancing*, thought Ally, smiling at how cute they looked. She gave them a wave as the conga line passed by.

The spirited finale ended with out-of-breath dancers clapping and back-slapping each other. Ally caught up with Linc, and they ducked out through the French doors onto the front porch to cool off. They were laughing.

"Definitely out of my comfort zone," said Linc, shaking his head.

Several other guests had the same idea, and soon the porch was full. Happy and Hobart, who had been making their way through the crowd inside, were shaking hands when they too stepped outside to catch their breath. Ally was quick to congratulate them.

"That was amazing," she said.

"We've been practicing for weeks," confessed Happy. "Hobart wanted to make this evening a tribute my Irish heritage."

Two men came over and offered their compliments on the performance.

"Ally, Linc," said Happy, "this is Lyon Lenning. He's the screenwriter, and Ezra Silverstein is the producer-director of *An Old Virginia Christmas*, the movie.

They were deep in conversation when Deke came running up. "Okay, Ally," he announced loudly, "I know now where I've seen you before. I just heard. You're the girl who was kidnapped and held captive with Hobart Castlebury here in this mansion." He seemed proud of himself.

Ally was not impressed. She glared at Deke. She'd hoped to get through this week without again having this kind of unwanted attention. She'd actually noticed herself getting better since being back here with her friends. She'd felt that Union Gap was helping her heal and put this episode behind her.

Everyone around her was quiet. People now moved closer to find out what was going on. They were staring and started peppering Ally with questions.

"Is it true?"

"You're that girl?"

"What was it like?"

Linc was watching Ally. He was ready to step in if necessary.

Hobart was clearly not happy. He scowled at Deke and suggested they move this conversation into his office.

Hobart and Happy, Ally and Linc, Lyon Lenning, and Ezra Silverstein, dragging Deke Saxton by the arm, went back inside and across the hallway.

In Hobart's study with the door closed, Linc confronted Deke. "I don't know what your intent was, outing Ally that way," he said sharply. "What happened here six months ago was a nightmare, not something to brag about. Ally's been away from Union Gap since that time, trying to put it all behind her. This needs to stop. Now!"

Hobart added, "I'm used to being in the spotlight. Ally's not. She's very special to me. Deke, you need do as Linc asks."

Deke threw up his hands. "Hey man, I'm sorry. Ally, I just wanted to let you know that I really had seen you someplace before. It wasn't a pickup line. Once I heard, I remembered the story and seeing pictures of you on the news."

Ally was more angry than upset. She glowered at Deke. "Much of what was on the news was crap," she retorted. "Furthermore, tonight is not about me, and I'm really pissed you'd try to make it so. We're here to celebrate the movie, not go back to a time we're all trying to put behind us."

Deke's boss Ezra chimed in. "Deke," he said sternly, "give them your word."

"Okay, okay, I'll keep my mouth shut," said Deke.

"Thank you," Ally replied. "I'm holding you to your word."

"While we're all here" said Lyon, "I'd like to ask a question about something else. There's all kinds of stories going around."

They all looked at him, waiting. Finally, Hobart nodded. "Go ahead," he said.

"The diamonds," said Lyon. "Whatever became of them? Everyone's speculating."

"Ahh, the so-called Talone family jewels," Hobart said. "They've been nothing but a thorn in my side."

"To put it mildly," added Happy.

"If indeed they ever existed," continued Hobart, "they've not been recovered. The fiend Erik Reno searched this house top to bottom, as did the authorities."

"Are there any theories?" asked Ezra.

"Oh, lots of theories," said Hobart. "Some believe they're still here somewhere, well hidden and yet to be found. Some speculate they were found, maybe by a cleaning person or even law enforcement, but never reported. Still others doubt the diamonds ever existed."

"What do you think?" asked Linc, clearly interested himself.

Hobart sighed, debating whether to share his thoughts. "I have my own idea," he said finally. "One which may sound unorthodox." He chuckled. "But keep in mind, I'm known to be eccentric."

"Do you want to share it?" asked Ally.

Hobart winked at her. "For you, I will." He began: "After the tragic death of my beloved Ruby, I was compelled to move to this big old monstrosity of a house. By that, I mean I felt as though I was being driven by a force beyond myself. And I've felt that same powerful presence within these walls many times since. It's not an evil presence, just the opposite. It's comforting. You can call me an old fool, but I believe the spirit of my dead wife directed me to come here, and I feel Ruby's presence all the time. It's the reason I've stayed here and devoted myself to making this a place where I can do good things. As a tribute to her."

Ally put her hand over her mouth. They all looked at her. "What, dear?" prompted Hobart.

"Hobart, I don't think you're an old fool. I've not told anyone this…"

"Please, go on."

"I don't know," said Ally, debating whether to continue. "I'm a journalist, I deal in facts, not theories or rumors, or speculation, or ghost stories, but…"

"You're among friends," prompted Hobart, "and what's said here, stays here. Right?" He looked around. They all nodded in agreement.

"Right, Deke?" asked Ezra.

"Yeah, sure. Scouts honor," promised Deke, holding up three fingers.

Ally hesitated, then said, "I've never believed in ghosts, and I never gave a second thought to the stories I heard about this mansion being haunted by the ghost of Ruby Rosa but…" She paused.

Hobart took her hand. "Tell me," he said gently.

"When we were locked in that room downstairs," she continued, "it was just like what you described, Hobart. There were times I was on the verge of giving up. But then I'd feel a strong presence pushing me to think and do things I never felt I possibly could."

She went on: "I remember crying and feeling hopeless because I couldn't find anything to use as a weapon. And then, Hobart, you were talking kind of crazy about using a table leg as a club. You were coming out of your drug-induced state. Your speech was disjointed, and you were barely coherent. But, I checked underneath the table nonetheless and the legs were just attached with wing nuts. I was able to dislodge one without any tools. I used it to whack Erik Reno and get a head start when I made a run for it."

"I don't know where that talk was coming from." said Hobart.

"I know. It was like someone else was speaking through you."

"What else?" asked Hobart.

"Another time, I was making myself sick thinking about having a physical confrontation with Erik Reno. But, I knew I had to because I wasn't going with him. I was so scared my legs felt like Jello. I started to crumble. Again, something outside myself kept pushing, urging me to get to my feet and walk it out."

"So, what do you think?" asked Hobart.

"I've had six months to try to rationalize this, and I have a couple of thoughts. First, I believe the diamonds are a curse. They were illicit gains to begin with, and Ruby was going to make things right by turning them over to the authorities. Erik told me that's why he killed her. After her murder, a lot pieces started falling into place. And, all of it seemed to be because of the diamonds."

Hobart cut in. "You're right, Ally. Gianna was murdered because of the diamonds. Then a string of events happened, all because of the diamonds, that ultimately resulted in Erik being arrested for both murders. I like to think Ruby is standing guard over the diamonds, using whatever spectral influence she has to punish those who want them for their own greedy purposes…"

"And," Happy chimed in, "to protect her beloved Hobart against those who wanted to hurt him."

"Thank you," Happy," said Hobart, "but I also believe Ruby was looking out for Ally. "Officer Dempsey happened to be in the right place at the right time when he saved Ally from Erik Reno's death grip. Coincidence? Or, something else?"

"Exactly," said Ally. "These are all facts, a series of unlikely events that actually happened. You might say it's coincidences. If you believe in coincidences."

"But, you don't," said Hobart.

"I honestly don't know," said Ally. "But, I've thought about something else, too. If none of this happened, Linc and I wouldn't have met." She turned to him. "You're the best thing that ever happened to me."

Linc put his arm around her. "I've often wondered myself about the events that brought us together. If anything good came of all this it's you coming into my life."

Then, silence filled the room. Finally, Ezra said, "This is quite a story, Hobart. Would you be interested in sharing your theory? It would make a great segment for the documentary we're working on about unexplained occurrences."

Hobart laughed. "Maybe. If it were done right. I think Ruby would love it. She and I have never shied away from the limelight, you know."

"Lyon," said Ezra, "we're going to need a screenwriter."

Lyon gave a thumbs up.

"Deke," said Ezra, "write this down: 'The Ghost of Ruby Rosa'."

Fifty

Back in their suite, Ally and Linc stepped out onto the balcony where they had a view across Big Gap Lake to Stonewall Mansion, still lit up. It was getting cold outside, and Ally buttoned her coat. Linc put his arm around her.

After the kerfuffle in Hobart's study, they took a few minutes to eat while saying their good byes. They planned to head back to Richmond in the morning and feigned exhaustion. Ally told Fern they'd stop at the farm on their way out to drop off Linc's tux for Kyle to return when he took his back. Fern hugged Ally and made her promise that she and Linc would be back for the wedding.

"Absolutely," Ally promised. "We wouldn't miss it."

Mac teased Ally, saying he was looking forward to seeing her Pulitzer. Maggie told Ally to call her anytime for guidance. "Although," she winked, "it may be me calling you for advice."

Happy and Hobart begged Ally and Linc to come back soon. "Thank you, Ally," said Hobart, "for sharing your thoughts. Whether anyone else believes in ghosts or not, you and I both know that Ruby was with us, getting us through that nightmare."

Ally nodded in agreement, despite her personal doubts.

Tim wrapped Ally in an embrace. To Linc, he said, "Thanks for that chat we had. It helped. Please take care of my daughter."

"You know I will, Tim."

"When are you heading up north?" asked Ann.

"We're going back to Richmond tomorrow. Linc has to work

most of next week, and I'll be up to my eyeballs getting us ready to head up to Massachusetts later in the week."

"Safe travels," said Ann, hugging her daughter.

Ally wished them bon voyage on their cruise.

Then, she and Linc left to catch a ride back to the lodge.

Now, looking out from the balcony, Ally was feeling nostalgic.

"You know," she said, "a year ago Union Gap was just a sleepy little town off the beaten path. Now look."

"The town has changed, and a lot of people's lives have been changed," Linc remarked.

"None of us were here a year ago," Ally agreed. "Not you, not me, not Hobart. Now look at us."

"Sometimes," said Linc, "someone unexpected comes into your life and changes you forever. You did that to me."

"You did that to me too."

"I think this week's been good for you."

"I'm glad we came. It's been fun, and I think it's helped coming back. That talk with Hobart tonight gave me a new perspective."

"Are you going to tell me you believe in ghosts?"

"As I said before, I deal with facts. I'm here. You're here. We're together. Those are the facts. Ghosts? Coincidence? Random chance? Who knows? But I love Hobart's romanticism, his belief that his darling Ruby is still with him."

"I love you, Ally. You know that, right?"

"I do, and I love you too."

"So, when you referred to me as your husband-to-be... Shouldn't we make it official?"

"You mean get married?"

"That's what I want. Going into this next chapter…it's a big step. I want you to know I'm with you. I support you all the way."

"Linc, you've always been there for me. I know that. You've wiped away my tears. You've never once turned me away in the middle of the night when I needed to be held or those times when I just needed a hug or a friend or a smile or someone to share my personal thoughts with. I love you for all that and so much more. But…We've talked about this."

"Tell me."

"I want to be your equal partner, not a 'wife' that you have to…" She grimaced. "To bail out of embarrassing predicaments."

"Equal partner? I don't know what that means. I've never seen you as a lesser person because of what you went through or the effects that experience had on you, or even your leaning on me for support though this. I would do anything for you."

"But, Linc, I want to be normal."

"That's a strange thing to say. You're perfect, warts and all."

"You're funny, but you know what I mean."

"You seem to have navigated this trip well with all the memories. Especially tonight with Luke LeMere dragging you onto the dance floor and Deke calling you out."

"That's true. I didn't freak out or shrink back like I've been known to do. But, I'm also not ready to say I'm through with this PTSD business yet."

"Ally, we'll face whatever comes together. You may not realize it, but you've given me so much more than I ever hoped for. Before you came into my life, I was the person who always worked late, spent long hours at the gym, and volunteered for the unpopular travel assignments. I hated the dating scene and detested going home to an empty apartment. That's the reason I came to Union Gap for that press conference. No one else wanted to."

"I didn't know that. But, I sure am glad you did."

"These past six months, I've looked forward every day to coming home to you, sitting across from you at the dinner table and hearing about your day, sharing our intimate moments or just being with you. I can't bear the thought of life without you."

"I don't want that either."

"So, will you marry me? I'm proposing."

"Linc…" She started to protest.

He turned her face up to his, and they kissed. It was their special kiss, the kiss that always sent quivers of excitement dancing through her body.

Suddenly, bright lights illuminated their embrace as fireworks exploded over Big Gap Lake, signaling the midnight finale of Hobart Castlebury's gala extraordinaire.

Then they heard singing. Words from "An Old Virginia Christmas" carried across the water from Stonewall Mansion: *"… The mountains ring with music, the valleys echo laughter…"*

Lights, music. *Really?* Ally wondered.

And, in that moment, snowflakes began to fall.

Ally smiled to herself and shook her head in amazement. Then she laughed out loud.

"Lights, music, snowflakes," she said to Linc. "Have you been working with the ghost of Ruby Rosa and her otherworldly powers, to choreograph this perfect proposal scene? I sense she's sending me a message."

"So, will you…?"

"Okay, Ruby, she said out loud, I get it." To Linc, she added, "How could I say no to a proposal like this?"

They walked back inside.

It was time for Act II.

Fifty-One

It was Saturday, mid-afternoon, two days before Christmas, and excitement was in the air. Last-minute shoppers were browsing the businesses along the Lakewalk, while others were stocking up on toilet paper and milk at JD's Dockside Station in anticipation of a possible Christmas Day snowstorm.

At Jack's Pub, with every TV tuned in to the Weather Channel, Maggie and Mac McGuire were having a drink at the bar before an early dinner at the LakeView Lodge. They were celebrating receiving a query about the *Lakeside Ledger* from the Pulitzer Prize Board. *Who owns the newspaper?...Who is the editor?...*The request for information was in connection with a Pulitzer nomination for the paper's coverage of the Erik Reno Affair.

"I'll call Ally tomorrow with the news," said Maggie. She's going to be so excited." She pulled up a group text received earlier that day, with a photo of their former intern and her handsome "husband-to-be" standing on one of the arched bridges over the Charles River connecting Cambridge and Boston. They were smiling. Ally had added a comment: *Long day on the road yesterday, but we beat the storm. Merry Christmas from Massachusetts!*

The news about the Pulitzer nomination was sure to make her Christmas very merry. It also started the McGuires reminiscing.

"Mac," said Maggie, "remember the early days when you were city editor at the *Harpersburg Journal* and I was the newsroom grunt? Wedding write-ups, garden club meetings, family reunions...I was assigned all that small town stuff."

"Until the day I sent you off chasing bank robbers," said Mac.

Maggie laughed. "Lucky break for me, our crime reporter and staff photographer were off on another mission. You dropped a backup camera on my desk and said 'Go!' The police cars were in hot pursuit of the robbers, and I was bringing up the rear. Then, the getaway car crashed through that fence and into a chicken coop."

"My god, I remember you almost got arrested yourself, crashing onto the scene."

"I was yelled at and chased, but I got the damn Page One picture." She laughed again, remembering the suspects, covered in feathers and handcuffed, being loaded into the squad car.

"And you got a promotion!"

"And I got the attention of the handsome city editor. You finally noticed me. And took me seriously."

"And here we are. Remember when we thought nothing happened in this little town? Now Union Gap is on the map and our little *Lakeside Ledger* is a force to be reckoned with."

"You're still handsome, Mac."

"And you're still hot, Maggie."

"I love you, Mac."

"I love you, Maggie."

Off-duty Police Chief Odell Hawkins, sitting two seats down, interrupted. "Hey, you two love birds might have to be cut off."

Mac laughed and paid the tab. With a "Merry Christmas" to Odell, he put his arm around Maggie and they headed out the door.

At Stonewall Mansion, final rehearsals were underway for the First Annual Community Christmas Eve Variety Show being presented by the Stonewall Studio for the Performing Arts tomorrow at the civic center. Hobart Castlebury was working with members of the cast who were part of an abbreviated version of *A Christmas Carol*. Hobart was both directing and starring as Ebenezer Scrooge.

Darrell Dempsey had been there most of the day rehearsing under Castlebury's stern direction for his role as the Ghost of Christmas Future.

"Not again," groaned Dempsey, clearly frustrated.

"Bah!" bellowed Castlebury in his commanding Scrooge voice. "When Ebenezer says, 'Will you not speak to me?', the Spirit of Christmas Yet to Come—that's you—neither speaks nor moves. You're mysterious, shrouded in darkness…You do not answer any questions."

Dempsey sighed heavily.

"Are you following me?"

Dempsey didn't respond.

"Speak up, Oh Spirit! Am I getting my point across?"

Dempsey threw up his hands. "You just told me not to answer any questions," he shot back.

Young Carlos Flores, who was playing Tiny Tim, burst out laughing as he sat on the sidelines with his mother Lucia. So did Darrell's girlfriend Kelly, who was sitting beside Lucia. The laughter was contagious. Darrell couldn't help himself and snickered. Soon even Hobart couldn't keep a stern face and begrudgingly managed a smile.

A feeling of merriment filled the room.

At Finfrock Farm, Fern was returning from a ride across the fields on Magic, her rescued Tennessee Walking Horse. She met Kyle beside the concrete foundation for their new house. As she dismounted, Magic stood behind her and put his head over her shoulder, waiting for her to stroke his neck and muzzle as his reward for a good workout.

"What's all this?" asked Fern, looking at stacks of lumber that had just been delivered.

Kyle put his arm around her and pulled her into a hug. "Well," he said, "if the weather holds, the framing crew will be here next week and all this will be the beginning of our house."

"Kyle," said Fern, "it's getting real."

"You mean real as in our 'amalgamation'?"

"Huh? Speak English."

Kyle spelled the word for her. "It's another word for marriage. As in uniting, merging. As in you and me."

"As in, 'Sweetheart, will you amalgamate me?' Now, that's romantic," said Fern with a laugh.

Kyle laughed too.

"Now," said Fern, "before you woo me to further boredom with your 'grandiloquence'—that means 'extravagantly colorful language'…"

"Hey, I taught you that."

"Yeah, well, before you do, I'm off to the Mean Beans to give the employees their Christmas bonuses and close up. I'm canceling Wined Down tonight to give them the evening off, and we'll be closed tomorrow and Christmas Day as well. And, remember, you're expected at Stonewall Mansion in about a half hour for your final rehearsal as Bob Cratchit."

Magic flicked his ears, snorted, and gave a high-pitched whinny, his way of reminding Fern that he was still waiting for his reward.

Fern and Kyle both laughed, enjoying the moment.

At Waterside Treasures along the Lakewalk, Fern's father Cletus was *trying* to help Daphne with an influx of last minute shoppers. Daphne was chatting nonstop with customers while Cletus bustled about, retrieving boxes from the storeroom in the back and restocking shelves. Daphne sent him to bring out a couple of boxes of brass bigmouth bass corkscrews, which were in high demand. Cletus returned instead with a couple of sets of brass bigmouth bass cabinet door knobs. Daphne started to scold him good-naturedly. But, a customer standing nearby saw the knobs and wanted them.

"These are perfect for the cabinets my husband's putting up in his 'man cave'," she exclaimed excitedly. "I'll take two sets. And the corkscrews as well, if you still have any left."

Daphne gave Cletus a big thumbs up.

"I'll be danged," muttered Cletus, shrugging his shoulders as he hustled back to the storeroom.

They were all smiling jovially.

Just as the afternoon sun was starting to dip toward the mountains, Happy O'Hurley closed up Books Galore Bookstore and slipped out the back door. She and her little dog Pippy started up a hill along River Ridge. They were on a little-used trail that could barely be made out but one that Happy and Pippy knew well. After a few switchbacks and stops for Happy to catch her breath, they got to a piece of level ground with a view of the lake and the town. Behind them was a large stone, a memorial to Happy's late husband, Professor Liam O'Hurley. Happy had spread his ashes here thirteen years ago and she and Pippy visited often.

Happy sat on a rock and held the little dog on her lap while she talked to Liam: "Well, Professor, we made it through another year, and what a year it's been. Who says nothing ever happens in a small town?" She chuckled to herself.

"Everyone's looking forward to tomorrow's Christmas Eve show being put on by the Stonewall Studio. And, I've put together a team to prepare Christmas Day dinner to thank Hobart and his crew for all they've done for the town. Hobart insisted we include people who don't have family plans to join us at Stonewall Mansion where we'll all be sitting around the long Windsor Court table. It'll be pretty traditional, but Clover Battersby—she's the cook at the Mean Beans—will be fixing some special Jamaican Christmas dishes. I'm excited to sample her curried goat, but not so sure about the 'mannish water'. That's a soup made with the goat's intestines and testicles. And get this…it's regarded as an aphrodisiac. Should be a hoot, don't you think?"

She changed the subject. "Kyle's book is coming along nicely. You were a great tutor on the Civil War, and he reminds me all the time that you're his inspiration. He and Fern have started building their house and planning their wedding. They're so good for each other. And, I'm so happy for them." Happy started tearing up.

Liam, I know you always said it was the lake that makes Union Gap, but if you were here today, I think you'd agree, it's the people. Some have been here all their lives. Others came and stayed. And, there's those who were only here a short while but left a lasting impression." She wiped her eyes with the back of her hand. "Now, look at me blubbering and getting all sappy."

She got up. "C'mon Mr. Pips, before I get so blurry-eyed I can't see the trail."

Happy, with her little dog trotting at her heels, started back down back down the hill, just as the sun was setting on the Lake at Union Gap.

"AN OLD VIRGINIA CHRISTMAS"

═══ THE SONG ═══

An Old Virginia Christmas

Chorus:

It's an Old Virginia Christmas, a back-to-basics Christmas,
A simple pleasures Christmas; the family's coming home.

The mountains ring with music, the valleys echo laughter,
The house is filled with stories of the places where we've roamed.

If Christmas is for giving, if Christmas is for loving,
If Christmas is for sharing all around the earth,

Then an Old Virginia Christmas, a good old fashioned Christmas,
A traditional family Christmas is Christmas for all its worth.

Verse 1:

From his penthouse in Manhattan, the streets look busy and bright.
He knows he should be grateful for having reached this height.

It's Christmas in the city, yet he suddenly feels alone,
Remembering Old Virginia and that little country home.

There never was much money for the toys he hoped Santa'd bring,
But the house was full of laughter, love, the pure and simple things.

He can smell Grandma's cornbread and hear songs of Christmas Eve.
He can still see all the family, together trimming the tree.

He knows his Wall Street fortune will never be able to buy,
An Old Virginia Christmas with its peace down from on high.

Chorus

Verse 2:

From outside her Malibu beach house, she stares out at the sea.
It's Christmas in California, where she's always wanted to be.

Yet she thinks about a Christmas past when freshly out of school,
She told her Daddy of her dreams, afraid he'd think her a fool.

He put his arm around her, and said, "My dearest little girl,
Our little country road's a path to anywhere in the world,"

Now even with newfound success, she recalls the joy back then,
When Christmas meant togetherness and the love of all their kin.

The ocean's roar, the pounding waves, can never begin to compare,
To Christmas in Old Virginia and the priceless moments there.

Chorus

Verse 3:

From New York to Los Angeles, the call is loud and clear,
To return to Old Virginia with her memories so dear.

For those who've left and known the world and found success and fame,
Christmas in our country home still beckons all the same.

It's an Old Virginia Christmas, there's peace through all the land,
Snow's falling in the valleys and upon our mountains grand.

Our houses glow with laughter, songs, and overpowering love.
For we have the gift of family and a blessing from above.

If Christmas is for peace and love and simple family pleasures,
Then here in Old Virginia we'll share our yuletide treasures.

Chorus

www.ingramcontent.com/pod-product-compliance
Lightning Source LLC
Chambersburg PA
CBHW031030030726
47497CB00004B/1081